THE NICK LAWRENCE SERIES

TARGETED VIOLENCE & MURDER 8

BRIAN SHEA

Severn River
PUBLISHING

Severn River Publishing
www.SevernRiverPublishing.com

This is a work of fiction. Names, characters, businesses, places, events and incidents are either the products of the author's imagination or used in a fictitious manner. Any resemblance to actual persons, living or dead, or actual events is purely coincidental.

ISBN: 978-1-64875-016-8 (Paperback)

ALSO BY BRIAN SHEA

The Nick Lawrence Series

Kill List

Pursuit of Justice

Burning Truth

Targeted Violence

Murder 8

The Boston Crime Thriller Series

Murder Board

Bleeding Blue

The Penitent One

Sign of the Maker

COLD HARD TRUTH

Never miss a new release! Sign up to receive exclusive updates from author Brian Shea.

BrianChristopherShea.com/Newsletter

Sign up and receive a free copy of

Unkillable: A Nick Lawrence Short Story

TARGETED VIOLENCE

A NICK LAWRENCE NOVEL

This book is dedicated to Barbara. You are my silent partner in this endeavor and have supported and nurtured my work. I'm forever grateful for all you do, and I'm blessed to call you my friend.

1

Sheldon Price stood outside the main doors of Connerton-Jacobs High School as he'd done at the beginning of each day for the last three years. He knew this would be the last time he would ever set foot inside its halls. The gangly, rail-thin junior stopped a few feet from the main door. The mottled reflection in the tinted glass doors stared back at him. His matted hair, glasses, and pimple-riddled face had only given more ammo to the arsenal of verbal abuse he'd endured every day since beginning his arduous journey into adolescence. The kindest of his abusive peers had called him Smelly Shelly, but there were many other names, each salt on the open wound of his psyche. He tried not to yield to its pain and found the old adage about sticks and stones was a load of crap. Words hurt. More times than he cared to admit he had curled into a ball on the floor of his bedroom and cried until his tear ducts emptied.

His father had left when Sheldon turned twelve. Not that his presence in his life would've added any balance. Being an All-American football player, his father never understood Sheldon's plight. His father was disappointed, more like disgusted, by his son's physical weakness. At times, early in his life, his father had openly mocked Sheldon's poor performance in all things sports related. *I guess the "awesome" gene skipped a generation*, his father had told a neighbor. Sheldon had overheard the comment and its impact still resonated to this day.

Sheldon's mother was a different story altogether. Sheldon had become the man of the house after his father's departure, and he cared for her on those days when she couldn't get off the couch. She'd slipped into a deep depression and never recovered. Her condition worsened when she began using sleeping pills to stay in a semi-comatose state. Sheldon did the grocery shopping, cooked the meals, cleaned the house, and even took a job as a stock boy at Jenkin's Hardware to float the bills when his father decided not to send his monthly stipend, which was becoming more frequent.

He looked at his reflection. *Man of the house*, he thought. He wondered who would look after her and worried that what he was about to do on this beautiful early spring day in Jessup, Tennessee, might be the final nail in her rapidly closing coffin. He shuddered, trying to shake the thought from his head. She would be devastated, but he'd left her a letter that would hopefully provide her some comfort in the coming aftermath.

His momentary lapse into introspection was interrupted by an unexpected impact. Sheldon's body lurched forward, almost causing him to topple. Staggering, he caught himself before face planting into the concrete.

Then he heard the all-too-familiar accompaniment from an all-too-familiar voice, "What's that smell?"

The shove had caused the last reserve of hesitation to dissipate from Sheldon's mind. His commitment resolved. He turned to face his attacker.

His eyes flashed with anger at the sight of Blake Tanner.

Blake hadn't always been this way. Sadly, Sheldon and Blake spent many an afternoon playing and exploring in the expanse of their neighborhood creek-fed woods. That was years ago and the memory of those days had faded into oblivion. The thick-shouldered athletic boy standing before him held no resemblance to his childhood friend.

"Oh look at this! Smelly Shelly looks angry. Hey, Dom, do you think he wants to fight?" Blake said.

"I really hope so," Dominic Purcell said. "Tell you what. We'll even let you take the first swing."

Sheldon stood still, but underneath the loose-fitting T-shirt his body trembled with fear. Like sharks after blood in the water, Blake and Dom circled him, closing the distance. Their breath smelled of toaster strudel and orange juice. The sweet smell contradicted the savage look in their eyes. Sheldon moved slightly, clutching his backpack's strap draped over his left arm.

"He's trembling. Look at him. He's probably going to piss himself," Blake said through gritted teeth.

"Great idea. How about you piss your pants right now and I won't cave your face in," Dom said balling his fist.

Sheldon felt his face warm in anger.

"You heard him. Do it!" Blake said, leaning in. A wide smile stretched across his flawless face.

Blake suddenly stepped back and his whole appearance changed as the school's secretary, Ms. Turtley approached. "Good morning, Miss Turtley."

"Good morning, boys," she said, glancing at the trio. Her eyes rested a second longer on Sheldon.

Sheldon was on the verge of tears. A blind person could see that the exchange taking place was not an amicable one, but she barely broke stride and continued into the school. He'd seen it too many times to count. The faculty seemed to look the other way when it came to Sheldon's abuse. Just like his father, most had probably never experienced his pain and had no reference for it. Or worse, they had been the Blakes and Doms in their own high school years and saw it as some twisted rite of passage.

"So, how about it? Is Dom going to pop those zits on your face with his fist or are you going to piss those pants?" Blake asked.

Sheldon weighed his options. His backpack now seemed heavier, and his mind raced for a solution. He knew that Dom would follow through with his threat. It wouldn't be the first time. Facing the unbeatable odds, he yielded and released his bladder. The warmth spread out from his underwear, permeating the front of his jeans. It quickly cooled in the early morning spring air.

"Holy crap! He pissed his pants!" Dom yelled.

Other students cast looks as they passed by into the school.

"Smelly Shelly pissed his pants!" Blake yelled, calling further attention.

Sheldon listened to the laughter as classmates passed by, pointing and gawking. The only thing he could do was fight back against the well of emotion and prevent the tears so desperately pleading for their release.

Blake and Dom gave each other a high five and chest bump while running into the school, but not before snapping a picture on their phones. Another viral Sheldon picture that would reach every kid before Sheldon made it to his first class. He exhaled, collecting himself. Today would be different. Soon they would understand.

Sheldon allowed his current circumstance to solidify his resolve. The need to cry had subsided. On any other day he would have turned and made the long, embarrassing walk home. He had tallied an impressive number of absences over the last three years, but nobody seemed concerned.

The second bell rang, the tardy bell, and Sheldon remained outside the school, staring at his reflection in the doors, the front of his khaki pants now darkened with urine. He looked at himself and wondered if he would survive. Part of him hoped that he didn't.

2

I'm not Smelly Shelly, not anymore. I'm Sasquatch_187. I'm the warrior elite and today I will cross over and become a legend. The first selected and hand-picked from a sea of others to make the leap, Sheldon thought to himself. A tenuous smile crept across his acne-covered face.

Sheldon's hand trembled as he gripped the metal handle of the front door to Connerton-Jacobs High School. He knew that once the door opened, everything would change forever. There would be no going back.

He'd been told fear was to be expected, but the reward would be unimaginable. He was a Patriot. He was the first soldier in a new war.

One deep breath and he jerked the handle as he exhaled loudly, almost grunting. The door resisted slightly, the suction from the weather-stripping released, and Sheldon stepped inside, entering into the main hallway. The overhead lights bounced off the heavily waxed laminate tile flooring, casting a soft glow. Purple and gold, the colors of the Connerton-Jacobs Cougars, covered the lockers lining the hallway. Those colors would forever cause his stomach to turn, and the sight of them now added fuel to his hatred of the place.

An obnoxiously loud squeak accompanied each step of Sheldon's left foot, his puddle of urine had soaked his left sneaker. His worn sneakers barely had any tread left, and coupled with the wetness, he moved more gingerly, taking shorter steps to accommodate for this. His backpack remained slung over his shoulder and, in the quiet of the empty hall, its contents banged loudly. He laughed, envisioning himself as a one-man band. A silly thought, that on other days, would have provided some degree of mental escape from his current circumstance. Sheldon could not allow his mind to drift. The plan was simple enough, but its execution would require his absolute focus.

He stopped in his tracks. At the far end of the hall he saw Darryl Hawthorne, the school security guard. Sheldon froze, hoping the barrel-chested man wouldn't notice him.

To his dismay Officer Hawthorne turned, smiled and waved. Hawthorne had interrupted many of Sheldon's bullying incidents and was probably the only person in the school who seemed to be looking out for him. The deep voice of the middle-aged guard had sent students running, though Sheldon knew he was a gentle giant.

"Hey, Sheldon," Hawthorne said with a broad smile. The whiteness of his teeth contrasted with the darkness of his skin and black, stubbled beard. "A little late this morning—oh damn, what happened?" Hawthorne's eyes had obviously caught sight of the pants.

Sheldon swallowed hard and failed to answer the big man. His nervousness caused him to sway anxiously, even though he knew Hawthorne wasn't a threat.

"How about we get you to the nurse's office? Maybe call your mom and get you a change of clothes?" Hawthorne asked with genuine concern. He began closing the distance to Sheldon.

Sheldon regained his composure. "No thanks Officer Hawthorne. I've got a pair of sweatpants in my gym locker," Sheldon said quickly.

It was a lie. Sheldon never dared to go into the dreaded boys' locker room, and on gym days would resign to wearing his sweaty attire all day. Thus one of the reasons he'd earned the nickname Smelly Shelly. It was a price he was willing to endure because he knew, for a boy like Sheldon Price, entering the boys' locker room would be the equivalent of a zebra entering a lion's den just before feeding time.

"Alright, just make sure you stop by the office and grab a hall pass before heading on to your first period."

"Will do," Sheldon said. As Hawthorne began walking away Sheldon called out to him. "Officer Hawthorne, thanks for always being kind to me."

"Sure thing, buddy," Hawthorne said, turning and walking away in the opposite direction.

Sheldon hated everything about this school. The design layout had all of the eight corridors converging to one central common area, referred to as the Commons.

The Commons had an octagonal design. Three steps brought students down to a smattering of couches, benches, and tables for them to study and socialize for the ten minutes between classes. It was roughly one hundred feet across and, for the socially accepted, the Commons served as a hang-out. Sheldon's schedule forced him into the Commons several times a day during the transitions. Popular kids loved it and reveled in the few minutes of socialization before the next block of instruction, but to kids in Sheldon's ranks it was a guaranteed block of public humiliation. Not today though. And never again.

Today the two hundred and twelve students of Connerton-Jacobs High School would learn a terrible lesson.

3

The Commons was vacant. Typically, few people lingered in the space during the first instructional block of the day. In the absence of other students Sheldon felt at ease. It was a strange sensation and one he'd not experienced previously.

Sheldon walked into the center and sat on a bright red couch, a spot reserved for only the most popular students. He knew the soft fabric would absorb some of the urine, and he rejoiced in the thought of some unsuspecting popular kid sitting in Smelly Shelly's piss. He unshouldered the backpack and rested it on the floor in front of him. It was heavy, but unlike normal days, it contained no books or notebooks.

He looked down at his watch. He had ten minutes until the bell would ring, releasing the horde of the student body into the hallways for class transition. He unzipped the backpack and peered inside. The instructions had been clear and simple. *Set it on the ground. Flip the switch to activate. Press the green button on the remote to detonate.*

Sheldon looked around and was pleased to see that the halls leading into the Commons remained vacant. He looked up at the black convex lens of the security camera and smiled for posterity. He knew that Officer Hawthorne was the only person who monitored the cameras and knew, seeing him only minutes before, that he was out conducting his rounds. He slid the heavy metallic frame of the device from his pack and gently put it beside the couch, toggling the switch upward. It hummed and a red light came on.

Sheldon dug his hand into the bag and retrieved the remote. He then went back into the backpack and removed the last item, his mother's Smith and Wesson M&P 9mm semiautomatic handgun. She had bought it the month after his father left them. She told Sheldon it was for home defense, but the gun sat in a shoebox on the top shelf of her closet. He took it a month ago and she'd never noticed. It came with a spare magazine which he had filled to capacity. Sheldon had never actually fired a real gun, but Sasquatch_187 was a pro. *How hard could the real thing be?*

The empty backpack now loosely covered the device and he slipped into position, tucking himself into a far corner hidden by a locker. He hoped it would provide enough shielding from the blast.

The gun felt heavy in his hand. The extra magazine was stuffed in his damp front pocket.

He waited.

4

The bell rang. The sound interrupted the silence and startled him, causing his pulse to quicken. Then he heard the sound he was waiting for. A loud rumbling filled the hallways. The eight arteries feeding into the Commons reverberated with the bang of lockers and voices. He felt a wave of nausea wash over him at the thought of what he was preparing to do, but the laughter of several students nearby quickly reminded him of why he was doing this. The first few students entered. His instructions had been to wait as long as he could. The Commons filled. No one noticed Sheldon wedged in the corner. This fact didn't shock him. He often felt as though he were a ghost moving among the living.

Couches were quickly filled by students that didn't care about the ten-minute time constraint allocated for socialization before scurrying off to their next class.

Sabrina Wilmont, Blake's girlfriend of the month, sat in the exact spot Sheldon had just occupied moments before. He watched as her nose curled and she gave an exaggerated sniff of her surroundings as she looked for the source. Her face contorted in disgust as she shot up from the couch and screamed, patting her butt. Blake stood nearby and began laughing at her. His laughter activated Sheldon Price's internal time bomb and he stepped out from the corner, revealing himself.

Without saying a word, he raised the gun, pointing it in the direction of Blake Tanner. He heard a ripple of screams from students seeing the threat, but the beating of his heart seemed to drown out the noise. Sheldon squeezed the trigger. With each kick of the gun he aimed in a different direction.

"Sasquatch 187!" He screamed his war cry, bellowing wildly.

His classmates began running, ducking, and screaming as they tried to predict the next volley of shots. Sheldon continued clicking several times before he realized the gun was empty. He reached into his pocket, frantically grabbing for the spare magazine. In his haste he mistakenly put his hand into the pocket containing the detonator. Before his mind comprehended the error, his finger hand depressed the green button.

The Commons erupted in a bright light immediately followed by a deafening bang, cancelling his ability to see or hear. Sheldon was no longer standing. The blast had knocked him into the corner and his head struck the metal of the locker he'd hidden behind. The secondary impact with the locker had propelled him forward onto the floor. The laminate flooring no longer shined and his reflection was distorted by the blood pooling out from him.

Sasquatch_187 was gone and Smelly Shelly stared back, scared and dying, until his eyes closed to emptiness.

5

It was cold. Not a cold that any thermostat or workout could fix. It projected from within his heart and coated his bones. The room's endless gray added to it. The only color came from the faded orange binding of the one book he kept on his otherwise empty shelf. The timeless words of Sun Tzu had been committed to memory, the book now only served as a reminder of its teachings.

Nick stretched his body and gazed at the ceiling, retracing the cracks as he'd done a thousand times before. The maze of coils designed to support his frame penetrated the cot's thin mattress, poking at him like a blind acupuncturist with a penchant for pain. He'd already gone through his morning workout routine and figured he would get in another round of exercise before his next meal.

The last year had been the hardest of his life. And Nick Lawrence knew hard. The first few months of confinement had left him depleted, sleeping most of the day and barely eating. During his trial he'd lost nearly thirty pounds. Each time he closed his eyes he willed himself to die. Each time he woke he realized it wouldn't be that easy. He'd been shot, blown up, and stabbed, so starvation seemed an unlikely cause of death for someone with his uncanny ability to survive.

One morning he woke to the silence of his surroundings and understood that he had died. At least a death in the proverbial sense. His trial had ended. Nick, a former agent with the FBI, was convicted of five counts of murder. The woman who had brought the case against Nick was a far deadlier killer than he ever was, but she'd amassed a treasure trove of evidence against him.

Nick suffered greatly at the hands of that woman. She destroyed him, tearing away any connection to the people he loved. She'd managed to disguise herself as a man and slip into his mother's medical facility. His sweet loving mother, whose recall of life's joys had mostly been washed away by the spreading decay of her dementia, was killed by this madwoman. His mother was the last living member of his once close-knit family. Her murder had initially eluded investigators, but DNA had tied her to the crime.

More devastating than his mother's murder was the loss of Anaya and their unborn child. Anaya hadn't died, but after losing their child something inside him died, and she never forgave Nick for what happened. The strength of their love was tested and failed.

A lifetime of service to his country cut down by the judicial process. He'd killed Montrose and several of his henchmen. At the time, it made sense. Killing Montrose was justice served for the young girls' lives he'd destroyed. The same system that had failed to convict a human trafficker had no problem in closing the case on Nick.

The guilty verdict was delivered after Nick's plea, and he was handed his sentence, destined to serve out the remaining years of his life with the types of criminals he'd worked so hard to put away. On the judgment day, eight months ago, he was reborn. Everything he had was taken, ripped from his hands. What was left was an empty vessel, and he committed to never losing again.

Since his rebirth Nick had regained the lost thirty pounds and added close to fifteen more, all of which was muscle. It was amazing what you could do in a six by ten space when you put your mind to it.

Nick rolled off of his cot, landing in a push-up position. His long hair flopped forward as he warmed up his joints with a quick thirty, and then he began putting in the work that would occupy the next forty-five minutes of intensity. Each workout focused on different muscle groups, enabling him to attack every session.

He'd not cut his hair or shaved his beard since the day he entered Masterson Federal Correctional Facility. His attorney had warned him about his appearance, saying that the judge would see him as a savage. Nick knew his case was a lost cause. Simmons had collected an impressive amount of evidence against him. It also didn't help when he, against his lawyer's recommendation, pleaded guilty to the murder of five people. Five consecutive life sentences later, Nick was still alive.

Time had been a cruel gift. Each ticking second carried its own life sentence. Nick had no cellmate. None of the inmates in D Wing did. The justice system had deemed his neighbors to be unfit for the general population, or gen pop, due to the violent nature of their crimes or the volatility of their psychological makeup. Nick apparently fell into both categories but knew the deeper rationale in placing him in relative isolation was because he'd been FBI, a fact that wouldn't be lost on some of the residents. It would be a huge feather in the cap of any inmate capable of sticking a broken piece of plastic into his neck.

Only twice a day were the prisoners of D Wing allowed to mingle, during the lunch meal and the games hour. Some psychologist had the genius idea of putting a group of killers together to play chess. Obviously, this person had never spent an evening of deep conversation with Bill "the Blade" Culver, who spent his twenty-two hours of isolation three doors down from Nick.

Nick knew Culver's story, as did most of the world. Culver had carved his way through thirty-seven known victims. He was selective in most of his attacks but sometimes rage got the best of him and impulse took over. It was for that reason he'd been caught.

In a moment of road rage, Culver had killed a Georgia State Trooper. The incident was caught on the dash camera and its brutality made him a legend. He had been shot by the Trooper, but it didn't stop Culver. He managed to disarm the lawman and used the Trooper's gun to beat him to death. The most disturbing scene in the video occurred when Culver stood, blood covered, and smiled at the camera. That image had been plastered all over the Internet. During a rare and candid interview Culver was asked why he killed the trooper and his answer was eerily simple, "Because I could." Among the prison population he was notorious. His large, three-hundred-pound frame was given wide berth when on the move. Although a disproportionate amount of his girth was comprised of fat, he was strong and surprisingly quick. Nick had witnessed him on more than one occasion address a newcomer who, unknowingly, crossed his path.

A newbie, some tough-looking skinhead, had bumped Culver acciden-tally while moving past him during the lunch wave. Before the guards could react, Culver had snatched the man by the neck and slammed him to the ground. While the guards attempted to separate the large man from his toppled prey, Culver had managed to crush the Neo-Nazi prisoner's wind-pipe. It was a devastating attack and was over within seconds.

Culver managed to avoid the death penalty by making a trade. He'd given the locations of one of his previous victim's gravesites in exchange for life. A grieving family's need for closure trumped a judicial need to execute a killer. And so, Bill "the Blade" Culver had guaranteed he would be a life-long member of Masterson's D Wing.

Nick sat on his cot allowing the sweat to drip freely from his face, forming a small pool in the space between his white sneakers. There was no clock in any of the D Wing cells and no clocks on any of the walls. Inmates were not permitted to have watches and therefore had no refer-ence for the passing of time. The only discernible timeline came in the way of the light and bell system. The lights came on every morning, announcing the start to a new day, and turned off after the lights-out warning every night, signaling its end. Each meal was announced by loud-speaker after a buzzer sounded. It was a recorded message and therefore never deviated in tone or content. Breakfast's and dinner's message directed prisoners to turn from the door and place their hands on the wall. If you complied, the meal slot, located at the base of the heavy steel door, would lift and the beige tray would slide into the cell. Inmates were not permitted to move until the meal door was closed. Anyone that refused to put their hands on the walls or failed to hold their position didn't get fed.

In the early days of his confinement, Nick tested the waters by not complying with the recorded directive. He lost many meal opportunities in those first months, which was one of the reasons he'd lost so much weight.

The guards did not treat him differently from the others in D Wing. He respected the principle of that, but also came to the realization he was by all accounts a prisoner. Nothing more, nothing less.

The lunch wave and recreation block had a different announcement. The buzzer sounded and the announcement to hold the wall was given, but unlike the click of the meal door during breakfast and dinner, inmates had to wait for the loud hiss and clank of the cell door to release. The doors would then slide open and inmates would be instructed to release their hold and step outside their cell. Guards would line the octagonal balcony at strategic points. The cells were housed on the second tier of D Wing, approximately ten feet above the space below, used for lunch and the board games hour of recreational time. The area used for lunch and games was adorned with heavy aluminum tables and chairs bolted to the poured concrete floor.

The buzzer sounded and was quickly followed by the announcement. *Inmates, step up and place your hands on the wall. Keep your eyes facing the wall until told to move.* Nick took up his position, placing his hands on the gray wall. He had done this so many times, he'd become convinced his hands had weathered a divot out of the rough concrete.

The next command given was fifteen seconds after the first. *Inmates, turn and face the open door. Keep your hands at your side and exit your cell.* Nick turned to face the open door and then upon direction, stepped to the landing outside his cell. Head straight and body rigid, in a prison version of the military position of attention, Nick waited until told to move. The robotic command was given, *Face inward and maintain your interval.* The remaining instructions would be provided by the guards evenly spaced along the tier, shepherding the convicts.

Nick wondered what today's mystery meat would be. Food no longer carried any semblance of taste. It was now only fuel for his body, for the machine.

He maintained his place in the line. Each inmate was to move through the chow line with no less than three feet in front and behind, shuffling slowly forward. This was to prevent the accidental bumping or proximity to others, which typically led to violence, and on the rare occasion—death.

Nick stepped up to the serving line. Unlike gen pop, meals served in D

Wing were done by the guards. Everything was controlled and everything was monitored. Nick raised his beige plastic tray to chest level and began sidestepping along. No choices were given. Each compartment on the formed plastic tray was filled by the guard in front of him. Talking was not permitted. One meat, one starch, one fruit, and one dessert. At the end of the line was a clear plastic cup with water. Nick completed his stutter step routine and moved to the table he regularly occupied. Soon the only inmate he'd connected with took a seat across from him.

Sherman Wilson was taller than Nick by two inches, but his six feet four inches appeared even taller due to the man's rail thin frame. Sherman wore thick coke-bottle glasses that gave him an innocent, almost nerd-like quality. He was anything but.

In the outside world Sherman Wilson had been an enforcer for a powerful street gang with ties to founding members of the Black Panthers. Sherman had been labeled a serial killer by the Department of Justice due to the number of bodies he had under his belt. Nick knew this to be an incorrect tag. Wilson wasn't a serial killer, he was a hit man. The only reason he'd been caught was because of a person he didn't kill. The irony of which was not lost on Wilson. He had refused to kill a witness to one of his executions.

Sherman had told Nick the story in a rare moment of openness. He was on a hit. Without going into too much detail, he'd explained that another crew had moved in and was taking up some of the trade in his gang's area. Sherman delivered the message with a bullet to the back of the dealer's head. A twelve-year-old girl on a back-porch landing had seen him carrying out one of his assignments. He saw her too, but refused to put a bullet in her.

The girl later positively identified him out of a lineup and bravely testified to it during the trial. Sherman said he respected the girl's strength of character and accepted his fate. The gang, however, did not, and Sherman found out his replacement had sent a message to the neighborhood by killing the girl and her grandmother. That was the last time Sherman Wilson claimed any affiliation to the gang.

It was because of Sherman's moral code Nick had come to trust the man. That and the fact that Sherman had stepped in and stopped a brutal attack on Nick when he'd first arrived at D Wing.

Word had quickly spread to the residents of D Wing that an FBI agent had joined their ranks. Most of the convictions served had been done so at the hands of a federal investigation, so the chance to take their pound of flesh was a top priority for some. Three inmates had conspired against Nick. The attack was fast and brutal. Nick had been struck from all sides simultaneously. The blows were well aimed and delivered with devastating effectiveness. One inmate snapped his tray in half and was attempting to slit Nick's throat with the jagged edge. That's when Sherman Wilson demonstrated his own set of skills. He moved through all three men, stepping on knees and manipulating elbows and wrists. The crunch of their snapped limbs was sickening. All three were hospitalized and never returned to D Wing.

Nick had asked him why he helped him, and Sherman had simply said, "It was the right thing to do."

6
***

"You're looking a little sweatier than usual today," Sherman said as he slipped into the chair in front of Nick.

"And you're looking a little thinner, Sherm," Nick said, giving a slight grin.

Sherman laughed. "If you're going to start pitching your inner warrior crap I'm going to get up and go sit with fat Culver."

Nick looked over toward Culver to make sure he hadn't heard the jibe. The large killer always sat alone. The rolls of his neck fat jostled as he devoured the food on his tray. Nick often wondered how the man continued to gain weight under these conditions. It was like watching those post-apocalyptic shows in which soft actors and actresses play survivalists. Satisfied Sherman hadn't offended Culver, Nick turned back to his friend.

"So, what's on the agenda today?" Sherman asked with a chuckle.

"Always a toss-up. So many options," Nick said.

"Maybe it's time," Sherman prodded.

"Don't start with me. Save your psychobabble for someone else."

"It's not psychobabble Nick. You need to get some closure so you can move forward."

"Closure? I closed that chapter of my life almost a year ago," Nick said, breaking eye contact.

"If you won't allow her to visit then the least you can do is write her a letter," Sherman said.

Nick looked back at Sherman, who stared unblinkingly back through the coke-bottle glasses, the size of his eyes amplified. It was like those lenses gave him some supernatural ability to peer deep into Nick's soul and he hated it.

"I regret telling you about her," Nick muttered.

"I'm glad you did. It made me feel a whole lot better about saving your cracker ass."

Nick laughed. It was a strange world he now lived in where the gangly, racially charged ex-hit man provided him with his only sense of humanity.

Nick had banned all visitors after his final relocation to Masterson Correctional. Anaya had sent several requests, but he denied them. He couldn't face her. He couldn't bear to see the disappointment in her eyes. His past decisions had come back to haunt him, and it had cost him everything to include his unborn child—their unborn child. He'd faced no greater failure in his life.

Declan had also tried to use his swagger with the Bureau to arrange a sit down, but, as was legally Nick's right as an inmate, he could refuse any unwanted contact. Nick had taken his new assignment as a resident of D Wing seriously and knew he would be unable to psychologically survive the remaining years of his life if he maintained his previous connection to the outside world. So, he severed it, completely isolating himself to the recesses of D Wing and his new inner circle of Sherman Wilson.

The great warrior philosopher, Sun Tzu, gave him wisdom.

The ability to gain victory by changing and adapting according to the opponent is called genius.

7

He watched as she got off the bus. The light blue scrubs were wrinkled, her bun had come loose, and her thick black curls spiraled out. An indication the shift she'd just completed was not an easy one. She was a certified nursing assistant, CNA, at a local hospital. She picked up as many shifts as she could, but living in Connecticut was not easy on her salary.

Watching her meander toward her apartment building, he knew this was just one part of her very busy day. Only a few hours' reprieve before she'd be back on another bus heading to her second job. Most people would spend the interim sleeping, but not Shakira Anderson. She would be taking the block of time to spend quality time with her toddler, Jamal Jr. He watched her as she walked along the row of brownstone buildings, long-since converted from single family homes of the fifties into apartments mishandled and run by slum lords. It was a dangerous neighborhood. He knew this first hand. Its streets were familiar and so was the criminal element plaguing them.

Shakira paid no mind as she passed by his car, walking in a half daze of exhaustion. The grind of life had aged the woman beyond her twenty-six years of life. Declan watched her with a combination of deeply rooted guilt and unabashed reverence. His decision to shoot Jamal Anderson, nearly two years ago, had left her without a husband and her son without a father. The money he'd anonymously bestowed upon her had been tucked away into a savings plan for her son. He knew this and was glad it would benefit him in the distant future. But as he watched the condition of her life, he wondered what future would her son have growing up here? Declan wished that she had used a percentage of the sixty thousand to move into a better neighborhood and decided he would contact the attorney to free up some of the money to do just that.

Declan checked in on her from time to time. It was some sort of penance he'd created, forcing himself to bear witness to the unforeseeable consequence of his split-second life and death decisions. It was Declan Enright's twisted form of self-help therapy. His wife, a licensed Psychologist, had warned him of the damage this would do to him. But Declan was as stubborn as he was brave. She knew it and had long ago caved on this front.

He racked his brain to come up with an additional solution to alleviate his tortured soul. Deep down he knew nothing would ever completely resolve the void created when taking another's life. He'd done this numerous times in his previous life while serving among the Navy's elite SEAL Teams, but warfare is its own burden and Declan managed to shoulder the weight better than most. Taking a life as a cop had a much more intimate feel, personalizing its aftermath. And so here he sat, taking in the sight of Jamal's widow, making his ritualistic atonement.

Shakira moved along the rows of concrete steps, one of which was occupied by several men in their late teens or early twenties. A couple cat calls rang out as she moved past. He watched her ignore the banter, keeping her head down and pressing forward. Apparently, this did not sit well with one of the men. He stood up, throwing his hands in the air in dramatic fashion. The rear of his jeans sagged, exposing a pair of purple polka-dot boxer briefs. A bulge in his front waistline concealed by the partially tucked shirt indicated he was most likely carrying a gun. Declan opened his door as he heard him yell, "Bitch, I said I'm talking to you!"

Shakira kept stride but looked back. Fear flashed across her eyes, but Declan watched as she tried desperately to hide it.

The man hopped down two steps to the sidewalk and threw his hands out wide and gestured toward his crotch. "Get your big ass back here!"

Shakira's pace quickened as the goon's two minions stood up, joining him on the sidewalk. All three now trailed behind the woman, closing the gap. Declan silently slipped in behind the trio, maintaining pace but staying several feet back. They didn't notice his uninvited arrival to this party. *Why would they?* He thought. Declan spent the better part of his adult life as a ghost, operating in units that were built around the ability to move without detection. It was one of many trademark skills he possessed.

"Yo! You didn't hear my boy? He said to bring it back!" A fat counterpart said.

Shakira broke into a slight jog as she approached the front steps of her building. She reached into her purse as she ran, rummaging for her keys while bounding up the steps. She got the door open and slipped inside.

She pulled hard in an effort to close it behind her, but the saggy-bottomed thug wedged his foot between the frame and the door before it shut completely. Shakira held the interior door handle in a futile effort to stop the trio from entering. The door was ripped open and her hand came free. She fell backward to the foyer floor and screamed. She scurried back like a crab, scrambling to escape.

The three men entered, focusing on the woman on the floor before them. Shakira Anderson rolled to the side and began scampering to her feet just as one of the men kicked her legs out from under her. The fat one licked his lips overtly as if he was preparing to feast.

"I like a girl with a little fight in 'er," the one with the polka-dotted boxers said. "Take her to the basement."

The fat thug grabbed her by the ankles and pulled hard, spinning her toward the adjacent stairwell. It was dark and the super had failed to change the bulb months ago. Shakira screamed again, attempting to get the attention of one of the neighbors. In an area like this people typically did not get involved. Especially if the troublemakers were gang affiliated. The repercussions could be deadly. No doors opened. No do-gooder exited the safety of their apartment to render aid.

During the commotion, no one had noticed Declan slip in behind the three men huddled over their prey. He said nothing as he set to work.

He'd sized up all three men while he was following behind them. The biggest known threat was the skinny kid with the gun and he needed to be dealt with first.

Declan kicked hard at the back of Polka Dot's left knee and simultaneously pulled him backward by the shoulders. The unsuspecting man toppled easily back to the hard tile of the entranceway. Declan dropped his right knee hard on his neck, driving the man's face into the flooring. He was dazed almost to the point of unconsciousness, and Declan seized this opportunity to rip the gun from his waistline. The man relented under the weight of Declan's knee. With the gun in hand Declan drove the butt of the small caliber pistol down on the struggling man's temple, rendering him completely unconscious.

The man that had been standing next to Mr. Saggy Pants turned, trying to make sense of the last few seconds of madness. As he turned, Declan launched at him, crashing his elbow hard into the man's face. The blow sent him back into the row of metal mailboxes affixed to the opposite wall. The combination of impacts was devastating, and the man slid down the wall and slumped on the floor. A trail of blood smeared the wall, leaking from the back of the man's head. His eyelids fluttered rapidly and his eyes rolled to the back of his head, indicating he was temporarily out of the fight.

The fat man, seeing Declan's assault, had released Shakira's ankles, and his right hand was moving quickly toward his waist. Declan saw the glint of a large knife. Declan reacted, throwing the gun in his hand at the man's face. The fast-moving hunk of steel found its mark striking the man between the eyes, instantly breaking his nose. The introduction of pain and flow of blood caused the fat man to drop the knife and the blade clanked loudly against the tile.

The fat man was stunned and his head arced back. He gripped his nose with two hands, the blood poured out through the gaps between his fingers. His large body teetered momentarily before yielding to the force of the assault. The man staggered back, losing his footing at the edge of the basement stairwell. He fell down the same flight of stairs he'd tried to take Shakira Anderson down. He lay upside down and unmoving in a heap at the bottom.

Declan outstretched his hand. Shakira took it with a look of utter bewilderment. He gently brought the woman to her feet. "It's okay. You're safe now."

"Thank you," Shakira said softly, surveying the three men in various states of incapacitation.

"I think you better head to your apartment and I'll get this cleaned up," Declan said, scanning the three downed men.

"How can I repay you?" Shakira asked gratefully.

"Move."

"Move?" She asked.

"It's not a safe place for you. And definitely not after this. You'll be receiving some money in a few days to get you a better situation. Until then do you have somewhere to stay?" Declan asked.

"Money? A place to stay? Uh... yes," Shakira rambled, understandably overwhelmed.

A soft groan ebbed out of the fat man at the bottom of the stairs. Declan shot her a look. "Time for you to go."

Shakira nodded and scurried down the hall toward the stairwell leading to her second floor apartment.

Declan quickly went about retrieving the gun and knife from the floor and searching the thugs more thoroughly to make sure there weren't any other weapons. He used their shoelaces to hog tie the three. A good Navy man can always pull off some knots. Especially when you're trained to do it holding your breath for two minutes while submerged twenty meters below surface.

He didn't want to try to explain in great detail to the local cops what he was doing in the neighborhood, so he used the fat one's cellphone to call the police. He gave a loose interpretation of what was going on and what crime was being committed at the time of his citizen's arrest.

He opened the door to leave. Before departing he turned to the three men who were now conscious but tightly bound. "If you ever bother that woman again, I'll come back. And next time I won't be so nice."

Declan slipped out of the door and walked back toward his Bureau-issued sedan parked several buildings away. A lean man, clean-cut with a slight gray along his temples, was leaning casually against the passenger side door.

"Hey friend, you're leaning on my car," Declan said nonchalantly as he got closer.

"I know," the man said.

"Whatever you're selling, I ain't buying," Declan said. His cavalier tone flashed to impatience.

"You really are a shit magnet."

"Not sure what you're talking about," Declan said, sliding his hand close to the Glock 23 subcompact holstered inside the rear right side of his waistline.

"Easy Declan. No need for that," the man said.

"Do I know you?" Declan said, his hand unmoved.

"Not by face, but by name."

Declan eyed the man cautiously but said nothing.

"I'm Jay. I felt like it was time for you and I to meet face-to-face."

"How do I know you are who you say you are?" Declan said, knowing the need to vet everything.

"I called you a while back using your wife's number to contact you."

Declan moved his hand away from his gun and relaxed slightly, but not completely. When a CIA spook appeared out of nowhere, it carried with it an inherent level of danger. "So, why now? Why here?"

"It's complicated," Jay said.

"It always is," Declan mumbled.

"We need to talk."

"Okay. So talk," Declan said.

"Not here. I have a car waiting," Jay said, gesturing to a heavily tinted SUV parked down the street.

"What about my car?"

"I've got someone to drive it back to headquarters for you," Jay said.

"Is this the part where you tell me I've got no choice?" Declan said, raising an eyebrow.

"We've always got choices. This is a one-time offer and I'd like you in on it," Jay said matter-of-factly with no hint of a veiled threat. "Take it or leave it."

Declan sighed. "Nick trusted you. So, by default I do too."

"It's funny you said that."

"Why?" Declan asked, cocking his head.

"Because Nick's the reason I wanted to talk to you."

Declan tossed his keys to a thick-necked, ruddy-faced man who said nothing as he exited the rear of the SUV and walked toward Declan's sedan.

8

The news was playing out on a flat screen television hanging from the wall. Each channel carried the same story and similar images. The security footage had been leaked, as was the plan, and the black and white image played out in forty-two inches of high definition quality. Students were running as the gunman began firing randomly into the crowd. It was pandemonium, all captured on tape. Then came the explosion like a visual exclamation point, driving home the tragedy with devastating effect to the millions of viewers around the world. The camera flashed into a bright white and then faded to black, returning to the panel of experts prepared with canned responses.

The live feed was from the outside of Connerton-Jacobs High School, playing in the backdrop while politicians and former federal agents weighed in with their two cents. This was typical of these events and had become the staple of every news junkie's day, giving them their dose of terrible tragedy. The mental recovery from seeing images and scenes like the one depicted was starting to have minimal impact. Viewers became desensitized as violent extremism had begun to occur more frequently.

The repeated videos on a loop showed students and teachers running. Police, Fire, and EMS converging and triaging the victims. Tearful cries of anguish as groups of survivors were surrounded by supporters. Vigils were held and memorabilia covered the makeshift shrines signifying the tragic end of innocent lives. Then came the interviews of the traumatized as victims came forward to share their moments of horror.

A press conference had been announced where answers were promised to be given. Local authorities and community leaders banded together in a unified visual front. The President would make a public address condemning this act and others like it. All of it had been done before. All of it would be done again. And with little, if any, effect.

The group seated in the conference room watched and listened, absorbing the devastation played out before them.

"Twelve dead and twenty-nine wounded," Tanner Morris's voice grumbled, interrupting the newscaster's synopsis. "And what do we think of this?"

The room was silent, except for the shifting of chairs as the people seated around the hand carved mahogany table turned to face the man. Each person seated at the table managed equally important roles in the organization, but the man at the head, Tanner Morris, was on a totally different tier. One of the most unique rise-and-fall-and-rise-again stories in Fortune-500 history. Tanner had designed multiple successful startups, dabbling in a variety of markets. For a man who grew up in the blue-collar Midwest as a mechanic's son, he'd gone on to amass a small fortune. He did it all without ever attending college. Technically he never completed high school, but he did earn his GED.

Tanner Morris hit his first million before the age of nineteen. Things seemed to come together with relative ease until tragedy derailed his path.

Tanner's daughter Wendy, the youngest of his two children, committed suicide. It wrecked him—his life became a collision course of drugs and alcohol. One night he crashed his car, killing three people when he crossed into oncoming traffic and hit another vehicle head on. He served five years for the vehicular manslaughter. It had been a hard five years, but he rebuilt his empire. Although his focus had drastically changed.

The images flashing across the now-muted television screen were a result of his brainchild.

He knew no one at the table would dare to assess this first test run. At the end of the day, only he could weigh in on the success or failure of the operation. No one spoke. The assessment was being weighed, evident by the lines squiggling across his furrowed brow. Tanner Morris could easily be mistaken for a banker if it wasn't for the blue ink of the tattoo stretched on the side of his neck, a little memento from his prison affiliation with the Brotherhood. He was not a white supremacist nor did he hold their beliefs, but when caged with dangerous men survival was key.

"Did our test run equal a success?" Morris asked again, demanding a response.

All of the others in the room nodded solemnly.

"I agree. And you think that we are ready to widen the scope of our operation?" Morris asked gruffly.

The four members of his counsel spaced around the ornate table each shot quick glances at one another, a weak effort to decide who should answer. The eyes of the others locked on the small-statured floppy-haired technician, Simon Belfort. He looked like he'd be more comfortable surfing a wave in Hawaii or serving someone a latte as a barista. But one thing was for certain, Belfort was a tech genius. He'd proven that time and again on various assignments. Belfort was also loyal, and for those reasons Tanner Morris hand picked him to run the technical aspects of this endeavor.

"I—I say yes. We're ready. Analysis of the statistics point in that direction. Several Prospects are in the queue," Belfort squeaked. He desperately shuffled the stack of paper in front of him looking through his data, searching for the answer to the question that was sure to follow.

"Several is not a number. I need a number. Quantifiable data has numbers not generalities," Morris said calmly. But everyone in the room knew that lying just beneath the surface was a percolating rage. The group had learned to watch for the telltale sign Morris was about to launch into one of his legendary emotional eruptions. The veins alongside his neck would bulge and his face would redden.

Belfort cast a quick glance, looking up from his paperwork, and his tension eased a bit, seeing Morris's face was still calm. The early warning alarm of a tempestuous outburst had not been triggered.

Finding the sheet he was looking for, Belfort sat up and cleared his throat. "Sorry about that, Mr. Morris. As of this morning we have locked in on thirty-one prospects from seventeen different states. I've got over one hundred and sixty-two potentials who are closing in on the challenge stage."

"What is the percentage of people who reach the challenge stage that move on to prospect level?" Morris asked.

"We've seen an improvement in the percentile as of last week with forty-eight percent moving forward into prospect status. That's up sixteen percent," Belfort said pridefully and equally relieved to be able to deliver the answer with stats.

Morris nodded. "That brings me to my next question. Where do we sit financially?"

No one needed to look around the room as to who would answer this question because there was only one who handled this aspect of the company. Sarah Barnes, the company's chief financial advisor, tapped her iPad and the pale light of her device's screen illuminated her pockmarked face. What she lacked in beauty she made up tenfold in brains. "Our profits remain steady and we stand at one point two million for last quarter. I project we will exceed that during these next few months based on the last few weeks."

"I need Prospects in all fifty states. A Prospect is only a high-potential candidate. Our ultimate goal is to get them through to the Patriot level. Is that clear?" Morris eyed each and every member of his council, stopping at Graham Morris, his son. "Graham, you need to up your game son. I must have those Prospects turned into Patriots. Can I count on you?"

"Of course," Graham said coldly.

Graham, who'd been extremely gifted as a child, graduating high school at fifteen and college by nineteen, had also demonstrated a rare talent for the psychological manipulation of others. Tanner Morris had tested the limits of his son's ability and was very pleased with the end result. Facing a brutal and costly divorce, Tanner deployed his only living child to exploit the weakness of his soon-to-be ex-wife.

Graham spent months subliminally implanting thoughts into his mother, a woman he despised. She wasn't mean or cruel. Those traits would have been understood by Graham. He hated the woman because above all other things she was weak. Graham had found a penchant for hurting the weak. It started with an injured squirrel he'd found when he was six. Dispatching the creature through slow torture, the experience was one of his formative memories and he recalled it fondly to this day.

His father had caught him on occasion during one of his experiments, usually with a neighbor's cat or dog. He preferred cats because of the sound they made. Tanner Morris had turned a blind eye to his son's predilection, enabling his drive.

Graham deployed a barrage of psychological attacks on his mother. She didn't love him anyway. He saw the way she looked at him. It was far from the reverence she held for his sister Wendy. Two weeks after Graham began his social experiment with his mother, Alice Morris committed suicide. He'd realized he derived an immense pleasure from this new technique for exploring his deviance. Like his first squirrel, his mother's death had been a cherished and life changing experience.

After destroying his mother's life, the bond between Graham and his father had been unbreakable.

Graham had been tasked with shaping Prospects. He'd only test run one Prospect and taken him all the way to Patriot status. The methodology Graham had deployed proved to be effective. The news of Sasquatch_187's deployment had been a marked success and was relatively easy. He looked up at the scene on the television and smiled at the outcome of his latest experiment.

"How much time?" Morris asked.

"Tough to say, but now that we have proof positive on the approach, then I'd say we might have your fifty Patriots within two weeks," Graham said confidently.

"Alright," Tanner said giving a dismissive wave of his hand. "That's it for now."

The group stood and filed toward the ornate door of the small conference room. "Tank, stay for a moment," Tanner Morris said to the large man.

Thomas "Tank" Jones was the only member who couldn't pass for anything but a dangerous ex-military type. His stout five-foot, six-inch frame was packed with more muscle and tattoos than seemed humanly possible. The high and tight haircut coupled with his sun damaged skin added an element of ruggedness. The intensity of his look was exacerbated by a large scar stretching across the left side of his face that stopped at his ear. The top third of that ear was missing, lost on some distant battlefield.

"Yes?" Tank asked. His voice a rasp from years of yelling and chain smoking.

"He's still alive?" Morris asked.

"He is. From what the news accounts are saying... yes."

"We need to rectify that," Morris said, drumming his fingers on the varnish coating the wood conference table. "We can't have him talking about the game. There can be no exposure until we make the announcement. And there can be no link to us."

"Consider it done." Tank nodded, turned, and walked out of the room. A man of little words, but deadly efficiency. Tanner Morris never micromanaged him, giving Tank free reign to accomplish each task with minimal oversight.

Tank smiled as he walked out of the room. Having a new mission, regardless of its purpose or target, gave him great satisfaction.

9

Nick pressed his hands on the wall and heard the door's release. The days blurred into one repetitious cycle. Every time the lights came on it was like someone hit the reset button on his life.

Excellence consists in breaking the enemy's resistance without fighting. He'd read those words too many times to count and it reminded him to fight back. Resist being swallowed by the darkness, he told himself. Nick wouldn't allow himself to concede to the tedious weight of his circumstances.

He'd pushed himself extra hard during his pre-lunch workout and his palms were moist with sweat, barely maintaining their purchase on the smooth gray acrylic paint of his cell's wall. *Inmates, turn and face the open door,* the voice on the PA commanded. The familiar pause before the next static-etched command sounded, *Keep your hands at your side and exit your cell.*

Nick stepped out of his cell and onto the landing as he'd done two hundred and ninety-seven times since being relocated to Masterson Correctional. His poorly constructed sneakers and faded orange jumpsuit were the extent of his worldly belongings.

Nick stood on the yellow painted line centered on the four-foot stretch of the landing. The railing running along the balcony had five horizontal bars spaced at one-and-a-half-foot intervals, bringing the height to seven and a half feet, a little over a foot above Nick's six-foot-two stature. It was done to prevent the potential of an inmate being tossed to the lunch and recreation area below. No one had attempted such a feat in the short time since Nick had taken up residency, but Sherman had said the bars weren't always as high. The implication needed no further explanation.

Face inward and maintain your interval. The last of the announcements given for a while—until the lunch hour ended and they'd be returned to their cages. It was surreal for Nick to see himself among this population. He'd spent the better part of his life hunting men like these and now he ate beside them. He pushed the thought from his head. Nothing good would come from dwelling on a past he couldn't change.

Tray in hand, Nick began his side step shuffle along the chow line. The guard gave a moment's pause before manipulating the tongs to retrieve a slab of gray meat. Something was off. Maybe it was the way he looked at him or the extra careful nature in which the guard selected his food. But one thing Nick Lawrence excelled at was his ability to read people, and he trusted his instincts above all else.

"Make sure you take time to digest your steak," the guard said, breaking the cardinal rule of no communication.

The comment caught Nick off guard but he said nothing in response. Nick continued moving down the line, as he'd always done, until his tray was full. He stepped away from the chow line and the guard, moving toward his table. Sherman Wilson would be joining him shortly.

Nick tore at the meat with his hands. No knives, plastic or otherwise, in the D Wing. The flimsy spork was the only permitted eating tool and the guards inspected each inmates' plate and utensil before disposal to ensure that none of the small plastic points had been broken off. A prisoner's ingenuity was an amazing thing, especially when he was interested in killing another.

So, Nick abandoned the spork and used his fingers, separating the meat into several pieces. The jailhouse version of Salisbury steak came apart easier than a normal cut of beef and the piece Nick held was flimsier than most—he immediately saw the reason why.

A bit of plastic was lodged in the center of the beef. It was the size of a pack of sugar. Nick quickly took a big bite of the meat, shoving the plastic into his mouth with it just as Sherman dropped into his seat. The watery juices trickled across his hand.

"Well, you sure are hungry today. All those push-ups you do increases your appetite," Sherman said. The former hit man cracked a wide smile, exposing the bright white of his teeth.

Nick nodded and tried to smile back while chewing. His tongue manipulated the piece of plastic into the space on the right side of his mouth between his teeth and cheek. Nick swallowed the meat, being careful not to accidentally ingest the item.

"Nothing like Salisbury steak. It must be Tuesday. Or Wednesday? Maybe Saturday?" Nick said, reciting a joke they'd used more times than he cared to admit. Somehow to them it always proved a source of entertainment and Sherman chuckled.

10

The remainder of the lunch hour had passed without much fanfare. Nick returned to his cell and waited until the heavy steel of his door closed. The door had a small vertical window, six inches wide and one foot high. The pane of glass was heavy and was used for the guards' random visual inspection of the cells. There was no way to communicate with other prisoners, not that Nick wanted to. In other installations inmates created their own form of Morse code, banging on pipes or walls. They used mirrors angled out of the bars to eyeball others, lip reading words unspoken. Not in D Wing. The walls were thick and the space between each cell had an additional layer of soundproofing. There was no exposed piping near the sink and toilet.

The silence actually turned out to be one of Nick's favorite aspects of his time at Masterson. He was grateful he didn't have to hear the constant whine of attention-seeking jailbirds. In those twenty-two hours of isolation, Nick Lawrence explored the depths of his mind, searching for answers that had long since eluded him.

Nick put his hands to his mouth and coughed loudly. His left hand now contained the small piece of plastic. He stood and retrieved The Art of War from his bookshelf. *Is it a book shelf if it only contains one book?* Nick pondered as he looked at the now-empty shelf. These ridiculous questions had become more common as the days of isolation stacked up. He'd found he could lose hours to his conundrums. But when your life is suspended in a timeless void, those hours hold no value.

He opened the book and placed the thin piece of plastic between the pages. Nick turned his back to his cell door, concealing his actions from view of any passing guard. Upon examination, Nick noticed the plastic was a vacuum sealed pouch. Looking closer, he could see it was a tightly folded bit of paper.

Satisfied no guard could see, Nick removed the plastic square, bringing it to his mouth. He used his teeth to gnaw at the packaging, tearing at the grooved edge. It took a couple of failed attempts before getting the corner to separate. Nick pinched and twisted at the small opening with his fingers. The airtight seal released and the plastic loosened. He was careful not to rip the contents. Someone had obviously gone through a great deal of trouble to get this to him and he was intrigued. Nick tapped the folded paper into the seam of the book and looked over his shoulder, ensuring a guard wasn't peering into his cage.

He understood the implications of the discovery of any potential contraband during a random inspection, so Nick slipped the plastic wrapping into his mouth and swallowed hard. The rough edges scratched at his throat as he worked it down. He set the book down which now held the mysterious note and moved over to the sink. Nick pumped the handle down three times, creating a trickle from the faucet. Cupping his hands, he filled them with the tepid water and hastily slurped at it. He gagged once as he pushed the contents down his esophagus.

Clearing his throat, Nick returned to the book on his bed and opened it back up to the page containing the note.

He unfolded the thin white paper and stared at the hand-written words.

Nick,

You need to accept Declan's request to speak with you. He's already filed the contact order. You need to hear what he has to say. I'd be dead long ago if it wasn't for you. Time to repay my debt.

Jay

. . .

Nick sat back in deep thought, pondering the message. He then tore the note into small pieces, forcing each one into his mouth. He swallowed hard, his saliva did the work of disintegrating the paper, making it easier to get down than the plastic.

He looked at the open book. Sun Tzu's words taunted him. *Opportunities multiply as they are seized.*

Nick closed the book. His decision had been made.

11

Tank sat outside of Jessup County Memorial Hospital and watched as the media circus frothed at the hopes of an exclusive interview or candid shot from one of the shooter's family members. This was not the hospital where the critical victims of Sheldon Price's shooting were being cared for. The severely injured students were transported and treated at Vanderbilt University Medical Center. It was the closest Level 1 trauma center in the Volunteer State to the incident.

The media had initially flooded the victims in recovery, but the wave of media interest had receded in the last few days, shifting focus to the possible recovery of the killer. The world was apparently more interested in the mind of such a person than the survivors' plight.

His blood boiled as he watched the activists parading around the media vans with their hand-painted signs calling for second amendment reform. Every shooting brought forth this group of fanatics. He liked guns and appreciated his right to carry one.

Tank breathed deeply and calmed himself by thinking of the brutality he'd just unleashed on Doctor Gray. Violence always centered him.

Tank had been surveying the hospital for the last six hours, patiently waiting for his opportunity. Dr. Gray had exited the south side of the medical facility, avoiding the media cameras. He was roughly Tank's size, albeit the good doctor's thickness came in the way of fat. It had been a relatively easy thing, killing the physician. Tank found it to be a far easier thing than most people realized. He was glad more didn't understand its simplicity because it lessened the competition for gainful employment.

A tap of the doctor's bumper on a stretch of roadway with no traffic. The pudgy doctor had exited to examine the damage to the rear bumper of his Prius. Tank fired his silenced pistol twice into the back of his head and stuffed the body into the trunk of his rental, rented under a name and license that didn't exist. Tank didn't need to kill the doctor. He could have just as easily rendered him unconscious and left him tied up. *But what's the fun in that?* He only needed the doctor's identification and security badge to navigate the increased security surrounding Sheldon Price. And now he had them.

For a reason only known to him, Tank felt more composed and relaxed after a kill than at any other time. He truly believed he was the reincarnate of some great warrior and the only way to bring balance to his psyche was to satiate his bloodlust. In a rare moment of unguarded conversation he'd revealed this to the woman he loved. She laughed. She was now dead too. And afterward Tank never shared his private thoughts again.

12

Tank clipped the doctor's credentials to the white lab coat and moved toward the hospital's south entrance. A crisp breeze whipped across the parking lot and the cold air cut through the thin green scrubs he was wearing under the coat. He felt naked and wondered how doctors and nurses spent their days wearing this thin pajama-like material. Tank refocused himself, entering the building through the same doors the now deceased Dr. Gray had exited less than an hour before.

Tank knew his unique scars might catch the attention of others, so he affixed a light green surgical scrub cap, masking most of his damaged face and ear. He carried a thick file folder on a clipboard he'd swiped from a nursing station as he passed by a distracted medic talking with an attractive young nurse. Tank moved quickly and it gave him an air of importance, not making eye contact with any staff he passed. Doctor Gray's credentials were flipped to avoid being detected by a known associate.

He stood by the elevator located away from the main lobby area and pretended to be intently reading the file before him. Two orderlies had already pressed the up button and paid no attention to Tank. Doctors and nurses were commonplace in a hospital. Not too difficult to blend.

"My opinion, they should let the bastard die," one of the orderlies said.

Noticing Tank lingering behind them, he looked over his shoulder at Tank. "What do you think doc?"

"I'm actually on my way up to see the little bastard right now," Tank said with a smile.

The orderlies laughed at Tank's affirmation. His snide comment resonated with the two orderlies, and by the simplest of manipulations he'd garnered their respect. The doors to the elevator opened and Tank followed the two men inside.

"You said you're going to five doc?" the orderly asked.

"Yup. Time for the little bastard to get his medicine," Tank snarked.

All three men laughed.

He was glad the men had engaged him. It made locating Sheldon Price that much easier. Otherwise he'd been left to bumble his way from floor to floor, greatly risking an increased exposure.

The orderlies had exited on the third floor without a further word. Tank rode the rest of the way in silence. The elevator dinged, announcing his arrival to the fifth floor. He stepped out into the low murmur of voices and whirring mechanics of a variety of life-saving machines.

Tank took a moment to scan his surroundings. He was looking for the one thing he knew would identify Sheldon Price's room from all others— police. It wasn't long before he saw the two uniformed police officers standing guard at the far end of the floor.

His purposeful walk began again, and Tank moved past the floor's nurses' station without giving them a second look. The officers turned at his approach and seemed unconcerned. Their guard obviously lowered at Tank's ensemble.

The officer on the far side of the door remained seated. The one closest to Tank stood. Tank flashed Doctor Gray's credentials quickly and dismissively in a manner balanced between routine and annoyance. The officer seemed less than interested in examining them carefully.

"Afternoon doc. I'm going to need you to sign the log. You know the drill," the officer said flatly.

"Sure thing," Tank said with a smile as he took the clipboard from the young officer. Tank looked at the scribble of the other signatures on sheet and laughed to himself. Doctors really can't write legibly, which worked in his favor. Tank made his mark.

"Got the mask on huh?" the seated officer said inquisitively.

"Oh yeah. Got a bit of a cold. I don't want the poor boy to catch his death," Tank said with a laugh, knowing the cops would resonate with his dark sense of humor.

He'd assumed correctly as both men chuckled at the joke, and he handed the log back.

The officer pushed down on the handle, opening the door. Tank slipped inside, closing the door behind him.

13

The room was quiet, except for the beeps and buzzes from the machines bookending Sheldon Price's bed. Tank approached, examining his file folder as he closed the distance. Price stirred, groaning as he rotated his body toward him.

"Hello Sheldon, I'm Doctor Gray. How are you feeling today?" Tank said, doing his best to deliver a believable guise consistent with standard bedside manner banter.

"I'm okay I guess," Sheldon said weakly. His voice came in muffled rasps. His face was bandaged, leaving only his right eye exposed.

"We need to talk." Tank's demeanor changed and became gravely serious. Sheldon must have noticed because his one eye widened slightly.

"Okay. What about?"

"Who did you talk to?" Tank asked quietly.

"Talk to? About—what? I mean who are you?" Sheldon asked. His voice quivered.

"Who did you tell about Rebel Dogs? About Sasquatch_187? About the Patriot level?" Tank spat the questions in rapid fire succession.

"N-n-n-nobody," Sheldon stammered.

"Are you sure?"

"Nobody. Oh Jesus! Who are you?" A tear fell from Sheldon's right eye.

"I'm the last face you'll ever see," Tank said quietly, moving a razor-sharp scalpel across the boy's throat, opening the neck on the opposite side from where Tank was standing.

Tank stepped back quickly avoiding the arterial spurt. He pulled the curtain to block the view from the hallway. It would take Sheldon price approximately thirty seconds to bleed out from the wound, long enough for him to clear the floor before triggering the monitors' medical alerts. Tank moved to the door and exited.

"Hey boys, I'll be right back. I forgot something in my office. Can I grab you a cup of coffee from the lounge?" Tank said, already moving at a quick pace down the hall.

"I'll take one. Black, two sugars," the seated officer said.

"Sounds good. Black two sugars," Tank called back over his shoulder as he shuffled away.

He bypassed the elevator and pushed the door to the stairwell. As the door closed behind him, he heard an alarm sound and the automated Code Blue announcement blare over the speakers. Tank made quick work of the stairs and pushed out into the first-floor lobby. Tank crossed the shiny yellow floors leading out toward the south exit and out the same doors he'd entered less than ten minutes before.

Thomas "Tank" Jones calmly drove out of the parking lot of Jessup County Memorial Hospital as several cruisers barreled in. The sound of police sirens worked the media personnel into a crazed frenzy. Tank watched in the review mirror at the chaos he'd created. He looked down and noticed a small drop of blood in the knuckle of his right index finger.

Deeply satisfied, Tank smiled.

14

It had been eight months since Nick had set foot in the small room. Last time his lawyer had occupied the chair facing him. Nick looked at the rugged features of the man who now filled that space. It was not the face he'd expected to see after reading the note.

The two men hadn't seen each other since the day they'd shared a vodka toast to their fallen friend, Izzy Martinez. It was the same room where Nick had spent his last moments of freedom. He remembered how the taste of the Tito's had soured in his mouth when his closest friend and fellow agent had walked him out the door of that room and into the cuffs. The end result of that journey landed him here inside the confines of Masterson Federal Correctional Facility.

Nick no longer blamed his friend, but the ability to reach that resolution had taken months of contemplation. Nick had looked the other way on a bank robbery Declan had committed. He'd realized the good in the man and looked past his mistake, leaving the case unsolved. Nick had gone against everything his training and experience had taught him in making the arrest, but he owed him his life, and on the battlefield the lines are not black and white. Some of his burden had been alleviated when he learned Declan had used the money to help a devastated family, confirming in his mind he'd ultimately made the right decision.

The biggest irony was Declan now worked for the Bureau and was attached to their world-renowned Hostage Rescue Team, or HRT. Declan was an agent and Nick a convict. Life presents some strange twists of fate.

Declan had walked him out to an awaiting team of FBI agents. As reflection gave way to clarity, Nick realized his friend had done this for his benefit. Nick understood Declan feared the arrest could go badly and he didn't want Nick to get hurt or possibly killed. But beyond that, Declan Enright wanted to be by his side at Nick's darkest hour. And for those reasons he forgave his friend, holding him in the highest regard.

The bond of their friendship was strong, and the fact that his friend, sitting across from him now, had gone through these efforts one year later to meet with him proved it to be unbreakable.

Nick sat, separated by a small heavy steel table buffed to a dull glow, reflecting the soft incandescent light above. The chairs and tables were bolted down. This was more important here than anywhere else in D Wing. Nick was convinced many an inmate would've tried to hurl them at their lawyer. Any object a Masterson convict could move was considered a potential weapon and therefore the facility was filled with counter-measures.

"Jesus, look at you," Declan Enright said.

Declan's eyes widened, betraying the shock at seeing Nick's hardened exterior. Long tendrils of dark greasy hair reached his broad shoulders. The beard, thick and matted, covered his cheek bones, the long squiggly ends dipped to the middle of his throat. He looked like a lumberjack returning home from a two-month logging expedition. The last time Declan had laid eyes on him, Nick had been a clean-cut FBI investigator. Oh, how time had changed things. But one thing Nick's rough and tough exterior couldn't change – his eyes. It was a true statement that they were a window into the soul.

Nick looked his friend over. Declan Enright was ageless, frozen in time, and somehow capable of maintaining the same physical stature indicative of the Navy's elite. He looked as though he'd just dusted the Coronado sand off of his pants before strutting into this interview room. The aura of confidence beaming from him caused other men to question their virility.

"You look... the same," Nick said flatly.

"I'd ask how the food is, but apparently they're stuffing it with steroids," Declan said, chuckling softly at his own joke.

Nick stared blankly and didn't respond. He was weighing this meeting in his mind. Eight months of isolation and then a message from Jay puts his friend in front of him. It was no small task to get the note to him and so he assumed something serious was coming. Nick waited.

"Well, I can see you're not in the mood for small talk. So, let's get to the meat and potatoes of why I'm here," Declan said, leaning in.

Nick looked back toward the closed door and the back of the guard's head that was visible in the small pane of heavy glass.

"Not to worry. They can't hear anything we're saying." Declan tapped the watch on his left wrist. "This watch sends out a signal, disrupting the audio recording. Don't ask me how it works beyond that. A courtesy of our mutual friend," Declan said.

"You'll still have only a few minutes before the guards come in. Once they realize there's an issue with the recording system, they'll terminate this interview or relocate us. They don't screw around in here."

"Then let's get on with it," Declan said. The thin smile dissipated, and Declan took on a serious look.

Nick sat back, resting his hands evenly on his thighs, still quivering slightly from the exertion of his early morning workout.

"We're breaking you out."

"You've lost your goddamned mind. Impossible," Nick said.

"I wouldn't be here if it wasn't for you. I'd be the one rotting behind bars on the bank job. I would've lost everything if you hadn't helped me out. And my daughters would be growing up without a father," Declan said softly.

Hearing the word father caused Nick to twitch and his stomach knotted. He'd pushed the memory of his baby far from his mind. But hearing Declan's reference to his own children forced it to the forefront and the tragedy of losing a child. The inexplicable pain was difficult to contain, but Nick focused on the man in front of him and pushed down his sadness.

"Apparently, from what Jay's told me, he too owes you his life. He didn't go into any great detail which I guess is par for the course with a CIA spook. But he did mention you took a few bullets for him and that he would've been dead otherwise," Declan said. "Neither one of us want to leave this world without repaying our debts. And we've come up with a way to do that."

Nick shook his head. "It's impossible. I'm not going to Shawshank my way into the shitters. I'm telling you whatever cockamamie scheme you've come up with will fail. You're living in fantasy camp."

"I said the same thing, but Jay... well that guy's at the next level. You're about to find out what your friend's been up to since you last saw him." Declan paused, clearing his throat. "I will say this—your life will never be the same once we do this. Never," Declan said with a finality that Nick had rarely seen.

"I'll entertain you on this, but only because I've got a pretty open schedule today," Nick said, giving a feeble attempt at humor.

"You're going to die today."

Nick gave his friend a double take.

"I'm going to tap the tip of your shoe. It's going to transfer a small adhesive pouch. Contained inside is a pill. Don't ask me what the hell it is, because they told me and I've never heard of it. Apparently, something Jay's team has cooked up," Declan said, speaking in rapid fire succession.

"Jay's team?"

"No time to go into that now. If you're right about them cancelling the interview then we have limited time." Declan said.

Nick felt the hard impact of Declan's foot against the toe of his shoe.

Nick looked straight ahead, giving no reaction to the contact. The transfer was complete.

"You're going to take that pill and then tie your bedsheet tightly around your neck. You're going to do all of this tonight ten minutes after lights out just before the guards do their first visual room pass. We'll handle the rest," Declan said.

"What's the pill going to do?" Nick asked.

"It's effectively going to slow your heartbeat to an unrecognizable level, at least by human touch. Meaning the guards won't be able to tell. That's why the timing is essential. They need to find you right away. There's a limited window before that pill's going to have a permanent effect."

"Permanent?" Nick said.

"Like I said—leave the rest to us."

Nick swallowed hard, digesting this plan.

"Do you trust me?" Declan asked.

Nick paused and looked hard at the man before him. "Like nobody else."

"Then get ready to be reborn."

As if on cue, the door to the room opened and two guards entered. "Excuse me Agent Enright, but there is some type of issue with the recording system in this room. We are making arrangements to have you transferred down the hall to another room."

"No need. We're done here. Thank you," Declan said dismissively.

At the direction of guards, Nick stood. He shot an affirmative glance at Declan as he was quickly shackled, connecting a long chain from his cuffs on his wrists to the ones on his ankles. The metal around his ankle rubbed uncomfortably as he was guided toward the door.

Nick shuffled down the hallway bookended by the two guards.

He moved in the direction of his cell. Regardless of the success of this mission, one thing was certain, this would be Nick Lawrence's last night as an inmate of Masterson Federal Correctional Facility. Dead or free—he'd be leaving.

15

The Shelton Public Library buzzed with the murmurs from the mass of Pebble Brook High School students who'd made the short jaunt over after their school's dismissal. It was a common occurrence and most of the teens used it as hangout. This behavior was more typical during the winter months when Sand Hill Park was too cold for comfort.

For Albert Hutchins the library was an everyday routine regardless of weather or season. It wasn't a hangout for him. It was a safe haven from the outside world, a cruel and brutal place that had left him broken and dejected.

Most days he beat all the other students because he never stopped at his locker, or as he referred to it, the beating booth. Albert ensured he avoided his locker at all costs, carrying the books for every day's subjects in his over-sized and extremely burdensome backpack. He would linger in his class until the hallways cleared and then make a beeline for his next class. This tactic increased his transit safety most of, but not all of the time. Any time he'd been trapped outside of the eyes and ears of the faculty it was bad, very bad, for Albert Hutchins.

At sixteen years old he had already developed a slight hunch from slogging through his day with thirty pounds of materials. His shoulders always expressed relief when he'd release the straps at the end of his day, dropping the burdensome load.

There was one computer he always sought out, isolated from the terminal hubs arranged for the more social of his classmates. His sanctuary was set back, shrouded by large bookcases containing volumes of books he had never read. Sheldon used to read and found he could lose himself inside the pages. That was until he found online gaming. It enabled him a deeper and darker escape from his pathetic reality.

He took up his seat at his terminal and slipped his headphones on, the worn pads of which effectively closed him off from the outside world as he began his transformation. A few clicks of the keyboard and Albert Hutchins was now his alter ego, Bully_Slayer#1.

Albert spent most of his after-school time as his alternate personality, sometimes finding it difficult to disconnect. Numerous times in the recent past he'd been snapped from his gaming trance at the librarian's closing announcement. It usually took Albert the ten-minute walk home before he was able to clear his mind enough to engage in human interaction, which under the circumstances of his current living conditions was less than desirable.

His foster family was better than the last. At least the father didn't pay him midnight visits. He'd lived with the Walker family since the start of high school, but never truly fit in. He was berated the moment he walked through the door as they took out their daily frustrations. He understood his place in the pecking order around the house and also knew his value. Albert Hutchins was a government stipend for the Walker family. Nothing more, nothing less.

He'd long ago stopped caring about his life or the direction it took. His immersion in online gaming alleviated some of his despondency, but only slightly. That was until he found Rebel Dogs. The game allowed him to create a world worth living in and Albert Hutchins found something he hadn't had in a very long time, a purpose. His goal when playing was to kill every bully he encountered within the gaming platform's realm.

Albert spent countless hours learning the user gamertags of his Pebble Brook classmates. He kept a secret journal listing who they were in real life and how many times in his alternative life he'd killed them in his alternate universe. The tally grew exponentially with each passing day and he reveled in his dominance.

Not too long ago he had overheard Andy Bloom, his archnemesis, complaining to a friend about the Bully Slayer and how he'd love to find him in real life and kick his ass. The irony is, Andy, unbeknownst to him, had on many occasions already followed through with that threat. But for every time Andy had punched, kicked, or embarrassed him, Albert had killed him in Rebel Dogs ten times over.

The game world was designed as a free-range open play format with levels of achievement earned through actions, enabling characters to gain experience points and level up. If you wanted to steal a car, you stole a car. If you wanted to be a police officer and fight crime, you went after the guy who stole the car. If you wanted to take a hammer and drive it into the head of your enemy, well—you became like Albert "the Bully Slayer" Hutchins.

Points were awarded for each achievement earned, and every once in a while the game's admins, or administrators, would install a challenge. Successful completion of such challenges would give you badges and increase your ranking. Sometimes a challenge would be something simple like seeing how many street robberies you could complete under a set time constraint. There were a wide variety of other challenges, but the one in which Albert excelled at were Savage Countdowns. During this type of challenge, Albert was rewarded for dealing as much death to the other gamers and artificial unmanned characters as he could within the time limits. Over the short span of time he'd been playing Rebel Dogs, Albert had moved up in the rankings quickly.

Once a player's ranking reached a certain number then a title would be earned. Plebe was the lowest and assigned once a profile was created. Andy Bloom was a still a Plebe. Prospect was the next level up and extremely difficult to achieve and Albert reached it two days ago. He'd been elated and wanted to share the news with someone else, but he had nobody in his life he could confide in. That was, until yesterday when Albert had logged in to his profile and saw there was a message waiting for him in his gaming inbox.

The message was from a fellow Prospect, Graham_CrackerHacker. Another human being had actually sent him a message. The feeling at getting such a message was overwhelming. Graham_CrackerHacker was the first person to show him any interest in his recent memory. Today, he had sat in school all day yearning for the day's end. He stared at the clock all day, watching the seconds tick by until he was free. Albert almost considered skipping school, but knew if he did the librarian wouldn't let him in. He knew this because he'd been caught doing that before. As soon as school ended, Albert dashed out the doors and now sat staring anxiously as the game loaded. His leg bounced nervously in anticipation and he was excited to see if his new friend had written him again.

The game intro complete and his profile accessed, Albert saw there was not only one message, but three. His fingers tingled with exhilaration as he accessed them.

The first: *Are you there?*

The second: *Let's play.*

The third and most interesting to Albert read: *Are you ready to go to the next level???*

Albert messaged his response: *Yes. Where are you?*

The question was not about Graham's actual physical location, but more importantly his location within the game. Gamers could pick from active campaigns or games happening in any of the variety of environments. It was easy to get lost in Rebel Dogs' vastness, but Albert knew of the popular locations that his classmates used. But Graham_CrackerHacker was not from his school and therefore he needed to find him in the virtual world.

There was a way to tap on a gamertags and geolocate another character. Once that is done a gamer can join up the other player and interact. That's how, in the past, Albert had effectively been able to spawn near his schoolmates and kill them. He could see Graham_CrackerHacker's avatar link and click on it, trying to link up. Every attempt had failed to connect. Albert felt rejected. His hopes at meeting a new friend was not working out as planned. He slumped in his seat as a message notification dinged and Graham was number one, flashing in his inbox, indicating a new message had just been received.

Graham: *Ready? Click and see.*

Albert clicked Graham's character tag, a skull and cross bones, and

Bully_Slayer#1 now stood next to Graham's avatar, who was configured to look like a ninja. Once two characters were linked, the two could chat freely. This was the first time Albert was able to chat with anyone in recent memory, and he couldn't type fast enough.

Albert typed feverishly: *How are you? Thanks for connecting. How old are you? How long have you been a Prospect?*

Albert stopped after hitting send, realizing he looked desperate and possibly a bit crazy. He didn't want to scare off the first person who'd befriended him in more than a year.

Graham did not address any of the questions asked. He only answered Albert's question with a question of his own: *Are you ready to be a Patriot?*

Albert knew there was a final level, but no matter how many kills he'd amassed or challenges he'd completed he couldn't seem to figure out how to get there. Until now.

Albert messaged: *How?*

The chat bubble above Graham's avatar pointed toward the outside of a school.

It didn't look too much different from the school he attended. Albert surveyed the virtual scene on his monitor zooming in on the autos, unmanned characters, as they filed into the school. It looked relatively boring, as if he were watching the beginning of a regular day at Pebble Brook High. Albert could tell the autos from the manually controlled avatars because the unmanned characters had no personalized name tags hovering above them.

Albert: *What's the challenge?*

Graham: *KILL 'EM ALL.*

Albert stared at the screen and his heart beat faster. Not out of nervousness, but from the sheer excitement of it all. He'd envisioned this day in real life and relished the thought of getting to play it out now. And unlike real life, he wasn't alone. Graham, his new best friend, was standing beside him.

Albert asked: *Weapons?*

Every challenge came with additional weaponry or tools.

Graham: *Check your inventory.*

Albert made a click to the satchel icon and it opened. Inside was a device, most likely a bomb, and a pistol.

Graham: *ARE YOU READY?*

Albert typed, feeling cool and powerful. *Hell to the yeah!*

Graham: *LET'S DO THIS!!!*

The timer activated and a small countdown clock populated the upper right corner of the screen, ticking down from three minutes. Bully_Slayer#1 and Graham_CrackerHacker moved in tandem toward the front doors of the school. Graham's avatar dropped behind, letting Albert take the lead as they entered.

Albert manipulated his avatar through the crowd, shoving aside the simulated students lingering in the hallway. He moved to a more population-dense area. To get the highest kill ratio in the shortest amount of time he needed to strike in a place with the most students congregating. He found the perfect place to begin his assault, the cafeteria.

The Bully Slayer switched to first person point of view, or POV, knowing it's always better to kill from that perspective. He withdrew the pistol from his inventory and aimed. Albert used the keyboard to manipulate his aiming points as he began firing into the group of students.

He was good. No, he was great, placing head shots on the virtual students. The autos reacted to his shooting and began running for the doors of the cafeteria. Albert fired at them, piling bodies at each of the exits and making it impossible for the characters to leave. The simulated student body was trapped with the Bully Slayer. Like shooting fish in a barrel, he emptied the gun and reloaded several times. With every pull of the digital trigger, Albert envisioned Andy Bloom's face.

Out of bullets, he retrieved the bomb from his inventory. The doors were now blocked for him too. The countdown timer was ticking down with only a few seconds left. Albert "the Bully Slayer" tossed the bomb into the center of the café and detonated. His screen went blank.

Albert sat in silence staring at his muted reflection in the smudged blackness of the flat-screen monitor.

Then a message in bright green letters populated the screen.

PATRIOT.

Albert involuntarily held his breath as he took in the seven letters exemplifying his life's biggest achievement.

In smaller letters beneath the word came a message:

Are you ready to take it the next level? Are you ready to be a legend in the real world?

Albert Hutchins wasn't sure what that meant, but wanted this feeling to continue. He slowly and deliberately pressed each key of his simple response.

YES.

16

"Open cell 301!"

Nick heard the words but the sound filtered in like someone screaming underwater. Then without warning all sound dissipated.

"No pulse. Get him on the gurney," said Sergeant Gary Fredrickson, D Wing shift supervisor. Panic filled his voice. No supervisor wanted an inmate to die on their watch. Not a good thing for the resume, especially for someone vying for the next Lieutenant's position. "Christ! Move his ass!"

The two large guards each positioned themselves at the shoulders and feet of Nick Lawrence. They grunted their exertion, hoisting his large frame to the lowered gurney. The two medics, who'd luckily been at the facility on an unrelated matter, were able to redirect to D Wing to assist. Fredrickson looked two shades whiter than normal, which made the pasty face of the overweight man look translucent.

Fredrickson's goal was to get the inmate in the ambulance before anyone pronounced him dead. Then it would be a medical death and not a failure of his leadership. As arbitrary a difference it may seem, Fredrickson knew those details sometimes saved careers. With only a few years left before reaching his pension he couldn't afford the fallout. The frantic federal corrections sergeant started pushing on the back of one of the medics, trying to expedite the process.

Outside the cell, Fredrickson led the way, practically jogging along the yellow line of D Wing's second tier landing with the two medics following close behind. The right front wheel of the gurney was loose and wobbled noisily as it pulled to the right, banging loudly into the rail lining the landing. The larger of the two medics, a broad-shouldered ginger-haired man in his late thirties, adjusted the cart carrying the body of Nick Lawrence and corrected the alignment of the poor-quality bed on wheels.

Sergeant Fredrickson brought the medics to the large elevator adjacent the chow line area. He'd radioed ahead and the doors were already being held open by one of the guards.

Fredrickson ensured that inmate Lawrence was properly shackled to the gurney. He advised the medics that he'd called ahead to Mercy General, only a few miles down the road, to ensure security would be standing by to take them to a secure room in the ER. The thinner medic who was now guiding the front of the gurney into the awaiting ambulance nodded.

"Not a problem. We transport inmates back and forth all the time," the thin medic said.

"Not from D Wing. We run things a bit different tonight. I would normally have a guard ride with you, but I'm short staffed on this shift. I will have someone ordered in to assist, but it will take a little bit for me to arrange that. The hospital security staff should be sufficient until that happens. Whatever you do, those cuffs do not come off him. Do you understand?" Fredrickson said.

"Understood."

The rear doors to the ambulance closed. The sally port doors of Masterson Federal Correctional Facility clanged loudly as they opened, and Fredrickson watched as the ambulance sped away toward the first of three gated checkpoints. The sirens echoed in the stillness of the night.

"Get it running. Time's running out," the large medic said, checking the IV line.

"It'll take a minute, but we should be seeing some signs of life soon," the thin medic said.

The ambulance had pulled to the side of the road and the lights and sirens were turned off as the two men worked to revive the man strapped to the gurney. The large man reached to release the shackles that were binding the inmate to the railings.

"You think that's a good idea?" the smaller man said.

"What are you scared of?"

"Um... he's a big guy. I'm not sure how he's going to react. Sometimes people don't respond well to being dead." The smaller man moved back a bit. "Go ahead, but you're in charge of wrangling him in if things go awry."

The larger red-haired man smiled, confidently. "It'd be just like wrestling a gator."

17

The silence broke like a tidal wave above his head. Without warning the absolute quiet had pitched to full volume. The tranquil darkness that, seemingly only moments before, had completely enveloped him like a fluffy blanket lifted abruptly, the shock caused him to convulse wildly. His heart beat wildly and felt as though it would jump from his chest. Nick's body trembled violently like someone staving off hypothermia.

The mask attached to his face hissed loudly, filling his lungs with cool air. He welcomed it and inhaled deeply as if taking in his very first breath.

"He's coming out. Get ready," a voice said from somewhere around him.

Nick's eyes watered at the introduction of bright white light, blurring his vision. Disoriented, he swung his head looking for the source of the voice he'd just heard. His mind reeled, trying to comprehend his current circumstance, but his thoughts were encased in a fog that wouldn't seem to lift.

"Try to relax," a different voice said. This man's speech was deeper and thicker than the other. There was a very distinct accent that accompanied the words, but the identification of it was too far from his memory.

Relax? Nick thought. *How the hell does one relax under these circumstances?*

"It takes some time to adjust to everything that's just happened to you. Death isn't an easy thing to come back from," the thick accented voice said.

Death? Nick battled with the comprehension of the comment as he closed his eyes, giving in. The recall of the events leading up to his current predicament started to filter in, but it was a disjointed account like trying to remember a dream. But with each passing minute his mental acuity returned and with it a sense of calm.

He opened his eyes again. This time his vision cleared, and he adjusted to his surroundings. Closest to him was a muscular, fair-skinned man with bright red, almost orange, hair. Nick twisted his head back, finding the source of the other voice. This man had short dark hair and was thinner than his counterpart. The thin-framed man looked athletically fit and had a seriousness to his eyes. Nick could readily tell both were hardened men.

Nick nodded to both and exhaled, remembering the plan and now understanding their role in it. The humidity of his breath fogged the clear rubber shell of the mask, still providing him with cool oxygen.

"Welcome back. You've got an IV drip that you're going to need a little bit longer. And I recommend the oxygen stays on too. Your brain will thank me later," the large man said. "I'm Bob and my friend over there—for now, you can call him Joe."

Nick nodded, knowing it was useless to try to talk through the hiss of the mask.

"I'm going to unshackle you. Try to stay calm," Bob said. "I'd hate to have to watch you die again."

Nick wasn't quite sure if the large man was kidding and nodded his understanding.

The cuffs released. Nick only moved his hands and feet enough to clear the shackles away. He remained supine and relaxed, rubbing his wrists.

A cellphone chimed and the man called Joe answered. He listened without saying a word and then ended the call.

"They're here. Ready?" Joe asked.

"Nick, listen carefully. We've got to transfer you to another vehicle. I'm going to help you because you're going to be fairly off balance for the next hour or so while your body comes back to homeostasis. That death pill is a real bitch," Bob said with a chuckle.

Nick gave a weak thumbs up.

Seconds later the rear doors to the ambulance swung open. Nick's body fought against him and did not cooperate, making the task of propping himself up extremely challenging. His disorientation made movement harder than he imagined and he immediately realized the truth of Bob's words. *Death isn't an easy thing to come back from.*

His eyes took a moment to adjust to the darkness outside. In the wash of light pouring out from the ambulance he saw a familiar face standing there to assist in steadying him as he exited and attempted to stand.

"I thought you looked like shit the last time I saw you, but you've taken that to the next level. Death is not a good look for you, my friend," Declan said with his infamous cocky smile.

Nick grabbed Declan's shoulder with his right arm and used his left to push the oxygen tank like a crutch along the dirt-covered breakdown lane of the roadway. The man called Bob followed closely behind holding his IV bag in one hand and supporting Nick at his left elbow.

A small box truck was parked, idling only a few feet away. The short distance felt like a marathon in Nick's current physical condition.

Declan and Bob got Nick up the ramp and laid him down on the hard paneling of the box truck's rear compartment, stripping him out of his jumpsuit and throwing a blanket over his naked body.

He then watched as Declan and Bob removed a tarp covering something on the other side of the small space of the box truck's interior. Nick saw a stack of three bodies. Two of the bodies were clothed, wearing the same medical uniforms Bob and Joe had on. The third body was naked and Nick watched as Declan and Joe awkwardly slid the jumpsuit over the third body. The size of the dead man was comparable to himself.

Bob hung the IV on a hook above Nick's head and then returned to assist in hauling the three bodies out of the rear of the truck.

With the last of the bodies out, Declan closed the doors. "Sleep tight buttercup," he said, latching the door.

Nick was once again surrounded in darkness. He knew the truth behind the age-old saying that it was always darkest before the dawn.

He rested, preparing his mind for what his next dawn would bring.

18

"It's working better than I thought. And that's a hard thing for me to say, because I was pretty confident in the potential. I just didn't think it would be this easy," Graham said. "I guess there are a lot of messed up kids out there."

"So, where does that put us in terms of timing?" Tanner Morris asked his son.

"Ahead of schedule. I'd say it's time to send the message," Graham said eagerly.

Morris looked at his son, weighing his suggestion. He had contemplated the ramifications of this next and final step. In fact, he'd been obsessed over it, but now that the objective was within grasp, he hesitated. It had been six years since he'd formulated this plan. Six years since his life had been derailed and put him on this very destructive path. *How many acts of violence needed to saturate headlines before this cultural and systemic indifference was reformed?* Tanner Morris thought to himself and knew he was about to find out.

Tanner knew the type of child he'd raised. He knew his influences on the monster he'd helped create and the deviant behavior he'd fostered for his own benefit. Looking at Graham he felt no sense of fatherly pride. His son was on a preordained journey of violence, a fact Tanner had known since the day he caught him torturing the neighbor's dog. He'd covered for his nonconformity then and wielded its potency now.

His daughter, Wendy, had not been like her brother. She was the polar opposite, an angel with not a malicious bone in her body. And *they* had taken her from him. The cruelty of others had been too much for her delicate nature. The void in Tanner Morris's life created in the wake of her death was deep and dark—a ponderous gap as wide as the Grand Canyon. The ex-convict entrepreneur hoped, against all reason, his plan would fill that hole.

"I'll bring in the others. Tank should be back in town this afternoon." Tanner looked at his son and recognized the lustful spark in his eyes, a spark only satiated by death. "We'll move up the timeline and begin prep for the final phase."

"For Wendy," Graham said.

Hearing her name gave Tanner Morris pause and he closed his eyes briefly, picturing the soft round cheeks and deep blue of his daughter's eyes. He exhaled loudly, releasing the memory. "For Wendy," he said, steadying his voice and resolve for what was to come.

19

Nick heard the conversations of others. He sat up in his darkened space and looked around. The fog lifted and his body no longer had the lagged response from earlier. Whatever he had ingested to induce his simulated death had worn off.

Nick realized he was no longer on the uncomfortable floor of the box truck. The soft leather of a couch had replaced the hard wood flooring. The oxygen mask he'd been wearing when he drifted off into oblivion was now gone. Running his fingers along the outside of his left hand, Nick felt the attachment of the IV. In the dark, he traced his fingers up the rubber tubing to the depleted soft plastic of the empty bag, hanging from the thin metallic hook of an IV holder. He tore off the tape and withdrew the needle from the vein in his hand. Not a big fan of needles, Nick shook off the wave of nausea accompanying this feat. Not being able to see clearly in the dark had assisted his ability to do this without becoming overwhelmed.

His eyes, having been closed for some time, adjusted quickly to the limited lighting of the room and he was able to vaguely make out his surroundings. Using the light coming in through the space under the door, he observed a sturdy desk and high-backed leather chair rounding out the extent of furnishings, in addition to the couch Nick was seated on.

The cool of the floor seeped up through Nick's bare feet. He was still naked. The blanket he'd been covered in was now in a heap on the floor. He stood and stretched, his joints popped as he adjusted himself. On top of the desk was a pile of clothes and pair of sneakers. He dressed, surprised at how well the clothing fit, and moved toward the door. His hand rested hesitantly on the knob, knowing that when he opened it he'd be stepping into a brand new world.

Nick entered the room, shielding the light from his eyes with his hand. All talking ceased as the former FBI agent turned inmate stood in the open space of what could best be described as an operations center. A ten-person conference table was set in the middle of the room. Scattered along the walls on both sides were cubicle-styled work stations separated by gray partitions.

Six people were seated around the table and all present turned to face him. The way they sized him up and down, he felt as though he was still naked. At the table's head was a face Nick hadn't seen in several years. The man stood and smiled.

"Welcome back from the dead, my friend," Jay said, broadening his smile.

Jay walked out from behind the table and approached. Nick remained still, taking it all in, still processing the situation.

"I know this is a lot to swallow. I'm going to bring you up to speed, but first let me introduce you to the team," Jay said, closing the gap and giving Nick a hearty embrace.

"How long was I out?" Nick asked, trying to account for lost time and to get his bearings. The room he was in had no windows and therefore he had no ability to discern the time of day.

"Not too long. About ten hours," Jay said, looking down at his watch.

"Ten hours? I can't remember the last time I slept for more than four at a clip," Nick said.

"Death is an exhausting process. Plus, I think you've been long overdue for a rest," Jay said, patting Nick's back. "Sorry it took me so long to get you here."

Nick cocked his head at Jay. "Where is here?"

"All in good time. Like I said, let's meet the others," Jay said, guiding Nick forward toward a vacant seat.

Nick approached the table and took a seat nearest the only other person he trusted in the world, Declan Enright.

"Nick, let me first say you're in the company of dead men," Jay said.

Jay resumed his position at the head of the table. The person closest to Jay gave an exaggerated clearing of her throat.

Jay chuckled. "Correction, you're in the company of dead men and women. Better?"

"I think it's more politically correct to say dead people," the woman said, laughing softly at her own joke.

"I'm Barbie. I handle logistics," she said with a nod.

Nick returned the nod. She was attractive, but not in such a way that would draw too much attention. It was her air of confidence that added to her mystique. She had strawberry blond hair and light blue eyes, bordering on gray. Her jawline was taut, indicative of a high level of fitness. She sat upright like an astute student eagerly waiting to answer the teacher's next question.

Sitting to her left was the smaller man from the ambulance, the one who'd called himself Joe. He spoke next, "I know we already met. I'm Spider. I handle interrogations."

Hearing the name Spider, Nick almost laughed out loud but stopped himself when he saw the seriousness in the dark-eyed man's stare. Nick couldn't help but feel as though he'd just entered the Justice League's secret lair. He half expected Batman to walk in.

"We met earlier. I'm Gator and I run the pre-op planning," the large red-haired man said.

Nick had heard the heavy accent before but couldn't place it in his mental haze. Louisiana or somewhere close to that locale. The nickname made sense based on the man's size and vernacular.

"I don't have a cool code name. These ass-clowns call me Wizard, naming me after the '80s movie with Fred Savage. I've filed my complaint with corporate." Wizard eyeballed the group with an exaggerated glare, a joke he undoubtedly had used on more than one occasion. "I handle all computer and technical issues. In short, I'm their hacker."

"Don't sell yourself short. You're not just any hacker, you tapped into the federal reserve database and siphoned millions," Jay said, cocking an eyebrow.

"Oh yeah, that. Well, it was for a good cause," Wizard said, laughing.

"And what cause was that?" Barbie asked.

"Me," Wizard said, grinning widely. "If you can't treat yourself, then you're not living."

"Well, you're not living anymore," Gator said.

Wizard chuckled loudly. "True. It was a terrible fire."

"I'm Declan and I'm an alcoholic," Declan said with a flat monotone delivery.

The group erupted into laughter and, as if rehearsed, in unison chimed, "Hi Declan."

The sound of his friend's voice combined with the cocky wit displayed in this room full of strangers had a calming effect on Nick. The awkward tension dissipated almost instantly.

"I know this is a bit odd. But trust me when I say this—you are in the company of some of this country's most underrated and unsung heroes. What we do here is... unique," Jay said, scanning the group members. "We operate outside of the normal parameters of other governmental law enforcement agencies. In doing so, we are able to react quicker to threats and deploy tactics not acceptable under the typical policy guidelines."

"So, which agency governs you? There's always some type of oversight. Homeland? Department of Justice?" Nick asked.

"Neither," Jay said.

"Then who sanctions you?" Nick surveyed the room. "Who funds your operation? Running something like this has got to cost a pretty penny."

"That's for a later discussion. You're not asking the right question," Jay said, looking intensely into Nick's eyes.

Nick stood at the end of the table. All eyes were on him, Declan included. "Why me? Why am I here?"

"I thought you'd never ask," Jay said, breaking into a smile. "I owe you my life. A debt not easily paid. And one I take very seriously."

Nick gave a subtle nod, knowing Jay's reference and remembering their first encounter years ago in the mountains of Afghanistan. A bloody bond that only the truly battle-tested could understand.

"I couldn't let you waste away in a cell. A cell we both would be sharing if you ever spoke about the intel gathering aspect of your assault on Montrose and his goons," Jay said.

"We'd all be in a bit of trouble on that one," Wizard said.

Nick immediately realized the support Jay had provided back then was not through his CIA channels, but by this ragtag group. He looked again at the big man from the bayou. Something was familiar but initially unplaceable, and then it dawned on him. "You were at the hospital in Austin that day."

"Yup," Gator answered in his thick backwater accent. "I wondered if you'd remember."

Nick shook his head in disbelief. Gator had been the one who Jay had sent to retrieve the tracking device. And Wizard, or Wiz, must've been the one who reverse engineered it, enabling him—well, more Declan and Izzy —to save Mouse from the traffickers.

"Jesus," Nick sighed.

"I know it's a lot to take in. Especially after just coming back from your recent near-death experience," Jay said. "Take some time to process this and wrap your head around things."

Nick sank deeper into his seat.

"So, how about it?" Jay asked, expectantly.

"How about what?"

"Becoming a part of this dysfunctional family?" Jay asked, grinning.

Nick shot a glance to Declan, who returned it with a solemn nod of his head.

"I don't see why you'd need me," Nick said dismissively.

Jay unfolded his hands and leaned in, resting his elbows on the sturdy table. "For starters, I've never seen a more tenacious investigator. I'm going to give you an opportunity to apply that, without restriction, to some of the worst offenders this country has to offer. And more importantly, I know you. I know you've been battle tested, and what you're capable of doing. You operate at a totally different level, like when my life hung in the balance. When the proverbial shit hits the fan, I want you by my side."

Nick accepted the compliment with a slight bow of his head. "Well, I guess I'm dead so there really isn't a life to go back to."

"I'm going to take that as a yes," Jay said. "Now the only thing left is to name you."

There was a murmur from the group as they began to voice their ideas. One voice, clear and louder than the others, dominated. "Wolf," Declan said. "I mean look at him. It's either that or Shaggy Dog."

"I like it," Jay said. "Wolf it is."

"Jesus, even the new guy gets a better nickname," Wizard whined.

"Meeting adjourned. We need to check the chatter and I want an update on progress with The Seven's last meeting location."

The group rose and the members dispersed to their cubicles. Declan walked over to Nick and clasped a strong hand on his shoulder. "Crazy stuff, huh?"

"That's the understatement of a lifetime." Nick gave a smile, but it came out flat. "Did I hear Jay correctly? He said The Seven. Are we talking about the same group Khaled worked for?"

"Yup, the one and only," Declan said. "Ever wonder how terror groups disappear from the headlines? Apparently, this group is the answer."

"No nickname for you?" Nick asked with cock of his head.

"I have one. The same one I used back in my days as an operator," Declan said in his typical swagger. "They call me Ace."

Nick remembered Declan's old call sign from his days in the Navy's most elite ghost unit, Alpha One. "What about Val and the girls?" Nick asked, genuinely concerned that this new position would compromise the devoted family man's home life.

"I'm not dead if that's what you're asking. Jay saw no need to fake my death. He knew me well enough to know there'd be no way I'd volunteer for this under those parameters." Declan continued, "Jay actually, through channels unknown, got the Bureau to officially reassign me on a temporary loan from HRT to a specialized security detail. It's beneficial having someone in this unit who can operate in an official governmental capacity if and when the situation dictates." Declan flashed his badge, clipped at his hip.

The hum of work filled the strange office space as the others set about their tasks. Nick surveyed his new world, a world where he was no longer Nick Lawrence.

He was now the Wolf.

20

The man pulled hard at the cigarette in balance between his fingers. In the quiet of the car he could hear the crackle of the tobacco as it burned. He'd been sitting down the street from the house for several long hours. The package arrived forty-five minutes ago and he could see the soft brown wrapping of the nondescript rectangular box occupying a portion of Debbie Johnson's tattered welcome mat.

Debbie Johnson no longer lived there and had vacated the residence months ago, at the conclusion of an extensive eviction process. The details of her life meant little to the man other than it provided a temporary usable address. His job was to select locations unlikely to draw suspicion so that deliveries could be made and picked up without notice. It was a seemingly simple task, but one filled with potential disaster. With several of the other cells neutralized, his role had become increasingly more important to his employer's cause.

He'd been hand-picked for a new and more important role. The group's reclusive leader had reached out to him directly. Receiving the call had been the equivalent of speaking to Allah himself. He remembered the coldness of his voice and the fire his words had evoked inside him.

I need you. Without you we will fail. And that cannot happen. You are our last great hope and your deeds will be remembered for all time.

He tried to contain his excitement at the prospect of the upcoming mission. After today, Ibrahim would be able to serve his people in a way he'd never dreamed possible. Today's package would not be handed off to another. Today's package was for him. The instructions had been clear. His name would forever be etched into the stones of history. His people would sing his praise and the Americans would tremble in fear at the indomitable strength of The Seven.

The heat of the burning cigarette warmed his stained fingers as the embers closed in on the moist filter. Without wasting a moment, he retrieved another from the pack balanced on his thigh. He used the nearly spent cigarette to light his next, a true definition of a chain smoker. He flicked the butt out the small opening in the window, adding to the pile accumulating outside the door of his powder-blue Subaru Forester. He liked the "soccer mom" anonymity of this car.

It was hard for him to wait, but his instructions had been explicitly clear.

Wait a full hour. Ensure no counter-surveillance. Retrieve the package and proceed to the staging area.

The remaining minutes of that hour ticked by in timeless fashion. He scanned the area, looking for the exhaust of an idling vehicle. Ibrahim's Forester had been off for hours. He'd been prepared for the cool spring air, layering warm thermals under his jeans and sweatshirt. The only indication he was in the car was the smoke seeping out from his window, but he decided it was a minor risk at exposure. *How could he be expected to pass the time otherwise?* he had thought before lighting the first cigarette out of the now nearly empty pack.

Nothing on the street indicated he was being watched. The last car he'd seen had pulled onto the street twenty minutes ago and parked. The occupants, an elderly couple, shuffled into their multifamily brownstone without a look in his direction. The street was quiet, and the timing of the delivery had been purposeful. The carrier's instructions were clear. *Deliver between one and two p.m. Leave on doorstep.* Ibrahim had tracked the package using the postal app on his cell phone and was pleased when he watched the delivery truck pull down the street at 1:17 p.m. That was fifty-seven minutes ago.

Satisfied he was alone, Ibrahim stepped out of his vehicle, dropping the cigarette at his foot. He pulled the baseball cap brim low, obscuring his face from any potential video cameras in the area. Ibrahim moved purposefully down the uneven sidewalk in this quiet neighborhood located in the heart of Virginia's historic district of Old Towne Alexandria. His pace slowed as he neared the former residence of Debbie Johnson. Conducting one more visual scan of his surroundings, Ibrahim moved up the three weathered stone steps to the landing where the package rested.

The box was surprisingly light for the size of the box, but he knew the deadly contents contained therein and its devastating payload. He cradled the awkward shape of the box against his chest and returned the way he'd come. Keys in hand, he hit the trunk release and the back of the small-sized SUV's tailgate raised as he approached. He leaned forward, placed the box on the black carpeted lining of the trunk. He stood erect, stepped back, and closed the trunk, hearing the click of the latch.

Ibrahim's head was forced forward, striking the heavy tint of the trunk's window. His vision was peppered with speckles of light, like glitter flickering in the dark. The pain from the impact to his neck was crippling and his knees had buckled. He never felt the needle plunge into his neck. The glitter-filled haze faded to absolute darkness as one thought fluttered across Ibrahim's mind. *Failure.*

21

"Well that went smooth as bread pudding," Gator said.

"What about his car?" Nick asked.

"It will probably be tagged as a non-residentially parked vehicle or considered abandoned. Eventually it'll be towed and then sit in some lot indefinitely. No evidence of a crime. And no evidence of us being there."

Gator drove. The big man looked odd behind the wheel. Like he belonged in a gorilla cage and not wedged behind the dark finish of the Durango's dashboard. He struck a large pothole and the vehicle bounced violently. Nick's eyes widened.

Gator gave a hearty laugh. "Don't worry. I checked and it's not armed."

"That's a relief. How long's our friend back there going to be out of commission?" Nick asked.

"Probably an hour. Maybe a bit longer."

Nick nodded. "So, who funds our little group? I mean we had a Gulfstream on standby to shoot us across the country from Texas to the D.C. area. Private jets seem like a hefty budget item on an expense sheet," Nick said sarcastically.

"That's not really in my wheelhouse. Jay would be the one to ask if you're really interested. I find it better not to go looking that gift horse in the mouth, ya know?" Gator said in his thick accent. "I just know that we operate at a level well beyond any unit I've ever worked with. I like my new station in life and so I don't push too hard for answers I may not want the answer to." His last comment didn't carry the typical lightheartedness Nick had come to expect from the man.

"Understood." Nick looked back at the blanket covering the bound man sprawled across the seat and weighed his next question carefully, "So, how'd you end up here."

Gator let out a long sigh, "Well, you are the inquisitive type. I guess that makes sense. Jay and Declan said interviewing was your forte. I know the whole call sign thing seems a bit extreme, but it's done in part to provide an extra layer of protection."

"Protection?"

"If we end up like sleeping beauty back there. Stuffed into some bad guy's car and dragged off to who-knows-where to have who-knows-what done to us," Gator said.

Nick nodded, understanding the implication. "It just seems like you all know a hell of a lot about me and I just thought..."

"I'll say this. Jay found me when I was at a low point. Not too much different than you," Gator said.

"How so?"

"I was locked up too," Gator said, looking over at Nick. "Overseas. I did some wet work for an off-the-books CIA op. It got some bad press and I became the Army's patsy for the fallout. They labeled me a war criminal."

"Jesus," Nick muttered.

"Tell me about it. So, without boring you with details, I died. Like you." Gator cleared his throat. "And here I am. Just like you."

"Jay's op got you jammed up?" Nick asked.

Gator looked ahead. "He's loyal to those who are loyal to him. He told me you're cut from the same cloth in that regard."

Nick gave a half smile.

"He also said you're a hard man to kill. And to me those are two qualities that can't be taught," Gator said with a nod of approval.

"Thanks. Hopefully, I can live up to my reputation."

"Your buddy Declan—correction Ace—spoke highly of your abilities in regard to interrogation," Gator said.

"I guess. Seems like a lifetime ago now," Nick said dismissively.

"Well, you're about to see some next-level shit with Spider," Gator said.

"I understand everyone's nicknames except for his. Why Spider?" Nick asked.

"Because he traps people. The more you squirm and try to wiggle out of his interrogation, the more tangled you become, like a fly trapped in a spider's web." Gator laughed. "I wouldn't want him poking around in my head. That's for damn sure. Not too sure what the hell he'd find."

"I guess this guy's not going to have that luxury," Nick said, thumbing in the direction of their unconscious prisoner.

"The Spider is already spinning his web. And this little fly doesn't have any idea what's in store for him."

22

To say the room was dark didn't do justice to the word. The twelve square feet of space was void of any light. Even as Nick peered in through the thick glass of the one-way mirror, he couldn't make out the faintest outline of the man who was strapped to the chair inside. The only reason he knew the man was in the room was because he and Gator had been the ones who put him in there.

Nick thought of the box truck and his awakening into this strange new life. The man in that room was soon to wake from his sedative-induced slumber into the murky blackness surrounding him. How strange it would be to open your eyes and see nothing. The man would be blind to his unfamiliar circumstance. Then there was the silence to contend with.

Gator had referred to the room as The Cube and explained that their unit used rooms like this often and had them at various sites, or vaults as they called the office, which were staggered across the continental U.S. He had also shared the room's design. The walls were triple layered, basically a club sandwich of poured concrete and next-gen soundproofing. Gator said that they'd tested its effectiveness. A gunshot couldn't be heard once a person was sealed inside. The man strapped to the bolted chair could hear nothing and see nothing. Blind and deaf is terribly disorienting. The longer this man sat, the deeper he would sink into madness.

"How long has he been in?" Spider's smooth voice interrupted Nick's thoughts.

Nick looked down at his watch. "Two hours."

Spider looked down at the tablet in his hand. "He's been awake for ninety-three minutes."

"How do you know that?" Nick asked.

"The sensors built into the chair monitor his vitals among other things," Spider said as his stoic face broke into the slightest of smiles.

"I told you this guy goes next-level with this stuff," Gator chuckled, slapping his large hand in the center of Nick's back.

Nick nodded, catching his breath after the big man's jovial blow. He did not want to be on the bad side of Gator's fist if he ever wielded those giant meat paws in anger. It'd be like getting hit by an anvil.

Spider tapped the flat glass screen with his finger and the interior of The Cube burst into a bright light, penetrating through the heavy tints of the one-way mirror. Nick looked away, caught off guard by the sudden radiance.

Nick's eyes compensated for the light and he looked back into the room. The man strapped to the chair writhed in agony. Tears streamed down his face. The white light bathed his tan skin. Nick watched intently as the man shook violently, swinging his head back and forth obviously desperate to find a reprieve. The chair, bolted to the ground, did not budge. The man's eyes were tightly closed and his cheeks curled, desperate to create a barrier to the light. By the man's reaction, his eyelids were having little effect at stopping his torment.

Then another tap on the tablet from Spider's finger and the light was immediately replaced by darkness. Spider tapped on the screen again. This time nothing seemed to happen. Nick peered over at the screen, trying to see if he could figure this new phase.

"Sound." Spider said, coolly. "Very loud."

Nick heard nothing. He pressed his hand firmly against the wall of The Cube and felt no vibration. He stepped back, impressed at the design.

"Like I said. You can't hear a gunshot through those walls," Gator boomed.

"Any coffee left?" Spider asked.

"I think Wiz just made a fresh pot," Gator said.

Spider turned and walked toward the break room, carrying the tablet under his hand like a book. Nick followed.

The break room was clean and had a variety of different coffee makers. Nick eyed the assortment and watched as Spider went straight for the large percolator, nestled between a Keurig and an espresso machine.

"All this fancy crap, and this seven-year-old percolator makes a better cup than all of them," Spider said.

"I hate to admit, but I've been a Keurig convert," Nick jested. "Although I have to admit I've had to adjust my tastes for the past year."

"Try this and tell me I'm wrong."

Spider handed over a blue mug filled with the steaming dark liquid. Nick cradled it with both hands. He held up his cup briefly in a sort of mock cheers and then took a sip. He swallowed the hot aromatic beverage and nodded his agreement. "You win. That's a life-changing cup of coffee."

Spider poured his and then placed the cup on the granite countertop. He looked down at the screen and flicked open the application designed to control and monitor The Cube. After entering a code into the digital keypad, the Cube's control panel populated the glass. Spider's fingers nimbly navigated the icons, this time he tapped several different controls before putting the tablet on the counter. He turned his attention to the coffee.

"I've never seen anything like that used in an interrogation before," Nick said.

"Our paths aren't so different you know. But as with the way things are within this unit, pasts hold no real relevance to our present," Spider said. "Although, you will need to learn my trade."

"Why's that?"

"Because I may not always be around," Spider said solemnly.

"Planning on retiring anytime soon?" Nick said, trying to lighten the tone.

"This unit has an unusually high turnover rate," Spider said. "And *retirement* is one way of putting it."

"How long do you keep someone in The Cube before entering?" Nick asked, taking the cue that today's interrogation would serve as an orientation lesson.

Spider took a long deliberate sip from his mug. He eyed the tablet and then looked at Nick. His eyes were dark and complimented his olive skin, indicative of an Italian descent. An air of intensity shrouded him and only seemed to lessen when he would break the façade with his almost imperceptible grin.

"Depends. In this particular case we have a tight timeline. That bomb has a destination and this group is known for redundancy, ensuring a failsafe. Although, that was before we began to intervene. The numbers of The Seven have greatly dwindled in the last two years since you last had contact with them."

Nick watched the grin bend the edges of Spider's lips upward.

"Let's go spend a little time with our visitor and see how he's doing," Spider said, moving out of the kitchen area, tablet in one hand and coffee in the other. He strode to The Cube with the casualness of someone walking their dog.

Nick looked at the one-way mirror. Pulsating flashes of light shot out through the mirrored pane of glass. He approached and looked in at the man trapped inside. The strobe effect was intense, and the man flailed more wildly than before. His face had tuned a bright red in anguish and his mouth opened and closed. Nick could tell the man was screaming, although no sound penetrated The Cube.

"Heavy metal music is now accompanying the light show," Spider said, matter-of-factly.

Then the room went dark again. Within thirty seconds the strobe started again.

"He may not be ready yet, but time isn't on our side. I'd normally continue this for another couple hours before making contact. But we do what we can with the cards we're dealt," Spider said, turning off the lights and sound with a quick barrage of finger strokes of his tablet. The overhead light came on and the room now looked like an ordinary interview room. A table separated the restrained man from the other chair in the room. Spider pressed his index finger on a panel next to the door. There was a beep and then a hiss as the seal released. The door slid silently along the track. It reminded Nick of the cell he'd called home for the past year. *But as Spider said—our pasts no longer matter.*

Nick watched from behind the one-way glass as the door's mechanics shut the door behind Spider, entering the room to face off with the restrained man.

23

"You son of bitch!" Ibrahim screamed. His voice squeaked. The rasp was a combination of his lifetime of smoking which was further exacerbated by his recent bellowing.

Spider ignored the man and sat, adjusting himself into the soft cushioned chair and pulling himself neatly to the table. He set the tablet on the table and looked at the man seated before him.

Ibrahim was wet with perspiration. His tan skin was blotched darker from the physical exertion in his futile resistance to the light and sound immersion he'd received. His breathing came in ragged spurts. He looked down at the floor, away from Spider's intense eyes.

"We are going to talk about some things. Most of which you do not want to talk about," Spider said, speaking slowly and calmly. "Do you understand this?"

"I'm not saying anything! You can go to hell!" Ibrahim spat the words.

Spider cocked his head to the side, evaluating the unsuspecting fly trapped in his net. His face held no trace of emotion. He allowed a moment of silent reflection to pass before speaking again.

"That would be a shame. If you're not ready to talk, then I'll have to leave. If I leave then it starts again," Spider said whirling his index finger in the air. He could see the restrained man's understanding register in his face.

Ibrahim opened his mouth to say something and then closed it. He sighed deeply and the heave of his chest showed his resignation.

Spider had read the intelligence report gathered by Wiz and knew that Ibrahim was psychologically weak. He knew it would take very little to overwhelm the man's will to fight, especially after the last couple of hours he'd spent inside The Cube.

The room could challenge the strongest of minds. Spider knew this because he'd managed to spend seventy-two hours in there before teetering on the brink of insanity. The other members told him he was foolish to do it, but he had explained that to understand a weapon's potency you must experience it first-hand. It was a lesson he'd learned from his hapkido instructor. *You can't effectively deliver a strike until you've felt its impact.*

"Would you like me to leave?" Spider asked, the veiled threat was obvious.

Ibrahim said nothing but raised his head slightly, sheepishly making eye contact.

"Good. Now, with that out of the way, we can begin our conversation," Spider said. "I need you to understand how things work inside here. Once you fully comprehend the capabilities of this room and how it can be used, we can begin a meaningful dialog."

Ibrahim's eyes fluttered as he quickly scanned the bare walls of the room before settling back on Spider.

"The chair you're strapped to is very special and relatively unique in its design. It's reading your vitals, body temperature, weight distribution, and muscle tension as you sit there. I tell you this, so you understand the importance of truthfulness. I'm very good at detecting deception without any of this, but I like to remove all doubt. You'll find that I am very thorough in my job. Your body will tell me when you're being honest and when you're not. I need you to understand this because your honesty is the only thing keeping you from returning to the dark."

Spider tapped the screen on the tablet and looked at the display. He examined the sensory input, watching as the man's breathing rate increased along with his heart rate. A lot of physiological reactions were taking place inside Ibrahim's body. Spider was satisfied the previous two hours had the desired effect.

"I can see you don't want the darkness again," Spider said softly.

"What do you want from me? Who are you?" Ibrahim hissed.

"We'll get to that. Or maybe not. Your questions are irrelevant. I will ask and you will answer truthfully. Do you understand what I told you? About this room, your chair, and the importance of telling the truth?"

"Yes."

"If we get to an impasse and you're unwilling to be truthful then I'll have to step out. You don't want me to do that," Spider said. "Resistance is wasted energy."

"Whatever you think you can do to me, they can do worse," Ibrahim said flatly.

"Let's start there. Who is *they*?"

Ibrahim hesitated, breaking eye contact.

"Well, we're not getting off to a good start. I can see you don't understand the position you're in. I'll give you some time to think," Spider said, pushing his chair back.

Ibrahim's eyes immediately widened, panic stricken at the sudden movement of his interrogator. "Wait. Please don't leave me in here. I just need a minute. Please! They'll kill me! You know that? If you've done your research, then you know how dangerous they are."

"Weren't you just about to blow yourself up? And you sit there worried about death. I thought they picked you because of your resolve. Sounds to me like they picked the wrong man for the job," Spider said, casting an eye of judgment.

"I'm prepared to die!" Ibrahim yelled.

Spider tapped the screen, ignoring the man's outburst. He looked at the vitals and smiled. "No, you're not. You're terrified. Of me. Of them. You're definitely no martyr. They must be really desperate to pick you for such a task."

"They picked me. They know who Ibrahim Al Faziq is and what I'm capable of!" His hands dug into the armrests, nearly peeling back his fingernails.

"Who is *they*?" Spider asked again. "Let's assume I know, and this is my first test of your truthfulness. Lies have consequences."

"The Seven!" Ibrahim said through gritted teeth. A froth of spit bubbled out, coating his lower lip in the white substance.

"Now that wasn't so hard was it? I hope everything I ask you isn't going to be this difficult. It'll be a very long conversation if you decide to behave this way. You need to get past the fact that you've failed. To be honest, we probably saved you from botching your mission. Consider yourself lucky," Spider said.

"Lucky?" Ibrahim asked.

"From what I see there was a good chance you would've screwed up and then they'd probably take out your failure by punishing your son. Can you imagine what they'd do to him?"

"My son? How do you know about my son?" Ibrahim asked, his face contorting into a pained expression.

"We know everything about you."

"If you touch my son, I'll—"

"You'll do nothing. Understand that. Get that through your head and know that your threats are wasted on me and the people I work with. Your son is fine for now, but how long I'm able to guarantee his safety will depend on your cooperation," Spider said, emotionless.

Ibrahim sat speechless.

Spider tapped an icon on the tablet. The Cube's speaker system came to life.

"Father? Is that you? Father? Where are you? It's so dark in here. Help me please!" Spider ended the transmission and looked up at the restrained man.

Ibrahim's last reserve of resistance leaked out of him in the form of tears streaming down the deflated expression on his face. "Please—he's my only son. He's only a boy. Only fifteen. Don't hurt him."

"He's in a room just like this. Waiting. Just like you waited. It's dark in there," Spider said evenly. "How long can a child's mind handle the dark before falling apart?"

"You're sick! He's just a boy!"

"What were you going to blow up? Children and families would've been killed. I don't want to hurt your son, but like I said that depends on you."

"Anything. Just don't hurt him. I'll tell you anything you want," Ibrahim said, his shoulders went slack, and his head slumped in defeat.

"Pretty cool stuff, huh?" Wiz said.

Wiz's comment startled Nick who was fully engrossed in the audio feed from the interrogation. Nick was sitting at his cubicle. He wore headphones and had been listening to Spider's interrogation. Although the room was silent, there was a microphone and video recording device in place, allowing others in the unit to monitor.

"We've got his kid in one of these Cube things? What the hell is going on here? I'm all for saving lives, but torturing kids?" Nick said angrily.

"Relax. It's fabricated. His son's at home with his mother. I was able to reconstruct the message from conversations we'd intercepted. Pretty damn effective though?" Wiz asked.

"Very," Nick said, settling his nerves.

"I told you. The Spider's got skills," Gator boomed as he walked by with a large burrito in hand.

"I guess I got some things to learn," Nick said, slipping the headset back on to listen to the interrogation.

24

"At least it wasn't on the other side of the country. I hate flying and avoid it at all costs. But sometimes these ops don't afford me that luxury," Gator said, his bulk conforming to the confines of the SUV driver's seat.

Nick looked over at the large man and chuckled to himself at the sight. He couldn't imagine the man's muscular girth would fit comfortably in any vehicle. They should have towed him on a flatbed.

The prep for this op had been very detailed, especially considering the limited time frame before its execution. Jay was initially convinced the snatch of Ibrahim would've adjusted the timeline and bought them some time. Then Wiz intercepted some chatter and confirmed Spider's assumption that The Seven didn't have much faith in Ibrahim's ability to complete the task. When Ibrahim hadn't responded to them, they'd assumed he'd chickened out. A second man had been tasked with carrying out the attack. Redundancy was critical to any mission success and The Seven were desperately looking for a win.

Gator and Nick sat in the postal delivery truck in the back lot of the Post Office on Cameron Street. The windows were heavily tinted, blocking any view in through the windows. The bottle-nosed front end faced a four-foot concrete privacy wall separating the rear of the postal parking lot from another strip of businesses.

The red-bricked sidewalks were quiet, as they should be on a Sunday morning in Alexandria's historic Old Towne. All of the neighboring businesses were closed at the moment and most would remain so for the day. Only one building had activity from its arriving patrons.

The Christ Church, built at the conclusion of the Revolutionary War, had stood the test of time. It was the church attended by sitting presidents until the turn of the 21st Century. It was, however, chosen by The Seven for a different reason. During World War II, Roosevelt and Churchill had attended the church in a ceremony to commemorate the World Day of Prayer for Peace. The Seven, in the manifesto set for release and intercepted by Wiz, sought to taint this landmark and make it a call to war.

The team had arrived a few hours earlier under the cover of darkness. A microdrone had done overflight surveillance before they entered the area. The same drone now acted as their overwatch. Cameron Street was the side of the church where Ibrahim had been directed to stage his phase of the attack. That intel was the reason Nick and the large man from the Bayou were manning their current post.

Gator and Nick were positioned at a good vantage point to the street and church. Declan and Barbie had just walked into the building to attend the church service. They were tasked with scouting a secondary assault team.

Spider extracted an incredible amount of detail from their captive. The plan called for an external detonation in the form of a car bomb, a task originally meant for Ibrahim that now was assigned to his replacement. The force of the blast was designed to crumple several of the load-bearing walls of the historic structure, collapsing the church's pulpit and forcing panicked parishioners toward the front doors. Two additional martyrs would be inside and tasked with detonating a secondary device as the people exited, effectively turning the ornate church into a fiery tomb.

The Seven's plan was complicated. It called for simultaneous actions by each team operating without any on-site communication. A vehicle, the replacement to Ibrahim's powder blue Subaru, would pull up and activate its hazards. The driver had been instructed to give the appearance of being broken down or out of gas. He'd idle in the lane closest to the church on Cameron's one-way street. The man in the car would be instructed to wait for five minutes after the church doors closed and then detonate. Those were the instructions Ibrahim had been given and the team had to assume would still be in place.

Nick and Gator had to close the gap and take out that threat without allowing him the opportunity to activate the detonator. Declan and Barbie had the tougher job of eliminating the interior threat in a crowd full of civilians. Wiz controlled the drone from his cubicle and would use it to jam any potential remote detonation capabilities while Gator disabled the car bomb.

25

Declan moved into the church's interior. The air was thick with a damp mustiness coated by the overwhelming fragrant incense. The combination of conflicting odors was comparable to someone masking body odor with perfume.

Barbie held his hand, giving the illusion the two were a happy couple. The cool early morning air allowed for both to wear long overcoats. The ensemble enabled them to effectively conceal the weapons strapped to their waists without drawing any unusual glances from the other patrons. Declan took two long, controlled breaths as they slowly approached a row of pews near the back of the church.

Hands held, they both scanned the crowd. A man of middle eastern descent stood near the back wall, alone. His eyes were closed, and he appeared to be praying. Declan assumed he actually might be, but figured his prayer was more for strength rather than salvation. Either way he was definitely one of The Seven's two inside men. He too, wore a jacket and the bulk of it was most likely due to the explosive rig strapped to his chest. Declan gave a squeeze of Barbie's hand and then traced his pinkie finger across her palm, indicating the direction of the man he'd targeted. She shot a glance at the man and then squeezed his hand twice indicating she understood.

Barbie located the second man. He was in a pew two rows up from them. This man also wore a puffy winter coat.

"Hey hon, I'm just going to hit the restroom," Declan said, releasing Barbie's hand.

Barbie nodded and Declan slid past her, exiting to the center aisle. He moved purposefully, proceeding to the rear of the church without looking at the man in the back, who would be Declan's target. He entered the restroom and locked the door.

Declan withdrew the pistol from his waist. It had a longer draw because of the silencer threaded to the barrel. He'd decided it was a better idea for him to prep this weapon into position while out of the public's view.

Barbie's large handbag was empty except for one item. At the bottom rested a pistol, also affixed with a silencer. The purse enabled easier access at the point in time when she'd need to retrieve it.

The silencers would minimize any initial shock wave of panic from the civilians present. After the assault, crowd control and their subsequent escape would be the next biggest hurdle in this operation.

26

"A small minivan just rolled to a stop on Cameron. Hazards on. Target acquired. We're moving," Nick said. His voice was clear, and all of the other members of the team would receive the message through the flesh-colored wireless earbud inserted in his left ear.

In the short time he'd been involved in this unit, the technology available amazed Declan. That was no small feat, impressing someone who'd been hand-plucked from the Navy's elite SEAL teams for selection in the ghost unit, Alpha One. The earbud was actually more like a Band-Aid, an eighth of an inch in diameter adhered to the skin. To see it, someone would've had to be standing next to him and staring into his earlobe. The sound quality was unrivaled in anything he'd used in the past. Nick's last transmission sounded as though he was standing beside him. Wiz told him it had another unique capability in its proprietary design. The earpiece would adjust volume to outside influences like gunfire or explosions, enabling them to hear clearly under the worst of combat conditions. Or as Jay had put it, *if the shit hit the proverbial fan.*

The processional hymn began. Declan exited the restroom and watched as the priest ambled slowly behind a young altar boy swinging the decorative incense ball against the chain. The smell intensified, adding to the lingering remnants he'd smelled earlier.

Declan had his hands inside his coat pockets. In his right he held the silenced 9mm. He had cut out the interior seam of the jacket's pocket, enabling him to maintain a solid grip on the gun without exposing any of it.

He stopped short before crossing from the hallway into the interior of the church and into view of the target. The heavy wood of the church's front doors banged loudly as they closed. The Seven timeline had begun. Five minutes until the car bomb was set to go off.

"Can I help you find your seat sir?" A well-dressed usher asked.

"No thanks. I think I'll stand close to the restroom. I've got a bit of a stomach bug. A little Montezuma's Revenge," Declan said.

The last comment had the desired effect. At hearing about his sickness, the man moved away from Declan and stepped deeper into the church and off to the right. This gave Declan an unobstructed entrance point when the time came.

27

For a big man, Gator moved like a cat, nimbly closing the gap between their postal truck to the idling minivan. Nick intentionally lagged behind as they'd planned during their rehearsal preparations. Gator wore a postal delivery uniform and approached the man in the vehicle, walking around the rear of the minivan to the driver's side. They'd banked on the fact that the man in the vehicle would be too nervous to notice the uniform as being out of place for a Sunday.

Gator tapped on the glass of the driver's side window. "Hey there, fella! Can I give you a hand?" Gator asked in his thick Louisiana accent.

The man almost jumped at the interruption. Seeing the uniform, he softened slightly and shook his head. Sweat poured from the man's forehead. Although tan in complexion, he looked pale and was obviously overcome by his unnerving task. Blowing one's self up was no simple undertaking.

Gator laughed loudly. "Really friend, it's no trouble whatsoever. Pop the hood and I'll take a look for ya."

The man in the car shook his head again, and the fear originally lining his face now shifted to anger.

Gator stood by the window drawing the man's attention as Nick deftly moved to the front of the minivan.

Nick raised the pistol in his hand and took aim at the man's forehead. The man turned and Nick fired three times. The silencer muted most of the sound. Most of the noise came from the 9mm rounds as they penetrated the windshield. The glass had one hole with cracks spiderwebbing out from its center. The second and third rounds had followed the path of the first one, a testament to Nick's precision.

The man's head had rocked back at the initial impact but came to rest in a slumped forward manner. The headshots had served their intended purpose, bringing death to the bomber and immediately interrupting the brain's function as to prevent the man from detonating the device in hand.

"Target one down. Working on disabling the package," Gator said through the bone mic taped to his throat.

"Two minutes," Jay's voice transmitted. "Ace and Barbie are up."

Declan heard the transmission and eyed the back of his partner's head, waiting for her cue. The trick of killing two men at the same time was a skill few were capable of. More challenging was to do it surrounded by hundreds of unaware civilians. Both Declan and Barbie had Homeland Security badges affixed to their hips and had rehearsed their follow-up. But the execution of such dynamic plans always carried inherent, and often unforeseen, variables.

The congregation stood as the priest greeted the crowd. Barbie stood with them. Declan watched her intently as she began deliberately moving her head up and down as if answering a question. Once, twice, and on the third bob of her head Barbie's right arm swung up quickly. The purse dropped to the wooden bench seat as her arm extended with the silenced pistol in hand.

Declan stepped out from around the corner and into the church, planting and pivoting his foot while taking up a stable shooting platform. His gun's front sight came up on the target as he moved. Two shots exited his weapon as his marked man turned his attention to Barbie as she fired on the other target.

The shots found their mark and both men collapsed. The man Barbie had shot fell forward and was bent over the hardwood backing of the pew in front of him. Her target had been more difficult than Declan's. In the split second allotted, she had to ensure the angle of shot would have a safe backdrop.

As predicted, shrieks erupted at the sight of the two dead men. Several parishioners nearest Barbie's target had been painted in the man's blood, adding to the fervor of the screams.

Declan and Barbie shouted at the crowd, "Homeland Security! Calmly exit the main doors of the church! Do it now!" As they gave their rehearsed commands both of them exposed the badges on their hips.

Declan and Barbie quickly moved to their respective targets. The rigging of the bomb vests each martyr wore were identical and simple in design. At the sight of the bombs, a new wave of panicked cries rippled through the crowd. They separated the detonators from each brick of C4, rendering the bombs safe. The church cleared out into the street and quiet was restored to its interior.

Declan and Barbie made for the exit nearest the pulpit, and furthest away from the recently departed crowd. They reversed their jackets and donned knit caps as they stepped from the church. The quick change gave them a modicum of disguise as they worked their way to their postal van.

Gator drove out of the area as Wiz guided them by drone, avoiding the responding police cruisers. Nick let his hair out of the tight ponytail, and it fell wildly about his face and shoulders.

"Jesus buddy, your name really fits," Declan said.

"How's that?" Nick asked.

"You really look like a wolf."

The group laughed, releasing the tension of the morning's mission. Nick's first official indoctrination had been completed. He replayed the event in his mind as the church disappeared into the background.

28

Back at the office everyone went about their business with the same casualness as if they'd just returned from getting coffee. Nick was still adjusting to this new life and sat quietly at the conference table. It had been a long time since he'd fired a weapon and taken a life. It was a burden he never took lightly, no matter the target.

"You good?" Declan asked, pulling up a seat and plopping heavily into it.

"Yeah. Just taking a minute to let this whole cloak and dagger thing sink in," Nick said. "Not really my forte."

Declan shed his typical cavalier demeanor and dropped his cocky smile. Straight-faced he said, "You did good today. Lots of innocents would've died if you hadn't taken that shot."

"I know," Nick said. "Thanks."

Declan looked down at his watch. "I've got to run. Val's been without me for a while. I'm heading home for a bit. I've got to make the six-hour drive up to Connecticut. Hoping to make it there by dinner. I'll be back in a few days or when the next mission spins up. Need anything?" Declan asked.

"Nope. Say hi to Val and the girls for me."

"I can't."

"Huh?"

"You're dead, remember?" Declan's smile returned. "Unless I told them I've been hanging out with your ghost. Not sure how that'd go over."

Nick feigned a smile as Declan departed.

"Speaking of the dead. Since our last operation left no one alive to interrogate, I guess that frees us up a bit," Jay said, obviously having heard Declan's comment when exiting his office and entering the main space. "How'd you like to go to a funeral?"

"Whose?" Nick asked.

"Yours."

29

"Tobie we're late! Let's go!" Kemper yelled up the stairs.

The sound of gunfire and explosions erupted from the second floor.

"Tobie Daniel Jones get down here this instant! Now!" Kemper Jones boomed.

The effort caused his face to redden. He hoped he didn't have to stomp up the stairs in the uncomfortable suit he was wearing. He hadn't had many occasions in recent years requiring this level of dress. His daily attire was usually a button-down collared shirt and a pair of 5.11 Tactical khakis with some flex built into the waist.

The last time he'd adorned the charcoal suit's coat and pants was when he had been promoted to detective several years back. Its fit had been tight. Now, it almost cut off the circulation to his legs. A valiant attempt to button his pants had left him winded and extremely frustrated. He'd finally given up, resolving to leave it unbuttoned. His belt was the only thing keeping the trousers up. He fumed and decided he'd be damned before he would climb those stairs to get his son, fearful the effort might render him pantless.

"Coming!" Tobie shouted over the volume of his video game.

"Now!" Kemper shouted in response.

Tobie looked at the words on the screen in front of him. He was elated. A few friends at school had achieved this and he'd been trying ever since.

The message read: *Congratulations PROSPECT!*

He noticed a new message alert from a player whose gamer handle was Graham_CrackerHacker. Tobie could hear his father losing his patience and fearing another blow out, logged off. His dad had been on edge ever since Agent Lawrence had been locked up, and the news of his death had a devastating effect. He worried about his dad, but wasn't sure how to help. During his rotational stays at his dad's apartment he'd been spending more time immersed with his online gaming than any real quality time with his old man. He regretted the decline of their relationship and hoped they'd find a way to reconnect.

Throwing on his navy-blue blazer coat, Tobie Jones bounded down the stairs two at a time.

"Son, I swear on everything good and holy, you're going to be late to your own funeral," Kemper said, trying to calm his frustration. There had been some recent tension between the two and Kemper knew most of it stemmed from his ex-wife's recently remarrying. His son was a good kid but he could tell the change in lifestyle was having an impact.

Tobie rolled his eyes and brushed past his father. "Come on dad, we don't want to be late."

Sarcasm, a teenager's ultimate weapon, and as of late Tobie deployed it on his father with increased regularity. Kemper shook his head, shaking off the jibe as he huffed after his son into the unseasonably warm air. March in Texas was a strange transitional period and provided a short, almost imperceptible, shift from winter into summer.

30

"Wiz already has it cued up," Jay said, waving his arm in the direction of the tech genius hunched over his keyboard.

Nick said nothing. He stood and followed Jay over to where Wiz was seated.

"I took the liberty of launching a drone from our facility outside of Austin," Wiz said, looking up from the array of screens before him.

"Austin?" Nick asked.

"Anaya received a death notification from the prison. At the initial phases of your incarceration, you'd listed her as your only next of kin to be notified in the event of your death."

"Jesus, I totally forgot about that." Nick's stomach sank at the thought of delivering another blow to the woman he'd loved and had planned on starting a life with. His past cost them their baby. And now his death, although staged, would pick at the emotional scab.

"She arranged to have you buried in a cemetery close by to her home," Jay said.

Nick sighed.

"Everyone always wonders what their funeral would look like. Funny thing about death is nobody ever gets to find out. But you get a sneak peek, watching it first hand," Wiz said with a geeky smile.

Nick leaned in, looking at the empty grave and the mound of freshly upturned dirt piled beside it. The casket hovered above the hole, cradled by two thick straps wrapped around the rolling cylinders running parallel to the length of the brown wood of the box. A caretaker in dirt-covered gray overalls stood off to the side and out of the way standing under the shade of a tree. Near the foot of the casket stood a heavyset middle-aged man in a cheaply made suit. Nick did not recognize either man—obviously they were employed by the funeral home or cemetery. The 4K image fed from the drone hovering silently above was as clear as if Nick had been perched in a nearby tree.

"How about we give him a minute alone?" Jay asked, nudging Wiz.

Wiz looked at Jay and then over to Nick. He nodded and stood, vacating his seat. Wiz gestured for Nick to take his spot in front of the monitors. "Try not to touch anything. I get the feeling you're not the most tech-savvy of people. The drone's autopilot is set and will remain in its current position, automatically adjusting for winds and other environmental variances."

Nick said nothing as he slipped into Wiz's chair, adjusting himself.

It was strange, almost surreal to look out on his burial site. Nick was aware the ceremony was a ruse to further mask his disappearance from his former life. He looked at the solitude in which his body was to be buried. Minus a few, those closest to him were dead. An empty funeral spoke volumes to the life he had lead, or at least to the choices he'd made.

Anaya Patel entered the drone's field of vision. She wore a dark dress. Her long black hair shimmered in the sunlight and her mocha brown skin contrasted with the bright white of the flowers she cradled in the crux of her arm.

The sight of her had a crippling effect. A rush of emotion flooded him, feelings and thoughts he had tucked deep during his year's incarceration came to the forefront. Nick leaned closer to the monitor.

Kemper Jones appeared in view, trotting across the rough St. Augustine grass. Nick watched as his portly friend's hustle was impeded by his tight-fitting suit. The Austin detective's bulk bulged out at various spots. Knowing the man as well as Nick did after working several cases of depravity together, he was aware of his disdain for such dress. Nick appreciated his friend's effort but couldn't help chuckle at his appearance. Kemper Jones' teenage son followed in step behind him.

Nick watched as Kemper gave Anaya a long, heart-felt embrace. He longed to feel her skin against his and smell its sweet familiarity. The thought was a fleeting one and he sadly knew the reality, that he would never hold her again.

Anaya and Kemper separated, and they looked in the direction of the casket. A moment passed where time seemed to stand still for Nick. Had it not been for the fluttering branches of a nearby tree, he would have thought the screen image was frozen.

Anaya nodded to the man in the suit who, in turn, nodded to the caretaker under the tree. And with that Nick Lawrence's funeral service, or lack thereof, came to its close.

The caretaker pulled the lowering wench and the casket began its controlled descent into the ground. The three attendees looked on with heads bowed. Anaya broke from her solace and took a step toward the hole, tossing in the flowers.

Nick looked more closely and noticed she had something else in her left hand, something he hadn't seen until now. It looked like a small stuffed animal. Anaya pressed the plush blue bear to her lips and threw it atop the brown wood of the casket. She gently caressed her stomach, touching the emptiness.

"Wiz, can you zoom this thing?" Nick called over his shoulder.

Wiz appeared and tapped a few keys on one of the nearby keyboards. He then grabbed a controller. "What do you want to see?"

"The stuffed animal on top of the casket," Nick said, straining his eyes hoping to get a better look.

Wiz manipulated the controller, and the image enlarged without losing any of the clarity. The camera zoomed in to such a degree Nick was able to read the tag attached to the bear's collar. *Nick Jr.*

Nick had shut out everyone in his life after his arrest. In doing so, he'd never learned whether the baby they'd lost was a boy or girl. At the time he deemed it one additional layer of emotional protection, a way to dissociate and distance himself. The newfound shock of this revelation rocked him to his core. He'd lost his son, a boy they'd never had an opportunity to name.

Cut down before he had a chance at life, a twisted consequence to his actions several years before.

Nick closed his eyes but not before a tear found its exit. The salty discharge trickled down his face, becoming lost in the tangles of his unkempt beard.

"Sorry man. We just figured it would give you some closure," Wiz said softly.

Nick allowed the sadness to pass and opened his eyes. With one swift move of his arm, he removed any trace of the tear. Wiz had typed in some commands and the drone's live feed was now offline. A still image remained on the screen. Anaya's face, wet with tears, frozen in front of him. As painful as it was to see, a small part of him felt relieved she still cared for him and, maybe, still loved him. The way things ended had been tragic, and he never thought he would see her again. He was grateful for the opportunity, even if it was under these extremely unusual circumstances.

Jay clasped Nick's shoulder, the same shoulder he'd taken three bullets in when saving the former CIA operative's life. "I think you could use a drink?"

"I can't think of anything better," Nick said.

31

The dim light added a nostalgic element to the Irish pub. The low rumble of conversation and laughter blended with the instrumental music piping through the speakers overhead. Nick followed Jay to a table against the wall.

"How many years has it been since we've sat in this bar?" Jay asked.

"Too many," Nick said. "A lot's changed since those days."

"No truer statement." Jay stopped talking as a waitress approached. He ordered two Black and Tans. As she walked away, he continued, "I know this is a lot to take in, but I think you're going to find that this is a good fit for you."

"How long have you been running this team?" Nick asked.

"I switched over about five years ago. There was a need for what we do. The country needed the ability to react quickly and decisively against rapidly evolving threats. I was picked to assemble the team. And the unit has evolved over the years through personnel and operational reach."

"Who do we work for?" Nick asked quietly.

Jay didn't answer. The waitress returned, placing the beers in front of the two before disappearing into the small crowd.

"That's a hard question to answer. Simplest answer, we're sanctioned at the highest levels. At the same time, we don't exist and therefore are expendable. If something breaks bad or one of us is killed, then we are on our own," Jay said. He then paused, taking a long pull from the mug. The dark of the Guinness swirled against the amber lager of the Harp as he set the glass down.

"I guess that makes sense. If it breaks wrong, then there would be no ties. Nobody to take the blame, but us," Nick said.

"Something like that," Jay said. He hesitated momentarily and then continued, "I couldn't watch you disappear into the abyss of that prison. I owed you."

Nick let the beer roll down his throat. "Speaking of my exodus from Masterson. Those three bodies used to replace Gator, Spider, and me."

"Not what you think. We didn't go off and kill a few people for the ruse. Jesus Nick, give me some credit," Jay said with a shake of his head.

"Well then how's it work?" Nick asked.

"We've got connections and are able to get bodies when needed. Most come from people who've donated their body to science. We are able to enter a variety of databases and have the manifests changed. The hardest part was finding close physical matches. You and Gator are atypical body types."

"Okay, but how did you pull off the medical transport? Wouldn't the jail realize the ambulance was phony when none of the neighboring hospitals or ambulance companies had been dispatched to Masterson?" Nick asked, rubbing his temples in a concerted effort to understand.

"Yes, but we mitigated by creating confusion. When you were a teenager did you ever tell one of your parents you were going to a friend's house? And the friend would say they were going to your house, but in reality you were going to a party somewhere else?" Jay asked.

"Yeah, but I don't get how that analogy applies to this," Nick said.

"We've basically done the same thing. Wiz manipulated the incoming and outgoing information from all of the involved departments. The medic employee files for Gator and Spider were embedded into an actual ambulance company. Long story short, three people died when the front right tire blew, and the ambulance struck a tree. We staged a fire which made the bodies unrecognizable," Jay said, smiling and obviously content with his summation.

"You went through all that trouble for me," Nick said, shaking his head.

"You know I would've been dead in the deserts of Afghanistan if it hadn't been for you. I don't take the debt of that day lightly," Jay said.

"I think we can call the debt paid."

"A life debt never feels fully repaid," Jay said sincerely. He cleared his throat and said, "I'm sorry about the funeral thing. I just thought it might give you some closure."

Nick nodded slightly. "I never really said goodbye. Thank you for giving me that. Crazy you're able to get a drone up and control it remotely. That's some military-level stuff."

"You have no idea what you are walking into with this unit."

"I'll adjust. I guess I don't have much choice," Nick said, running his condensation-covered hand through his long hair. "So, what's next?"

"Most of our operations come from assignments handed down from my boss. We also gather our own intel on prospective targets. Wiz scours databases looking for patterned criminalized behavior with large scale threat implications. If we come across something that might meet our operational capabilities, then I forward it up. Nothing we do happens without a green light. That means your extraction was sanctioned."

"Did you say boss?" Nick asked. "I thought we didn't answer to anyone?"

"Everyone is accountable to someone. Don't waste your energy on that equation," Jay said with a half-smile.

"What if I want out? What then?" Nick asked softly, looking down at the drink in his hand.

"You're a free man. You give me the word and you'll walk away. New identification and new life."

"With your boss's approval," Nick added.

Jay said nothing.

"Declan has a family. How long do you think he can operate like this?" Nick asked.

"He's a hell of an asset."

"That's not an answer," Nick said, draining the remains of his pint in one gulp.

"I guess that decision lies with him then," Jay said.

"He's only doing this because of me. I know he feels like he owes me too."

"Maybe. Probably. I don't know," Jay said. "I know one thing—he definitely believes in what we're doing. He sees the futility and bureaucracy when it comes to hunting the real threats. We cut the red tape. We can move at speeds beyond any other domestic agency's capabilities."

"I know. I got a taste of that this morning," Nick said. "It's just a bit beyond my norm. I'm an investigator, not an assassin."

"Were."

"Huh?"

"You *were* an investigator," Jay said. "Nick Lawrence, FBI agent, is dead."

Nick said nothing but intently looked into his friend's eyes. He'd found a way to adjust to life as an inmate and knew time would help him with this latest transition.

Jay flagged the waitress's attention and held up two fingers. Moments later two more black and tans appeared. The two men tapped the glasses together.

"Happy funeral day," Jay jested.

Nick laughed, "To many more."

32

The news stations had continued to air their coverage of Sheldon Price's school attack. Interviews of survivors trickled in as victims sought their fifteen minutes of fame. One particular boy's recounting of the events had caught the attention of Tanner Morris as he sat in the ornate conference room. The boy's name, Blake Johnson, was plastered on the digital banner beneath his face.

"There was all this shooting and explosions and stuff. Crazy—just crazy. I'm lucky to be alive," Blake Johnson said, looking distraught.

"You mentioned to me off-camera about something the shooter yelled before his rampage began. Can you share with our viewers what Sheldon Price screamed before opening fire on you and your classmates? Do you remember what he said?" The news anchor asked in rapid fire succession.

"Sasquatch 187," Tanner said.

"Sasquatch 187? Do you have any idea what that means?" the reporter asked.

"Nope. But I'll tell you this. Sheldon was a loner and a weirdo. I just wished I had been able to stop him," Blake said with false bravado.

"You're a very brave young man! And you should be proud of yourself," the reporter said.

Tanner Morris hit mute and then turned, facing the members of his small council. "The test runs are complete. It's time to launch the final phase of our operation. Graham tells me he's secured Patriot level candidates in all fifty states."

The room was silent. The truth behind that statement carried a gravity and each member knew it. The only one who appeared genuinely pleased was Graham Morris.

"It's time to send the manifesto. It's time to wake this country from its slumber and open their eyes," Tanner said.

"The broadcast is ready," Graham said.

Simon Belfort, the technical genius who worked behind the scenes, chimed in, "It's anonymized and will be untraceable. Well, I'm sure they'll eventually track it down, but I've set it up so that even when they do it will never lead back to us."

"Very well. Send it," Tanner said.

Belfort nodded and left the room. He returned a few moments later. "It's done."

Graham Morris smiled broadly and had a glint of madness in his eyes. It was a look Tanner had seen in his son many times in the past. The blood lust of his only heir worried him, but he pushed the thought from his mind and turned his attention back to the television mounted on the wall.

Tanner Morris turned up the volume on the newscast and sank into the worn leather of his chair, waiting for the media to deliver his message.

33

"We've got a problem," Wiz said aloud to all present.

"What's up?" Jay asked.

"Check it out for yourself. It's breaking on all the stations right now," Wiz said, looking up from his computer and clicking on the television.

At the top of the screen a bright red banner with the bold-faced words BREAKING NEWS came into view. A panic-stricken blonde reporter in a light-blue power suit looked wide-eyed as she shuffled papers and cleared her throat.

"This station has just received a disturbing message. We are still in the process of confirming its authenticity, but we wanted to bring it to you immediately. Remember, you heard it here first!"

Barbie smirked, "Why does the blonde always have to be the dipshit?" For affect, she flipped her strawberry blonde hair in an exaggerated arc like an actress on a shampoo commercial.

"Not all. Just this one," Gator said in his thick accent.

"Shh. You'll want to hear this," Wiz said.

"The message you're about to hear is a disturbing one and this station recommends that if young children are present please have them leave the room at this time." The reporter waited for approximately ten seconds, adding to the dramatic effect of her delivery. "We'll play it for you now."

A mechanical voice replaced the refined reporter's delivery:

"This message is to those who have preyed on the weak, picking on and isolating those classmates who you deemed unworthy of your friendship. A reckoning is coming.

This battle has been long fought but has remained invisible to many and condoned by societal silence. Every day children are victimized by the brutal attacks of their peers. These attacks, both physically and emotionally, have demoralized and irreversibly damaged innocent children.

Our schools have become breeding grounds for bullies. Our educational system has turned a blind eye to these travesties. Governmental attempts to address this through catchy slogans and feel-good initiatives have failed. Teenage suicide is on the rise, largely in part due to the damaging emotional trauma.

Attacks like the one perpetrated by Sheldon Price are not isolated incidents and are occurring with increased regularity. 'Why' you ask? Because you stood by while the damage to these young minds was committed. You created these monsters! Sheldon Price was a test run. He was the first soldier we've deployed in our war. He is the first, but he will not be the last. You are unprepared and incapable of stopping what's coming next.

Monday, April 1st, will be a day where you will suffer unimaginable loss. This country was founded on the blood of Patriots and through similar sacrifice this country will be reformed. No school is safe. No state is exempt. No longer will we stand by. The system has failed them. This is our time to rise up and rebel."

The blonde looked defeated after delivering the message. She faced the camera and the normally verbose woman was speechless.

Wiz muted the television. "I think it's legit."

"Either it is or isn't. Why do you think it's real?" Jay asked.

"It's completely anonymized, and I can't locate the source. It's bouncing all over the place. This ability to hide their digital footprint makes me concerned."

"What the hell does the message mean?" Jay asked, scanning the members of his unit.

"Not sure. It sounds like a coordinated attack, but I'm not exactly sure how they plan to pull it off," Wiz answered. "I'm looking for other specific chatter on social media and the like, using similar phrasing. I'll hopefully have more for you in a bit."

"Well, it's going to be hard to filter it out after that. Everyone in the world is going to be talking about it," Jay said.

"Listening to the message, we can at least piece together a rough idea of what the plan is to accomplish," Nick said. "We know the date. We know the targets are schools, most likely high schools if the Price attack was actually a test run. And we know it's a large-scale nation-wide attack."

"How in hell could anyone pull off an operation of that magnitude?" Gator asked.

"He already told us," Spider said quietly, inserting himself into the debate.

"How so?" Gator asked.

"He said Sheldon Price was a test. Somehow, Price was mobilized to carry out his attack. Whatever method they used to connect with and manipulate him, they've obviously done with others," Spider said. "That is if this is a real threat and not some hoax."

"It could be a bluff. Or it could be someone using the shooting to further some anti-bullying agenda," Jay said.

Wiz was shaking his head. "I don't think so."

"Why not?" Jay asked.

"Because Spider's already figured it out," Wiz said.

"I did?" Spider asked.

Wiz nodded. "How do you connect with a teenager?"

"Facebook, Instagram, you name it. Take your pick of the social media roulette wheel," Nick said.

"Or this," Wiz said, pushing back in his chair and exposing the image on one of his monitors.

REBEL DOGS in dark red letters with an image of a wolf's head in the backdrop appeared on the screen.

"What's that?" everyone asked, almost in unison.

"It's a free online first-person shooter game," Wiz said.

"I'm not seeing the connection," Jay said.

Wiz smiled broadly. "You won't believe what the game's tagline is. Rise up and rebel." Wiz cued up the speech they'd just listened to and fast forwarded to the end, hitting play, *"This is our time to rise up and rebel."*

"Holy shit!" Nick said.

"Couldn't it be some angry kid? I mean, who would use a video game tagline in a manifesto?" Barbie asked.

"Right. I know it sounds fishy, but I seriously doubt a kid could've anonymized the message put out to the media. I intercepted it and tried to trace it back to its source. It's changing IP addresses every couple of seconds. That's some crazy encryption. So, on that alone I'm concerned," Wiz said, sounding impressed.

"Why tell us when? Why give us the Sheldon Price link?" Barbie asked.

"Good point. Maybe it's a bluff. Or maybe, whoever's behind this has no plans of following through," Nick said.

"I don't think we should wait and see. That deadline is a week away," Gator said.

"I need to make a call," Jay said, retreating to his office and closing the door. "And Wiz, send a message to Declan. We'll need to get him back here asap."

Nick's eyes followed Jay. He wondered who was on the other end of the line. He understood the need for secrecy but still wasn't comfortable taking orders from an unknown source. He caught Spider looking at him with his dark unreadable eyes.

"You can't turn it off, can you?" Spider asked in a hushed tone.

"How do you mean?" Nick asked.

"That need to know. It becomes as important as the air we breathe. The investigator inside you needs answers."

"The investigator inside me is dead," Nick said. "He was buried today."

34

Albert left school at lunch time. He went to the nurse and told her he wasn't feeling well. She'd called Susan Walker, his foster mom, but she wasn't able to come and pick him up. He knew that would be the case and had in fact planned for that. After being cleared to leave, he walked the short distance to his home.

Passing by the Shelton Public Library, Albert wanted nothing more than to slip inside the safe confines of its walls and become the Bully Slayer. He refrained, the orders he'd received had been very specific. It was Wednesday and a package would be arriving soon. Graham_CrackerHacker had told him the exact time it would be delivered. The timing guaranteed it would be delivered two hours before any member of his foster family would be home.

Albert sat anxiously in the window sill and waited, peeking out from the blinds. At 1:36 he watched as a brown delivery truck pulled to a stop along the curb in front of the cracked walkway leading to his front porch. The man walked to the door, carrying a large box. He rang the doorbell twice and tapped something on his mobile delivery device. The man placed the box down on the tattered welcome mat and turned and walked away.

Once the truck was out of sight, Albert scooted out to the porch and retrieved the package. His heart raced with the excitement of Christmas morning, or more accurately what Albert had always envisioned Christmas morning to feel like. His recall of such holidays was dim and sad.

The package was heavier than he anticipated, and Albert's cheeks reddened with the unexpected exertion. He put the box down inside the threshold of the cluttered hallway. Albert's fingers tore at the bubble wrapping covering the exterior, exposing a benign cardboard box. He slit open the box and stared in awe at the contents.

Inside was a small metallic box. It too had been wrapped in a layer of bubble wrap, but this time Albert took extra care in tearing it. Off to the side of the device was a padded manila envelope. Albert pulled it out from its wedged position and ripped it open, freeing the contents. A black handgun and three loaded magazines fell to the frayed hallway runner covering the poorly conditioned wood flooring. A white slip of paper had fallen out and lay under one of the magazines.

Hey Albert,
Remember the instructions. I'm proud of you.
Your Friend,
Graham

Albert focused on one word in the message. *Friend.* A word he hadn't heard in such a long time that he'd forgotten its value. He folded the note and stuffed it in his back pocket. Graham had told him to burn the box and letter in a message he'd sent through his Rebel Dogs account, but Albert Hutchins couldn't bring himself to burn the letter.

He got up from the floor and went into the living room to retrieve his backpack. The weight of his books was comparable to that of the package's contents. He shouldered the backpack and put the gun and magazines back into the box with the bomb. Hoisting the box, Albert awkwardly ascended the stairs to his bedroom. He gladly set the heavy box back down on his unmade bed. He then dumped the books out, making room for his gifts.

Albert returned to the package, removed the device and placed it gently into his backpack. The cold metallic device made him nervous, but Graham had assured him the bomb would remain inert until he flicked the switch. He slipped the remote at the bottom of the box into the side pocket of his pack and then picked up the gun. The bomb fit snugly into the backpack with enough room at the top to cover it with a book.

Albert walked over to the full-length mirror. He pointed the gun, taking up an action stance he'd seen in movies and video games. Albert had a diminutive stature but looking at his reflection in the mirror with the gun in hand made him look bigger. He felt an unfamiliar strength.

And then he thought of Andy Bloom.

35

Tobie Jones read the message from Graham_CrackerHacker. His dad had always warned him about chatting online with people he didn't know, but this message seemed safe. It was just a guy looking to team up.

Tobie accepted the link and joined the campaign. Graham's avatar was a ninja and it approached Tobie's character, DocDeath501. A chat bubble appeared, and Graham asked, "Are you ready to be a Patriot?"

Tobie read the question and was elated to have amassed enough points to move toward the game's final level. Only one kid he played with in his high school had reached that level—Darren Jackson. Tobie knew Darren and had always been nice to him, although never felt he really knew him well. Others in the school treated Darren poorly, and Tobie, never one to shy away from sticking up for the underdog, had intervened on his behalf several times. Most recently, his intervention had cost Tobie an after-school detention. A price he'd happily paid for punching the kid who had knocked Darren's books out of his hand.

"Let's do this!" Tobie answered through his avatar.

The screen shifted settings and Tobie's avatar was now stood facing a school.

"What's this?" Tobie asked.

"Patriot level!" Graham said.

"What do we do?" Tobie asked, watching the computerized students entering the building.

"KILL 'EM ALL!"

Tobie sat in his room and stared at the screen. It didn't seem like any advanced level stuff. It seemed strange. A timer popped up in the upper right corner of his monitor and immediately began counting down from three minutes.

Tobie manipulated his avatar and approached the entryway to the school. He didn't arm his character because none of the simulated characters had weapons. He entered the school, expecting some type of surprise attack. Nothing happened. The computerized students moved through the hallway in the same fashion as if they would on a normal day of school. He didn't understand the purpose.

"KILL 'EM ALL!" The message bubble appeared above Graham_CrackerHacker.

"???" Tobie typed into his avatar's message box.

"KILL 'EM ALL!"

Tobie only liked shooting games where bad guys shot back. This seemed uncharacteristically sadistic. Tobie refused to shoot. Even though it was only a game, killing unarmed noncombative characters didn't feel right.

FAILURE flashed on the screen as the timer ran out.

Tobie shook his head in annoyance and logged out of the game.

36

"Three days since we've been authorized to move on this thing and we aren't getting any closer to figuring it out," Jay said aloud, but most of his frustration was directed at Wiz.

Nick could tell Wiz felt the frustration. The group hadn't left The Vault since the authorization to seek and eliminate the threat had come down the invisible pipeline. Declan had returned and now all six members of the team were huddled over their respective computers searching for something that would guide their next move.

Everyone knew the best hope rested on Wiz's shoulders and it was evident in the fact that the hacker hadn't slept or showered in the last few days, barely moving from his workstation to relieve himself and add to his caffeine level. The stress of a potential widespread attack on school children had the group's nerves on edge.

"Something's got to break. An attack of this magnitude can't be done silently. There's got to be a link. But there's nothing of substance. The game is encrypted. I can't access it! Crazy stuff," Wiz hissed in frustration.

"Maybe we're going about this the wrong way. If you're right about the game being the link then what about the physical address?" Declan asked.

"What physical address?" Wiz asked.

"I mean you're trying to access the game's database, but what about a physical address for merchandising. Most businesses have one, right? We just need to locate it," Declan said.

Wiz looked up from his screen as if seeing the world around him for the first time.

37

The rain fell more steadily, soaking through Albert's T-shirt. It was a cold rain and he shivered as goose bumps prickled along his pale skin. His head was down, which was not unusual because he did his best to avoid eye contact at all costs. But his social oddity left him vulnerable. Ever since receiving the package two days ago he'd been more distracted than normal, his mind constantly wandering to the task that lay ahead. The only place he found any semblance of distraction was inside the sanctuary of the Shelton Public Library.

He rounded the corner of the building's familiar gray stone façade, having taken the shortcut from the school. Every day's commute from school to the library was filled with land mines of potential threats, all of which came at the direction of Andy Bloom and his horde of brainless minions who followed his every move.

The water dripped down his forehead and into his eyes. He entered through the library's main doors and the instant warmth from the entranceway's radiators fogged his glasses, blurring his vision. Albert stopped and removed them, rubbing them on the inside of his untucked shirt. He raised the cleaned glasses to his face, but before he could put them on a blur of movement caught him off guard.

Andy Bloom's fist struck the side of Albert's head. The unexpected impact knocked him off balance. Shooting pain radiated out from the point of impact with dizzying results and Albert staggered awkwardly away from his assailant. In his daze, he tripped and collapsed to the ground. Albert felt the crunch of his glasses, still gripped in his outstretched hand, as he attempted to break the fall.

"I'm so sorry I didn't see you there," Andy taunted.

The sound of Andy's clearly recognizable voice and scattered laughter from his cronies was too much for Albert to bear. He felt the tears welling up and fought hard against their release. He scrambled to his feet, retreating madly into the torrential downpour. Outside, the sky seemed to understand his plight, masking his tears with the heavy rain.

Albert ran. His feet clamored through puddles as he sobbed uncontrollably, hyperventilating from the combination of exertion and torment. He entered his home, slamming the door behind him. He crumpled into a heap, alone and angry.

Albert's mind raced. He only needed to wait a couple more days and he'd have his revenge. The Bully Slayer would show the world that Albert Hutchins was not one to be messed with.

Albert felt the broken glasses in his hands and attempted to put them on. They hung loosely. The left hinge was snapped, and the end piece flopped loosely against his face. He grabbed a piece of tape from the kitchen's junk drawer and did his best to tighten it.

Albert stood facing the mirror in the hallway. His image was distorted through the cracked right lens. His wet hair and clothes, bruised cheeks, and broken glasses gave him the deranged look of a madman. His chest rose and fell in dramatic fashion as he surveyed the image.

Why wait until Monday? He was the Bully Slayer! Albert thought angrily.

Albert ran up to his room. He dropped to his knees alongside his bed and wiggled his hand between the mattress and box spring. His fingers found the cold metal of the gun's slide and he pulled it free. One of the three magazines Graham had provided was already loaded into the gun, but Albert made sure he didn't chamber a round. He was scared it could go off while he was sleeping. The extent of his firearms knowledge stemmed from game play and carried little in the way of real-life experience. Graham had sent him instructions on how to load the gun through Rebel Dogs' message system. It seemed relatively simple. Once the magazine was clicked into place all he had to do was pull the slide back and release.

Easier said than done. Albert struggled with the slide and decided he needed two hands. He used his knees like a vice grip to firmly hold the base of the gun while he pulled with both hands. After several failed attempts and some cuts along the palm of his hand, he'd managed to retract and release the slide. Definitely not as cool as he'd thought, disappointed in his weapon-handling prowess. It would've been embarrassing if he'd tried to do this at the school on Monday. Satisfied a round was now chambered, Albert slipped the black Smith and Wesson MMP into the front of his waistband. The weight caused his pants to sag and he ratcheted his belt to keep things in place.

Albert looked at himself again in the mirror above his dresser. The grooved metal of the weapon dug uncomfortably into his bony hip and he adjusted it several times, trying to find the best position. He changed out of his wet T-shirt, throwing it on the ground and missing his over-flowing laundry basket. Taking a moment, he eyed the black butt of the gun protruding out of his pants before pulling on a dry shirt. Satisfied he'd effectively concealed Graham's gift, Albert Hutchins walked down the stairs and back out into the gray afternoon light.

The rain had stopped. It wouldn't have mattered either way to Albert. His mind was focused on one thing and one thing only, Andy Bloom.

38

"Oh my goodness! Look at what we got here!" Andy taunted as Albert approached.

This time as the gangly teen walked, Albert's head wasn't down. For the first time in a very long time, he held his head up high and walked with something he hadn't experienced in years—confidence. Sadly, he was bright enough to know the confidence exuded didn't stem from some inner growth but rather the gun tucked in his waistline, chaffing his right hip.

Bloom's followers circled around, smelling the potential for confrontation. They began jockeying for the best vantage point from which to view the abuse. Cellphones were in hand and pointed at the ready, preparing to film another embarrassing moment in the sad life of Albert Hutchins.

"I like your new glasses! Where'd you get 'em? Bums "R" Us?" Andy Bloom snarked.

Albert stopped five feet away from his nemesis, the one person who'd made his last three years a living hell. Five feet away stood the person he hated most in this world. His arms and legs tingled with the adrenalin coursing through his veins. Albert's ears pulsed with each beat of his racing heart. He said nothing.

"I asked you a question, turd!" Bloom began a theatrical swelling of his chest and flailing his arms out wide, welcoming the challenge. "And when I ask you a question, I expect a damn answer!"

"Break his face, Bloom!" a boy off to Albert's left yelled. He paid no attention. His only focus was on the person in front of him.

Time seemed to stand still as Albert made his move, shoving his hand into his waistband and finding the hard grip of the semiautomatic handgun. Bloom took a step in his direction, oblivious to what was coming.

The gun now free, pointed out toward Andy Bloom's face. It shook violently in Albert's hand as his nerves caused his body to convulse. He brought up his left hand in a meager attempt to steady himself.

"You think a pellet gun's gonna scare me?" Bloom looked at his group and smiled. "Now I'm gonna hurt you really bad!"

"No," Albert said, his voice squeaking under the strain.

"What did you say?"

"No!" Roared Albert. The shaking subsided slightly, and he remembered who he was.

"Albert, Albert, Albert, you truly have lost your mind," Bloom taunted.

"I'm not Albert," he hissed. "I'm the Bully Slayer, bitch!"

Albert saw something in Bloom's eyes. It was something he'd never seen before in his tormentor. Fear.

Albert never heard the gunshot.

Bloom fell backward and was rolling from side to side, clutching desperately at his chest. The dark red spread across his tan shirt. Agonal gasps filled the air, but no final words from his enemy. *This was definitely not like the gaming world,* Albert thought.

Albert looked around, wild-eyed. Most of Bloom's friends had scattered at the sound of the gunfire. Their loyalty to their leader was readily apparent.

Albert tucked the gun back in his waist. He stood over Bloom's writhing body until it came to a stop. He then turned and walked slowly back in the direction of his foster home.

39

"We may've gotten our first real break!" Wiz announced to the group. "Check out this video. Some kid in Iowa put it on Facebook Live and it went viral."

The group huddled around Wiz's workstation and watched as their resident techie hit play.

The video was obviously taken by a cellphone held vertically when recording. The camera man, who undoubtedly was a teenager, was not steady-handed. The amateur production quality didn't take away from the brutality of the scene playing out on the flat-screen monitor.

A tall, rail-thin teenager with a slight hunch was squared off with another more athletic boy. There were a group of students surrounding the two, taunting and laughing. The video appeared to be capturing the early stages of a fight, and from the looks of it, a very one-sided fight. It was clear to anyone watching, the gangly teen was the victim of this group's assault. The video footage was taken to further any damage inflicted through the speed of social media.

Nick and the others waited, assuming there was more to the video than a few teens taunting another. And then it happened. Nick saw the tall boys body language change, taking a stronger stance and standing more erect. Nick watched as the prey became the predator. The boy had withdrawn a gun, holding it pointed out toward the clean-cut athletic kid.

The screams and taunts continued from the others circling the standoff, and included in that volley of insults was the cameraman's voice, recorded clearly. "Look at Albert! He brought a toy gun!"

All of the voices fell silent as the awkward boy with the gun shouted something and then the familiar sound of a single gunshot resonated through the speakers of Wiz's computer. The athletic boy fell back and the video became a disjointed whirl of images as the cameraman ran away from the shooter.

"And how does this disturbing video, although extremely tragic, help us?" Jay asked.

Wiz rewound the video clip to the moment the teen had pulled the gun. And paused it. "Listen carefully to what he says before pulling the trigger. I've removed all the other voices and isolated the shooters."

Wiz hit play.

"I'm not Albert. I'm the Bully Slayer, bitch!" The boy with the gun said. The words were clear.

"I'm still not seeing how this relates to our current situation," Jay said.

Wiz smiled, pleased with himself. "Everyone, meet Albert Hutchins. Or as I've better come to know him, Bully_Slayer#1."

"Bully Slayer number one?" Nick asked.

"It's his handle, or online gamer name. And would you like to guess what gaming platform he uses this on?" Wiz asked, cocking his eyebrow.

"Rebel Dogs," Nick mumbled.

"Correct!" Wiz exclaimed.

"Holy crap!" Jay said, excitedly.

"And there's more. Police found a bomb in his bedroom. A fully functional bomb with remote detonator. The FBI was called in. I've already scoured their evidence database and confirmed it was similar in design to the one used by Sheldon Price's attack," Wiz said.

"So, the threat is confirmed. And now we know how they plan to carry out the attack. But how do we stop fifty bombers scattered across fifty states?" Declan asked, inserting himself into the conversation. "It took us days to get to this point."

"I've got that covered," Wiz said. "Remember you mentioned about looking for a physical address for the Rebel Dogs' headquarters?"

Declan nodded and the others intently listened.

"I came up with zilch. And then Albert, the Bully Slayer, appeared on scene. He screwed up. He'd kept the original packaging the bomb had been shipped in. It was stuffed in his closet and recovered during a search. The FBI photographed the box, to include the shipping label," Wiz said.

Wiz toggled his mouse and clicked on a digital file folder, pulling up the label's image.

"We've got your address," Wiz said with confidence.

Zooming in on the label, the others could clearly see the return address.

RD Consulting

1187 US-83

Liberty Hill, Texas 78642

"You're a damn genius!" Jay boomed, slapping the computer wizard's back.

"Yes. Yes, I am," Wiz said.

Jay turned and surveyed his group like a quarterback calling an audible before the hike. "Spider and Barbie, I need you to take a trip out to Iowa and meet with our friend Albert Hutchins. You know the drill, and Wiz will get your credentials ready."

Spider and Barbie both nodded.

"Gator, Declan, and Nick are going to head to the address on that shipping label. Maybe we'll get lucky and stop the delivery of some of these devices." Jay said. "Looks like you get to take a trip back to your old stomping grounds Nick. Liberty Hill, Texas isn't too far away from Austin?"

"I never thought I'd be going back," Nick mumbled.

"Time's ticking. There are only two days left before the attacks are to take place," Jay said. "I'll make the arrangements. You'll be flying in a private jet out of Reagan National."

"Great," Gator said, shaking his head in frustration at the thought of air travel.

"I guess I'm staying here?" Wiz asked rhetorically, looking at Jay. "I know the answer already. Just once I'd like to get out there and kick some ass."

"You can take my ticket," Gator said sarcastically.

"Don't worry, I'll be here to keep you company," Jay said with a laugh.

Wiz rolled his eyes. "Now that I know Albert Hutchins' Rebel Dogs gamer handle, I should be able to access his account. If I can, maybe I can backdoor my way into the company's server."

Jay was about to speak, but Wiz spun and started typing furiously into his keyboard. He was immediately lost in a sea of coding algorithms.

The rest of the unit's members readied themselves for their respective trips.

Nick prepared himself for setting foot back on the soil where he'd recently been buried. He thought of the funeral and then of Anaya.

40

"Good afternoon, I'm Agent Russo and this is my partner, Agent Smith," Spider said to the receptionist of the Shelton Police Department. "I believe your department received word of our visit." He smiled, sliding his FBI credentials in through the slit underneath the thick, bullet-resistant glass to the officer working the desk.

The officer, a thin man with ruddy complexion, took the badges and wrote the information into his log book, noting the time. "Yes sir. If you'll have a seat. Hutchins is in with his attorney at the moment."

Spider and Barbie sat in the metallic benches of Shelton Police Department's main lobby. They'd done a little research on the small town of Shelton and its representative law enforcement agency. The town, with a population of less than three thousand, was protected by a twelve-man department. Not very much in the way of crime for the small town. That was until Albert Hutchins shot Andy Bloom. The officer at the desk looked tired, a sign the tiny department had been overwhelmed by the recent circumstance.

"Should we be worried that he's speaking with an attorney?" Barbie asked in a hushed tone.

"Nothing to worry about. In my prior life I've interviewed many a perp in the presence of a lawyer. We shouldn't have a problem getting the information we need," Spider answered confidently.

Just then, the secured door nearest the main desk opened and man in a light-colored suit exited. Spider eyed the man, assuming this must be the boy's attorney. The suit was stretched to capacity, filled by the man's large-muscled frame. He did not look like a man who was comfortable in such attire. But what caught Spider's attention wasn't his clothing, it was the scar stretching across the man's face and ending at his misshaped ear. The thick man passed without giving a glance in their direction.

As the lobby doors closed behind the scarred man, the thin officer at the main desk stood up and ran toward the back of the office space and into an adjoining hallway, disappearing from view.

Moments later the desk officer barreled out of the same door the suited man had just departed. He withdrew his firearm and ran toward the exit.

Spider and Barbie stood, bringing their Glocks to the low ready, unsure of what was happening.

"Son of bitch!" yelled the desk officer, exiting out to the sidewalk.

"What's going on?" Barbie asked as they followed behind.

"Hutchins is dead!"

"What?" Spider asked.

"His lawyer killed him. Choked him to death in the room and just walked out," the officer panted, frantically scanning the area for the killer.

A squeal of tires shattered the quiet of Shelton's evening. A black Dodge Charger slid sideways out from the police department's parking lot and onto Main Street. The desk officer raised his gun and then lowered it without firing a shot at the fleeing vehicle.

Spider and Barbie ran toward their gray Impala. Barbie took the wheel and the two sped off in the last direction of the Charger. Sirens sounded from the lot behind them, but they were convinced the understaffed and under-trained members of Shelton's police force wouldn't be able to keep up.

The good thing about Iowa in the early spring was the dust. There hadn't been a heavy rain yet and it left the roadways coated in the dried dirt of trucks and combines, vehicles that spent most of their days off road. The effect was a trail of dust kicked up by the Dodge's tires like a jet's contrail, enabling Barbie to find the vehicle as he navigated the flat landscape of his unfamiliar surroundings.

Barbie treated pursuit driving like mogul skiing. To avoid any and all obstacles one must look beyond, giving the brain time to make calculations and adjustments. The engine roared as she accelerated the Impala to speeds exceeding one hundred miles an hour. The traffic was light, enabling her to close the gap with minimal difficulty.

She nudged closer, closing the distance to a car's length away. Barbie prepared to make her move, but the Charger's engine gave it a boost in speed that her Chevrolet couldn't match and the black muscle car started to increase the separation again.

The stretch of roadway was long and straight with smaller roads intersecting from neighboring farm lands. A rusted Ford pickup was stopped at an intersection a mile ahead. The farmer pulled onto the road without yielding to the two high-speed vehicles fast approaching.

The truck's wide right caused the driver of the Charger to brake hard, kicking up a cloud of dust. Barbie seized the opportunity and closed the gap.

Barbie brought the Impala along the left side of the Charger. Her move was quick. She accelerated and whipped the steering wheel hard to the right. The front right corner of Barbie's Impala struck the left wheel well of the Dodge.

The effect was immediate. The Dodge had slowed to avoid the collision with the red truck. The perfectly timed Pursuit Intervention Technique, or PIT maneuver, spun the black Charger one-hundred-eighty degrees. The reversal of direction at the high rate of speed seized the fleeing vehicle's engine. Barbie completed the move by continuing her forward momentum, driving the front end of her Impala into the nose of her target.

Barbie accelerated hard, forcing the Charger off the road and down into a shallow water-runoff culvert. The vehicle and the large, scarred man inside, were now pinned.

The Impala's windshield exploded in a hail of gunfire. Barbie and Spider were already moving, bailing out of their respective doors and finding cover behind the rear of their vehicle.

A pause in the gunfire either meant the large man was reloading or on the move, or both. Spider pressed himself flat against the ground and took up a prone supported shooting platform beneath the right rear tire.

Barbie, in a tight squat behind the left taillight, raised her gun without exposing her head and torso. She fired blindly in the direction of the Charger and toward the last known position of the driver.

Barbie's suppressive fire gave Spider a momentary window as the large man exited the Charger. The big man's legs, now visible under the open driver's side door, made good targets for Spider's well-trained eye. He fired two controlled shots, each finding their mark and striking the big man's kneecaps.

The large man crumpled to the ground. Lying beneath the door in the crux of the culvert, he tried desperately to move out of the line of fire. But he was too slow.

Spider fired again. Two more shots. This time the rounds struck the man's broad shoulders, flattening him and rendering both arms useless. The large man roared in protest to his incapacitation.

"Drop the gun or the next one's going in your skull!" Spider yelled.

"Screw you!" spat the big man.

Spider never repeated a command. He'd found it lessened the desired impact of its statement. He waited, silently counting down from ten.

The big man must've had his own mental countdown going. One with a shorter fuse. He fired at Spider's position. The damage from the wound to his shoulder made his shots inaccurate, but close enough to be a threat.

Spider fired one round, ending any further negotiations or prospect of interrogation.

41

Tanner Morris sat in his office and listened to the newscaster's brief of the president's most recent address regarding the terror threat.

"The president has called for schools across the nation to close on Monday April 1st. He said this April Fools' Day will be one remembered in history, but not for violence. He's calling for reform, creating an oversight committee whose sole purpose is to come up with an approach to neutralize the rampant mistreatment of our student population with regard to bullying. He called his anti-bullying campaign the single most important piece in stopping the widespread rise of incidents of mass-casualty violent extremism."

Morris flipped the channel and another newscast showed images from anti-bullying rallies taking place across the country. A unified national vigil was planned to take place on Monday, calling for a moratorium on school violence.

Each channel carried some variant of that message. Tanner Morris clicked off the television and sat back, sinking into the soft leather of his James River Leather Executive chair. He closed his eyes absorbing the impact his vision had on the country's outlook. He felt contented.

His peaceful respite was interrupted as Graham entered unannounced.

"Albert Hutchins is dead," Graham said.

"Okay," Morris said solemnly to his son.

"Tank's dead too," Graham added.

"What? How?" Tanner Morris asked, sitting forward.

"A couple FBI agents killed him in a shootout."

"This isn't good," Morris said, rubbing the sides of his temples.

"I don't think it really matters much at this point. There's no way of stopping us now," Graham said confidently.

"Maybe it's time to shut this thing down." Tanner Morris looked down at the finely crafted desk, breaking eye contact with his son and avoiding his judgment contained therein.

"You've got to be kidding! Shut this down? Have you lost your damned mind? All the work we've done. The years of planning. We are so close," Graham said through gritted teeth. He began pacing madly in front of his father's desk.

"Look at all the news stations. Look at the coverage. We've made our point! Our message has been received. The world took notice and heeded our warning," Tanner said, still avoiding his son's glare.

"What about Wendy? Her death doesn't matter to you anymore?" Graham seethed.

Tanner Morris looked at his son. Anger flashed across his face. The veins in his neck bulged and his cheeks turned blood red. "Don't you dare ever question my devotion to her!"

Graham stopped pacing and squared his body to his father, seated before him. "You're not shutting this down. This is my masterpiece and it's going to happen with or without you."

"What did you say?" Tanner Morris rose up, shoving the chair into the wall behind him.

Graham didn't move, standing still in the presence of his enraged father's impressive frame. He pulled a gun from a holster concealed on his back hip. "Take a seat," he said calmly.

"A gun! You're pulling a gun on me you son of a bitch!" Tanner boomed. He saw the familiar look in his son's eyes. The same look he'd seen when he caught his son killing the neighbor's pet. He sat.

"Good. Now you're going to sit quietly and listen carefully to me," Graham said. The gun remained pointed at his father's chest.

"I know that look. You crazy bastard!" Tanner said.

"Not a very nice way to treat your only living heir," Graham snarked.

"As of this moment in time you're dead to me," Tanner said. His voice carried less conviction staring down the barrel of a gun.

"It's sad to hear you say that, but to be quite honest I think you would've come to that conclusion at some point anyway. And in the spirit of honesty —I have a little story to tell you."

"What the hell are you talking about now?" Tanner asked.

"It's about your precious Wendy."

Tanner cocked his head, confused at the reference.

"Your whole plan to exact revenge on her tragic death was misguided," Graham said with a smile.

"I don't understand."

"You will," Graham said. "You always loved her more than me. She was your little angel. All I wanted was a piece of what she had. And then you caught me in the early phase of my experimentation."

"Experimentation? You strangled cats!"

"Well let's agree to disagree," Graham chuckled. "Anyhow, I know whatever chance I had at earning your love died that day."

Tanner Morris sighed loudly, displaying his frustration with the banter.

Graham ignored his father and continued, "Poor Wendy was picked on at school because she was fat. It hurt her. Wrecked her emotionally. Kids are mean. But not as mean as you thought."

"What are you getting at?"

"She was depressed, but she wasn't suicidal," Graham said.

"They pushed her over the edge. The kids who emotionally abused her on a daily basis ruined my little girl," Tanner murmured.

Graham shook his head slowly and deliberately. "They did hurt her feelings. And yes she was sad. But that final push didn't come from them."

Tanner's brow furrowed.

"I can see you're thoroughly confused. Let me help you connect the dots," Graham taunted. "Who convinced sweet little Wendy to take all those pills?"

"No!" Tanner Morris shouted.

"I can see you know the answer is true. I worked on her weak little mind just like you had me do to mom," Graham said, eyeing his father coldly. "It was easy."

"I'm going to kill you." Tanner spat the words.

"Shh. You're wasting what little time we have left on futile threats." Graham looked at the gun in his hand. "Remember when I came to you and told you I'd found her lifeless body? I do. I remember the anguish in your face. I treasure that memory almost as much as standing over Wendy as she took her final breath."

A tear rolled from Tanner Morris's eye and down his reddened cheek.

"So, now you can clearly see why I can't shut down this thing we created. It was never for Wendy. It's always been for me."

Tanner Morris launched at his son from behind the desk. His movement was surprisingly quick for a man of his size, but it wasn't quick enough.

One shot rang out from Graham's gun, striking his father's forehead, instantly killing him.

His body slumped across the desk. Blood quickly filled the beveled grooves of the etched wood of the expensive hardwood desktop. Graham placed the gun in his father's right hand, stepped back, and waited.

The office door swung open as Sarah Barnes ran in. Seeing Morris's body she stopped short, a look of horror on her pock-marked face.

"I couldn't stop him," Graham said. "He started yelling about Albert Hutchins screwing up the plan. He muttered something about failure and then he shot himself."

"My God! Oh my God! What the hell?" Barnes asked frantically. "We need to call an ambulance. We need to do something for Chrissake!"

Graham closed the door and locked it, turning to face Sarah Barnes.

"What the hell?" Barnes asked, obviously confused.

Graham closed the distance between the two, standing close enough to feel the warmth of her breath as she rapidly breathed in short fearful gasps. The accountant did not handle the stress of her current situation well. Her body began to tremble, and it excited him, not in a sexual way, but that of a hunter in the presence of his prey.

"Before you die, you're going to transfer all of the company's money into my account," Graham said.

"Do what?"

"You heard me. Open up the tablet in your hand and pull up the account. I'm going to watch you make the transfer," Graham calmly demanded.

"Are you crazy?" Barnes asked. Her voice quivered.

"You're the second person to call me crazy today," Graham said, looking past Barnes as he nodded his chin in the direction of his dead father.

"If you're going to kill me anyway then why should I bother making the transfer?" Barnes asked.

Graham smiled. He smelled the remnants of Doritos on her breath. He liked those connections. He knew from this point forward that any time he smelled the nacho-cheese-flavored corn chips he would remember her death.

"You'll do what I ask because otherwise I won't be so quick about it. And you won't like that." Graham moved closer, his lips grazing the bottom of Barnes's ear. He whispered, "You won't like that at all."

Sarah Barnes stood frozen in fear. Graham had slipped a knife into his hand. It was his favorite tool and carried with it a sentimental value, used on his first human victim. He had intended to use it on his father. The gun was only meant as a control measure, but when faced with Tanner Morris's rage-filled attack he'd been left with no choice but to shoot.

"Please don't! Graham, I've known you for the last six years," Barnes pleaded, tears streaming down her face and her lower lip quivered uncontrollably.

Graham swiped his left index finger across her cheek. He stuck it in his mouth and savored the saltiness, feeding off her fear before taking a step back. He didn't speak, but only glanced at the tablet in her hand.

Sarah Barnes could barely hold the tablet steady enough to type in the banking passcode. Graham brought the knife up toward her neck as a reminder. Barnes made the transfer and turned the tablet to show him. Graham opened his account from his cellphone and verified the deposit. Satisfied, he slipped the phone back into his pocket.

He looked at Barnes and then at his watch, wishing he had time to play. Without a word, he swiftly slashed the blade of the knife across the woman's throat. Her eyes widened as her life ended in the cascade of an arterial spray.

Graham opened the door, eyeing the company's technical expert, Simon Belfort, who sat typing away at his computer station. He wore Bose noise-cancelling headphones. The volume he kept his speakers set at would be loud enough to drown out a plane crash. Graham exited his father's office, closing the door behind him.

Graham stood behind Belfort, who must've seen his image in the monitor because he startled and turned to look, taking off his headphones.

"Hey Simon, sorry to scare you. Did you finish the final message? I just talked to my old man and he's on board."

"I just finished. Here it is," Belfort said, pointing at the audio file's icon on his screen. "I've set it up so all you have to do is hit send. Just like before, it'll go out to all of the same news stations."

"Thank you."

"To be honest, I'm glad we're calling off this thing," Belfort said.

"Did you get my account linked to all the Patriots on our list so that I can send them the notification?" Graham asked casually.

Simon nodded. "Sure did. You've got total control through your login. It looks like you don't need me anymore." He chuckled.

Graham laughed too. "You don't know how right you are."

The knife slammed down into Simon Belfort's heart. Graham snaked his left arm around the thin neck of the dying man and squeezed. He enjoyed feeling Belfort writhe and twist. He enjoyed feeling the struggle subside as the game designer yielded his life to death's call.

Graham grabbed his laptop and gave one last look back at his tapestry of death before leaving the Rebel Dogs headquarters.

42

"Movement on the front door. It's the same guy I saw go in half an hour ago. He's got a laptop in his hand," Declan said. His message relayed to Nick and Gator using the same bone mic and earpiece system from the church takedown. Nick was on the opposite side of the building, covering the rear doors. Gator was a block down the road in a diner parking lot.

"Roger that, Ace. Do you want me to follow or stay put?" Gator asked.

"Stay with the building. It's the only known we've got at this point. We don't want to lose whatever's in there. After the guy clears the lot let's hit it," Declan said, removing his pistol and resting it on his thigh.

Both Gator and Nick acknowledged the transmission.

"He's leaving the lot in the same tan Mazda he arrived in. You should have eyes on in a couple seconds," Declan said.

"Got him. He just passed by my position," Gator said. "I'm heading your way."

Declan saw the big southerner enter the parking lot.

"Now," Declan said.

Declan accelerated his vehicle, meeting Gator's on a blind side of the building near the main entrance. Both men were out of their respective cars within seconds of pulling to a stop, their weapons at the ready.

Nick called out, "At the back door. Charge set. Ready for the count."

Declan took lead and Gator stacked up behind him, placing his big left hand on Declan's shoulder as the men staged by the door. Declan checked the door's handle. It was locked. He set the breaching charge. "Charge is set. Front is ready. Standby. On my count."

Declan paused, listening for any movement. Silence followed.

"Three. Two. One."

The blast cut through the door, splintering the heavy wood and separating the locking mechanism from the frame. Declan moved into the building. The interior was setup as an office space, relatively open in design and sparsely furnished with a few workstations set up. The layout was not so different from the Vault his unit operated from. He took the left side and Gator reading off him took the right.

They quickly cleared the main space. One man was sprawled in a pool of blood, laying on the floor by a computer terminal.

"One down," Declan called.

Nick entered the main room from a narrow hallway. "Rear clear," he said as he entered, facing Declan and Gator.

The three turned their attention to the closed door at the end of the work space. Declan took the left side. Nick and Gator stacked on the knob side. Declan slide his hand to the doorknob. He turned it slowly. It was unlocked.

Declan made eye contact with his counterparts and nodded. They acknowledged and mouthed a silent count. Three, two, one.

Declan opened the door and pushed hard with his left hand, swinging it inward as Nick and Gator immediately entered, filling the room with their weapons pressed forward.

"Clear," Nick said, surveying the bodies of the man and woman.

"All clear," Declan said.

"Mother of God! What in hell happened in here?" Gator asked awestruck.

"I don't know. But I'm kicking myself for not having you tail that guy in the Mazda," Declan said.

"Let's see what we can gather," Nick said as he looked back and forth between the three dead bodies. "One thing's for certain. Whoever did this is one sick bastard."

43

"Are they okay?" Nick asked, speaking into the phone on the table.

Nick, Declan, and Gator were at a Vault location forty miles east of where they'd found the bodies of the Rebel Dogs employees. The Vaults were staggered throughout the country, giving the unit the ability to operate at full capacity with fully functional op centers. Each Vault contained a variety of equipment and weapons to effectively carry out those missions.

"Yes. Neither of them was hit during the exchange of gunfire. Not so much can be said for the other guy," Jay said, from the other end of the call.

"So, I guess there'll be no interrogation for Spider to conduct?" Gator chimed in with a laugh.

"Not unless he can communicate with the dead," Jay said. "Spider and Barbie are going to remain in that area a bit longer. Hopefully, there are some clues that will help us narrow our leads. Albert Hutchins was our best lead. But now that he's dead we need to look elsewhere. The clock is ticking on this thing."

"Not sure where we go from here," Nick said.

"Well, I've been able to confirm one of your dead guys from the warehouse. It was Tanner Morris," Wiz said in the background.

"Are we supposed to know the name?" Declan asked.

"If you read Forbes, then yeah. But from the sound of it, I would venture to say that's a big no," Wiz said.

The three men looked at each other and shrugged. "Never heard of him," Declan confirmed.

Wiz said, "Anyway, the guy was one of those young entrepreneurs who hit it big early. He crashed and burned after his youngest daughter died. Even did a stint in prison for a DUI manslaughter case. After that he'd supposedly made back some of his fortune but has been very reclusive. His only living family member is his son Graham. I'm guessing by the description you gave, that's who you saw leave the headquarters building, just before you entered."

"Maybe the son got wind of his dad's plan to attack school children and took it upon himself to end it?" Nick postulated.

"You might be right. Nothing is known yet. So, assumptions are all we've got right now. Wiz has been working to gain access to the Rebel Dogs server. Once he gets inside, we should be able to confirm some things," Jay said.

"You might want to turn on the news," Wiz said excitedly.

Gator took up the remote in his large hand and clicked the TV power button.

An animatedly expressive reporter was in mid-sentence, "—it looks like the threat may have been resolved. Our station just received another message and we're going to play it for you now."

The mechanical voice of the digitized audio file played:

"Our voice has been heard. The message has been received. Legislators have taken notice. Schools are vowing to take a stand against those students within their walls who choose to damage the innocent. The rebellion has turned peaceful for now. But know this, we are always watching. Do not slip in your resolve or we will be there to remind you. Tomorrow, Monday April first, will come and go without violence. Your children will be safe to return to school. We're glad you saw the err of your ways and changed course. Your ability to do this has saved countless lives. This will hopefully be the last message you'll ever receive from us."

The news anchor, dressed in a dark suit and bright red tie, looked into the camera and smiled.

"Well folks, it appears that whoever was behind this threat has had a change of heart. Schools will remain closed on Monday as law enforcement verifies this message and confirms the threat to our nation's children has officially ended," the anchor said enthusiastically.

Gator muted the sound on the television and the group turned their attention back to the conference call.

"Thoughts?" Jay asked.

"It'd be nice if this is the case. But I'd like to find Tanner's son and have a little conversation with him to know for sure," Nick responded.

"Agreed. Wiz is working on locating an address for him, but it appears he's more of a recluse than his father. The last picture we were able to locate of him was from a charity banquet, several years ago, before his father went to prison," Jay said.

"Maybe they never really intended to do any of this. I mean coordinating with students from around the country. Are there really that many angry kids willing to blow up a school?" Gator said, shaking his head in disbelief.

"That and the fact that this group announced the planned day of attack. Anyone in their right mind would assume school systems would take precautionary measures and shut down campuses. Who warns a target before a strike?" Declan asked.

"Maybe that was the point. Make some impact with Price and Hutchins and let hysteria take over," Gator said.

"Or maybe Monday was never the plan. What if all this was done to lull us into a false sense of security?" Nick asked.

"One thing's for certain, we better find Graham Morris before the school bell rings on Tuesday morning," Declan said.

The group fell silent, knowing their work wasn't done yet.

44

Graham Morris sat inside his motel room. It was a disgusting place located on the outskirts of Austin. He tolerated the substandard conditions—a necessary sacrifice, knowing the need to keep a low profile until he left the country after his masterpiece of carnage was completed. He'd paid for the room with cash and had already changed his appearance, darkening his hair and shaving off his goatee, to visually match his new passport and other credentials. A new life awaited him and with it, a new hunting ground for his animalistic desire. Closing his eyes, he smiled at the thought of it. Opening them, he put the thought of his future endeavors on hold. Everything hinged on tomorrow.

A few taps of his laptop's keyboard and he'd logged into his Rebel Dogs user account. Simon Belfort had given him unlimited access, linking his settings to administrative capabilities.

It was the eve of his masterpiece's unveiling, and almost two days had passed since he'd killed his father. With no further messages sent to the media and all investigative leads exhausted, the media was labeling the threat an elaborate hoax. This pleased Graham greatly.

Tomorrow morning he would prove them wrong. His father taught him to never underestimate an enemy's ability until you've looked him in the eye. How many had looked into his green eyes in their final moments? Only he knew the number, a tally soon to grow exponentially. Everyone had mistakenly underestimated Graham Morris, to include his father.

The bright screen of his laptop cast its glow upon the dreary surroundings of his temporary living quarters. With twelve hours to go, Graham hit send on his final message, calling his Patriots to battle. His heart beat more rapidly in anticipation of tomorrow's culminating event.

Graham stared at the screen, impatiently waiting for the first response to populate Graham_CrackerHacker's inbox. He looked down at his watch. Several minutes had passed. This was not typical. The weak little pissants usually responded in seconds to any message he'd sent. Their pathetic lives were desperate for his friendship, like a desert flower waiting for the first drop of rain. And he definitely didn't expect this lag with the final phase already underway. He went into the message log's sent box, verifying it had left the digital outbox. All the messages were marked as sent.

Ten more minutes passed by without a response. Graham became unhinged, pacing the room wildly. Grabbing a cigarette from the pack on the dresser, he opened the door to step outside for a smoke. Halfway out, he heard the ding of his computer's inbox alert.

Graham spun and rushed over to the bed where he'd left his laptop. The message was from a familiar player. It was from a Patriot, but one he'd never expected to hear from again. That was because this Patriot was already dead.

Bully_Slayer#1, the user name of the recently deceased Albert Hutchins, had sent him a message. He hesitated to open it for fear that it might contain some malware capable of corrupting his hard drive. Curiosity got the better of him and he clicked the mail icon in the upper-right corner of his screen, opening it.

Bully Slayer's message, simply stated:

Graham, your attack has been called off. GAME OVER!

Graham stood up, throwing aside the computer. He ran over to the drawn blinds and peered out, half expecting to see a line of police cars and SWAT trucks. The parking lot was empty, minus a few scattered vehicles parked in front of the sparsely populated motel. These cars had been there when he'd arrived earlier. Convinced he was momentarily safe, he retreated into the room.

Frantic, Graham grabbed his gun and packed up his belongings. He picked up his laptop and started to stuff it into his suitcase. An idea crossed his depraved mind and he stopped suddenly, opening the computer and accessing his Patriot database. Seeing what he was looking for, he closed it and left the hotel room.

Graham sped off into the night, heading toward his only chance of success.

45

"How many do we have located and detained so far?" Jay asked.

"I already told you. I'm not getting these reports in real time. There are delays in the data entry and my ability to retrieve them," Wiz said, agitatedly. "Forty-four accounted for. Looks like we've nabbed all but six. No. Wait. I just got another message. Five. We're looking at five at large."

The unit's resident technical expert looked more haggard than before. He'd used Albert Hutchins' gamer Bully_Slayer#1 account to hack into the digital backdoor of the Rebel Dogs server he'd been data mining, searching for any links to Patriots. It was a terrifying realization when he'd found the threat had not been a bluff. There were fifty Patriots, from each state in the nation, with the exception of Iowa, where Hutchins had launched his attack three days ahead of time. Fifty children willing to attack and kill their innocent classmates. It was a scary revelation.

After accessing the server, Wiz had located the message blast sent to all the Patriots. The plan had never been to launch an attack on April 1st. The 2nd had always been the target date. Without Hutchins' screw up, he'd never had been able to tip the scale in their favor. They'd have been blindsided by the attack.

The Patriot list contained the real names of each player and their physical address. Each had been sent the same package Sheldon Price and

Albert Hutchins had received. Wiz, through Jay's unnamed superior, was able to disseminate the list to state and local law enforcement. Raids were being run across the county and Wiz had been crossing names off the Patriot list once an apprehension was made. He was waiting confirmation of those last five still on the loose.

"I'm glad we left those guys in Texas for an extra bit of time. One of the last five returns to an Austin address," Wiz said. "Maybe luck's on our side on this one."

Jay looked unusually stressed. "I'd prefer the local agencies handle it. We don't want to expose ourselves unnecessarily."

"Still, it's always good to have a contingency plan should things break bad," Wiz said.

"Agreed," Jay said. "Still no trace of Graham Morris?"

"No. But he got the message I sent him. I got a digital receipt a few minutes ago," Wiz said.

"Well, he's priority one for every law enforcement agency in-country and his face is plastered across every news station. I can't imagine it being very long before he turns up in custody or dead. Either is fine by me."

Wiz slurped from his can of Mountain Dew and turned his attention back to his computer. "Jay, I think we've got a problem."

"What's up?"

"Darren Jackson is missing," Wiz said.

Jay looked over Wiz's shoulder, reading the intercepted transmission. "Where?"

"He's the Patriot from Austin," Wiz said.

"Send the information and address to Nick," Jay said.

A couple keystrokes later Wiz looked up, "Done. I also was able to locate a recent photo of the kid from the school's database. He's a Junior at Woodrow Wilson High."

"Let's hope he turns up," Jay said.

"And there's another problem."

"What now?" Jay's patience stretched thin.

"They did a search of Darren Jackson's house. Neither bomb nor gun were located," Wiz said.

"We've got an angry teen who's recently been radicalized and is now roaming the streets of Austin with a bomb," Jay said, letting out a sigh of frustration. "That's a recipe for disaster if I've ever heard one."

46

"I'm driving you and that's final!" Kemper said.

Tobie threw his hands up and stormed out to the car. "I should've never shown you that message! You're such a spaz! It doesn't mean anything."

Tobie had the day off from school yesterday because of the national threat. Kemper had taken the day off, hoping he could spend some quality time with his son. He'd hoped to reconnect with his son and break down the growing emotional distance. His plan had failed and Tobie spent most of the day in his room and Kemper spent several hours typing up his case notes.

The unspoken tension continued this morning, coming to a head when Tobie showed him a message from one of his classmates.

"Haven't you been paying attention to the news this past week? There's been threats to schools across the county. I'm going to alert your Principal and then check this kid out when I get back to headquarters," Kemper said, following after his son.

The two got into the Austin detective's beige unmarked Ford Taurus. Kemper sat and looked over at his son and tried to calm his voice, softening his tone. "Listen, when some kid sends you a text telling you not to come to school today. A message like that, coming the day after a planned attack, then, yeah, I'm going to be a little bit concerned."

Tobie gave his all-too-familiar roll of the eyes and said, "Dad, you're totally overreacting. Darren is a quiet kid. He'd never do anything like that. It was April Fool's Day yesterday! He was probably just trying to be funny and prank me. Something dumb like that."

"Let's hope so," Kemper said, pulling out of his apartment complex's parking lot.

Tobie tapped his finger on dashboard's digital clock and smirked. "And Dad, you might want to use your lights and sirens."

"Why?"

"Because we're going to be late," Tobie said, a broad grin stretched across his face. "Dad, you're going to be late to your own funeral."

Kemper Jones laughed out loud at his son's mock impression as he pulled the Taurus into the heavy congestion of Austin's morning commuters.

47

"Nothing. Declan used his Bureau credentials and made contact with Austin PD. The sergeant he spoke with told him Darren Jackson left the house around eight o'clock last night and hasn't returned. He was picked up by someone driving a tan Mazda. She told police her son had left carrying his backpack," Nick said, relaying the information into the phone. "The kid has since dropped off the face of the earth."

"Shit," Jay said. "We've got to assume the Mazda belonged to Graham Morris and that he is with this kid now. The only positive is, we may be able to kill two birds with one stone."

Nick looked over at Declan seated in the driver's seat. Sleep deprived, both men's eyes were bloodshot from the long night of searching. They were parked in the lot of Woodrow Wilson High School, where they'd been for the last two hours. Gator was in a separate vehicle near the lot's only entrance.

"Wiz just confirmed Darren Jackson is the only Patriot on that list who hasn't been picked up by law enforcement," Jay said.

"Then this is our best chance at stopping this thing. Once and for all." Nick said, hoping his words were true. To fail would be unforgivable.

"I know, but this move is a big gamble. Keeping the school open puts every one of those kids at risk," Jay said. The long night and frustration accompanying the lack of sleep was evident in the tone and crackle of his voice.

Nick rubbed his eyes and yawned. "True. But if we shut this school down now then Graham may go to ground. We'd be left holding our breath. Each day could be another attack, another school, and we'd be back where we started, in the dark and totally unprepared. I'd rather we end it here and now."

Another sigh from the unit's commander, "There's no room for error on this one."

"Understood."

"And Nick, good luck," Jay said.

"Luck has nothing to do with this," Nick said, ending the call.

The plan was simple. The best ones always were. The devil always presented himself in the details.

Gator was in position, parked in a spot under a tree located only a few spaces from the only entrance to the school's parking lot. He'd be responsible for calling out the arrival of Graham's Mazda when it entered. Nick and Declan were parked in the center of the lot. Two larger vehicles bookended their small sedan. They'd be the initial takedown team once the target vehicle came to a stop. Speed and the element of surprise would be the advantage they'd hoped to achieve.

Most of the student body had made their way into the school at the sound of the first bell. A few of them meandered by their cars, most likely caught up in their mindless teenage banter.

Five minutes later, another bell rang, and the few remaining students trickled into the red-bricked building.

48

"You can do this! You're the last Patriot," Graham said to the boy in the passenger seat. "I'm counting on you my friend."

He watched the teen carefully, evaluating his physiological response. His body trembled as he sat with eyes downcast, cradling the heavy backpack on his lap. Darren Jackson was weak, and Graham despised him. Nothing would give him more pleasure than squeezing Darren's frail neck until his life ended. But Graham also knew the only chance of redeeming any modicum of satisfaction rested in the boy's ability to complete this task. And so, he'd spent the better part of the night into the early morning hours motivating and manipulating the teen's fragile mind.

"I can do this," Darren said, meekly.

"Yes, you can!" Graham said, giving the boy a firm grip on his shoulder. "The world is never going to forget your name. You're a true hero."

Graham watched as Darren Jackson's posture straightened. He'd decided the boy was as ready as he'd ever be. He looked at his watch. The tardy bell should've already rung and most, if not all, of the students would be inside by now.

Graham Morris drove out from the side street, where they'd been parked for the last hour, and began the final three-block commute to Woodrow Wilson High.

49

The engine was off. Neither man broke the silence. Without question, Nick knew they were in the eerie calm that precedes a storm. The mental preparation before the execution of a tactical operation was important. Visualization had long since been an integral part of Nick's pre-mission routine.

The quiet was shattered with Gator's thick Louisiana accented transmission, "Mazda in sight. Two occupants. Approaching from the east."

"Copy," Nick acknowledged.

Both men readied themselves, adjusting slightly in their lowered seats. Nick inhaled deeply, oxygenating his brain and readying himself for combat.

"Targets confirmed. Morris is the driver and Jackson's riding shotgun," Gator said.

"Copy that."

Nick looked over at his friend in the passenger seat. Declan turned his head and smiled. The calm with which he faced danger always impressed Nick, and he was glad they were teamed up on this day.

"They're pulling into a spot two rows back and ten spots to the right of your location," Gator said. "Not sure you're going to have a visual from your position."

"Copy."

Nick and Declan waited for a ten count. "Moving," Nick announced as both men exited into a crouched position.

"No movement from the Mazda. Both targets are still inside," Gator called through his bone mic.

Nick crouched behind Declan and the two men stayed low, snaking their way to the row of vehicles containing the Mazda.

"We've got a problem," Gator said.

Nick and Declan halted their progression, taking a knee behind a Chevy Suburban.

"Heads up guys. An unmarked just pulled in the lot," Graham said.

"I thought Jay coordinated to ensure all agencies, state and local, remain out of the area. This was supposed to be jurisdictionally claimed by the Feds," Nick said.

"Well, I guess this guy didn't get the message."

"Where's the unmarked now? Disregard. I see it," Nick hissed. "Shit!"

"What?" Gator asked.

"It's Kemper Jones. And his son," Nick said, exhaling heavily.

"Well this will be an interesting reunion," Declan said.

"Obviously, Kemper wouldn't bring his son if he knew about the threat. His kid must go to school here," Nick said.

"What are the odds?" Declan asked. "I thought you had a penchant for bad luck, but this takes the cake."

"Apparently you and I aren't the only shit magnets in town," Nick joked.

The two gave a quick laugh. And, again, began moving toward the target, only eight cars away.

"The kid's on the move!" Gator called out.

Darren Jackson, laden with his heavy backpack, was ambling away from the parked Mazda toward the front entrance of the school. He walked with the rigidity of a robot, moving deliberately as if each step forward required its own independent decision.

"I've got the kid. You two stay on Morris," Gator called out.

Nick and Declan maintained their low profile but quickened their approach on the Mazda. Gator's car screeched through the lot, rapidly closing the distance on the unsuspecting teenager. The noise of the approaching vehicle caused the boy to stop and turn.

Gator hopped out of the car, pointing his gun at Jackson. Immediately the big man from the Bayou began giving commands to the teenager. Darren Jackson stood frozen, his face drained of color.

"You don't want to do this, kid! I promise you that whatever he told you is an outright lie!" Gator's delivery was calm and controlled. His pistol pointed at Darren Jackson's head.

"I've got to. You don't understand!" Jackson screamed. Tears began to fall, and his knees buckled.

"Let me help you," Gator said, reassuringly. "I can only do that if you take off the backpack. Come on Darren. Please hear me on this."

The boy dropped to his knees. Sobbing uncontrollably, he unshouldered one strap of the large pack.

Nick and Declan, only two cars away, prepared to take Graham Morris. In unspoken unison, they both slowly raised up behind the Mazda, taking a point of aim at the back of Morris's head.

Declan boomed, "Graham step out of the vehicle, keeping your hands where I can see them. Do it now."

The plan had been to take Graham Morris alive, a request that had come down from Jay's superior. Apparently, in the world of politics, the decision had been made that bringing in the man responsible would look better in someone's PR campaign than showing the nation another dead terrorist. But the politicians weren't standing six feet behind a deranged murderer.

In the ever changing fluidity of a crisis situation, each action had a potentially dire consequence. Time was measured in milliseconds. And Morris's silent refusal to exit caused Nick to take the slack out of the trigger.

The explosion's blast wave knocked Nick backward, sending him onto the hard asphalt of the parking lot. The impact had a dizzying effect, and he shook his head to clear it. His ears were ringing, adding to his sudden disorientation. As he began to get his bearings, Nick scanned his surroundings. Declan was down, wedged in a heap near the Mazda's driver's side rear wheel. Either his friend was unconscious or dead. Impossible to tell from his position, but he hoped it wasn't the latter.

Nick's vision cleared and he saw fire and twisted metal in the parking space where Darren Jackson and Gator had, only moments before, been standing.

The driver's door to the Mazda popped open and Graham Morris casually stepped out. His face was bloodied from bits of shattered windshield, amplifying his appearance. Nick evaluated the man, deeming him the poster-child for lunatics and madmen.

Graham smiled, looking down at Declan's body, twisted and unmoving.

Nick suddenly realized his gun was no longer in his right hand. He must've lost it in the blast. Desperately, he scanned the lot's surface. A split second later he saw it, ten feet away from him under the front axle of a small red compact car. He looked back at Graham, standing over his friend with a gun in his hand.

Knowing he'd never be able to recover his weapon in time to save Declan, he did the only reasonable option that came to mind. A quote from Sun Tzu popped into his mind, *"Let your plans be dark and impenetrable as night, and when you move, fall like a thunderbolt."* The ancient Chinese master tactician and strategist had server him once again.

Nick Lawrence roared, launching himself at Morris.

The guttural scream and sudden burst of movement had the desired effect, causing the armed Morris to look up, briefly distracting him from his task at hand. The gun, no longer pointed down at Declan, was now pointed at Nick's large frame.

A shot rang out, the sound of which was muffled from the concussive auditory damage caused by bomb's recent detonation.

Blood spatter covered Nick's face, blinding him and causing him to crash head first into the Mazda's trunk. Nick fell to the ground.

Wiping the blood from his eyes he visually scanned his body for the wound. He found no gunshot entry point. He stood to face the gunman.

Graham Morris was no longer standing. He was now sprawled atop of Declan, blanketing him. Blood leaked onto the black asphalt, filling its cracked surface. Nick's brain worked fast to connect the dots, which immediately became clearer at the sight of the man who'd fired the shot.

The portly Austin detective stood with his duty weapon still pointed in the direction of Morris's lifeless body.

Nick stood still, looking at the detective, a man he'd come to trust and respect over the many cases the two had worked together over the years. More importantly Kemper Jones was the man who, one year ago, had saved Anaya's life. And here he was again, stepping up in Nick's time of need.

Kemper lowered his gun, holstering it as he looked in Nick's direction.

Nick watched as his brisket-loving friend visually evaluated him. Nick's long hair and blood-covered face added to his unintended subterfuge. Kemper's eyes widened with recognition. Nick smiled faintly, trying, without much success, to alleviate the awkwardness.

"Nick?" Kemper mumbled.

Nick was at a loss for words and only could manage a meager shrug.

"How?" Kemper asked. His voice a muffled whisper.

"Long story," Nick said. "And one you probably don't want to know."

A groan from the pile on the ground interrupted the uncomfortable reunion. Nick and Kemper each took a step back, Kemper's hand on the butt of his holstered gun.

Declan pushed the dead body of Graham Morris off his back and stood.

"How long were you guys going to leave this dead guy on top of me?" Declan asked, adding his trademark cocky smirk. "Oh hi, Kemper. Funny seeing you here."

"Declan," Kemper said, nodding.

"Is this your handy work?" Declan asked, looking down at the dead man.

Kemper nodded.

In the distance, sirens alerted the local cavalry's arrival. The parking lot of Woodrow Wilson High was soon to be a cavalcade of local, state, and federal law enforcement officers as they converged to jockey position for control of the scene.

"Probably best I get going," Nick said.

"Take our car. I'll stay with Kemper," Declan said, flashing his FBI badge affixed to his hip. "I'll handle the cleanup. There's going to be a lot of explaining to do."

Without another word, Nick retrieved his gun, holstered it, and hustled back toward the car he'd arrived in.

He sped by his two friends and out of the school's lot.

"Are you sure you're okay, son?" Kemper asked, hugging his son for the second time in less than a minute.

His son's eyes no longer held the contemptuous glance typical of his recent crossover into teenage angst. Kemper knew the blast had scared him, but it wasn't the blast he was worried about. Kemper Jones's son had watched him kill a man. Regardless of the evil he'd dispatched, witnessing the death of another human being was a devastating thing to behold. And one that would impact his son for the remainder of his life. A lasting impression worsened by the fact its execution had been carried out by his own father.

"Are you okay?" Tobie asked, gently separating from his father's embrace.

"Yeah. I'll be fine. But it's never easy," Kemper said, looking back in the direction of Morris's body, covered in a sheet of black plastic.

"Are you sure?" Tobie asked again, concern in his voice. "Because you look like you've seen a ghost."

Kemper gave a slight laugh and shook his head, "I think I just might have."

50

Nick and Declan regrouped back at the unit's Northern Virginia Vault site, the same location where Spider had conducted his interrogation.

Nick had a newfound respect for Jay, impressed by the way the former CIA spook, with technical assistance provided by Wiz, had been able to manage such a complex operation. The group, under Jay's adroit supervision, had thwarted the worst large-scale coordinated attack in U.S. history. Nick couldn't begin to comprehend the devastation the nation would've faced if Graham Morris had been able to deliver his payload.

One thing was for certain, this ghost unit, to which he now belonged, was the only reason there weren't images of thousands of dead children plastered across every news channel. The live feed from the news currently playing in the background only showed one scene and the headline read:

Three Dead in Failed Attempt.

FBI and Local Law Enforcement Thwart Attack.

The entire group had assembled around the conference table, minus one. The large frame and gregarious nature of the ginger-haired man from the Louisiana Bayou was absent. In the short time together, Nick had come to like and respect the man. Although, he realized that he knew very little about him.

Jay stepped out of his office with a bottle of champagne. Unceremoniously, he uncorked it with a loud pop. Each member seated around the table had an empty glass or coffee mug in front of them. Jay moved around the table, pouring an ample amount of the golden bubbly liquid. Jay filled his own glass and remained standing at the head of the conference table.

Raising his glass, Jay said, "To William Robichaux. He paid the ultimate sacrifice. His second death will be remembered only by those in this room. Today, we give him back his name and release him. Until Valhalla!"

The group slammed their glasses down hard. Nick and Declan followed suit. In staggered unison they loudly repeated the phrase, "Until Valhalla!" A reference to the Norse mythologic hall where chosen warriors, who die valiantly in combat, are carried to upon their death. It, or some variant thereof, was a common saying among soldiers.

The circle drained the contents of their respective glasses in one large gulp before placing them back on the table. Nick surveyed the remaining members, moving his eyes from one to the next. He'd silently hoped never to learn the full names of the others in this group. Especially if that knowledge only came ceremoniously through death.

"We need a name," Declan blurted, interrupting the silence with his comment.

The rest of the group looked back at the man. "Huh?" Nick asked.

"Seriously guys? You call these office spaces, scattered around the country, Vaults. The interrogation room is called The Cube. How have you not come up with a name for this ragtag group of dead men?" Declan asked, ending the somberness of the ceremony.

The levity broke the heaviness of the moment and Nick watched as tense shoulders and serious eyes gave way.

"We tried early on but nothing stuck," Wiz said. "Then we figured maybe having no name gave us an added layer of anonymity."

"Well, I for one, think it's needed," Declan said, adding his cocky smile. "If we're out doing superhero crap at least our team should have a cool name."

Jay gave a slight laugh, "Okay, what'd you have in mind?"

"I've got no idea. Hell, my old unit was named after a steak sauce. So, I'm probably not the best guy to ask," Declan said.

The group laughed. The weight of Gator's death lifted slightly.

"You already said it," Nick said softly.

"What do you mean?" Jay asked.

Nick looked out at the group. "Valhalla," he said, pausing briefly. "Think about it, we're already dead. Each of us warriors in our own right. Seems fitting."

A slow nod of approval worked its way around the table.

"I like it. So, if we're calling ourselves the Valhalla Group and I'm the one who called you here, then I guess that makes me Odin," Jay said, referring to the Norse God.

"Great! Someone else gets a cool nickname," Wiz huffed. "Since we're in a creative mood, do you think we could change mine?"

"No!" the group shouted, laughing at the hacker's obvious frustration.

"Valhalla Group it is," Jay said, banging his porcelain coffee mug down on the table like a judge's gavel. "Next on the agenda is to locate Gator's replacement."

51

The strange funeral service ended, and the group separated. Jay gave everyone a couple weeks to decompress. Declan was eager to get back to his loving wife and three beautiful daughters.

Nick had been given a new identity with credentials to match. Nick tried to think of somewhere to visit, but every fiber in his body called him back to the one place where he knew he shouldn't go. Texas was now more complicated than ever with Kemper's knowledge of his existence.

"How'd it go with Kemper?" Nick asked.

Declan shrugged. "We had a complicated scene to clear up and getting our story straight took a bit of work."

Nick gave a nod.

"Plus, I think he's smart enough not to ask questions he doesn't want the answer to," Declan said.

"Talk about poor timing," Nick said.

"Well, his poor timing is the reason you and I are alive," Declan said with a smile.

"True."

"You know the man better than me. Do you think he can be trusted to keep your secret?" Declan asked, his tone serious.

"I do. He's a good man and I trust him completely," Nick said.

Declan gave a thoughtful look. "Well, we are looking for a new member for the team."

"I don't think he'd bite. Not so sure this sort of thing is in his wheel-house," Nick said.

"Okay then. Just a thought."

"I do have another idea on who might be a good fit, but I'm not sure she's ready," Nick said.

"She?" Declan asked.

Nick smiled. In that moment he realized where he'd be going for his respite. He'd missed the last opportunity to visit Pigeon, Michigan. This would be an opportunity to make good on that. Nick had been given a second chance at life, just like the girl he planned to visit. And he knew Wiz would be pissed off if she joined their group.

Because she already had a cool nickname.

MURDER 8

A NICK LAWRENCE NOVEL

To Margaret, for being an amazing sounding board for my wild ideas and helping me find a way to bring Mouse back into the fold.

1

It had been a while since Amber Litchfield had taken a night off from studying. *Med school begins the day you walk into your first undergraduate class,* her father preached. A man who'd built himself from poverty to power over a lifetime of toil. She respected and loved the man, but in recent years missed the connection the two established before his most recent position devoured the majority of his time. Amber never resented him for his drive but only wished she'd been able to steal him away occasionally.

Tomorrow would be good. She planned to meet him at their favorite spot. Boston Chowda Company, located at Faneuil Hall, had the best clam chowder. Amber salivated at the thought of the sourdough bread bowl it was served in. Her father always got the lobster bisque. She'd never acquired the taste for it, but that never stopped him from trying to get her to order it.

The stack of books spread across her desk brought her crashing back to the present. She'd been cramming for midterms all week and still had a thesis paper to write on the morality of gene engineering as it related to correcting disorders in humans. Her eyes crossed as fatigue set in. Amber prepared to take a break with some popcorn and a little Netflix binge-watching before she went to bed. Not the typical Saturday night for a freshman surrounded by Boston's wild nightlife.

Those plans got derailed when Clem, her roommate, barged in half-drunk. "Girl, you're not spending another night curled up in this room!"

Amber rolled her eyes. Clementine Hungerford was Amber's polar opposite, spending the first semester of her college career majoring in partying and minoring in boys. Clem came from a strict household. On her own, with parental reins loosened, she unleashed herself upon the world. Clem made a point of breaking every rule her parents ever gave her. She'd kept a log tallying which rule and how many times she'd broken it. As of late, underage drinking was taking a major lead as she tallied quite a streak over the past month.

Amber, on the other hand, had been given some latitude in her upbringing, and never saw much need to go overboard. Although she wasn't a complete angel, either.

On the occasions she dabbled in some experimentation, she found she liked pills more than drinking. Her rationale was purely academic. If she drank, then her next day's studies suffered. But pills had no lingering hangover and she was able to be a functional human being the following day.

"Clem, don't do this to me tonight! I've already showered and got my PJs on," Amber pleaded.

Clementine dove onto Amber's bed, sprawling herself atop the thick, fuzzy, pink comforter. Her breath exuded the odor of whatever concoction she'd been drinking earlier. Amber guessed Clem had been partying in one of the other dorm rooms.

"Listen, you're never going to get laid sitting in this room," Clem said, grabbing Amber's pillow and giving it an exaggerated make-out session.

"Maybe I don't want to. Did you ever think of that?" Amber snarked back.

"Yeah, yeah. Get your clothes on. We're going to a party." Clem blew her a kiss.

"Ugh! You're impossible!"

Clem shrugged, throwing her hands up. "Maybe, but you love me."

"Fine," Amber said, storming about the room, gathering up some clothes. "But I'm not staying out all night! And if this party sucks then I'm leaving you and coming back here."

"Fair enough, but I don't think you're going to hate it," Clem teased in a singsong.

"Why's that?"

"Because Derrick's going to be there." Clem smiled deviously.

Amber tried, without success, to hide her excitement as her cheeks flushed. She'd met Derrick during orientation, and they'd hit it off but nothing romantic ever happened. Clem knew she was head-over-heels for the boy and his attendance would guarantee she'd come.

"Where's the party? Some frat house?"

Clem shook her head. "Nah. Just this guy who lives off campus. From what I hear he throws the craziest parties. Ice luges and tiki bars. That kind of stuff."

"We'll see. Last time you took me to a *cool* place we were packed into a tiny apartment like a bunch of sardines." Amber cocked an eyebrow.

"This will be different. I promise."

"You said that before, too."

The passing train rattled the sign nearest her as Amber walked the T platform alongside the stumbling Clem.

"How much did you drink tonight before you came to get me?" Amber asked.

Clem giggled, "Not enough."

"How much farther? I have this strange feeling you have no idea where we're going."

"Have faith in my phone's GPS," Clem said, slurring slightly, holding up her phone.

"Okay Magellan, lead the way."

Just then a pocket of rowdy boys walked by and up the front steps of a brownstone building. Clem pointed. "See. We're here."

Amber could hear the heavy bass of the music through the windows. She couldn't imagine anyone living in this part of the city who wasn't a college kid. It would be impossible to sleep through the noise.

"Here we go again," Amber muttered to herself.

"Now let's go find your boyfriend," Clem said.

Amber's face reddened. "He's not my boyfriend."

"Who's not?" A male voice said from behind them.

Amber spun to see Derrick's broad smile and dimpled cheeks. Her face turned three shades of red, and she could feel the warmth pierce through the cool night's air. He gave her a friendly hug and then did the same to Clem.

"I see you've got an early start," Derrick said to Clem.

"Don't be jealous," Clem shot back. "Did you bring any party favors?"

"Of course." Derrick tapped his jacket pocket. "I've actually got something new."

"Oh, I like the sound of that."

"Amber?" Derrick asked.

"Maybe later. Let's get inside and check out the party first."

The three entered the apartment after getting buzzed in. They followed the sound of the music. It was deafening inside and completely packed with people. But Clem had been right about the layout—there was a tiki bar and an ice luge. The crowd of college kids surrounding both attractions were impassable. Amber hated crowds. No way was she going to fight her way through to a drink any time soon and she desperately needed something to take the edge off from her quickly rising anxiety.

"What'd you bring?" Amber yelled into Derrick's ear. The bass thumped loudly, drowning her out.

"What?"

"What. Did. You. Bring?" She emphasized each word and tapped his pocket for added effect.

Derrick nodded his understanding. "White Lightning!" He yelled back into Amber's ear.

She thumbed in the direction of the bathroom. He nodded. They slithered through the crowd. Clem followed behind.

The noise was still oppressive but more tolerable once inside the bathroom with the door shut.

"I think my ears are bleeding!" Amber yelled.

"You don't need to yell any more. I can hear you." Derrick laughed.

"Sorry. So, what did you call the stuff?" Amber asked.

Derrick pulled a small Ziploc bag from his pocket. It held a bright white powder. "The guy called it White Lightning."

"What is it? Coke?" Clem asked.

"No, he said it's something different. It's supposed to make you super chill."

Amber eyed the bag. "Have you ever tried it before?"

"No, but this guy's always given me good stuff in the past."

"How do you do it?" Amber asked.

"Snort it. He told me you can shoot it, but I don't like needles."

"Okay. Well, I could definitely use something to take me down a few notches," Amber said.

"I'll put a little bit on your knuckle and then you can just sniff it off. The guy said you don't need much to get a good high."

"How much is too much?" Amber asked nervously.

"Jesus, Amber, if you're too scared then I'll do it." Clem put her hand out.

"Relax. I'll do it. I was just asking." Amber put her hand above Clem's.

Derrick tapped out some of the powder on to Amber's knuckle. A small mound of the fine granulated substance crested her skin.

"It tingles," Amber said.

Derrick's eyes widened a bit. "Very cool!"

Amber dipped her head slightly, then carefully brought her hand to her nose. She pressed her left finger alongside and sniffed hard, pulling the powder up into her nostril. Amber's hazel eyes watered and she rubbed the end of her nose vigorously, wiping the remnants of powder away.

Amber moved over to the mirror and ran the water. She washed her hands and splashed some water on her nose to rinse away any evidence.

"So, what do you think?" It was Derrick's voice, but it came out garbled, like she was underwater.

Amber turned to face her two friends. The vibrations from the music were more intense. She felt each boom of the bass in her ribcage. The room began to spin.

"Something's wrong. I can't feel..." Amber couldn't finish her sentence. She wasn't even sure if she'd said anything at all. A thousand thoughts swirled around in her head, but her mouth wouldn't cooperate with her brain and no words came out.

All sensation in her extremities tingled like being poked by tiny needles. Then, a moment later, sensation dissipated altogether. Her mind raced for order as she felt herself floating and falling simultaneously. Lights flickered, then faded completely. All sound stopped and the thumping in her chest receded. Her last thought was of her father.

"Oh my God! Amber!" Clem screamed.

Derrick knelt at her side, cradling Amber's head. Blood pooled where she struck the floor face first. It caught them both off guard.

"We've got to move her!" Derrick yelled.

"What? Move her where?" Clem said, hyperventilating.

Derrick lifted Amber up and awkwardly balanced her dead weight against his body. "Are you going to help me or what?"

"Help you how?" Tears streamed down Clem's face.

"We're going to go to jail for this!"

Clem's eyes widened. "Jail?" She began shaking her head wildly.

"We've got to get her out of here." Derrick pleaded desperately.

"What do you mean?"

Derrick suddenly looked angry. His eyes narrowed. "Get your ass over here and hold her up with me! We're going to walk her out of here. It won't be the first time friends have carried a drunk person out of a party."

"She's not drunk! I think she's dead."

"That's why we're going to jail."

"Not we. You! You brought the drugs!" Clem yelled.

"Yeah, but you were right there with me telling her to try it."

Clem swallowed hard. She slipped Amber's dangling arm over her shoulder. "I can't go to jail. My family would disown me."

"Then help me. It was an accident. We know that, but the cops will never believe it."

"So, what's your plan?" Clem wiped the tears from her face.

"We dump her somewhere," Derrick said sadly.

"Dump her?"

"If anyone asks, we'll just say we brought her outside for fresh air and she decided to walk home. We'll go back to the party and stay for a while."

"My God, we're monsters," Clem whimpered.

"It's either that or the future you and I have planned ends here tonight."

Clem said nothing but nodded solemnly. The two carried their friend's limp body through the crowd. The few partygoers who cared enough to notice only jeered. "Looks like somebody can't handle her liquor!"

Out in the cool night air, the two moved down the steps onto the sidewalk. A half-block down from the party was a poorly lit alleyway lined with several large dumpsters.

The two paused, looking for any witnesses. Surprisingly, the foot traffic had dwindled with the rapidly dropping temperatures.

The two stumbled into the darkness of the alley with their burdensome cargo.

❦

2

"We've got a few minutes before you go live. I'd like to go over the day's schedule with you again. It's going to be tight and I think we need to look at moving one or two things," Gloria Baker said.

She had a rapid cadence in her delivery and Senator Buzz Litchfield appreciated her economy of time. Gloria was also assertive, another trait the hard-nosed legislator considered important in his entourage. At times she crossed the line, reaching a point of overbearing annoyance, but this was not one of those times.

"Okay. Hit me with it," Litchfield said gruffly. Another woman, the makeup artist, deftly brushed some bronzer along his cheek line. The ex-military man had long ago given up resisting this pre-camera treatment. During one of his first televised advertisement campaigns Litchfield refused the make-up. When he later saw the ad, he'd been shocked by how terrible he looked. The camera washed out his rugged good looks, giving him the appearance of being sick. His daughter said he looked like a zombie. Ever since, he allowed the stage hands to primp any way they saw fit.

"After your speech we've got an interview with the *Herald*. I think it's important. The piece they're writing will focus primarily on your anti-drug reform," Baker said.

"Does anyone read the *Herald* anymore? Or newspapers in general, for that matter?" Litchfield snarked.

"I do. And yes, the data from a recent poll shows that fifty-three percent of your constituents still read the newspaper on a daily basis. Although, probably more of them are doing it online these days," Baker added, not looking up from her schedule. "Then we'll keep that."

"Next," Litchfield said.

"Lunch with your daughter. It will be the second time we have rescheduled her in the past three weeks if we move it. Your call."

Litchfield sighed. He'd been generating some momentum in recent months and what little time he'd had in the past for his personal life evaporated at an alarming rate. "Keep it. But text her and make sure she isn't late like last time."

"Will do." Baker jotted a note on her pad. "After that you're going over to meet with Father Macintyre, who runs the outreach center and clean needle program for junkies."

"Gloria, we don't use that term. It's demeaning and lowers our image in the eyes of the voters. We are pushing reform through awareness. Opioid addiction is a disease. And what do we call people suffering from disease?" Litchfield asked in a patronizing tone.

Gloria Baker glanced up from her notepad, "The sick, ill, or afflicted. Sorry about that, sir. Won't happen again."

Litchfield nodded sternly. He hounded his people to be mindful of the terminology used. He warned how quickly the wrong phrasing could compromise the good works they were doing. If the media caught wind of anyone in his camp referring to those chemically dependent members of society as junkies, it would cause a storm of criticism. Litchfield had his sights set on another job, and to achieve that lofty goal, he needed to be perfect.

"That should take less than an hour. After, you have the Opioid Reform Committee meeting. That typically takes several hours. So, if there's any fat you want to shed in the itinerary, I think we should push your dinner plans with Congressman Waterford to another time."

"So, what you're telling me is that we've gone through my entire schedule for the day and the only item on the agenda worth moving is dinner? I'd like to eat. Sounds like we're keeping things as is," Litchfield said dismissively. "And get me Wilcox. I need to speak with him."

Baker scribbled onto her pad. "Will do. I saw him in the break room earlier."

A few minutes later, as makeup finished her paint job on the weather-beaten face of the Marine Infantry Colonel turned politician, Avery Wilcox entered the room.

Wilcox was tall and lean. He'd managed to keep his chiseled shape years after separating from the service. During his last tour of duty, Wilcox commanded a special operations group of Recon Marines tasked with seeking out high-threat targets. Litchfield and Wilcox connected early in their careers and had risen through the ranks together, moving in similar circles. And Buzz Litchfield, through the unbreakable bond forged on the battlefield, trusted no man more than Avery Wilcox. It was for that reason alone Litchfield had made him his aide-de-camp.

Wilcox wasn't much for politics and initially refused the offer to work for the senator. Litchfield pushed his friend, knowing his skills could be valuable in a multitude of ways. The former Marine not only handled odd jobs, he was also Litchfield's security manager and personal bodyguard.

"You rang." Wilcox's voice was throaty and intense, the sound of which scared the younger of Litchfield's employees.

"I wanted to check the status of things."

"Everything is in motion as discussed. You'll have some of the numbers you're looking for in the coming days," Wilcox said.

"Excellent. Onward and upward."

Wilcox nodded.

The closed door to his dressing room opened and Gloria Baker stood in the entranceway, looking at her watch as she tapped her pen against the end of her notepad. "Excuse me, sir. They're ready for you."

"Well then, let's not keep them waiting." Litchfield stood.

The senator, at six foot, three inches, towered over most. His physical stature dominated his portly peers in legislative meeting rooms. As far as iconic political figures went, Buzz Litchfield was a rising star.

"Good morning, ladies and gentlemen of the press. Thank you for taking the time to be here today. Hopefully, the coffee provided wasn't too bad. I don't want you taking it out on me in your columns," Litchfield said with smile. "Especially you, Janice." He gave a mock glare at Janice Evans, a reporter who'd been less than kind in some of her early articles about him. She seemed to be coming around as of late and the wording had shifted to more favorable descriptions of his political efforts.

A light-hearted chuckle arose from the crowd of reporters and cameramen. He'd always found it was good to start with a bit of levity before delving into a serious conversation. The pollsters liked him and even some of the more abrasive reporters softened to his mannerisms.

"As most of you know, I've been assigned to head the Opioid Reform Committee. Initially, upon taking this responsibility, I had no idea what was in store. The learning curve has been massive and the war against drugs is far different now than it used to be. Funding for this war has cost this country billions per year and left us with little to show for it. That's why I've been working to change the country's approach to legality and treatment for abusers. I like to look at things simply. Maybe that's because I'm a simple man." Litchfield paused and smiled for effect.

"If someone craves ice cream and there's an ice cream store on every corner, then that person will have no problem getting his fix. If that store closes or moves out of town, then maybe that person goes a day or two without his frosty treat. If enough time passes, maybe that person realizes he doesn't need ice cream anymore. That's my methodology on how we should approach drug dealers. I am pushing to make the penalties for distributing drugs higher, with bigger consequences on the back end, working to raising the minimum sentencing for such crimes. I'm also empowering local law enforcement and prosecutors around the great state of Massachusetts to go after the dealers linked to overdose-related deaths. Dealers linked to a fatal overdose will be charged and prosecuted for manslaughter. I will hold these dregs of society accountable for the damage they do."

Litchfield swiveled his head around the room, pausing for a millisecond at each camera. "This next message is for any of the drug dealers who may be watching. We as a people are tired of you preying on the weak. We are tired of the damage you're doing to our communities. The voices of my constituents have been heard. I will not stand by any longer. Any death your product causes will be laid at your doorstep. Hear me loud and clear. We are coming for you!"

Nods and even a few claps came from the reporters in the room. Many began to slide forward in their seats, poised to launch at the opportunity to ask a question.

Litchfield continued, "But to treat the problem by going after the distributor is only a partial solution. In my humble opinion, it's the reason why past committee leaders have failed. My approach is two-pronged. Go after the dealers and help the afflicted. Families across this state have been impacted by the ravages of abuse, none more prevalent than with the scourge of opioid addiction. Crimes like larceny and burglary, typically associated with the drug community, continue to plague our cities as desperate addicts seek the means to support their habit. The overdose rate grows every year and continues to be on a steady rise. The Center for Disease Control long ago labeled it an epidemic. It's time we recognized this and took an alternative approach. The opioid crisis is the Black Plague of the twenty-first century."

Litchfield took a sip of water and cleared his throat. "In the past, abusers would be arrested on possession charges and rotate in and out of the penal system, tying up both law enforcement and prosecutors. Our prisons grew overcrowded. A large percentage of that population is comprised of those arrested on minor possession charges. It's a failed approach and has been for a very long time. Some people say my plan is crazy. Well, do you know the truest definition of insanity? Doing the same thing over and over again but expecting a different result. The drug enforcement efforts of the last thirty years were insane. Now is the time for change.

"I've been working closely with members of Boston Police Department's Narcotics and Homicide units to pilot this new approach. Those sentinels of justice are on the front lines in this battle and are supportive of my initiatives. Dealers responsible for an overdose-related death will be priority targets of investigative efforts. The sick, those found in possession of useable amounts of narcotics, will not be prosecuted. I've created an initiative called 'Hope Restored,' designed to work with drug addicts through a network of crisis intervention centers. Treatment facilities across the state have agreed to support this program. If a drug-addicted person is willing to seek treatment, they will not be arrested. In lieu of arrest, the BPD's Narcotics team will transport them directly to one of the supporting Hope Restored centers so that person can immediately begin receiving therapy.

"If I can dry up demand, then the dealers will be out of business for good. Mark my word, the tide is about to change. We are going to take back our streets! We are going to bring home our family members lost to addiction! We are going to make this country whole again!" Litchfield belted out the last words of his speech, slamming his fist on the podium to punctuate its message.

A multitude of reporters fought for an opportunity to have their question fielded. Litchfield picked one who in the past had been supportive. "Go ahead, Abraham."

"Thank you, Senator. Could you explain how this initiative will be more cost effective than others in the past?" the pudgy, dark-haired reporter asked.

"Good question. Some of the numbers are easier to crunch than others, but I'll do my best to give you the *Reader's Digest* version. For starters, the clinics are already in operation, so all we are doing there is adding more clients. Did you know the average cost of housing one inmate for a year in our state is roughly fifty-five thousand dollars? My initiative plans to drive the prison population down by twenty-five percent in the first year alone. Another cost is overtime and man-hours used to fund local crime reduction efforts. I know some of the unions have voiced concern, but this initiative will lower overtime as criminal activity slows. We'd also reduce the burden to hospitals who deal with the constant flow of non-fatal overdose-related patients that inundate emergency rooms on a daily basis. In short, this initiative will save money in the long run by unburdening some of the taxpayer strain."

Another reporter seated in the back yelled her question above the ruckus of her cohorts. "Senator, what do you say to the rumors that you've created this initiative as a platform to run in the next presidential campaign?"

Litchfield's cheeks reddened slightly, and he was grateful for the make-up's mask, hiding his reaction to the question. "I don't know where that rumor came from, but I would first attribute any questions to my initiative being politically motivated as complete and total poppycock. Second, when it comes to pursuing the highest position in the land, I'm honored that..."

Litchfield stopped talking as Avery Wilcox stepped up onto the platform and approached him. He could see a look of seriousness beyond the norm in his most-trusted associate. Wilcox leaned in and whispered into Litchfield's right ear, "Sir, we have a problem."

Litchfield turned to face the man. "Can't it wait?" Litchfield hissed, unaccustomed to such interruptions.

"No, it can't," Wilcox said. His face pained. "It's Amber."

"Amber?" Litchfield's voice, louder than intended, had been picked up by the podium microphone, and the reporters sat forward, eagerly awaiting something juicy like vultures smelling decay.

"We've got to go," Wilcox pleaded.

"I don't understand." Litchfield's typical composure fell away. Buzz Litchfield no longer looked like the shining star of the Democratic Party. He was a father, desperate and terrified.

"She's dead. BPD found her this morning in an alleyway near campus."

Litchfield's legs buckled, and Wilcox caught him by his arm. He was escorted from the podium's platform and faced Gloria Baker, her eyes wet with fresh tears.

In the hallway, away from the watchful eyes of the reporters, Buzz Litchfield broke free from Wilcox's grasp. He breathed deeply, trying to control the rapid beat of his heart. His eyes watered. The man, foreign to such emotional outbursts, was overwhelmed. He squatted into a crouch, covering his face with his hands.

And for the first time since he could remember, Buzz Litchfield wept.

3

Sleet fell more rapidly as the gray sky's mid-morning light filled the alleyway. Miranda Li squatted, shrinking her diminutive stature even more so. Small and thin, the Asian-American homicide detective had never let her size stop her. She'd dominated her peers in all things police related. Her tenacity and drive did not go unnoticed. Boston PD's Homicide had been impressed with the way she handled a death investigation during her second year on the street as a patrolman. She'd found evidence overlooked by senior investigators on the scene of a brutal execution of a fellow cop. That find ultimately broke the case wide open and brought a cop killer to justice. At the time Li had been a cop for less than two years, and her efforts in the case had given her a legend status among her peers. Homicide requested her and she'd been with them ever since. For the last seven years Li had tallied the highest conviction rate in the city, proving to any naysayers that she wasn't a one-hit wonder.

"Are photos complete?" Li asked one of the crime scene techs.

"Almost," the tech replied.

Li cocked her head. "Did you get a picture of this?"

"Not sure. What is it?" the tech squatted beside Li.

"Looks like a small bit of plastic sticking out from under her back. Probably a bag of dope, but the placement's odd."

"Huh," the tech responded.

Li stood and made a notation in her notebook. "Make sure you get a picture of it before we move her."

The tech angled the camera and adjusted the lens, snapping several photographs. The sleet pelted at the blue plastic of the popup canopy set over the alleyway's crime scene which contained the body of Amber Litchfield.

A jogger had stumbled across the body during his early morning run. The patrol division secured the scene and held it until the homicide detectives arrived. The first officer on scene went through Amber's purse, locating a school ID and driver's license. They'd begun a canvass of the area and learned the girl was seen at a party a few brownstones away. Apparently, a few diehard partiers were still there when police arrived at the apartment. One of the guys recognized the girl and said she had been wasted. He remembered seeing her carried out by a couple friends. The patrol's partner was on campus, canvassing Amber's dormitory.

Amber Litchfield's body remained in the same position in which she'd been found. Her legs were bent and slumped off to the right. Her back was flat against the asphalt surface of the alley with her head slightly propped against the brick face of the wall. She was between two large, green, metal dumpsters. Her body was coated in a thin layer of ice by the time Miranda Li and her team arrived.

The on-scene supervisor, Sergeant Bryce Talbot, had run the scene prior to Li's arrival. He was a no-nonsense kind of a boss. Miranda worked under his direction during her short time on the streets. He was a good cop but tended to see things in black and white, looking for the simplest answer so that he could clear a case and move onto the next call. Today would be no different.

Talbot stood under the awning, wearing a long, department-issued, rubbery raincoat. His arms were folded and his face was firm. "Looks like the girl partied a little too hard last night. Toxicology will probably come back as some drug and alcohol combination."

"Maybe. Maybe not," Li said casually.

Talbot shifted his weight, giving a barely perceptible roll of his eyes. "I guess you see it differently?"

"Something's off with this."

"Like what?"

"For starters, I don't like that gash above her eye." Li referred to the blood encrusted wound above the girl's right eye, along the brow.

"Maybe she fell and hit her head on the dumpster or wall?"

"Maybe, but I don't think so."

"Why's that?" Talbot asked.

"There's no blood on the dumpster or the wall," Li answered.

"That doesn't mean anything. This nasty bit of weather could've washed it away," Talbot said with an air of satisfaction.

"As bad as that cut looks, we'd be seeing some evidence on or near the body. And there's nothing. It looks like somebody cleaned that cut up a bit. I'll bet we'll find some towel fibers embedded in that wound when we process the body."

"Anything else?"

"The small baggie under her back," Li pointed out.

"What baggie?" Talbot asked. His eyes widened.

"There's a small plastic bag, most likely coke or heroin."

"See? It proves my theory. Overdose. Plain and simple," Talbot said smugly.

"It's the placement that bothers me. Looks like somebody placed it there."

"What makes you say that?"

"If she did overdose and was holding the bag when the drug took hold, then it would either still be clenched in her balled fist or dropped. If dropped, it would most likely have been further down by her feet and not up near her back." Li paused for effect. "But, then again, maybe I'm wrong."

Talbot smiled. "You haven't been wrong much."

Li gave a little laugh. "It's my curse. Maybe that's why I can't seem to keep a boyfriend for very long. You men hate to be told you're wrong."

Talbot's radio keyed up. "Sergeant Talbot?"

"Go ahead," Talbot said into his lapel mic.

"Um, Sarge. Looks like we found another scene related to the alley," the patrolman relayed.

"Understood. Hold the scene and I'll notify Homicide." His smile widened and the salty sergeant shook his head. "Looks like your intuition has served you well once again."

"Like I said, my curse."

"Looks like this case just got a bit more complicated." Talbot looked past Li toward the crime scene line at the end of the alley.

Li turned to see a man she recognized but had never met. Today's meeting would not be pleasant. Buzz Litchfield was arguing with the two patrol officers assigned to man the line and hold the scene. Apparently, the political giant was not accustomed to being told no.

"I'll handle it." Talbot began to make his way toward the commotion.

"It's okay, Sarge. I've got it." Li took the lead.

Upon closer proximity she could hear the verbal assault the rookie patrolman was taking. To his credit, the officer seemed to be taking it in stride.

"Listen here! That's my daughter in there! You're going to let me in or so help me God I will make your life a living hell!" Buzz Litchfield boomed at the officer.

"Sir, I apologize, but civilians aren't allowed past this point. It's an active crime scene," the fair-skinned officer said firmly.

"Civilian? Do you know who I am?" Litchfield's face turned bright red.

"Sir, like I said..." the officer began again.

Miranda Li interjected, "Senator Litchfield, I'm Detective Miranda Li. I'm in charge of this investigation, and I'm terribly sorry for your loss."

Litchfield turned his attention toward Li. "Well then, Detective, I'm going to need to see my daughter!"

"The officer is correct in what he told you. This is an active crime scene and any entrance of non-essential personnel puts this scene's integrity at risk and potentially contaminates any evidentiary findings. My goal is to find every possible detail so that I can paint as clear a picture of what happened as possible," Li said calmly.

"Detective, that's my baby girl over there," Litchfield's voice cracked, and his rage was instantly replaced with a deep despondency.

"Please know that nobody will work harder on this case than I will. You don't want to remember your daughter like this." Li pulled a business card from her breast pocket. "My work and cell number are on that card. You can call me day or night and I will answer."

Litchfield took the card and handed it to the man standing beside him. Litchfield's assistant then pulled a card, handing it to Li.

"Call me with any updates you have in this case and let me know when I can see my daughter." Litchfield turned away.

Talbot, who'd positioned himself beside Li during the exchange, said, "I don't envy you on this one."

Li nodded, pocketing the senator's business card.

"Detective, photos are done." the tech approached.

"Okay, thanks." Li moved out of the sleet, back under the reprieve of the vinyl canopy.

Li slipped two pairs of latex gloves onto her hands. Double-gloving reduced any potential transfer from investigators. The exterior pair would be removed and disposed of after each piece of evidence got bagged. Then a new pair would replace the discarded. It was a tedious process, but one that ensured a minimal risk of contamination.

The first item of interest for Li was the clear plastic bag. Li called over to the technician with the camera. "Jerry, I'm going to roll her. I need you to take a photo when I do."

"I'm ready whenever you are."

Li got down on her knees. The icy slush covering the alleyway soaked through her pants, sending a chill up her back. She was already cold, but adding wetness to the mix created an extra layer of misery to this morning's scene.

Miranda placed her gloved hands on the girl's shoulder and hip. The icy coating cracked under her grip. She gave a shove. Moving the dead girl's body required more effort than normal. Hours of icy rain coupled with the early signs of rigor gave the girl rigidity. The slight frame of Amber Litchfield gave way to Li's force and her body shifted to its side with a cracking sound.

The small Ziploc bag became exposed. The click of the digital camera behind her assured its current position was documented. Li took her right hand off the girl's shoulder and peeled the bag from the ground.

When she released her grip of the girl's body, it remained in its new position, resting on its right side. Li stood and looked at the bag's contents. A bright white powder lined the bottom quarter. There were no markings or dealer stamps on the exterior. Li knew most dealers stamped their bags as a method of brand recognition. It also made it easier for investigators to find the source.

Li placed the Ziploc inside a plastic evidence bag and sealed it. She labeled it with the case number and time of recovery, initialing the bottom before handing it over to the technician.

Detective Li then removed both pairs of gloves and pulled out her cell. She needed some expert advice on this case and knew just who to call.

4

"I hate hitting a house on days like this," muttered a voice in the cramped space of the raid van.

"When it's nasty outside, the roaches move indoors. This is the best kind of day to hit a house. Lookouts won't be posted outside. Gives us the tactical advantage," Sergeant Daniel Sorenson said, his explanation slightly muffled by the black balaclava covering his face.

Sorenson had taken over Boston's elite Tactical Narcotics Team a year ago. The team was comprised of eight members, not counting Sorenson, and handled the execution of high-risk drug raids. The city's SWAT team used to handle these operations, but several years ago, during a controversial shooting, the administration overreacted, restricting their involvement to barricade hostage situations and dangerous felony warrant service.

The van parked on an adjacent block, and they waited for the surveillance team to give the all-clear. Sorenson's men were seated along benches lining the side walls of a stretched Econoline. The interior space had been modified to accommodate the operators. Their bodies were crammed tightly together with the bulk of the heavy bulletproof vests adding to their discomfort. Each member wore a facemask to conceal their faces from suspects during these assaults. It also added an element of intimidation to the group, one of the hallmarks of any self-respecting tactical unit. Two members carried M4 Commandos, the short-barreled sister to the Army's M16. These two were assigned to the perimeter and would cover exterior windows from the ground, also providing rear security for the entry team in the event any target bailed.

Scott Smith, the team's breacher, had been an academy mate of Sorenson. Smith had an uncanny ability to splinter the most difficult doors with relative ease. More important, he was Sorenson's right-hand man and confidant. Smith's size and strength were a stark contradiction to his even temper and soft-spoken demeanor. Sorenson bounced all of his op plans off the big man before every mission. Smith never hesitated to speak his mind or question tactics. Although they didn't always see eye-to-eye, Sorenson appreciated his friend's candor.

The remaining members of the team had been hand-picked by Sorenson. It had been one of his contingencies before taking the supervisory position. The results of his selection and the accomplishments of the team had impressed the department's top brass. The TNT's efforts resulted in the highest seizure records in recent history, and the success of their unit had gained them quite a reputation among the drug dealing community. For a short period of time, Sorenson had had a twenty-five-thousand-dollar bounty on his head. That dealer was now serving a forty-year prison sentence. The death threat went away overnight.

"Sarge, we've got movement. Zeek's car just pulled up," the voice on the radio said.

Ezequiel Garcia, or Zeek as he was known on the street, was a local dealer in Boston's Dorchester neighborhood. Sorenson had grown up not far from today's target address. Much had changed in the years since his childhood.

Zeek had recently moved up in the ranks of his small distribution operation after his boss was shot and killed. Zeek was believed to be the shooter, but it had not been confirmed. Since Zeek's rise, he had made some aggressive moves to control more of the market. The result had sparked a turf war and thus caught the attention of Sorenson's team.

Zeek was a mid-level distributor of heroin. A reliable informant had given Sorenson the info on a large delivery Zeek was receiving today. The snitch was himself a drug dealer, and Sorenson knew the information was given so TNT would eliminate the competition. It was the gray area of narcotics, and Sorenson navigated it carefully. He turned a blind eye to his informant's deeds to focus on more important targets.

With the time and location of the pickup given, Sorenson got an anticipatory search warrant. If Zeek showed up with a package in-hand during a one-hour window of time provided by the informant, then the warrant, signed by a judge, would go into effect. And that time had arrived.

"We're set," Sorenson replied.

The murmurs and whispered conversations of his team hushed. All the horseplay and mindless banter ceased in the final minutes before any operation kicked off, each man collecting his thoughts.

"Zeek's alone. He's got a red duffle bag. Moving inside. Doors closed. No more visual," the voice said over the radio.

"Moving now." Sorenson nodded to the team's driver.

The van pulled out from the curbside space.

"Taking a left onto Zeek's street," Sorenson announced over the radio. "Pulling onto the street. You should have eyes on us in a second."

"We see you now."

"Thirty seconds out," Sorenson said calmly into the radio, eyeing each member of his team. They acknowledged with subtle nods. Smith winked at him as he rubbed his battering ram, affectionately named Debbie. Sorenson smiled; the facial gesture was hidden under the black cloth of his facemask.

The van stopped in front of the light blue multi-family house.

"Now!" Sorenson commanded and the back doors of the van swung wide.

The four men on each bench peeled out of the back, hitting the ground and moving in a tight column toward the front door landing of the residence.

Stacked on the door, the lead man checked the door, turning the knob. He looked back. "Open. Moving."

The door opened inward and the team filed in behind. Sorenson stayed in the middle of the moving stack of operators. He'd learned he was able to maintain better control of his men from that position, but he missed being on point.

The team made their way up the stairs, doing their best to control the noise created by the gear they were wearing, hoping to maintain the element of surprise. The poorly conditioned wood staircase fought their efforts creaking loudly under the weighted footsteps.

The unit espoused a credo of speed, surprise, and violence of action. The goal would be to put those words into action today.

"Always the third floor," Smith hissed, cresting the landing behind the point man. "Can't these morons ever get a place on the first floor?"

Smith took his position, aligning his left side against the door. Taking a wide stance and gripping the formed steel brackets used as handles, he brought Debbie up to chest height. Smith manipulated the sixty-pound ram with relative ease. He lined up the blunt end of the ram for its first strike, taking aim at the sweet spot, the space between the door knob and the deadbolt.

The team stacked themselves on the stairwell. Sorenson squeezed the shoulder of the man in front of him sending the non-verbal message to initiate the breach up the chain. The point man at the top of the stairwell nodded at Smith, who waited patiently with his massive ram at the ready.

The ram reared back and Smith, using his hips, swung the ram in a controlled arc toward the door. Body and tool working in fluid concert, he delivered a powerful blow, denting the door's paneling. But it remained intact. Smith repeated the process three more times, each strike equal in magnitude to its predecessor. But the door didn't budge.

"It's reinforced! The door's braced!" Smith yelled, after another blast from Debbie.

Sorenson's informant hadn't mentioned anything about a door brace, but a snitch's information was only so reliable. Sorenson made a mental note to have a little conversation with his informant when this was over. But the present circumstance needed to be remedied, and quickly. The longer they spent on the outside, the more time Zeek had to destroy evidence, or worse, prepare for a gun fight. The latter was less likely, but always a possible consideration on operations like these.

There was a window on the right side of the landing, leading to a fire escape. Sorenson had noted it during the reconnaissance done in preparation for the raid. The rusted metal zigzag on the exterior of the structure didn't look up to code, and by its dilapidated condition appeared to have not been used in a very long time.

"You three stay on the door with Smith," Sorenson said to the men stacked ahead of him. He then turned to the two operators behind him and said, "Follow me."

The two entry team members standing behind Sorenson stepped to the center of the stairwell. Sorenson turned back toward the landing and bounded up the last few steps to the top. The window designed to access the fire escape was nailed shut. Definitely not to code, Sorenson thought.

He used the butt of his pistol, breaking the glass. Quickly clearing most of the hanging shards from the wooden frame, Sorenson stepped through and onto the rickety fire escape's third floor landing. The narrow metal platform ran alongside the right side of the dwelling. Sorenson edged forward, hugging the wall as the second member of the team came out the window. The added weight of the second man snapped two of the hinge brackets holding the platform level. Sorenson staggered, grabbing the rust-covered railing to keep from falling.

The fire escape creaked loudly. Sorenson looked back. "Get back inside. This thing's about to collapse!"

The black boots of his teammate disappeared back inside. Sorenson was now evenly spaced between the window he'd exited and the one connected to Zeek's apartment. Another one of the bolts affixing the metal landing to the side of the house came loose.

Sorenson launched forward, taking the last few feet to Zeek's window in two bounding strides. The platform began to shift away from the wall as he moved.

Without hesitation, Sorenson leveled his left shoulder at the closed window. Shattered glass tore at his clothing, biting at his skin as he toppled head first into the room.

Sorenson scrambled to his feet, finding himself in the small bathroom of Ezequiel Garcia's third floor apartment. He wasn't alone. Zeek was kneeling by the toilet with the red duffle bag by his side. The drug dealer was frantically tearing open the plastic bags and dumping the grayish-brown powder down the toilet. He looked up, wide-eyed, at Sorenson. The dramatic entry was obviously unexpected and caught the dealer off guard.

Sorenson brought his gun up, but the restrictive confines of the bathroom kept the weapon close to his vest. "Get on the ground!" Sorenson commanded.

Zeek said nothing, ignoring the order as he continued to pour the powder into the toilet's cloudy water.

Sorenson could see the large duffle was mostly empty now and the floor around Zeek was littered with the ripped plastic bags. Zeek reached for the flushing lever. Sorenson kicked outward and the bottom of his boot crashed down on the skinny man's rib cage. The resulting impact knocked the man sideways against the fiberglass bathtub and away from the toilet.

Sorenson holstered his weapon and dove down on the man, applying all of his weight to keep the squirrelly drug dealer from escaping. Although Sorenson outmatched the drug dealer in both size and strength, Zeek put up a hell of a fight. Desperate men have an impressive reserve.

A few well delivered knee strikes to the squirming man had the desired effect, neutralizing his movement and enabling Sorenson to ratchet down a pair of thick plastic flex cuffs.

Sorenson hoisted the drug dealer from the ground. Zeek bucked and spat but neither had any effect on his current situation. Sorenson shoved the man out the bathroom door, slamming him into the hallway wall. The loud, repetitive bangs from Smith's relentless strikes continued. He saw what had rendered their initial entry plan useless. A large two-by-four was set across the door. Heavy brackets mounted on the door's frame held the thick wood in place.

"It's me!" Sorenson called through the door.

The banging stopped. Sorenson popped the wood free with one hand while keeping Zeek pressed against the hallway's wall with the other.

The board banged on the poorly conditioned hardwood of the floor and the door swung wide. The team immediately flooded the apartment, maintaining a tight formation as they moved past Sorenson and his prisoner.

He could hear his entry team clearing the rooms and waited until he heard the *All Clear*. Once given, all members of the team repeated it, including Sorenson, acknowledging receipt of the message.

Sorenson brought Zeek into the living room where the other members of the team congregated.

"Clear that couch," Sorenson said.

The cushions were flipped. Criminals tended to stash weapons, and you never wanted to make the mistake of having them sit somewhere that wasn't properly cleared.

"Clear," Smith said.

Sorenson sat Zeek on the couch. The drug dealer said nothing, and his shoulders slumped as his head hung low in defeat.

"That was some John Wayne stuff, boss." Smith smiled.

Sorenson shook his head and laughed. His cellphone vibrated and he looked down to check the caller. He looked at his men. "Begin the secondary search."

Sorenson stepped into the hallway and answered the call. "Hey Miranda. What's up?"

"You busy?" she asked.

Sorenson pulled a piece of glass from his arm. "Not really."

"I've got something I may need your expertise for."

"Anything for you. What do you got?"

"Dead girl. Looks like an overdose gone bad. They're going to want to go after the dealer on this one," Li said.

"Let me know what you need from us."

"I've got two at the station now. Her roommate and some guy she was seen with last night. Maybe you could have a conversation with them or at least listen in on the interrogation to see if you recognize the dealer by name or description."

"Sure thing. This one getting a lot of press?"

Li sighed into the phone. "You have no idea. The victim is Senator Litchfield's daughter."

"You mean the anti-drug czar? His kid OD'd?"

"The one and only. There is going to be a big push to follow his new initiative of going after the dealer associated with a death. And I'm really going to need your team on this one."

"Consider it done. I've just got to finish up here and I'll head in to the station to assist on the interrogation."

Li ended the call and Sorenson returned to the living room.

"Have patrol come and collect Mr. Garcia. We've got to regroup back at the office," Sorenson said to Smith.

"Okay. Something big?" Smith asked.

"Priority One Target," Sorenson replied, as he went back to clearing off the glass and debris from his tussle with the skinny drug dealer.

This was an opportunity to highlight his team's capabilities, as well as his skills as a supervisor. The timing was perfect.

5

Nick watched through the darkly tinted plate-glass doors as the girl walked into the building. She carried an air of confidence belying her age. The sign above the door read *Your Journey Begins Here*. Nick laughed to himself. No slogan could be more misaligned to the girl who'd just entered the US Army's Saginaw Bay recruitment office.

Nearly three years had passed since he'd last seen her. How far she had come since her entrance into the country! The Walkers, her foster parents, obviously had taken good care of her since accepting her into their home. Mouse had shown an unfathomable resilience in light of the initial circumstances life dealt her. Raised in the ghetto of Juarez, crossing the border after the tragic death of both her parents, her journey to America had been an arduous one, but those events brought Mouse into his life and he was grateful for that.

The time drifted by slowly as Nick waited in his compact rental car. Spilling out over the top of dark sunglasses, his long hair was barely contained by a baseball cap. He wasn't sure about this reunion and wanted to pick the right time to approach her.

Nick arrived in Pidgeon, Michigan a few days ago. He'd been watching Mouse from a distance, trying to get a feel for her life now, and whether it was worth the risk to interfere. Wiz had done some research for him and found out she'd graduated high school at the top of her class. Not bad for a girl starting over in a foreign country. Since then, she'd worked at a neighborhood childcare center called Rainbow Junction. It was funny though to see the deadly little girl working with children. Enlisting in the Army seemed a more appropriate career path.

He wasn't sure this was a smart idea. He'd debated whether making contact with her would be detrimental. In the small Michigan town tucked into the picturesque Saginaw Bay, most of his time was spent hemming and hawing over this decision. He'd learned from a local gas station attendant that the area was affectionately referred to as the "Thumb." When asked why, the woman held up her hand, using it like a map, pointing to a spot near the middle knuckle of her thumb—the location of Pidgeon. Nick remembered the great pride the gas station employee had taken in explaining this to him.

His phone vibrated and he saw it was from Jay.

"What's up?" Nick pressed the cellphone against his face.

"Sorry to cut the R and R short, but I need you back. Something's come up and I need all hands on deck," Jay said.

"What do we have?"

"We'll go over it when we're all together. There's an airstrip not too far from your location. I'll send you the info when we hang up. There'll be a plane there in two hours. Be there."

"Okay." Nick knew there was no real point in pleading for more time.

"Will you be traveling alone?"

"Not sure yet."

The call ended. His phone immediately vibrated, alerting him to the airstrip coordinate location and flight information. Nick was angry at himself for vacillating over the decision to make contact with Mouse. He wished he had spoken to her.

Maybe another time, Nick thought to himself as he put the car in drive. Just then, the doors to the recruitment office swung open and Mouse stepped out onto the sidewalk holding a thick stack of papers. Seeing the girl changed his mind, and he seized the opportunity.

Nick slipped the car's transmission back into park. Mouse was still standing in front of the office. He approached. When he got ten feet away, the girl turned in his direction.

Nick stopped in his tracks.

"Mouse," he said quietly.

She gasped and ran at him. Mouse leapt into his arms. Her arms wrapped tightly around his neck. At eighteen, she wasn't much bigger than he'd remembered, and she felt light as he welcomed her embrace.

"I was wondering when you were going to get around to saying hi," Mouse said.

"What do you mean ' get around to'?" Nick released her to the ground.

"I've been watching you follow me around for the past few days." Mouse smiled broadly.

He'd forgotten how resourceful she was. Apparently, her observation skills hadn't diminished in the security of her new life.

"You are truly amazing," Nick said, looking down on the girl like a proud parent.

"I thought you were dead." Mouse cocked an eyebrow.

"Didn't you hear?" Nick asked with a grin, "I'm unkillable."

She gave a teenage roll of her eyes. "I'm pretty sure I had to save you at least one time."

Nick shook his head, giving a hearty laugh.

"So, you faked your death to escape prison just to check in on me? Nick, you didn't have to go to all that trouble. You could've just written me a letter."

"It's complicated."

"Everything always is with you."

Nick strained to come up with his next words. He sighed and looked around.

"You seem at a loss for words. What's on your mind? And, more important, what brought you here?" Mouse asked directly.

"I thought I'd come here and see how you were doing. Make sure you're okay." Sadly, he'd rehearsed his pitch too many times to count but now, with Mouse standing before him, none of it seemed right.

"Just spit it out."

"Are you happy?" Nick asked.

"Happy? Yes. The Walkers have been truly amazing to me, taking me in and treating me like family. They put up with my attitude and gave me space as I adjusted to normal life."

"Good. I'm glad to hear it," Nick said softly.

"But, if you're asking me if I'm content, then my answer's different." Her thin lips drew up at the corners.

"How so?"

"Something's missing. Hard to put a finger on it. I mean, look at this place. It's absolutely beautiful. I'm living with a loving family in a house on the freaking water. What else could anyone ask for? Right?" Mouse mumbled the last part.

"Is that why you just walked out of the Army recruitment office?" Nick gestured to the stack of paperwork in her hand.

"I guess." Mouse looked up at Nick with a flash of intensity in her eyes. "Raised the way I was doesn't quite jibe with normalcy. It's been really hard to shake my past. I guess the Army looked like a place where I could put all of my father's lessons to good use."

"Maybe. Maybe not. But if you really want to be all that you can be, then I may be able to help," Nick offered.

"How so?"

"Not here. I saw you took your bike. How about we throw it in the trunk and I give you a ride home?"

"Sounds good to me."

Nick popped the trunk. It was a tight fit, but after several twists of the handlebars he was able to get the bicycle in. Mouse was already seated in the passenger seat with the recruitment paperwork on her lap.

She said, "It's not too far from here, but you already know that. I saw you parked down the street yesterday when I was heading off to work."

Nick smiled. She didn't miss a thing.

"So, what's this opportunity you're so hesitant to talk about?" Mouse prodded.

"Once I tell you, everything is going to change. If you accept, then your life will never be the same. All you've come to know over the past two years will disappear," Nick said seriously.

"As great as these last few years in Pidgeon living with the Walkers have been, it's not who I am. You know that and I know that."

Nick saw it in her eyes—the raw truth. Mouse was a byproduct of her past experience and it defined her. He wouldn't be tearing her from her life. He would be returning her to the only life she'd ever felt comfortable in.

"I work for a group, totally off the governmental radar, tasked with taking down some of the worst of the worst. If you joined us, you'd have an opportunity to capitalize on the skills you possess in a way the Army never could."

"Where do I sign up?" Mouse asked.

"You just did."

"What about my foster family? What do I tell them?"

"Let me handle that," Nick said, pulling out of the strip of businesses and leaving the recruiting office behind.

"When do I start?" Mouse asked. Her voice squeaked with a hint of excitement.

"Wow, you ask a lot of questions. The Mouse I knew barely spoke a word." Nick laughed. "We're going to be on a plane with wheels up in less than two hours."

"This really is some secret government stuff. They make movies about this kind of thing."

"Just wait until you meet your cast of characters."

Nick pulled into the driveway of the Walker's house. The white rocks of the half-moon driveway crunched noisily under the vehicle's weight. Mouse looked over at him. She fidgeted with papers on her lap.

"So that's the story you're going to give them?" Mouse asked as Nick brought the car to a stop.

"Yup," he replied, releasing his hair from the confines of his hat. Long waves of dark brown hair fell across his face.

"Looking like that, you think you can convince them?"

"I can be very persuasive," Nick said playfully.

"Well, let's do this then." Mouse stepped out of the car.

Nick fell in step behind the small girl. Nick sized her up and guessed her to be an inch or two below five feet in height. Her frame was wiry, and he'd learned from Wiz's intel report she'd excelled at cross country during junior and senior years of school.

The darkly stained wood of the door was intricately designed. Nick was by no means an expert, but if he were to guess, the door had been made by hand. The Walkers spared no expense and the exterior was an example of that. Whatever lavish lifestyle wealth had brought them, they'd remained humble people with generous hearts. In a time when Mouse needed a safe place to begin anew, it had been this ornate door of the Walkers' that swung wide to welcome her.

Mouse pressed the bronze latch and pushed open the door. She turned back to Nick. "We don't lock our doors in the Thumb."

Nick rolled his eyes.

"I'm home!" she called out in a lyrical singsong.

A woman's voice rang back, "We're in the kitchen."

"I've brought a visitor." Mouse ushered Nick into the foyer.

She opened her arms wide as if she were Vanna White revealing the puzzle's solution. "Nice, huh?"

"Pretty impressive."

The entranceway had a small two-step rise carpeted in a soft blue that led to an oversized living room with a giant bay window at the far end. From where he stood, it looked as though the house was floating. Saginaw Bay's clear water shimmered in the sunlight. There was no wind today and the surface was smooth as glass.

"Follow me." Mouse moved up the steps, disappearing to her left.

There was a short hallway leading into an open kitchen layout. Seated on bar stools at the marble counter were the Walkers. Nick recognized them immediately from a picture Anaya had shown him after Mouse was first placed with the family. They'd looked like nice people in the picture and the live version confirmed his impression.

Nick hadn't been able to make the trip out to visit Mouse with Anaya. His life had been turned upside down. And by all accounts it still was. Missing the trip had an advantage for today's meeting. The Walkers had never met him and therefore wouldn't recognize him for anything but the persona he portrayed.

"Guys, I'd like you to meet Captain Paulson. He's got a really great opportunity for me," Mouse said.

"I don't understand. I know you sent a text saying you'd be a little late today, but we figured you were going to the movies or stopping for a bite to eat," Eileen Walker said.

"I didn't want to tell you until I had all the facts, but I've decided to join the Army," Mouse said excitedly.

"Join the Army? I thought we talked about you taking the year off until you figured out what you wanted to do. We always figured you'd apply yourself at college. You've got a real shot at making something for yourself. You know that," Gary Walker said, rubbing his lined forehead.

It was obvious the Walkers were successful people, and they undoubtedly had a thought or two on how to best set Mouse up for her future. The military was definitely not on their short list of prospective life choices.

"Mr. and Mrs. Walker, your daughter has an amazing opportunity to join a very special unit within the Army," Nick stepped forward, holding Mouse's recruitment paperwork as a prop.

"No offense, sir, but you don't look like an Army guy," Mr. Walker said suspiciously.

Nick ran his hand through his long hair. "No offense taken. And believe me, I know. That's one of the things I work hard at doing. Making sure people don't see me for who, or what, I am."

"And what are you?" asked Mrs. Walker.

"I'm an Army Captain and I work for the Army's Special Projects Division. As far as what I do specifically...well, most of that requires a security clearance. What I can tell you is that one of the things I do is look for fresh talent to bring into our program."

"Talent? Program?" Mr. Walker asked.

"Yes, I scout the country looking for certain attributes, filtering through recruitment files to locate potentials, then I recruit them for candidacy in our program," Nick said, gauging the Walkers' reaction. He could tell they were starting to buy into his ruse. He added, "When your daughter came into the office several weeks ago, I'd received a message from the recruiting sergeant, and I began a review of her eligibility to participate. I've not been as impressed with any of our other recent recruits as much as I am at her prospects."

Mouse blushed at the compliment.

"So, you're saying she began this process weeks ago?" Mrs. Walker asked dejectedly.

Mouse must've registered the hurt in her foster mother's voice and mouthed the words, *I'm sorry.*

"Yes. And you'll be happy to know that she's been accepted. Although she's eighteen, and can sign up without parental consent, I wanted to come here today and tell you personally. She told me about her past, and she also told me how you welcomed her into your lives with open arms. The support you've given her since coming into your care has been nothing short of amazing." Nick's last comment was heartfelt and was his way of personally thanking the Walkers for looking after Mouse.

"Well, I'm not sure what to say to all of this. It's a lot to take in," Mrs. Walker said, almost in tears.

"Honey, are you sure this is what you want?" Mr. Walker asked.

"Absolutely," Mouse said firmly.

"I guess your mind's made up."

"It is."

"When do you start?" Mrs. Walker asked.

"She leaves today." Nick braced for the backlash, knowing this blow would shake them. "I've got a plane standing by."

"Today?" Mrs. Walker muttered, tears suddenly streaming down her face.

Mouse went to them and tucked her head between the two people who'd spent the last few years caring for her. She hugged them tightly, wrapping one arm around each of her foster parent's necks.

Nick's work done, he retreated outside, giving them space to say their goodbyes in private.

Mouse appeared ten minutes later with a duffle bag in hand and a backpack slung over her shoulder. Nick had removed the bike, making space for her bags.

The two sat in the car, taking a silent pause. Nick looked over at Mouse whose eyes were still damp.

"They were really great people. Do you think I'll see them again?" Mouse asked.

"I don't see why not. You're not dead. Goes without saying, but they can never know what we do."

"I understand."

Nick could tell she was thinking something. "What's on your mind?"

"Not sure this wild man look is working for you. I think it's time for you to get a haircut." Mouse broke into a laugh.

"Well, they do call me The Wolf."

Mouse laughed harder. "Wolf or not. That mane has got to go."

Nick looked down at his phone's GPS. They'd be cutting it close on Jay's timeline. He pulled out of the crescent driveway leaving Saginaw Bay, and with it Mouse's best chance at a normal life, behind. Nick hoped he'd made the right choice by bringing her into the group.

Her life was once again in his hands. A responsibility Nick Lawrence didn't take lightly.

6

"So, you pulled me from the beautiful water of Saginaw Bay to a run-down industrial complex in Waltham, Massachusetts?" Mouse asked sarcastically.

"Looks can be deceiving. You of all people should know that," Nick replied.

Nick and Mouse sat in the car outside of the gray aluminum walls of a building. The small sign above the door said *Simple Flush Toilet Repair*. Wiz thought it funny to give all of their Vault locations business names related to garbage and sewage disposal. Nick remembered when he'd first joined the Valhalla group and the pride shown by the computer tech with this contribution. Wiz told him, "We flush out the world's biggest turds."

This business, with all the Vault's fake-naming conventions, couldn't be found in any directory, online or otherwise. To ward off the occasional, but highly infrequent potential customer, the double doors had an *Under Construction* sign taped to the exterior of the heavily tinted glass. The doors on the outside were always locked, and the glass was rated to stop high velocity rounds up to fifty caliber.

Nick looked at Mouse, "Come on. Let's go meet your new family."

She feigned a smile.

Nick could see the focus in her eyes. She was tough, but he knew the adjustment to the unit would take a little time. As Mouse had proven time and time again, she could adapt better than most.

The two exited the vehicle and walked toward the doors. There were no windows, just seamless walls of the flat gray siding. The siding was specially lined with some next-level sound proofing, rendering any eaves-droppers, digital or otherwise, completely ineffective. The interior walls were reinforced to withstand a rocket-propelled grenade.

Nick placed the face of his watch against a small gray panel on the wall and a loud metallic click from the door could be heard. He stepped over and pulled the door open. Mouse watched him intently.

"Cool watch," she said.

The two crossed the threshold. The door closed behind them with a loud click and mechanical hiss. It was dark. The tints from the exterior glass door allowed very little light to pass. The space was small, and once inside, the two faced another set of doors. These doors, comprised of heavy steel, had no handles. A gray pad, similar to the one on the outside, was located along the adjacent wall. Nick held his watch to this pad, as he had done before.

A hum and rhythmic ticking began. The seam between the doors separated.

Nick stepped into the Vault. He looked back at Mouse. She hesitated only momentarily before entering.

The room was buzzing with chatter and a television played the news in the background. The Vault's interior doors closed. The members stopped what they were doing and turned, almost in unison, to face Nick and his guest.

"So, this is Mouse?" Wiz asked playfully, getting up from his computer terminal. "The girl who comes to our little unit and already has a cooler nickname than mine."

She nodded and shrugged, shaking the outstretched hand the messy-haired computer tech offered.

"I'm Wiz," he said with a roll of his eyes.

Declan stepped out of Jay's office and locked eyes on the young girl. "Mouse!" he called over to her.

She squealed with excitement at seeing the man who personally saved her life in a hotel room several years before. The two hadn't seen each other since then and it was obvious to Nick that the bond forged in that desperate moment of chaos remained unbreakable to this day, a sentiment he understood better than most.

Mouse crossed the floor, quickly closing the distance, passing several other members of the team. She gave Declan a hug, similar to the one she'd given Nick when he'd seen her again for the first time.

"I can't believe you're here." Declan released the embrace and took stock of the girl.

"Me either. But I'm glad I am," she said.

"Well, there'll be time for catching up later. First, let's get you introduced to this ragtag group of lunatics." Declan turned his attention toward the group, who pulled up seats around a large conference table. "I'm sure you'll fit right in."

The group sat around the large oval of the oak table, as was tradition, so members could introduce themselves.

"Mouse, we're very excited to have you with us. I think you're going to find that you are in the company of some of the world's finest operators. Both Nick and Declan here have bragged endlessly about your skill set. We look forward to bringing you up to speed on how we do things around here. I think we'll be able to find a place for you to fit in among our ranks," Jay said.

"I, for one, am glad to finally have another lady in our midst. Hopefully, we'll get a little girl power around here to balance out the unbearable level of testosterone." Another woman smiled warmly. "I'm Barbie."

"Like the doll?" Mouse said, returning the smile.

"Like I said, these guys have been running the show for too long." Barbie gave a theatrical twirl of her long blonde hair. "I handle most of the logistics for the group. For example, I was the one who arranged for the plane to get you here."

Mouse nodded.

"I'm also the best driver in this group. So, you'll probably want to ride with me if given a choice."

"I'll second that. She can handle a car like a NASCAR driver. I'm Spider and I handle interrogations," he said in his even-keeled voice.

"We've already met. I've been given the cool nickname of Wiz because this group of morons likes to pay homage to the eighties movies starring Fred Savage," Wiz snarked.

"Never heard of it," Mouse said.

Wiz shook his head in mock defeat. "Exactly what I'm saying. Why couldn't they pick Morpheus or Neo?"

"Shut up, Wiz!" The group said in unison.

"Anyway, I'm the computer guy. They don't let me go out into the field." Wiz leaned a little closer to Mouse. "Probably afraid I'll show them up."

Jay said, "You know Nick and Declan. Of course, outside of these walls they're referred to by their call signs Wolf and Ace respectively. We use those to protect our anonymity.

"Declan and I are the only ones that haven't severed our ties to our former lives. Everybody else in this room is dead. Wiz generates new identifications as needed, but original names are long since buried. I'm Jay, but as of recently, I've been given the call sign Odin." Jay paused, looking around the Vault. "And this is the Valhalla Group."

Nick kept his eyes on Mouse, evaluating her for any possible signs of distress as she adjusted to her new surroundings. The girl was stoic, no trace of hesitation or nervousness outwardly displayed. He was impressed.

"Barbie will get you up to speed on things in a bit, but for now we need to get moving forward on our latest assignment." Jay unmuted the television.

The news anchor was in mid-sentence, "...all we can confirm is that a girl found in a Boston alleyway this morning was Amber Litchfield, daughter to Massachusetts Senator Buzz Litchfield. As you may know, the senator heads the Opioid Reform Committee and has recently launched an aggressive new program designed at going after drug dealers responsible for overdose deaths. The investigation into his daughter's death is still in the early stages and is currently being looked into by Boston's Homicide Division. We'll bring you the latest once we have more on this terrible tragedy."

Jay turned the volume back off. "We've been called in on this one. The powers that be want to make sure that whoever is responsible for the senator's daughter's death is dealt with appropriately. Our employer has information that the senator may have a very real shot at the next presidency. Goes without saying, but this is important for our unit."

"Why don't we let the local agencies run with it? I'm sure Boston's got a narc unit capable of tracking this down," Declan asked.

"Not my call," Jay said dismissively. "And the orders are clear. We're not to stop until the source of the distribution is dismantled. From the bottom to the top. But you're right about Boston's narcotics unit being involved. They're already on this case assisting with the investigation. And that's where we'll begin. Declan and Nick are going to Boston to join up with them. I figured with both of your investigative backgrounds it should be easy to assimilate. You've already been cleared through the chain of command as the FBI's direct liaisons for this investigation. Nick, Wiz has got your credentials all set, as well as the paperwork authorizing your involvement. I've arranged to have one of BPD's senior brass meet you at headquarters in an hour. He'll escort you in and make sure everything goes smoothly."

"Sounds good," Nick said. Leaning over to Mouse he whispered, "I guess my long hair makes sense now. I can blend in as a narc."

Mouse giggled and shook her head. "It still needs to go."

Nick smiled. He and Declan stood from the table and began gearing up.

"I don't think this needs to be said, but I'll say it anyway for posterity. This operation is going to have a lot of eyes on it. Let's do our best to maintain a low profile," Jay said, dismissing the rest of the group.

7

"Hi everybody, I'm Carson." The thin man looked down at his untied shoe.

"Hi, Carson," the group murmured in staggered unison.

Carson Boyd knew he still looked like a junkie. His hair was long and greasy, a testament to his shelter's recent plumbing issue. It'd been three days since he'd been able to take a shower, but none of the audience seemed to be in much better condition and probably didn't notice. Two weeks had passed without him using once. For the first time in a long time, Boyd felt optimistic.

Attending the group meetings off and on for several years, Boyd never spoke. Presenting was not a requirement, only a suggestion. Supposedly, it helped release the burden. An introvert by nature, standing in front of the scattered audience, his hands began to tremble.

His voice cracked slightly as he began. "I've been coming to this place for a while. Sometimes by choice and sometimes by court mandate."

A ripple of soft chuckles moved around the small crowd, seated before him in lined rows of folding chairs. The members of this group understood and several probably fell into one of those two categories as well.

Boyd cleared his throat and continued, "Never been much for talking, especially to a group of strangers. Maybe that's why it's taken me so long to get up in front here. Anyway, I'm having a good couple of weeks and felt it was my time to share."

Boyd looked out over the vacant listeners and stopped at the face of James Sobestanovich, the group moderator and Boyd's sponsor. Sobe, as he liked to be called, was a big reason for Boyd's recent success in maintaining his sobriety. A recovering addict himself, Sobe had turned his pain into his passion. He was known throughout the local community and revered among addicts. Sobe was hard on Boyd, and Boyd needed it. His most recent overdose nearly cost him his life. It took several blasts of Narcan to bring him back and when he came around in the emergency room, Sobe was standing by his bed.

"I guess my story isn't very special. I've been coming to these meetings long enough to know that. But it's my story and I need to tell it." Boyd exhaled loudly, releasing some of his tension.

"I wasn't always like this." Boyd pulled up the sleeves of his dark gray hoodie and exposed his forearms to the group. The dark spots of his track marks peppered a scattered line, some with a reddish tinge, showing his more recent injection sites and told the tale of his long battle with heroin. Depressed veins left pits across damaged skin. These were the brands of this terrible addiction. "These are just the ones you can see. Pretty much any place you've got a vein, I've tried to dig in a needle."

Nods and murmurs of agreement from the group as members showed their support and understanding.

"I hope this one here is the last." Boyd tapped the lump of raised skin.

An abscess of trapped fluid bulged at his most recent injection point. Heroin was injected hot, and the body, in particular the intravenous system, did not respond well to the hot loads. The abscesses were typically formed when the needle missed its mark.

"Correction. I don't hope – I know that was my last time." Carson released his sleeves to cover his arms.

The group gave a weak cheer and a couple claps. Sobe smiled in the background.

"In my former life I was a high school math teacher. College degree and working in an admirable field. It feels like forever since I was that man. A car accident left me in pretty bad shape. I was hit broadside and my knee got really messed up. After the surgery and physical therapy, I was still dealing with a lot of pain. My doctor started me on oxy to help manage it. Wasn't long before I started upping my dosage, using more than prescribed. I started needing more just to get the right effect. When my script would run out, I'd get sick. Then, I started missing a lot of work, calling out two or three days a week. When I ran out of sick time, and I showed up to work, I was either high as a kite or dope sick. Neither version of me was pretty. Long story short, I was fired when they caught me trying to buy from one of my students. Another teacher saw and ratted me out. Can't blame 'em. Who wants a junkie for a teacher?"

Boyd paused. Losing his job was not the hardest piece of his journey into addiction, and he hesitated in his resolve to share to the rest. He locked eyes with Sobe, who gave a deep reassuring nod of encouragement.

"Without a job, I lost my insurance and with that, my access to my scripts disappeared. The street price for pills is high. I was spending thirty bucks a pop. I quickly spent all of my money from my severance package. I moved back in with my mother after getting evicted from my apartment. She was good to me and really tried to help, but I wasn't in a good place. I couldn't afford my pill habit anymore and someone turned me on to the bag. Told me it was cheaper and a better high. Been chasing the dragon ever since."

"Amen," a disheveled man called out from the group.

Boyd continued, "And then I started to bottom out. I couldn't get a job. My only concern was getting high, and without money, I resorted to stealing. Mostly just breaking into cars at night and pawning what I could. But then I did something I'll always regret. I stole from my mother. Took my grandmother's wedding ring and pawned it. I think I got enough for a bundle. Forty bucks for my mother's most cherished item."

The retelling of his theft made him sick as the memory of his mother's face came into view.

"She put me out after that. I've been on the street ever since. It's been three years since I've seen her. I've been hustling ever since. Finally got a spot at a shelter. I've died twice. Last time was the worst. Don't think I'll make it through another round."

Boyd looked at the audience. The empathy in the faces of his listeners

confirmed they all had taken a similar journey. He remembered hearing
Sobe talk about hitting bottom, about stabbing another addict in a drug
deal gone bad. The guy hadn't died, but the stabbing landed Sobe in prison
where he managed to kick the heroin and find God, two very difficult things
to do under those conditions.

"That's my story of addiction. I hope it ended ten days ago when I
booted my last bag." Boyd stepped away and returned to his seat.

A round of applause echoed as he slumped into the uncomfortable
metallic chair. Sobe came up from behind and gave his shoulder a squeeze.

"You did great. Thank you for sharing with the group," Sobe said. "One
day at a time from here on out, brother."

Carson Boyd looked up at the man and smiled weakly. He was equal
parts hopeful and terrified at what his future held.

***

The meeting ended and Boyd walked with Sobe out into the muted gray
light of late afternoon sky. He stopped in his tracks as he saw the man
leaning against a car parked along the curb. He was still paying a debt to
the man, but this time he worried the price would be too costly.

Sobe turned, obviously noting his trepidation, and asked, "Everything
okay?"

Boyd nodded. "Yeah, he's a cop."

He could see the concern etched in the lines across his sponsor's
forehead.

Sobe gave him a look and pursed his lips. "You know I don't judge. But
the worst thing you could do right now would be to put yourself back in the
environment. Even if you're working with them and not using, just being
around it this close to getting clean could set you back big time. You know I
speak from experience? Think hard about this and if you want, I'll talk with
him."

Sobe had quickly surmised Boyd's relationship with the police and also
knew its pitfalls.

"I owe him." Boyd walked away from Sobe toward the unmarked
police car.

"I'm impressed." Sorenson gave a nod of approval and a small golf clap as Boyd walked up.

"Almost two weeks clean."

"Two weeks? How you feeling?"

"The methadone helps, but I think I've got a real shot this time. Don't remember the last time I felt this optimistic about it."

Sorenson nodded.

"Why're you here? Me being clean means I'm probably not going to be much use for you. I know you did right by me on that case and I really appreciate it, but I thought I paid my debt. You got two dealers off the street with my help. Remember?"

"Let's take a ride." Sorenson opened the passenger side door and gesturing for him to enter.

Boyd looked back at Sobe, who stood where he'd left him. Sobe gave a slight shake of his head. Boyd turned away and entered the open car. A moment later the unmarked car pulled away from the curb.

"I really need you on this one," Sorenson pleaded. "You're my most reliable informant. You're smart, you don't skim bags, and you get great video. I've got a big case with a lot of eyes on me and you're the best man for the job. Hell, I'll pay you double the normal rate for this one. That's one hundred twenty bucks for an hour's work. Better than what some lawyers get paid."

Boyd shook his head. "I really want to help you, but I'm clean now. I need to stay away from it for a little while. Maybe in a week or two I'll feel more comfortable about doing it."

"Like I said, this is a big case and I don't have two weeks for you to come around on this. How many times have I helped you out of a jam over the years?"

Boyd sat silently.

"How many?"

"I don't know."

"That's because there's too many to count. Listen Carson, I'm not telling you to use. I just need you to make a buy. Only one. This is the last time I ask this favor of you. Whatever debts you owe will be paid in full."

"One hundred and twenty?"

"Yup. And it's going to be really easy for you. You've bought from this crew before."

Boyd sighed loudly in protest. "You're killing me, man. I don't want to be around the stuff."

"In and out. It'll take you less than five minutes."

Boyd thought about having one hundred twenty dollars in his pocket. That was one hundred and twenty more than he had right now. He looked down at the busted shoes on his feet. The seams separated from the rubber soles. A couple Dunkin' Donuts napkins stuffed inside filled the gap. He thought about getting a new pair. It was the first time he could remember that he didn't think about using his snitch money to buy dope. That was the irony of being an informant. The cops would give him money to buy dope from a dealer. They would then pay him for his service, and he would then return to the same dealer using the money earned to buy dope for himself. The police had been funding his habit for quite some time.

"Okay, but this is my last time. I'm out of the game after this. Lose my number."

"Last time. Promise," Sorenson said, slowly looping the block. "Where do you want me to let you out?"

Boyd looked around, seeing none of the usual crowd, he pointed at the upcoming corner. "Here's good."

"You still got the cell I gave you?" Sorenson asked.

"Yup."

"I'll hit you up when we're doing this. But be available. It's coming soon."

Boyd nodded, exiting the vehicle. Without looking back, he called back to the departing unmarked police car, "Last time!"

He walked away thinking about new shoes as an old, more familiar thought, entered his mind.

8

A cloud of thick smoke hung above their heads as loud explosions and sporadic gunfire shook the walls. The only light came from the half-drawn window shade and the bright display of the television. They'd been playing the video game for the past several hours. During that same block of time they'd managed to make twelve-hundred dollars.

"Pass that my way, brah," Freddy Rivera asked. The crew's youngest member, age fourteen, and appropriately nicknamed Spaz, leaned across the couch, reaching for the joint in Merc's hand.

"Get out of here you idiot! Make one yourself and make a couple runs. Earn your keep youngun'," Merc scolded, taking his hand off the Xbox controller and shoving Rivera's face. The teen slipped off the couch and onto the floor.

The others laughed.

The leader, Sam Caldwell, munched a handful of hot fries, while his girlfriend, Gloria, balanced her ample buttocks on his left thigh. Caldwell was known throughout the Orchard Park area of Roxbury as Jinx. He'd been in the local drug trade as long as he could remember and had risen through the ranks, starting as a runner and working his way up.

Now, he and his small but dedicated crew ran the four-block area surrounding Orchard Park Street, home to the infamous Orchard Park

Housing Projects, torn down in the early nineties and rebuilt as part of a community revitalization effort. It didn't take long after the rebuild for the area to return to its previous condition. Jinx and his compatriots were a byproduct of the neighborhood's tough environment.

Caldwell had been born and raised right there on the same street. He was literally born on Orchard Park Street in a building not too far away from where he was now. His mother was high when her water broke and never realized she was in labor until Caldwell started crowning. She'd disappeared not too long after his birth. At twenty-two years old, Jinx had managed to outlive many of his friends. He'd never met his father, who'd been locked away since he was a toddler. Raised by his grandmother after his mother left, Jinx had been pleasant enough as a child, but as he aged, the streets called to him. He was captivated by the fast money and power he saw wielded by certain members of his neighborhood. He'd figured long ago, after the second time he'd been shot, he was most likely going to die there as well.

A weak knock at the door was heard. Jinx paused the video game to get another bag of snacks.

"Who dat?" hollered Merc in a deep, intimidating voice.

"Darla," a timid voice squeaked from the hallway outside the apartment.

Merc, the muscle for Jinx's crew, rolled his eyes. "This is the third time homegirl's been back today."

Jinx shrugged. "Money's money, brah. Gotta make that cheddah."

"True 'nuf." Merc kicked at Rivera's leg. "Get to work Spaz!"

Spaz snuck a quick hit off the joint before scrambling up and moving toward the door. Looking through the peephole, he eyed the woman standing in the hallway. He unlatched the deadbolt and let her in. As he closed the door behind her, he asked, "How much?"

Darla pushed her hand into her pocket and retrieved thirty dollars. The things she had done to earn the crumpled cash in her hand would sicken most people. The lollipop in her mouth removed the taste from the last ten earned. The dope helped numb those thoughts. Ironically, it was the dope that sent the suburban girl into the vicious cycle of prostitution.

"A bundle," Darla asked for ten bags of heroin. Her voice quivered.

"You know the price," Spaz said, smiling.

"It's all I got. You know I'm good for it, man." Darla looked past Spaz and said, "Jinx, you know I'm good for it!"

Jinx heard the woman but did not react. He turned the game back on and his eyes fixated on the carnage of the digital battlefield as he tapped wildly on the controller's buttons.

Darla turned her attention back to the thin teenager in front of her, "Maybe I can work the extra ten off another way?"

Spaz laughed a squeaky chortle; puberty was wreaking havoc on the boy. He turned his head toward the others on the couch and called out, "Guys, Dirty Darla is looking to work for it!"

Merc made a mock gagging gesture as if he were about to vomit and then broke into a laugh. He threw a couple hot fries in the direction of Spaz and the girl before joining Jinx in the game play.

"Looks like nobody wants what you're offering." Spaz laughed.

Darla stood waiting with the crumpled money in her hand. "Please. I'm really hurting. You guys got the best stuff. I'll be back with the money. I promise," she begged softly.

Spaz didn't answer.

"Just give it to her! I'm sick of her being here," Jinx yelled out, still maintaining his focus on the game.

Spaz retrieved a tightly folded stack of wax paper bags wrapped together with a small black elastic. A lightning bolt was stamped on the exterior of each of the bags. He snatched the thirty dollars from her and dropped the bundle into the prostitute's outstretched hand.

She turned to leave and then stopped. "Do you have any aspirin? I've got a killer headache."

"Girl, are you for real?" Spaz asked. Although he was only fourteen, to the diminutive Darla he was an intimidating force.

Darla flinched. "Please," she whined. "It's pounding. Been throbbing all day. I just need a couple ibuprofen or aspirin."

Spaz reached for the doorknob, "Bitch, I ain't your healer!"

Spaz opened the door, shoving Darla out into the hallway and into Carson Boyd, who stood on the other side.

Darla scurried away down the narrow hall. Spaz called out, "Bring the extra ten next time you come. Dumbass dopehead!"

The small, damaged prostitute disappeared down the stairs at the end of the hall, leaving Boyd alone with Spaz.

"Hey bro. What's good?" Boyd said.

"Carson. Ain't seen you 'round in a minute." Spaz eyed him carefully.

"Trying to fly right," Boyd replied, looking down and shuffling his feet in his busted sneakers.

"Guess it didn't take," Spaz mocked. He stepped back, allowing Boyd to enter.

Boyd stepped inside the small, poorly furnished apartment. "Hey Jinx," he said, retrieving his money from his pocket.

"Carson." Jinx shot a quick glance over from the couch.

Boyd had a set of keys in his other hand with a small key fob attached at the base of the keyring. He manipulated the fob so the butt of it stuck out toward the group on the couch.

"What do you need?" Spaz asked.

"Two buns," Boyd said.

"Eighty," Spaz answered.

Boyd held out the money in his hand without counting it. He already knew the price, and Sorenson had provided the four twenties.

"That's what I like to see. Somebody that pays the price and comes correct with the money ready to go," Spaz called out to anyone listening.

Spaz began digging into his pocket for the product.

"Carson's a good customer. Grab him some of the new stuff we got," Jinx said from the couch.

Merc got up from the couch, disappearing into the kitchen area and returning a moment later with two bundles in his hand. He walked over to the two at the door.

"What is the good stuff?" Boyd asked with genuine curiosity.

"H with a little bit of that Murder Eight. We call it White Lightning. Everybody's loving it," Merc said, his breath smelling of hot fries and beer.

Boyd knew the slang and understood he was getting heroin mixed with fentanyl. "Sounds good."

Merc handed Boyd the two bundles. Boyd looked at the powder visible through the packaging. This was whiter and cleaner looking than the typical cocoa powder brown he was accustomed to with normal heroin. He'd never tried the mixture before and was intrigued.

"Thanks." Boyd pocketed the drugs and turned for the door.

Merc returned to the couch and Spaz closed the door as Boyd disappeared down the hall.

Boyd exited the front door out onto the street. It was cooling down quickly as the daylight faded, the late fall giving way to shorter days.

Boyd walked for a few blocks before cutting down an alleyway. Behind a small dumpster he took out the key fob and turned off the recording. Boyd then retrieved the product from his other pocket. He removed one of the folded bags from the bundle and looked again at the contents.

He continued his dogleg pattern of movement until he reached the waiting car, parked outside of the Jinx's territory. It was a small Honda Accord with heavy tints. In the waning light he couldn't see anybody inside, but he knew Sorenson was there.

Scanning the area to ensure nobody was around, Boyd approached the car. The door latch clicked and he slipped inside. The car pulled away as Boyd closed the door.

"How'd it go?" Sorenson asked.

"Easy. He gave me something else. Said it was new," Boyd said.

"Who did the hand off?"

"Merc."

"You're telling me Merc put it in your hand?" Sorenson asked.

"Yup. Called it White Lightning. Heroin cut with fentanyl."

Sorenson grabbed a plastic evidence bag from the center console as he drove. He manipulated the bag open with his right hand while he maintained the wheel with his left. He waved it toward Boyd who understood the gesture, a routine the two had done numerous times in the past.

Boyd dug into his pocket and retrieved the two banded bundles of drugs. He dropped them in and Sorenson returned the evidence bag to the center console.

"Sign the form and you're good to go." Sorenson reached into the backseat and grabbed the confidential buy form required after the completion of any police-controlled informant buys.

Boyd sighed. He hated putting his name on the page but knew it was part of the process. He'd done buys for Sorenson ever since the two met during an arrest. The first time they met, Boyd was picked up by a patrol officer. He had a few bags of heroin on him and a stolen iPhone. Sorenson visited him in the holding area and offered to help him in getting his charges dropped if he assisted in putting a case against his dealer. After Boyd had worked off his case, Sorenson offered him money to assist in other cases. He received sixty dollars and a pack of cigarettes for every buy he did for Boston PD's narcotic unit.

Today's buy wasn't about the money. Although Boyd planned to take it. Today he was repaying a personal debt to the man driving the car. It was Sorenson who'd gotten him into treatment after his latest overdose. He told him it was part of some new citywide program. His newfound recovery was, in large part, due to him.

Sorenson handed Boyd six twenty-dollar bills after both men had initialed the sheet, documenting the buy and the payment for services. Boyd took the money. He didn't want to. He'd planned to tell Sorenson he did it for the debt owed, but seeing the money, he lost the will to refuse it.

"Got the fob?" Sorenson asked.

Boyd took the black key fob out of his pocket and placed it in Sorenson's hand.

Sorenson examined it. "It's off."

"I must have clicked it off when I put it back in my pocket," Boyd said, nervously.

The fob looked real. It had the Dodge symbol on the back and door lock buttons on the front, but the black plastic casing held a small audio and video recording device. When the door unlock button and the car alarm button were depressed simultaneously, the camera system would activate. To stop it, the buttons were pressed again. The only indication the recorder had been activated was a small blue light that could be seen through a slit in the side of the device. Boyd had been trained to hold the fob in his hand, covering the light and aiming the butt end of the fob toward the intended targets. According to Sorenson, he'd been able to secure excellent video over the years. And he never returned to the car with the camera off. He felt uneasy in Sorenson's questioning eyes.

"You're sure you got it?" Sorenson asked.

"I'm sure."

"Did he say anything I need to know?"

"Normal banter, but he did say this was good stuff. Called it White Lightning. It's got a little fentanyl mixed in."

"You sure those are the words he used? White Lightning?"

"Yup. Why?"

"This might be better than I thought."

"So, I did good?"

"Absolutely. I really appreciate the assist on this one Carson. Like I said before, this case is an important one."

"Sure thing. I appreciate you helping me get back in the program," Boyd said.

"Hopefully, this time it takes. I'd like to see Carson Boyd back in the classroom again someday."

Boyd nodded and then pointed out of the dark tinted window. "Up here's good."

The car pulled to stop, parallel parking curbside behind a much larger SUV. Boyd did one more check of his surroundings before exiting into the cool evening air.

"This was my last time," Boyd said.

"Sure thing."

Boyd closed the door and hustled away as Sorenson's unmarked disappeared into the light traffic.

Boyd walked along the sidewalk. His hands were shoved deep into his pockets and he felt the chill of the coming winter penetrate his clothes as a gust of wind whipped him. His fingers fiddled with the thin waxy paper in his pocket, toying with the one bag he'd skimmed from the two bundles. Never before had he pulled a bag from a buy. His heart beat faster.

He wanted to rip the drug from his pocket and toss it down the nearest sewer drain. He wanted to do that very badly, but another want trumped his willpower, the need to have one more taste before he committed to a life of sobriety. His willpower, compared to the pull of the drug's call, was beyond his ability to resist. He gave in to his weakness, bowing to the strength of the barely measurable weight of the powder contained therein.

Boyd stopped into a corner store and grabbed a bottle of water, using some of the money he'd earned. Leaving the store, he turned down an alley. He'd rid himself of his portable needle kit after his last overdose but knew where to look. It wasn't long before he found a smattering of used needles discarded alongside a trash bin. He sifted through, looking for an unbent one with minimal dirt. Finding the best in the batch, he picked it up and wiped the metal end against his shirt, as if rubbing the exterior of a used needle would somehow reduce his risk of exposure to the myriad of diseases that possibly coated it.

He moved along, making his way to a bench near a small public garden. Boyd loved how in the middle of the city there were small plots of land devoted to these breaks in the brick and mortar of the surrounding buildings. He was alone.

Boyd opened the bottle and took a long swig. He removed the bag of dope from his pocket and put his lighter on top of it to keep the lightweight bag from blowing away. Boyd set aside the water bottle on the bench, leaving it uncapped. He then placed the water bottle's thick plastic cap on his thigh. When he'd first begin using, Boyd carried a bent metal spoon used for cooking the heroin. Over the years he evolved his process at the recommendation of a fellow junkie. The caps of a standard water bottle were thick enough to withstand the lighter's heat without burning. Plus, carrying a water bottle was much less obvious than walking around with a spoon in your pocket.

Unfolding the waxy paper bag, pinching it at the center, Boyd tore it in half, exposing the trace amount of powder resting at the bottom. Most dealers in the area mixed the heroin with cocoa powder, giving it a brownish tinge. Sometimes Boyd could taste chocolate in the first few seconds after an injection.

The powder at the base of this bag was different. It was much whiter than he'd seen before and looked more like cocaine than heroin. He pressed at the edges near the portion of the glassine bag containing the powder. Tapping gently against the bottom corner, Boyd released the contents into the cap. He completed the ritual by adding a small amount of water to the powder.

Boyd looked at the off-white slurry contained in the cap. His heartbeat increased and he knew by looking at it there was no turning back. He picked up the lighter. First, he lit the needle's end, trying his best to sterilize it. Boyd then held up the cap at eye level. He held the lighter in the other hand and began passing the flame gently underneath. The fire licked at the white plastic coating and the water bubbled, condensing as it began to evaporate. Satisfied with his prep work, Boyd set the lighter down beside him and rested the cap back on his thigh.

He picked up the needle and dipped the tip into the concoction. Drawing back the plunger, he filled it with the warm fluid. He gave a quick look around. Still alone, he proceeded.

Boyd had few veins left that he could access, but found a slight bulge suitable for injection on back of his hand. He opened and closed his hand in rapid succession, forcing blood into the region and giving a rise to the target vein. He exhaled as he pushed the needle in, quickly releasing its contents into his blood stream. He sat back as the familiar warmth washed over him. He let go of the needle, dropping it to the ground.

His eyes drooped and his body slumped as the drug took hold. He'd made fun of a friend after shooting up, saying he looked like a melting snowman. That's exactly how Boyd felt now as the heat pulsing through his veins countered the cold of the air surrounding him.

Then he felt something strange. A pain shot out from his chest, his heartbeat deafening in his ear, rapidly pounding like a drum. Squirming awkwardly, he tried to get up from the bench. His body didn't respond to his mind's command and he flailed about, slipping off the black metallic seat and onto the cold ground. The pain worsened as his body convulsed. The chaos fell to a silent stillness.

Carson Boyd lay contorted between the bench and a garden plot. Lifeless and alone, he lay dead next to the needle, the one constant of his last remaining years.

9

It was early, but the Tactical Narcotics Team's office space was a blur of movement. Sorenson exited his office with a large Styrofoam cup of Dunkin' Donuts coffee in hand. He surveyed his team as he took a sip.

"Let's bring it into the briefing room," Sorenson called out.

The members began migrating toward the room in the far corner where a headless teddy bear was nailed above the door's frame.

It was ideal for up to twenty people, with ten two-person tables. An aisle down the middle divided the tables evenly in two columns of five. An overhead projector was mounted to the ceiling with a retractable screen near the front. A dry erase board was covered with briefing notes and hand drawn layouts, diagraming the operation. Today's briefing would be standing-room-only because some extra brass had requested to be in attendance, as well as several supporting units from patrol tasked with assisting in the raid.

Sorenson sat on the corner of a table at the front of the room. He was in a thick gray shirt and olive drab tactical pants. He waited until his team was seated and the additional guests had found a place, lining the walls.

"Good morning," Sorenson said. "Thank you all for coming. I'll be passing out an intel sheet with today's target and the intended takedown location."

A rumble of murmured responses trickled back from the group. Sorenson grabbed a stack of paper and prepared to deliver his operational plan when he noticed Superintendent Polis enter the room. A man who graced them with his presence on the rarest occasions, Sorenson only had one interaction with Polis in recent years, that being his promotional ceremony to Sergeant. Polis was accompanied by two men Sorenson had never seen before. The larger of the two had long, unkempt hair. Both looked like hard men. He assumed they were from some sort of task force, federal or state.

The superintendent pressed himself to the back wall with the other two men aligning themselves together, standing shoulder to shoulder. Polis nodded at Sorenson.

"Looks like we have everybody here. Let's get into it. Take a look at the flyer with this morning's target," Sorenson said, his thick South Boston accent shining through in his delivery. He handed off the papers to Smith who was seated front and center. The stack snaked around the room with each person taking a copy as it passed by. A few nodded at the picture on the flyer, obviously recognizing the player they were going after.

"This morning we're hitting the OP Hoodstars. We did a controlled buy last evening. With the help of a very tired and annoyed judge, we were able to secure an arrest warrant for a Terry Powell, probably more commonly known to you guys as Merc. He's the Orchard Park crew's enforcer. He beat a murder rap a year ago and has a tendency toward violence. And mark my word—this guy's dangerous. He won't go easily. So, we're going to try to minimize the threat and take him away from their base of operations. When we hit him, it'll be hard and fast."

Sorenson took a momentary break, sipping from his coffee. He liked to drink it while it was still hot enough to burn the back of his throat. "We're ripping him on a car stop. We've got a two-man surveillance unit up on the house as we speak. It's early but we got intel that Merc will be making a drop this morning. I want to hit him before that happens."

Sorenson turned to the board, pointing to the crudely drawn take-down plan. "This is what we've got. He drives a green Honda Accord. Right now, it's parked on the street where it's been since our eyes have been on it. TNT is going to do the brunt of the takedown work, but we need some things in place if we can't contain him."

"I want marked patrol units at these two corners." Sorenson directed the group's attention to the board behind him. "Excuse my cartooning skills, but the guys in my team are used to reading my gibberish. When we go live, I want you to shut down the street." Sorenson looked at the uniformed personnel seated behind his team. They nodded their understanding.

"We're hitting him before he has a chance to get moving. The timing on this thing is critical. Powell is known to carry a gun. So, we want to eliminate his ability to use it. TNT will approach from the rear. We're going to box him in prior to initiating the assault. After impact it's going to get loud. Flashbangs will be deployed to the undercarriage of his car followed by a quick break and rake of driver and passenger side windows. As soon as he's in custody I want patrol to collapse the roadblock and rally at the takedown location. I want to be off-scene quickly. The goal is to snatch him and get him back to the station before too many eyes relay what happened. We need to get the intel on their crew's distribution source." Sorenson paused to scan the group for questions.

"The rumor is they're connected to a large-scale fentanyl distribution ring. If you haven't heard, yesterday's death of the senator's daughter has brought this issue to the forefront. Based on what we've learned up to this point from my sources, this is the crew responsible for selling the bag of dope that killed Amber Litchfield. We're implementing the new initiative, targeting the dealers responsible for an overdose death. Boston PD is taking the lead on this. We're going to be the tip of the spear on a program gaining some national exposure. So, be at your absolute best today."

Sorenson sipped from his coffee and then eyed the room. "It goes without saying. This is a Priority One Target. Get geared up. We're moving out in a few minutes."

The room went from quiet to full volume in a split second. Chairs squeaked and scattered conversations started up as the group disbanded. Sorenson saw that Superintendent Polis and his two guests remained behind, lingering in the back.

Smith noticed and whispered, "Looks like you've caught the upper echelon's attention. I'm sure he's going to ask why you didn't use PowerPoint for your presentation. Those guys love that computer crap."

Sorenson approached the superintendent as Smith and the last few members of the briefing departed.

"Superintendent Polis, glad you could make it." Sorenson extended his hand.

"No PowerPoint?" Polis asked, raising his bushy eyebrows.

"I'm all thumbs when it comes to computers, sir."

"Better learn fast. I heard you're next up on the lieutenant's list."

Sorenson smiled, unable to contain his excitement at the prospect. He knew the success of his operation would be the feather in his cap securing his next rank.

"Let me introduce these two gentlemen." Polis turned his attention to the men beside him. "These are Agents Enright and Samuels from the FBI's Drug Task Force."

"I know most of the guys in the Boston office. Are you guys new?" Sorenson asked.

"They're tasked from D.C." Polis answered for them.

"Good briefing," Nick said, extending his hand.

"Thanks."

"I like the plan. Seems like your team has a real handle on this sort of thing," Declan added.

Sorenson nodded slowly. "We do. My team's been doing this for a while now and we're pretty damned good if I don't mind saying so myself. Why do I get the feeling I'm about to get railroaded?"

"Danny, these guys are going to be taking things over from this point forward," Polis said. "They're here on orders trumping any local jurisdiction. I'm sorry, I know your team was looking forward to this opportunity."

Sorenson didn't know the superintendent even knew his first name and was momentarily caught off guard. But the words that followed nearly caused him to vomit, and he fought back from speaking his mind.

"Are you kidding me? We've just been tasked with our first Priority One target, and you're telling me to stand down?" Sorenson almost spat the words.

"Like I said, we like your plan. You're running the takedown. We're going to hang back on that. Consider us an extra set of eyes," Nick said.

"Well thanks for letting me run my op," Sorenson snarked.

"Look, we've all been there before. We don't like putting you in this position, but we've got our marching orders," Nick said, without any trace of sarcasm.

"I guess I don't have a say in this?" Sorenson said, looking at Polis.

Polis shook his head. "Sorry kid, this one comes in from way above my pay grade."

Sorenson sighed and threw his hands up.

"I think you'll find we're pretty good guys to have around," Declan said with a cocky smile.

"We'll see about that."

Sorenson stormed out of the briefing room to prepare for the mission.

10

"Take Honey with you," Jinx ordered.

Merc turned with the backpack already shouldered. "Why, brah? I'm straight with 'dis."

"You know it always looks better to have a female in the car with you. You look less gangsta," Jinx shot back.

"Whatever. She don't look like no school teacher. Cops can spot the jects on her as easy as they can me," Merc said. Leaning into the kitchen, he said, "Get it together, girl. We rollin'."

A short time later Merc and Gloria Willis, affectionately known in the group as Honey, but better known as Jinx's property, set off. They made their way outside and paused on the stoop as they always did. Creatures of habit, the two slowly eyed the block for cops or enemies before stepping off.

"I hate these early runs," Honey whined. "Why can't these dopeheads hit us up after lunch?"

Merc shrugged his indifference. "You know how we do. These junkies need that early morning fix. Got to hit 'em when they wake. If we're not there to serve 'em, someone else will. Like that freaky dude Gollum, they need their Precious. And we got it. All day, every day."

It was a truth. While coke and weed dealers typically work late hours, heroin users would be up early, dope sick, and looking to score. Heroin dealers needed to make those early rounds. Plus, cops were less likely to take interest during the first few hours of the morning. The dayshift patrol guys were typically older and less aggressive. Easier to move about when the law was looking for his breakfast rather than a drug bust.

Jinx sold the other drugs like coke and weed. Runners, like Spaz, were sent to handle the late-night deals. But Merc, always an early riser, got tasked with the morning dope runs.

Ever since he was little, he woke up early. He knew the reason and never told anybody but Jinx. When he was young his grandmother died, and he ended up in a group home because nobody wanted to adopt him. Any foster care was short-lived. To put it bluntly, Merc had violent tendencies and he took it out on those around him. At the group home he learned a valuable lesson—the early bird gets the worm. If he didn't wake up before the bigger kids, he wouldn't get to eat. After several missed meal opportunities, he'd never been able to sleep past six again. And therefore, by default, he'd become the morning distributor of the Hoodstars dope.

He hated when anybody came with him. Merc liked those moments when he was alone with himself and he didn't have to be the wild-eyed badass Merc. He was just Terry Powell. Sometimes he would take the long way and drive by the house where he'd lived with his grandmother before she passed. He couldn't do any of that with Honey in the car. She'd see it as weakness, and he'd never hear the end of it.

Merc didn't see anything out of the ordinary on this particular gloomy Monday. "Let's get going. Looks like it's going to rain, or maybe snow. Either way, I hate driving in that crap."

"You want me to drive?" Honey asked.

"I don't know how many times I've got to tell you. Nobody is driving my car. And that goes double for you."

"One crash and nobody wants me to drive."

"You crashed into a dang police cruiser!"

"Big deal." Honey rolled her eyes.

The two walked in tandem to the green Accord parked along the curb in front of the building. They entered and Merc tossed the backpack onto the backseat. The dope inside was packaged in bundles and contained five stacks worth of the fentanyl-laced heroin, totaling five hundred individual bags. He'd sell out within the hour, but didn't like taking more than that on any one outing.

"You're just going to leave it in the backpack?" Honey questioned.

"Why? You worried somebody's going to rob me?" Merc said, pulling up his shirt and exposing the black butt of his handgun tucked in the front of his waistband.

"No. But what if we get stopped by the cops? Jinx always said it's better to put it in the trap."

"Yeah, well Jinx ain't out here slinging this crap, is he? And besides, it's a pain in the ass to trigger the open and close mechanism with those dumb magnets every time I want to grab a bundle," Merc snapped. The car contained a trap built into the airbag compartment. By placing a magnet on each side of the center console's cup holder and pressing the radio power simultaneously with the A/C on button, the switch would activate, and the airbag compartment would open. It was slow and Merc rarely used it, except when he was distributing out of state.

"But feel free to get out of the car. I don't need you anyway."

"Whatever." Honey folded her arms in quiet protest.

"Whatever is right."

"Well, let's get this over with," Honey said.

Merc slid the key into the ignition and put his seatbelt on.

Nick and Declan sat in their rental car. They were parked on an adjacent street running perpendicular to the target vehicle's location. They stared at the rear bumper of one of the two vehicles loaded with members of Boston PD's Tactical Narcotics Team.

Declan was at the wheel. Nick looked down at his forged FBI credentials, Nicholas Samuels, stenciled under the clean-cut photo image of Nick. Wiz had managed to access the Bureau's database and retrieve his old ID photo. Nick laughed and stuffed it back into his wallet.

"What's so funny?" Declan asked.

"Just looking at my fake ID. How far I've fallen. Now I just get to play pretend G-Man," Nick muttered.

"At least you're not rotting away in that jail cell anymore."

"True," Nick said, thinking back to his long year of confinement. "How do you think our little Mouse will do in our ragtag group of misfits?"

"She's incredible. I think she'll be an asset."

Nick let out a tense sigh.

"What? You don't think so?" Declan asked.

"It's not that. I guess I now feel responsible for her. If something were to happen, I'd blame myself."

"She's a big girl now. Hell, that kid's been through a lot. She's seen things that would make combat veterans like us cringe. And amazingly, she's come out stronger. Her ability to overcome obstacles is second to none, and I think this will be no different. Plus, Barbie's taken a liking to her and is already working on getting her up to speed." Declan's smile reassured Nick as much as his words did.

"How's it feel to be back in the wild world of narcotics?" Nick asked.

"You know how my last narc job ended. Cost me my career and brought me to an all-time low." Declan paused and gave Nick a serious look. "I'd be lying if I said it didn't give me a bit of stress. But this is important. If we can dismantle this ring, then we can save a lot of lives. That fentanyl stuff is bad news. It was just starting to make its way into the city where I was working but hadn't gotten much traction."

"I guess a lot's changed in the past few years."

"It certainly has."

The radio, a loaner for the Boston PD given to them by Sorenson and dialed into the tactical channel, crackled.

"We've got eyes on the target. Just exited the front of the building. He's got a backpack and is with a female," the voice said.

"Roger that. Let me know when he's in the car," a voice, most likely Sorenson's, replied.

Nick readied himself. Although they'd told Sorenson they were going to be observing the operation, he knew the importance of this target's potential and needed to ensure he didn't get away.

A brief moment passed before the radio came to life again. "He's moving toward the car. At the door. Entering. Door shut. Target is the driver. Female is the passenger."

"The op is a go! Moving!" Sorenson said.

Both of the vehicles in front of Nick and Declan released the brakes. The two vehicles stayed tight to one another and moved down the city street at high speeds, barely braking as they made a hard left onto the target's street. Declan pulled out but stayed back, giving Sorenson's group room to operate.

They closed the distance on the green Honda as the vehicle nosed out from its parking space onto the one-way street. The vehicle slowly pulled out as the first TNT vehicle drove alongside, darting in front and then cutting the wheel hard to the right. The front bumper of Merc's vehicle hit the passenger side of the unmarked cruiser. At the same time, the second team slammed into the backend, effectively pinning the car.

Members in the lead TNT vehicle climbed out quickly through the driver's side of the vehicle. They took position, stacking along the hood and trunk, pointing their weapons at occupants of the target vehicle. Nick noted the muzzle discipline among the team and was impressed.

Tires squealed as Merc floored the accelerator. Smoke from the burning rubber spilled out from beneath the back tires.

The team in the rear emptied out of the car. A flashbang clanged followed by a loud explosion. A brilliant flash erupted from underneath the front axle of the vehicle, accompanying the noise. The concussive effect shook neighboring parked cars, activating several alarms. A split second after the blast, two members of Sorenson's team approached the vehicle, one on each side. They carried cold-steel baseball bats and swung hard as they moved alongside, shattering both rear windows. Other members of the team aimed their guns at the occupants of the green Honda.

One voice could be heard above all others. Sorenson commanded, "Hands! Show 'em! Don't reach!"

Nick could hear the man's voice from down the street and was thoroughly impressed with the execution and precision of the assault.

"Don't do it Powell!" Sorenson commanded.

Nick saw the head of Terry Powell, aka Merc, dip. *This is bad*, he thought.

Nick and Declan watched as Sorenson sprung forward in a blur of movement. He holstered his weapon into his thigh rig and shot his arms inside the vehicle. Sorenson gripped Merc by the arm and neck, slamming the drug dealer forward.

Keeping him pressed into the steering wheel, Sorenson hollered to his team, "He's going for his waistline!"

A large member of the team ripped open the back door and disappeared inside. A scream poured out from the Accord.

A moment later Merc was extricated by Sorenson through the window. The drug dealer's arm flopped loosely by his side.

"You broke my damn arm!" Merc yelled.

"At least you're not dead," Sorenson snapped.

The TNT member who'd leapt into the backseat exited with a small black gun in his hand.

Sorenson slammed Merc to the ground as he bucked back, kicking and spitting. Two additional members assisted in cuffing the man. Merc wailed loudly as his injured arm was brought to the small of his back. Honey was pulled out and cuffed as well, although her lack of resistance made the process easier.

Declan pulled the car closer and stopped approximately ten feet away. Nick and Declan exited and walked over to Sorenson.

"I guess I didn't need you guys after all," Sorenson said sarcastically.

"Apparently not," Nick replied.

"But we need them." Declan gestured with his chin toward the arrestees.

"No chance. We're bringing them to the station. They've got to be booked and processed before they're going anywhere with you guys. We've got a warrant and it's got to get logged."

"I think you might want to check that," Nick said.

Declan sighed, "Look, we don't want to do this any more than you. But we've got specific orders and they come from a place that guys like you and me can't question. Let's not make this a pissing contest."

Sorenson didn't speak. He looked around at the other members of his team who were now gathering around their leader. Nick surveyed the burly group and knew, without question, they'd attack on command. Neither Nick nor Declan backed down.

"We're all on the same team here, guys," Nick said.

"Not so sure about that, but I guess I don't have much of a say," Sorenson said.

He nodded to the TNT operators guarding Merc and Honey. Without any words, the man in the black balaclava moved the two toward Nick.

Nick took Merc by the elbow and guided him to their rental car. Honey remained with Declan until Nick was finished securing Merc in the backseat. He ratcheted the seatbelt, restricting the thug's movement. Honey got seated on the other side and restrained in a similar fashion. With them situated in the car, Nick walked back over to where Declan was standing.

"Listen guys, whatever we get from these guys that we're authorized to share, we will," Nick said.

"I'll believe it when I see it." Sorenson turned his attention back to his team as they set about recovering evidence and cleaning up the scene.

Nick and Declan returned to their vehicle, now plus two occupants.

They drove away, leaving the Orchard Park Hoodstars' territory in the background.

"Where the hell are you guys taking us?" Merc asked.

Nick looked at his watch. Wiz said it would take effect within five minutes. Neither of the backseat occupants had noticed when Nick stuck the small circular Band-Aid to the inside of their elbows when he escorted them to the vehicle. The drug was transdermal and would be absorbed through their pores. Based on the stress they'd just endured, their pores would be open, and their elevated heart rates would circulate the drug. Once in the bloodstream, they would be unconscious for approximately two hours.

Nick didn't answer and just looked back at the two. The female prisoner was slumped against the window. Merc was large and therefore the chemicals took a little longer to take hold. His eyelids dropped and then would pop wide, like a trucker fighting to finish the last mile of an eighteen-hour haul. Then the man's eyes closed completely, and he slumped forward with the cross strap of the seatbelt restraining him. The fight against the drug-induced sleep was over.

Nick turned to the front. "They're out."

"Good. I didn't want to listen to that guy whine all the way to the Vault," Declan said.

Nick took out his encrypted cell phone and tapped quickly at the letters. "I just let Jay know we're inbound with our new friends,"

"This is shaping up to be an eventful day," Declan said with a chuckle.

Nick prepared himself for the task ahead. With two prisoners, it was likely he'd be doing one of the interrogations. He knew that Wiz would have a full intel packet worked up on the two by the time they arrived. Nick needed to make a quick study of his suspect so that he could leverage personal traits and life history during the rapport phase and twist it to his advantage.

Nick smiled to himself. Not only did he get to play at being an FBI agent for this mission, he also got to do the thing he did best, interview and interrogation. During his previous investigative life, he'd always affectionately called the interview room the box. Now these info- gathering sessions would take place in the Cube.

He glanced in the rearview mirror, catching a glimpse of the sleeping man in the backseat. *He's got no idea what's in store for him today*, Nick thought as Declan drove them away from the city toward their Vault location.

11

Nick waited patiently outside. He was still in a state of utter fascination with the Cube's design. During his time in the Bureau, he prided himself on his high percentage of interrogation to confession. His ability to extract information from tight-lipped criminals earned him a reputation among his peers as being a human lie detector. Even with those skills, he knew some of the details slipped through the cracks. As he'd learned through countless hours investigating the criminal mind, the devil lived inside of those details. If the Cube had existed in his world as an FBI agent, there'd be no telling how many more cases he would have closed. The Montrose Case would have had a different outcome and his life wouldn't have taken the tragic turn that it did. He would still be an investigator and, more importantly, he would still have Anaya. Their child would still be alive.

Nick spent the better part of his year moving past the karmic twist that destroyed the very fabric of his being. His time inside Masterson Federal Correctional gave Nick the opportunity to mentally wipe most of his past, locking his pain away in the deep recesses of his mind. So many of his repressed emotions and memories trickled back since he'd brought Mouse back into his life. The girl was a constant reminder—as was Declan—of a life he no longer had.

The room was dark. Looking through one-way glass, he couldn't see the man he and Declan had secured in the chair an hour earlier. He studied the digital tablet in his hand. A colorful display appeared on the screen, showing Terry Powell's vitals. The chair he was seated on registered the most minute movement, and from the looks of it, the prisoner was flailing about. With all of the movement—and likely screaming—being done by the man inside, not a single sound emanated from the Cube. The only way to hear anything going on inside would be to listen through the microphone recording the event. Nick had already listened to a snippet a few minutes prior and determined that the man inside had a unique ability to string together expletives in such a way that would make a sailor blush.

"Nick, are you comfortable with the tablet? Or did you need me to run through it again?" Spider asked.

"I think I've got it. I'm still not sure how much I plan to use all the bells and whistles this thing has." Nick shrugged.

"Do what you're comfortable with, but those little extras can make the difference when time is an issue." Spider spoke in his measured, controlled voice.

Nick was always impressed with the man's steady, almost stoic, nature. He'd yet to see a flash of anger or frustration in Spider's façade. He knew very little about his past life. Of all the members of the group, Spider remained the most distant. The one thing he did know was Spider could rip information out of the most resistant of suspects.

Interview and Interrogation was old hat to Nick, and he found himself fighting the use of the Cube's capabilities. He felt it was like cheating the process. Normally, Nick would spend an hour or two with a suspect just building rapport. Criminals always entered the interrogation room, or box as it was commonly referred to, with their guard up. The first part of any well-planned interrogation was to knock down those barriers. Nick excelled at rapport building, but not just because he could talk to people. That was part of it, but his real talent was in listening and observing. As criminals softened, he would pay close attention to details in their personal story. Some of those details were called hooks, things the person cared deeply about, and Nick would use them as emotional leverage whenever a barrier went up. The other thing Nick would listen and watch for was triggers, topics to avoid. These areas of a person's life, different for everyone, could derail an interrogation if the interviewer wasn't aware. Hooks and triggers were the bricks in the foundation of an effective interrogation.

Nick now interviewed with the Cube's gadgetry at his disposal. He was getting more comfortable in deploying it against his adversaries, but was hoping he could bypass it on today's interrogation and get back to the basics. Time constraints were the biggest hindrance to his model of interviewing.

"We're going to need you to work efficiently on this one. Boston PD isn't going to be happy if we keep their arrestees too long. I'd like to have these two back in their custody in a couple of hours," Jay reminded, stepping out from his office.

So much for getting back to the basics, Nick thought, nodding as he looked around. "Hey, where's Mouse?"

"Barbie took her shopping," Jay said.

"It's not like she came here with much. They called it girl bonding time," Wiz chimed in. "I never thought a mall trip would be part of this unit's op tempo but things are always changing around here."

Nick smiled at the thought of Mouse and Barbie wandering around a mall together. The age difference would make them look like mother and daughter. Although the fair-skinned, blonde Barbie, compared to dark-haired, tan complexioned Mouse would make it more plausible the teenager was a step-daughter. Regardless, it was a nice thought. Nick never thought bringing Mouse here would give her some semblance of normalcy and was grateful for it.

He refocused on the task at hand, tapping the screen and activating the Cube's interior lights. The interior of the room came into view. The brightness contrasted to the darkness of moments prior and Terry Powell flinched, his body contorting as he tried to adjust himself to the introduction of light.

The keypad on the outside of the Cube gave Nick access, and the thickly lined door rolled aside. Nick stepped into the room. Between his height and his broad shoulders, he filled much of the entryway's space. It must've been intimidating to the man shackled to the seat in front of him. Nick pressed a button on the interior wall. A mechanical click and hiss were heard as the door's automated closing mechanism activated. The door shut behind him, and Nick stepped forward to the man seated in the center of the room.

As was standard in the layout of the Cube, an oversized chair housed the subject of interrogation. The chair used thick restraints, similar to those used on a medical gurney, securing the prisoner at five points. The straps locked the person to the chair at the shins, the forearms, and one larger band across the chest.

Powell was hooked up to a wireless heartrate monitor and several leads were affixed to his chest, sending a constant biorhythmic feed to Nick's tablet. The seat cushion was constructed with multiple sensors capable of reading the slightest of movement. The band secured around Powell's head measured perspiration levels. The circular leads affixed to the man's temples were for the introduction of electro-shock compliance. Nick had never used them before and didn't relish the idea of having to. It felt like a throwback to the dark times of psychiatric medicine.

"What the hell is this place?" Powell yelled.

"We're with the FBI, and this place is an interview room," Nick said coolly.

"Ain't like no interview room I ever been in before." He looked around and then down at the straps and wires on his body.

"Have you been interviewed by the FBI before?"

"No."

"Well then, there you have it. Of course, things might look a little different. That's because we do things a bit differently around here." Nick wanted to maintain the illusion as long as he could. It would be better if Powell never wised up to his situation.

"What do you mean?"

Nick could see a hint of fear in the young man's eyes. The tablet confirmed his observation as Powell's heart rate began to rise.

"Let me explain some things to you. I think it's important you understand. You're in a world of trouble, the likes of which you've probably never experienced. I've done my research on you and know you've been through some tough experiences. That being said, should you decide not to cooperate, today will most likely top the charts."

Merc said nothing.

Nick tapped the tablet and slid it across the polished metal of the table. The monitor, showing Merc's vitals, filled the screen. Powell looked down at the glowing computerized image.

"You see all these numbers?" Nick asked.

Powell nodded, but said nothing.

"Those leads attached to you are capable of telling me what's going on in your body," Nick said, turning the tablet so the imprisoned man could see. "The chair tells me every movement you make, no matter how slight."

"So! What the hell does all that matter for, anyway? You can tell I'm angry? Good for you. I could tell you that myself!" Powell punctuated his rant by spitting on the floor.

"I'm telling you this because I want you to understand how important it is to tell the truth. The consequences for not being honest will be bad for you."

"It don't matter. I'm not telling you nuthin. You trying to intimidate me? You don't know me! You got no idea who you're dealing with, brah."

Nick tapped the room control panel on the tablet and the room lights went out. Nick turned off the tablet's display and the last remnants of light faded completely.

"Then you can wait in the dark."

Merc yelled, laying out another impressive barrage of rapid-fire curse words. Nick said nothing and made no sound. He waited.

Nick had read the summation of Terry Powell, aka Merc, compiled by Wiz and saw something he could exploit with the Cube's technology. Nyctophobia, fear of the dark, diagnosed by one of Powell's child psychologists. A real and palpable fear, not properly treated, left the man with a crippling reaction to darkness.

Powell's grandmother had raised him from birth. She was the only person in his life who cared for him as a child. Powell was six years old when she died. She'd been killed in the middle of the night during a home invasion robbery. Powell was also stabbed and left for dead. He survived the attack and was left with a visible scar across his abdomen. But the deepest damage of that night was invisible to the naked eye and lay beneath surface of this hardened criminal's tough exterior.

After his recovery, he was thrown into the system and bounced between group homes and foster care. But that night, at age six, had permanently scarred his psyche. Darkness was the man's kryptonite, and Nick used the knowledge to his advantage now.

The swearing slowed to a stop and was replaced by ragged breathing. Nick didn't need the tablet to tell him that the darkness had won. He could hear it in the whimpering a few feet away, invisible in the deep pitch of the room.

"Please," Merc mumbled softly.

Nick tapped the screen and the room once more became brightly lit. Nick closed his eyes prior to the introduction of light. As he opened them, Powell was head down and breathing deeply.

"I know you don't like the dark. But more important, I know why," Nick said.

Merc looked up. "What the hell is wrong with you?"

Nick read the anger in the man's face. "You need to understand. This conversation between us is going to happen. Whether that's now or twelve hours from now. One way or another we're going to find out what we need to know."

"I want my lawyer." Merc sat up straight.

Nick said nothing but gave a fraction of a smile.

"You deaf? I said I want my lawyer? You know you've got to stop this as soon as I say that! End of show! I say that to you, and you grab that tablet and walk the hell out of here! So, get to steppin."

"Do I? You're not understanding the position you're in. You are in no place to be making demands. The sooner you get that into your head the better off you'll be."

"Get me my lawyer! Now!"

"It doesn't work that way here. No lawyers. No phone calls. Nothing. Just you and me."

"What the—," Merc muttered.

"You are here until I'm confident I have what I need. The quicker you understand that, the better off you'll be." Nick stood up from his chair, tucking the tablet under his arm.

"Where are you going? You better be getting' my lawyer. And don't walk back in here without him. You hear?"

"I've got other things to do, Mr. Powell. I'll leave and give you some time to think about it." Nick paused for effect. "In the dark."

Nick walked purposefully toward the only door in the room. He began to press the interior keypad.

"Wait," Merc said through gritted teeth.

"For what?"

"Let's figure this thing out."

"Thank you for understanding."

Nick returned to his seat.

The room only contained three pieces of furniture: a flat metallic table, and the two chairs. Nick sat catty-corner to his prisoner and pulled his seat close enough that his left knee nearly touched Powell's. In a normal interview, Nick would spend time building rapport and establishing a psychological connection or bond between him and the subject. But with time a pressing factor and the Cube's technological enhancements at his disposal, it allowed him to bypass the traditional model and pursue a more direct route to answers.

"Let's get down to the business end of what's happening while you've been sitting in this room. The life you've known is over. Your crew is being dismantled. Everybody you worked with is being picked off one by one. You won't be alone where you're going."

"It's just dope, man. Business. Nothin' more, nothin' less. I'm just a soldier. You wasin' your time on me. I don't run it. I'm just an employee."

Nick shook his head. "I forgot. You never got a chance to look at the charges you're facing. You think this is just another drug case. Rest assured it's not."

"So I sold a little bit. My lawyer can square this away. Just you watch." Merc smirked.

"Sure. Good luck with that. The warrant you were arrested on today was for distribution. Those drugs you were on your way to sell are being tested at the lab as we speak."

"Not sure what you're drivin' at but doesn't seem like I'm worth all this effort." Merc gestured with his chin to the surrounding walls of the Cube.

"Trust me, it's worth it. And I'm confident the lab's going to confirm what we already know."

"Yeah? What's that?"

"That the composition of the drugs you were in possession of are identical to the one that caused the recent overdose death of a senator's daughter." Nick sat back, letting the words sink in.

"Whoa, man. Back the hell up! You all tryin' to lay a body at my feet?" Merc shook his head from side to side in dramatic fashion. "Nah! I ain't havin' that! No way! No how! This conversation's over. Get my lawyer and get me the hell out of this room!"

Nick remained poised. "Not your call. You and your crew have been putting that poison into people for a while now. Too bad it took us this long to come for you. Business or not. And then you recently upped your game. Didn't you? Mixing in fentanyl. Heroin wasn't good enough. You had to mix in something with fifty times the potency."

"Not my decision."

"Good luck explaining that to a jury. It's inconsequential whether it was your decision or not. You were the one on the street delivering it. So, you're going to have to do a hell of a lot better than that if you want to find some light at the end of your very dark tunnel." Nick chose his words wisely. The mention of darkness would have a psychological impact and be a subconscious reminder to remain truthful.

"I don't call the shots. I'm more of the messenger, or a glorified delivery boy. You ain't goin' after the pizza delivery driver if the cook poisoned the cheese," Merc pleaded.

"I would. If the delivery driver knew about the poison. Which is easy enough to do in your case. I guarantee one of the members of your little group might even go so far as to say you were the one cutting in the fentanyl."

Nick watched carefully. Merc's right eye twitched slightly, a microgesture indicative of his mind's discomfort with the topic. If Nick were taking this case to trial, he'd have noted the physiological reaction in a detailed interview summary. But that was no longer the role he played. His sole purpose was to squeeze the dealer for usable information in order to further their unit's specific task of shutting down the distribution line.

"There's another issue you have when it comes to beating the rap at trial." Nick stared intensely at the restrained man.

"Yeah? What's that?" Merc met his gaze.

"Your name."

"My name? What are you talkin' about now?"

"It's pretty unique as far as drug dealers go. I'm assuming it's short for Mercenary. A street name like that doesn't bode well for you in front of a jury."

Merc shrugged. "It's just a name."

"It is. You're right about that. It was also the name the college kid who bought the drugs from you gave the police. The same college kid who admitted to giving a small sample to the senator's daughter. Get where I'm going with this now?" Nick added a tinge of sarcasm to punctuate the delivery.

Powell's shoulders drooped, hanging low. His body language epitomized the idiom how the weight of the world sat on his shoulders.

"I can see you're coming to grips with the gravity of the situation you are facing. It's not a simple drug case anymore. You and your fellow gang are going to be charged with manslaughter. Who knows how many other bodies will be tied to the drugs you've been peddling when this is all said and done?"

"Landers," Powell said under his breath. He refused to make eye contact.

"Who's Landers?"

"Not who. It's a what. A bar. That's where we get the supply. Some fat-headed white guy we call Lumpy meets us there. He's our fentanyl connect. I have no idea how Jinx got hooked up with him, but the price is good, and it enabled us to really stretch our product."

"I'm going to need you to talk me through it. Take it from the contact to delivery." Nick paused, then added an incentive. "Listen, your cooperation may reduce your sentence. You work with us and maybe we'll be able to help you on the backside of this."

Nick knew Wiz was already hard at work, scouring for information about Landers. But some details could never be found through a computer database. The human intel factor was critical to operations like these.

Nick savored the opportunity to extract the details from guys like Powell; he looked forward to peeling the layers of information like that of an onion.

For the briefest of moments, Nick Lawrence felt like his old self. And it felt good.

12

Nick exited the small confines where he'd spent the last three hours, leaving the emotionally drained drug dealer to reflect in the silence of the Cube. This time he left the lights on. No need to prolong the psychological warfare once the battle was won. Terry Powell had given up every bit of information about the gang's operation. If Nick were still with the Bureau, the results of this interrogation would have been a slam dunk for the prosecution.

Nick was exhausted. He compared an intense suspect questioning session equivalent to running a 10k road race. The intuitive efforts drained him. Any good investigator knew this feeling well and relished it even more when it came at the end of a successful interrogation.

Spider sat at a computer station, typing away, most likely making his notations of the details gathered during his interview of Terry Powell's female counterpart. It was always best to document the information shortly after the conclusion of an interview, while the pertinent details were still at the forefront of the brain. Although the Cube interrogations were recorded, redundancy was good practice. Plus, nobody wanted to go back through hours of interview tape to get to the isolated information wrapped in a sea of superfluous conversation.

Nick walked over to a terminal and dropped heavily into the seat. He yawned loudly and stretched his arms upward. The mental vigilance and emotional control it took to effectively control the flow of information during Powell's session was a brutal undertaking. But the reward was absolutely exhilarating. During Nick's time with the Bureau, he'd become addicted to the post-interrogation euphoric high. Like any drug, he sought greater challenges to reach the same high. Those cases, while purposeful, had worn away a piece of his soul. He accrued the invisible wear and tear of the countless hours he spent immersed in the criminal mind.

"Nice job in there. I thought you were going to have to give him another round of isolation, but you've definitely got a talent for quickly controlling the ebb and flow of an interview."

The cool, collected voice of Spider snapped him out of his haze.

"Thanks. You were watching it?"

"I checked in on you when I finished with the girl. Hers was fairly simple and straightforward. Not as much resistance as Powell. I honestly don't think she's very bright."

"Did she give anything up?"

Nick knew it was a foolish question based on what he'd seen of Spider's ability with regards to interrogation.

"She did. But nothing like what you got. She had lots of information about their local operation but knew little about the next level distribution. Apparently, Jinx, the crew's leader, kept her in the dark on most of it. Sounded like Powell was the only person he trusted to handle the big stuff."

"I'm hoping that I tapped him for everything he had. I got the local angle too, but more importantly, I managed to get him to lay out the next rung in the distribution ladder."

"Solid stuff. Wiz has already begun to work his magic."

"Yes I have!" Wiz hollered out from the recesses of his work station.

The unit's resident tech genius was facing a semicircle of flat screen computer monitors.

"Since you're eavesdropping on our conversation, why don't you let us know what you've cooked up so far?" Spider asked.

"The cell phone from our male guest, Mr. Powell, had his contact from Landers' bar listed as Lumpy in his phone. I've run the number and it looks like it's a burner phone. It's a pay-as-you-go service with no name attached.

Probably has fifty of these phones lying about with a different contact listed for each dealer he distributes to. He hasn't dumped the phone from what I can tell. Which is a good thing. It means he probably doesn't know Powell's been hit. We're also now tied into this number and the main line at the bar." Wiz smiled, peeking out from behind a monitor.

"Meaning?" Nick asked.

"I've got our version of a wire-tap up and running as we speak. I own anything he does on his cell phone from this point forward. I'm putting up a drone in a few minutes. Similar to the one I used at your funeral. I'll be perching it on a nearby power line to provide us with a live feed of our new favorite bar."

"Do we have any identification on our friend Lumpy?" Nick asked.

"Sure do. I can see why our guest referred to him with such a wonderful moniker. I ran all associated names with the business and pulled any relevant pictures. Come and meet our next target." Wiz pushed back in his chair and turned one of his monitors to face outward. Meet Landers O'Leary."

Nick rolled his chair across the linoleum to Wiz's station. He stared at the bulbous nose and rolls of fat pouring out from the chin, filling to capacity the Department of Motor Vehicle's driver's license photo. By all accounts, the nickname of Lumpy was an appropriate label. There was one thing that surprised Nick while looking at the photograph. O'Leary was a lot older than he'd expected. The heavyset bar owner and distributor of drugs was sixty-two.

Declan exited Jay's office. The two had been in a closed-door meeting. His friend approached, looking more tense than normal.

"This is our next target?" Jay asked.

"Looks that way," Nick replied.

"This guy looks more like a retired mall Santa than a drug dealer," Wiz chuckled.

"Makes sense," Declan said, looking over Wiz's shoulder. "Just like using young kids for runners, an older person is like its own police-cloaking device. A street cop's not going to give this guy a second look. The guy's portly features and gray hair are camouflage."

"You may be right about that." Wiz brought up another screen. "Looks like he's been popped for some minor coke and weed cases in his early days, but he's maintained a low profile over the last twenty years. No recent arrests. A couple liquor license violations for underage drinking, but nothing criminal."

"Did somebody say underage drinking?" Mouse said, entering the Vault with Barbie close behind.

The two women had several bags in hand. Mouse put them on the conference table and joined the rest of the group at Wiz's terminal.

"Do a little shopping?" Nick eyed the assortment of bags, as Barbie unloaded her armful.

"Little? This girl can shop. And eat! You've never seen anything so small consume so much food." Barbie smiled broadly.

Nick was reminded of Anaya. On numerous occasions she had recounted the first time she'd met Mouse, and she commented on the amount of food Mouse had devoured after she'd been found on the side of the road by a trucker, nearly dead.

The group laughed. Nick looked out over this strange new world he'd entered into and the girl he had pulled along with him. With Mouse on the team there was a different feel, a sense of something he'd longed for but failed at miserably. Family. Uniquely odd and definitely dysfunctional, but Nick was beginning to feel at home.

Mouse must've noticed his nostalgic look, because she gave him a tender smile before turning her attention back to the group.

"If this bar caters to young girls, then I guess it's time I step up and prove my worth around here," Mouse said.

"I'm not sure you're ready for this," Nick replied, quicker than he'd intended. It was a gut reaction. Under other circumstance, it might qualify as parental instinct.

"Easy dad, I think I can handle the chubby old guy," Mouse replied with a sardonic undertone.

Nick sighed. But hearing her call him dad, even if it was done mockingly, had rendered him speechless.

"She's right," Jay said. "I like her thought process. If we want to really get close, we need to deploy someone who'd never be suspected as a potential threat. No better person to do just that than Mouse."

Mouse beamed with uncontained excitement. Nick frowned and his brow furrowed with uncontrolled worry.

"Time to get our guests back to Boston PD for booking. They've been here for quite a while and I don't want to raise an unnecessary suspicion," Jay said.

"They're both unconscious now. The transdermal patches were administered when we finished our interviews," Spider said, verifying the information with his tablet.

Nick and Declan retrieved the two prisoners. The Vault had a sally port access for instances like this. Merc and Honey were placed into the backseat of the car in which they'd arrived. Each was seat-belted in.

"So, what was your secret meeting with Jay all about?" Nick asked.

"Nothing."

"As much as we've been through, you're going to hold back on me?"

Declan shrugged. The normal cocky swagger gone. "It's Laney. She's having a difficult time with my long absences. So are Abigail and Ripley, but to a lesser degree. I'm not sure where I stand anymore. Just figured I'd talk to Jay about options."

"I'm sorry to hear that. I wish there was something I could do to help. But as far as that goes, Uncle Nick is dead."

"It's not just Laney. Val's doing great but being alone with the three girls for undetermined chunks of time is starting to wear on all of them. And then there's the inherent danger of what we do. Val knows every time I leave for one of these missions there is the chance I won't be coming back."

"I understand how you feel." Nick was lost for words and immediately knew the ones he'd chosen were the wrong ones.

"Not sure you really can." Declan paused. "Sorry, that came out wrong. I'm just trying to say that it's a lot harder than I anticipated. When I was in the military, running ops with the Teams, I didn't have the girls. I only had to worry about the mission and the guy next to me. I watched a lot of families fall apart overseas. Not sure how well I would've done if I had to balance home life with workups and deployments. When I met Val and we had Abby, I got out and focused on my family."

"So, what's your plan?" Nick asked.

"Not sure. I'm on loan from the FBI. So, I'm leaning hard toward the idea of going back. Get some semblance of normalcy, you know?"

"You know I'd never fault you for doing that? No judgement here. Your family is more important than all of this." Nick looked at the two drug dealers sleeping in the backseat. "We stop one threat and another will fill its place. A never-ending cycle. Family is forever."

"True."

"Plus, I have Mouse now. She's tougher than you anyway." Nick chuckled at himself.

"And today, we'll get to see her in action."

13

Nick pulled out his cell and dialed the number. It rang twice before the voice on the other end picked up.

"Sorenson," came the curt response.

"It's Agent Samuels. Just wanted to give you a heads-up that we're on our way back with your two arrestees from this morning's raid."

"Did they give anything up?"

"Nothing worth sharing as of yet."

Nick heard Sorenson sigh on the other end.

"Maybe we can work something out when I see you at the station," Nick said.

"I'll have Smith meet you there. I'm stuck on something else."

The phone crackled, making it difficult to clearly hear the narcotics detective sergeant.

"You're breaking up. Are you in a tunnel?" Nick asked.

"No. I'm at the morgue. My informant that set today's bust is on a slab. We can add another body to the count. Looks like he must've skimmed a bag during the buy. Found the bag by his body. Apparently, my snitch had no family willing to come in for the ID so I got to do the honors."

The line went dead, and Nick put the phone away.

"How's things on the local end?" Declan asked.

"Sorenson's informant died. Overdose. It sounds like it came from the buy that led to his arrest warrant." Nick thumbed in the direction of Merc.

"I guess when he wakes up his future's not going to look so bright."

"Pretty bleak."

Nick looked at the slumped figure of Terry Powell, aka Merc, and knew his hard life was about to get a heck of a lot harder.

The drop off and return trip had taken almost two hours to complete. By the time they'd returned, the rest of the group was moving at full speed. The Vault was a whirlwind of activity. Mouse stood near Jay and the two were engaged in conversation.

Mouse was wearing a low-cut black shirt lined with silver waves. She had on tight black leather pants and low heels. The shirt exposed a bit of cleavage. Nick wanted to throw a blanket over the girl. He still saw her as the tough fifteen-year-old and probably always would.

"What do you think?" Mouse gave a twirl. Thrown off by the heels, she stumbled and almost fell but was able right herself, finishing in theatrical style.

"I think you're missing some material from that shirt," Nick said.

"Well, I for one think she looks great," Barbie said.

"What's the plan?" Declan asked.

"Mouse is going in alone. The bar's located in the downtown area. It's a bit of a dive, but close enough to the colleges where a girl entering alone shouldn't draw any suspicion. Wiz whipped up a fake Connecticut driver's license and Boston College ID card. The driver's license is intentionally made to look forged. We don't think it will be a problem. She'll be up on our comms and she'll give us a live feed from the pinhole camera in the pendant she's wearing. This is just going to be a surveillance operation," Jay said.

The group listened intently, and Nick watched as Jay pulled up a map of the area.

"Nick and Declan are going to be parked a block away. Barbie and Spider are going to be posing as a couple and eat at a restaurant across the street. They're going to be there to give an extra set of eyes and be the quick reaction team should something break bad," Jay said, delivering the message casually.

Nick was uneasy about Mouse going in alone but figured it was a good opportunity to ease her into the operational procedures of the group.

It was just a surveillance op. How bad could things go? Nick thought. His mind immediately played out a hundred different scenarios, tragically answering his hypothetical question. His stomach knotted.

14

_____

It was that time of night when a bar and restaurant made its transition from the post-work crowd to the late-night partygoers. Mouse sat in the back seat of the tinted Lexus, slowly collecting herself. She made a last-minute check of the equipment, the invisible earpiece and bone microphone taped to her throat. She used the small mirror to inspect herself. Barbie had helped her put some makeup on and added a touch around the small adhesive on her throat, masking it further and making it look like a subtle birth mark to anyone paying too close attention. Satisfied, she closed the compact and snuck it back into her hand purse.

"Good to go. How do you read me?" Mouse asked.

Nick and Declan sat in the front and didn't respond. They knew she was checking the relay to other members who were out of sight.

"All good on our end. I've got a clear visual from your pendant camera of the straggly fellow in front of you," Wiz said. His voice came through her earpiece as clearly as if he'd been sitting beside her.

Mouse giggled. "I told him he needs a haircut. Glad to hear someone else in this group agrees with me."

"We read you loud and clear," Barbie said. "Just remember, we're across the street should you need us."

"I'm heading out," Mouse said.

She leaned forward and gave Nick a peck on the check. "Don't worry. I've got this. Declan, take care of this guy for me, would ya? He's a nervous wreck."

"Aye aye, Captain." Declan gave a small salute.

Mouse opened the door and stepped out into the cold night air. As she shut the door, she saw Nick mouth the words *be safe*. Mouse winked a silent response and stepped away.

Mouse rounded the corner. The cold seemed to have little bearing on Boston's nightlife, and pockets of meandering bar hoppers filled the walkways. Music and laughter poured out of the open doors of the bars and restaurants lining the downtown area.

She watched as a group of teens, not much older than herself, stumbled by laughing loudly at something said. Her mind wandered, and she thought what life would have been like for her had circumstances played out differently. She'd never know *normal* as these kids did. Not much to do about it now. Her upbringing had prepared her for a much different future, one that she was embarking on this very moment.

Mouse moved past the group and toward her target destination. Streetlights cast a yellow glow as a gentle mist began to fall. Her first time in heels took some adjustment, and Barbie had helped her with that, too. She'd gotten the hang of them, but just barely. They were one-inch heels with a wide base, giving her a slight boost in height. With them on she almost hit the five-foot mark. Mouse had been given the nickname from her father and it stuck. He'd also given her many other things in those formative years of her early childhood. Above all he'd taught her *big things can come in small packages.*

The front door to Landers's Bar was open, and a large bouncer sat on a stool outside. He was a thick man whose large frame was contained by a dark leather coat. His bald head glistened, and he eyed the people passing by with a wary look, not the most inviting welcome to those looking for an evening out on the town.

Mouse approached the man, and he hoisted himself off the stool. It creaked loudly as if to thank her for getting the beast off his perch.

"ID," the bald man said gruffly.

Mouse reached down and opened her purse, retrieving the ID Wiz had forged for her. She handed it to him with feigned timidity.

The man flipped the license back and forth with his oversized fingers. He squinted at the photo and then looked at her. His eyes then drifted down to the low cut of her blouse and came to rest on her breasts for a second longer than they should've. A smile formed and the man's rough face softened slightly.

"Did my friends get here yet? I'm supposed to meet some of my sorority sisters. Tall blonde? Big blue eyes?" Mouse asked casually.

The bald man broke his downcast gaze and looked Mouse in the eyes. "Don't think so."

Mouse shrugged. "They're always running late."

"Here you go." The man handed her back the license.

She took it and put it back in her purse. She assumed the exchange was over and attempted to step inside.

The bouncer didn't move. He remained in her way, blocking the entrance. "You know I'm supposed to charge you a ten-dollar cover but I'm feeling generous tonight. Why don't you stop by and see me on your way out?"

Mouse smiled coyly and the man moved aside. He'd obviously deployed this tactic on girls in the past and must've achieved some modicum of success to deploy it on her now. The bouncer's clout came in the meager control he achieved in being the gatekeeper to this dive bar in the heart of a vibrant city. As much as he disgusted her, Mouse pitied the man.

As she passed by, he mumbled, "And have somebody make you a better ID next time. That one's not going to work everywhere."

"Thanks," she said, walking into the bar.

It was poorly lit and relatively small. There were several tables scattered about the main room and a long, lacquered bar centered along the back wall where a few patrons were seated. This was definitely not the stopping place for most college drinkers. The majority of the crowd looked to be in their thirties and dressed in suits, most likely businessmen and woman ending their work day with a few cocktails. She looked at the clock above the mirrored wall behind the bar. Ten o'clock was early for college students, and she assumed it would fill with more people her age as the night progressed.

She found a spot at the bar right of center and a few stools away from a man who'd apparently had a rough day at the office. His hair was a mess and he was bobbing his head over the glass tumbler containing the remnants of whatever liquor he'd been ingesting to reach this pinnacle of drunkenness. His suit coat must've slipped off the stool because it rested on the floor and was soaking up someone's spilled drink, maybe his own. The man didn't even register her presence. He was mumbling some incoherent nonsense.

The bartender, a platinum blonde with ridiculously oversized fake breasts, approached. She eyed Mouse and then shot a glance out toward the bouncer.

"What can I get you, hon?" she asked in a throaty rasp. The woman's age was a mystery. Years of chain smoking had weathered her skin and yellowed her crooked teeth. Mouse assumed most men didn't pay much attention to her face. She presumably used her augmented curvatures to earn her tips.

"Vodka cranberry," Mouse replied.

She'd been to a few parties while living in the Thumb of Michigan. Although Mouse wasn't a huge fan of drinking, she did have an ability to tolerate vodka and cranberry juice, or Cape Codder, as one of her friends had called it. She had also learned her limits and was cognizant of its effect. One heavy night of drinking had left her vulnerable to the advances from one of her classmates. She had been aware enough to stop it before he'd taken full advantage of her inebriation. The boy walked away with a broken arm and she with an understanding of alcohol's ability to lower situational awareness.

Declan had told her that bars typically watered down their well drinks and it would have less impact, enabling her to stay focused. He'd told her to sip the drink and allow the ice to melt. It would give the appearance of being full.

While the woman poured the glass, most of which was filled with ice, Mouse took a moment to read the shirt she was wearing. In bold green letters stretched across her enormous breasts it read, *Seeing Double?*

Mouse laughed to herself just as Wiz spoke, "I love this bar already."

She slid the drink across to Mouse. "That'll be eight dollars, or do you plan on starting a tab?"

"I'll pay as I go." Mouse placed a ten-dollar bill on the counter next to a bowl of nuts.

"Leave a two-dollar tip," Nick coached through the earpiece.

Mouse smiled. "Keep the change."

The woman smiled back and then turned her attention to the drunken businessman. "All right Freddy, I think it's time you leave. Don't need you puking all over my bar."

The man perked up at the sound of his name but looked around as if he couldn't quite pinpoint the direction from which it came. He then looked down at the glass in front of him and slammed back the remaining liquid, spilling most of it on his shirt. He slipped down from the chair, mumbling incoherently. Staggering back a few steps he leveled his gaze on his suitcoat. He eyed the coat angrily, as if it were taunting him.

Mouse watched the man in a combination of interest and pity. He bent down to recover the jacket. His balance obviously impaired, he bobbed wildly, snatching at the sleeve. He hung on to the coat, dangling his right arm, while balancing against a stool with the other. His finger gripped at the fabric like one of those rip-off claw games at an arcade. Finally, getting hold of the item, he righted himself. The blood rush from his efforts reddened his face, adding to his wild look. He staggered out of the bar and disappeared into the night. One thing was for certain—nobody would notice Mouse's awkwardness in her heels. She'd blend right in with this crowd.

A half hour had passed, and she hadn't seen Lumpy. The bar was slowly beginning to fill. Mouse nursed her drink and looked at her watch occasionally, pretending to be waiting for someone.

The bartender served a few of the new arrivals and then returned to Mouse. She rested her breast on the bar and looked fatigued.

"You going to want another one?" she asked with a hint of annoyance.

"Sure." She sipped the last bit of the glass, which at this point was mostly water.

"Meeting somebody?" the bartender asked.

"Yeah. Some of my girlfriends were supposed to meet me here. Not sure where they are." Mouse looked back toward the door. The large bouncer was back on his perch, eyeballing the outsiders.

"Still want to pay as you go?"

"Yeah," she said. "Might as well. Not sure how long I'm going to wait."

The bartender removed the glass, replacing it with a full one. Mouse opened her purse to get another ten-dollar bill when she was bumped by a man taking up the seat next to her.

"I've got it," the man said. His voice was loud, carrying over the low rumble of the neighboring patrons.

Mouse looked up. To her right was the round, blotched face of Landers O'Leary. He could have easily taken up two barstools with his girth. He looked like a circus elephant balancing on a ball. She smiled politely.

"Thanks, but you don't have to do that."

He dismissed her comment with a wave of his meaty hand. "And I'll take one of whatever she's having."

The bartender gave her boss a shocked look. "Um, you want a vodka cranberry?"

He chuckled and smiled, exposing his stained yellow teeth, "Sure, why not? Maybe throw in a whiskey back."

"Thanks again," Mouse said.

"So, tell me, what's a pretty young thing like you doing in my bar?" Landers said.

"Your bar?" Mouse asked, pretending to be impressed.

"That's right." His smile widened, bunching the fat of his cheeks into deep ripples. "Landers's Bar. And I'm Landers O'Leary. Owner of this fine establishment."

"Well, Mr. O'Leary, pleased to meet you." Mouse raised her glass and took a small sip.

O'Leary downed his shot of whiskey first and then took on the vodka drink, his glass much clearer than hers and obviously containing more vodka than cranberry. The bartender was obviously well aware of her employer's tastes.

"Mr. O'Leary was my dad, and he was an asshole. Call me Landers."

"Okay, Landers."

"That brings me back to my original question. What brings you here tonight?"

"Supposed to meet some friends."

"Boyfriend?" Landers asked, cocking an eyebrow and sizing up Mouse from head to toe.

"No, just a couple of girls I go to school with."

"Looks like you've been stood up." Landers frowned.

"Seems so."

"How about I keep you company and maybe I can help salvage the night for you." Landers drained his glass and rapped his knuckles on the bar. The bartender immediately replaced his drink with a fresh one. "I've been told I'm a lot of fun."

The bartender shot Mouse a worried glance before returning to her duties. She was aware of his tastes in both alcohol and women. It appeared she disapproved of the latter.

"I don't like this," Nick said. He was obviously talking to Declan, but it came through her earpiece.

"She'll be fine. Let's see where this goes. Barbie and Spider are across the street if we need to intervene," Jay said, softly overriding Nick's worry.

"So, Landers, what makes you such a fun guy to hang around with," Mouse engaged the man.

She played with the pendant around her neck and the movement drew the man's attention back to her chest. Mouse hadn't much experience in the world of dating, but her life experiences had exposed her to some of man's carnal nature. She could tell her ploy was working and Landers O'Leary was interested. His eyes lingered on the small curves of her exposed cleavage, just as the doorman had.

"Looks like your friends aren't showing up. Why don't you finish that drink and we can get out of here?"

"Isn't this your bar? Where else would you want to go?"

"I've got a penthouse that overlooks the water. Only about a five-minute drive from here." Landers raised his eyebrows.

The innuendo was not subtle. Mouse wondered how many times the fat man had deployed these tactics with any success. If you swing a bat a thousand times, you're bound to get a hit once in a while.

"Absolutely not," Nick said over the radio. "Do not leave the bar with him. This is an intel gathering operation."

"Sounds like a plan," Mouse said to Landers. "I've just got to use the ladies room before we go."

Landers pointed to the hallway left of the bar as he guzzled another glass of vodka. His face reddened and his eyes had a glossy sheen as the alcohol began to circulate in his system.

Mouse made her way into the dank hallway. Flyers for bands were glued along the walls in the dimly lit passage. She smelled the pungent odor of urine as she passed the men's room. Once inside the bathroom, Mouse checked the stalls to make sure nobody else was present.

"I've got this," she said, knowing the entire group was listening.

"I don't like it. It's a command and control issue for us," Nick pleaded. "If you go mobile it could expose us as we try to keep up. We don't want to spook him before we've had a chance to figure out his operation."

"Listen, if I'm part of this team, then I should be treated as such. We just got our opportunity to get this guy alone. We should seize it." Mouse spoke softly. "Who knows what we'll find in the guy's apartment. This could speed things up for us."

It was quiet. Jay broke the silence. "She's right. Let's see where this takes us. Barbie and Spider are close and can watch the movement from the bar. Nick, you and Declan can do the takeaway when they go mobile in the car."

"If this goes sideways, we're stepping in," Nick said.

"Relax, I've taken on worse guys than him and come out on top," Mouse said.

Mouse looked in the mirror and smiled knowing that Wiz and Jay could see her through her pendant camera. She was confident in her abilities to continue and hoped it was conveyed in the image they saw.

She stepped out of the bathroom and walked directly to Landers. She grabbed her drink and finished it off. The bulbous nosed man looked impressed.

"Ready?" he asked.

"Absolutely."

Mouse only stumbled once on the way out of the bar. A marked improvement from her earlier practice with the heels. She giggled and braced herself, grabbing the elbow of Landers O'Leary. He smiled down at her.

"I think I had a little too much to drink." Mouse added a little slur for effect.

Landers laughed. "No such thing."

He ran his tongue across his lips as though he was preparing for a meal. She saw the look in his eyes. She'd seen it before in men like him. Landers planned to have his way with her. Mouse reveled in the man's mistake in underestimating her.

15

"We've got eyes on you," Barbie said. "Moving out the front door toward the alleyway on the north side of the bar."

It was a strange adjustment to hear her voice so clearly. She looked over at the man she was walking beside, half expecting O'Leary to hear the transmissions.

"Nice car," Mouse said.

Landers pressed a fob in his hand and the black Jeep Grand Cherokee's locking mechanism made a thunk, announcing its release. Mouse walked to the passenger side. The temperature had dropped ten degrees since she'd first entered the bar and her skin prickled with goosebumps. She wasn't completely convinced the reaction was solely from the cold. Something about the large man unnerved her.

"This old thing? Nah, you should see my other cars." O'Leary opened his door and hoisted himself into the driver's seat. He lowered the passenger window and looked at her. "Hop on in."

Mouse entered and the SUV pulled out into the moderate congestion of the nighttime bar traffic. Although many college bar enthusiasts travelled by foot, there were an equal amount who used cabs or Uber-ed their way, especially in the colder months. The street was lined with them. O'Leary yelled profanities out the window at both cars and people alike. Apparently, his patience for delay was as thin as his receding hairline. The man was a few years away from bald and the comb-over job was a failed attempt at holding on to his glory days.

"How far did you say?" Mouse slumped down in the leather of the seat. She dipped her head in a bob, adding to her drunk-girl act.

"Only a couple minutes. If these goddamned idiots would get moving," O'Leary raised his voice again, projecting the last part out toward the street. He rested his hand on her left thigh, lowered his tone, and added, "Don't pass out on me yet. I've got plans for you."

Mouse didn't respond. She only gave a weak smile and flickered her eyes as if to fight off sleep. She placed her hand atop his to prevent it from riding further up her leg.

O'Leary wasn't lying about the distance away from the bar. Once the brunt of traffic was behind them it was only a few-minutes' drive until they reached their destination. It might have been faster for them to walk, but considering the man's obesity, she understood his desire to drive. He pulled the Jeep to a stop in front of a building that stood out from its surroundings. Lights were set along a row of potted bushes to cast a blue hue on the stone pillars holding the front entrance's overhang. A red carpet lined the four-step rise to the main doors, bookended by polished brass handrails.

There was a pleasant-looking doorman wearing a maroon overcoat embossed with gold lettering. He approached with a smile. "Welcome home, Mr. O'Leary."

O'Leary said nothing to the man, only tossing his car keys to him as he walked past. The man caught the keys in mid-air and moved directly toward the Jeep without further comment. Mouse followed behind.

The interior lobby was bright and inviting, with warm-colored tile on the floors bouncing the light from the chandelier above. Another man, similarly dressed to the one outside, sat behind a desk centered equidistant between the main entrance and the elevators. He set down a newspaper and assumed an attentive position.

"Good evening, sir," the man at the desk said.

O'Leary barely gave him a glance as he moved toward the elevator. The man at the desk rolled his eyes after the large man had passed. Mouse saw and smiled. He blushed at being caught and returned her smile.

"Impressive," Mouse said.

"You ain't seen nothing yet," O'Leary said, grinning.

Mouse looked at the man's distorted image in the polished brass doors of the elevator. Then she looked at herself. Side by side the size difference between the two was shocking. He towered over her by almost a foot, and she guessed his weight at close to three hundred pounds. It was a David and Goliath matchup, but she was missing the sling and rock.

Mouse realized that he'd never even asked her name. *How many nameless girls had this pig of a man brought through this lobby?* A ding rang out, ending the awkward silence, and the doors opened. O'Leary and Mouse entered the elevator and the big man pressed the top button, number twenty-one.

The ride was quick. Soft music filled the elevator and Mouse recognized the familiar tune but couldn't place the name of the song.

Reaching their destination, Mouse followed O'Leary out into the hallway. There was one door on each end of the hallway. He proceeded to the one on the right and she followed.

"Not too many neighbors," Mouse said.

"No neighbors." O'Leary laughed. "It's the penthouse. That other door leads to the back end of my place. But I prefer to use this door. You'll see why in a second."

Mouse felt her heartbeat quicken. She subtly began tensing and releasing her muscles. A technique her father had taught her, one that served to spread the introduction of adrenaline caused by nervousness. He'd taught her to embrace fear because it quickened reaction time. O'Leary paid no attention to her as he fumbled with the key to unlock his door.

"Here it is," the grotesque man said. He stepped aside as the door swung wide.

Mouse stood at the threshold to the apartment. White stone tile led to a dropped floor living room with an oversized fireplace, surrounded by walls of glass. The lights of city flickered like fireflies on a summer night. Under other circumstances Mouse would have been in awe. But not tonight.

"Wow," Mouse said, stepping inside.

The door closed, and O'Leary ushered her in ahead and stood behind her. She felt his soft gut press against her back as he put his right hand on her shoulder.

Mouse slipped her hand up, gently caressing the thick, stubby fingers. His grip tightened and she heard him give a sigh, blanketing her in the sour whiskey and vodka that lingered on his breath. Through her earpiece she heard the others talking in rapid-fire succession, but she was a ball of focused intensity and blocked the words from distracting her.

Finding his index finger, she wrapped her hand around it. With her thumb pressing against his middle knuckle, she peeled his finger upward. In one swift move she jerked up while simultaneously applying pressure to center of his appendage. The snap was loud in the quiet stillness of the posh apartment.

Landers let out a wail. "You little b-!"

His rant cut short as Mouse delivered a blow with her left elbow into the heavy man's solar plexus. Mouse's father had taught her the solar plexus was an area of the body that was vulnerable to attack regardless of an opponent's size. In larger men it was an accentuated triangle formed at the meeting of chest and stomach. O'Leary was no exception and his girth provided a perfect strike zone.

Landers reacted to the impact, staggering backward and slamming against the door. She maintained purchase on his finger, twisting it in an arc as she spun to face him. Grabbing the meat of his palm with her left hand, she torqued his wrist toward him. The man's arm locked at the elbow and she applied pressure to the shoulder joint, driving his body downward as he resisted the pain in his arm.

With only one usable arm to break his fall, O'Leary's face struck the hard floor with a thud. Another bellow erupted from the man. This time there was no accompanying comment, or at least not one that could be discerned.

Wasting no time, Mouse wrenched his arm to the small of his back. She straddled his large frame, locking the injured limb with her right thigh. She released her grip on his wrist and snaked her thin, wiry arm underneath his throat and around to her left bicep. Mouse constricted her hold on the throat, pinching O'Leary's carotid artery on both sides while applying counter pressure to the back of his neck with her left forearm.

The large man flailed and bucked, but Mouse held tight. She heard a loud, repetitious banging on the door but ignored it. O'Leary's raspy wheeze subsided and gave way to three short gasps until there was nothing. His body stopped moving and Mouse released her choke hold.

Mouse stood and straightened her shirt. She stepped back, admiring her handy-work before turning to unlock the door.

Nick rushed in and immediately stopped short at the sight of the downed man.

"Jesus! Are you okay?" Nick asked, wide-eyed and panic-stricken. He scanned her for injury.

"Of course. It's not me you should be worried about," Mouse said calmly.

Declan moved past the two and secured the big man in handcuffs. He needed to use two sets of cuffs linked together to accommodate the man's girth. O'Leary groaned, releasing frothy spit tinged with blood.

Barbie stood behind Nick, smiling broadly. "Looks like our little Mouse is more of a lion."

"I guess any questions as to her ability to handle herself have been asked and answered," Spider added, standing beside Barbie in the hallway.

"Let's pack up our new friend and take him for a little ride," Declan said.

Nick and Declan hoisted the big man up, rolling him to the side and then hooking him under his elbows. O'Leary was gaining consciousness as blood and oxygen began their ascent back to his brain. He groaned as he was lifted to his feet, uneasy and woozy. Both men exerted themselves to keep him upright.

"What the hell is going on?" O'Leary mumbled, surveying the group surrounding him.

"FBI. You're under arrest." Declan flashed his credentials.

"What for?"

"Don't worry. There'll be plenty of time to discuss that back at head-quarters." Declan stuck one of the transdermal patches to O'Leary's wrist and nodded to Nick. "Better get going before the big man here takes a nap. I'd prefer not to feel this guy's dead weight."

Mouse followed behind. She looked back at the apartment and the spot of blood marking O'Leary's fall. Without a sling and rock, she'd managed to topple Goliath. Content, she shut the door behind her and fell in step with the others.

16

"Sir, do you really think this is a good idea? I mean...not sure how this will look to your constituents. Holding a press conference immediately following your daughter's funeral might be perceived by some as callous. There's still time to cancel if you'd prefer to reschedule," Gloria Baker said, sitting across from the senator in the stretch limo.

Litchfield flushed with anger, his eyes still moist from the interment of his only child. He eyed the woman seated across from him in her dark blue power suit, cradling her notepad. She appeared to be using it as a subconscious shield for whatever verbal assault he was about to deliver. In his mind he pictured choking the life out of her. Who was she to question his decision?

He exhaled slowly. Years of combat during his time as a Marine had taught him valuable lessons in composure, and he engaged them now. He'd also learned many lessons about leadership, one of those being to surround yourself with people willing to challenge your decisions. A leader surrounded by "yes men" was only good for one thing, and that was stroking an ego. Buzz Litchfield's ego didn't need any additional stroking. And he carefully considered Baker's comments, knowing her suggestion came from a place of genuine concern for his position as senator and also as grieving father. She was looking out for his best interest.

"I understand your concern," Litchfield said in a measured tone. "But I beg to disagree. The timing of my speech couldn't be more important. I honor my daughter's memory by going after those bastards that took her from me. Today the world will see beyond my rank and title as someone who has a vested stake in the fight. No more rhetorical banter. We are going to unleash hell on those responsible, and we're not going to do that with me tucking away! People will remember that as others in my shoes would cower meekly, I took a stand."

Baker nodded and slowly brought her notepad back down to her lap, registering the potential tidal wave of rage had subsided. "Very well, sir. Then we're on schedule for this afternoon."

———

The room was packed, definitely outside of the fire code limits on number of occupants. It was twenty-eight degrees outside, so the heat was on, but between the stage lighting and hundreds of attendees the room was unbearably warm. Reporters opened their collars. Sweaters and coats were used as seat cushions. Those standing in a tightly wedged cluster in the back of the room struggled against the congestion. Notepads and hats became makeshift fans.

Senator Litchfield was oblivious to the discomfort of the awaiting crowd as he sat in the isolation of his waiting room, rehearsing the notes of his speech. His public speaking began as a young Marine officer. He'd learned the essential ingredients to motivate and bend the will of subordinates. More than he cared to admit, his words inspired men to make the ultimate sacrifice. He bore the weight heavily. Today would be a different type of audience but the message would be similar. It would be a call to action in a different kind of war. He knew that today, above any other, was critical not only for his Hope Restored initiative but for his potential rise to the highest seat in the land. President Buzz Litchfield had a nice ring to it.

A knock at the door took him out of his zone of concentration.

Baker peeked her head in. "Sir, the press is ready. It's time."

Baker disappeared back into the hallway, closing the door behind her. Litchfield inhaled deeply and slipped his speech into his pocket. He had no intention of reading from the paper once he began. There was no way to appear sincere if he were to do so, especially when talking about his daughter. But keeping the paper close at hand gave him comfort. His notes, written in bright red, lined the margins. He worked every speech to the final minutes before presenting. It was like cramming for a final examination the morning of the test. Something about the pressure calmed him. One of his personal traits that helped him excel on the battlefield.

Litchfield took one last look at himself in the small mirror above the wash basin. With his short-cropped hair and defined jawline, the senator maintained a likeness to his former self. An ageless warrior who donned thousand-dollar suits rather than his general-issue fatigues, but a warrior nonetheless. He was as ready as he'd ever be. Greatness was born in moments like these, and he knew without a single doubt this was to be his moment.

He stepped into the hallway, where Gloria Baker and Avery Wilcox stood. His two best people, each uniquely different in their tasks, but each uniquely important to his success. His nod initiated the procession down the long corridor to the awaiting crowd. No words were spoken. Everybody in his staff knew not to interrupt the silent moments before a speech with idle chit-chat.

Outside the door he could hear the low rumble of the reporters on the other side. He closed his eyes, taking a moment to picture his daughter. The last memory of her, supine and doll-like, in the ornate casket where he'd laid her to rest. He called to memory the last time they'd talked. Her smile was contagious, and no matter his stress, she always managed to lighten the load. He'd been deployed overseas when Amber was born, but he could recall the first time he saw her upon his return. She melted the tough Marine in him and added a subtle gentleness to his gruff exterior. He was a better man because of his daughter and felt an unfillable emptiness now that she was gone. No parent should ever have to bury a child. The effect was immediate and done with purpose, calling forth his suppressed emotions to the forefront. As his eyes watered, he turned the knob and entered the room.

Litchfield took the three steps up to the podium with slow, dutiful care. He cast a blurry-eyed glance out toward the journalists and heard the barrage of clicks, capturing his despondent gaze. Everything calculated, an opportunity seized. His eyelashes wet with fresh tears, adding weight to the words yet to be delivered.

He took a sip from the water staged by the microphone. Placing it back down, he cleared his throat and rubbed his eyes.

"It is with a heavy heart that I stand before you today. As many of you know, I buried my beautiful Amber this morning." His throat cracked at the mention of her name. That was not planned, but he recovered quickly.

"She died as a result of the scourge that plagues this great city and our nation as a whole. Many of you are getting information about my daughter's death from your various sources. Some are bending the truth to sell headlines saying she was a wild party girl enjoying a life of privilege. I'm here to set the record straight. She was a driven student. Dedicated and passionate about learning. She had a kind heart and a true love of life. My daughter was not a drug addict, but somehow it found a way to reach her. The poison snaked its way into my daughter's hand like the apple in the Garden of Eden. A victim of her own naivety. Here is the sad truth behind the circumstances surrounding my daughter's death. She attended an off-campus party with some friends and tried, for the first time, a drug that claimed her life. Fentanyl, a synthetic opioid that's one hundred times more potent than heroin, found its way into my daughter's bloodstream. She died on a bathroom floor moments after ingesting it. Police are working to build a case against the distribution network responsible for this. I have no doubt in the capabilities of the men and women of the Boston Police Department."

Litchfield paused, wiping at his eyes again. He looked back out at the audience with a steely intensity. "Do you know what they call it on the street?" he hissed. "Murder 8 is one of many slang words used to label this poison. I've made a commitment to bringing an end to this epidemic. As I've said before, my Hope Restored initiative is already being deployed here in Boston. Treatment for the afflicted is underway and being used to treat hundreds as we speak. But that's not why I'm here today."

Litchfield shook his head slowly, his teeth clenched. He slammed the podium with a closed fist. Some of the reporters jumped, startled by his delivery. "I'm here today to send a message to those responsible. I'm here today as a father and as a victim. The message I bring is for the drug dealers peddling this evil. If you're out there watching this, then listen very carefully. I'm unleashing the full fury of every asset at my disposal to seek out and destroy your network. With the help of our law enforcement professionals, I'm coming for you! It's a no-win scenario if you continue to sell death on our corners. Those responsible for the death of my daughter will face the full force of the law. You won't be charged as drug dealers. You'll be charged as the murderers that you are. Victims like my daughter Amber will be avenged. Today, the citizens of Boston can rest assured that justice will be served, and our streets will be cleared!"

Applause rumbled across the room. Reporters dropped note pads and stood. An ovation from political critics was even more than Litchfield anticipated. He took a moment to savor this speech and its potential impact for the long haul of his political future.

Senator Buzz Litchfield stepped down from the podium platform amidst the cheers. Voices called out, peppering him with questions as he walked to the exit. He had intended to deliver the message and leave them begging for more. He walked away satisfied his objective was completed successfully.

Gloria Baker took to the podium to quell the crowd as Litchfield and Wilcox moved into the hallway.

"What's the status of the case with Boston PD? How close are they to finding the bastards responsible?" Litchfield asked.

"My contact said the case has been reassigned. Some federal jurisdiction issue popped up and they've been asked to stand down. They're in the dark right now," Wilcox said. "With my contact out of the loop, I don't have any fresh intel right now."

"Then gather your own!" Litchfield stormed away from his friend and confidant. Shouting over his shoulder, he yelled, "I want you to personally handle this thing! From now, until I say otherwise, this is your sole responsibility."

17

"Where the hell am I?" Landers spat the words. His speech was slurred, a byproduct of the synergistic effect from the combination of alcohol mixed with the chemical sleeping aid of the transdermal patch he'd been given.

"You are in an interrogation room located at a secure FBI off-site facility," Nick said casually. "We're going to have a little conversation. And I hope for your sake that you find the right words to help you out of your current predicament."

"What the hell are you talking about?" Landers looked around the small enclosed space of the Cube. "And where's that little bitch who broke my damn finger?"

Landers O'Leary looked down at the splint taped to his right index finger. The swelling to the man's hand gave the already thick finger a freakishly huge, almost cartoonish, appearance. The break had been along the joint and undoubtedly had torn some tendons during its occurrence. It would be a long time before the bar owner would be able to comfortably put that hand on another young girl again.

"Let's be civil. If you continue to feel the need to refer to her in that way again, I'll make sure I reintroduce you to her. And next time, I'll let her finish what she started. To that end, if I were you, I'd be more concerned about the here and now."

"I know my rights. I want my lawyer," Landers said, smiling. He leaned forward against his restraints. The thick straps pressed into the man's doughy skin, giving him the rippled look of the Michelin Man. "And my lawyer's one of the best money can buy."

Nick smiled back, locking eyes with the man. "No lawyers here. We do things a little differently."

"No lawyers? You said you were FBI. I know you have rules. Hell, you guys are the boy scouts of the police world. There are protocols you are supposed to follow!"

Nick ignored the man. "Shall we begin?"

"I don't know how to make this any clearer to you. I ain't freakin' talking until my lawyer gets here! And know this, I'll have your badge for the little stunt you pulled back there in my apartment! This finger is going to pay out big time. Heck, I might be able to pay off my bar thanks to you and your little female friend."

"I don't have a badge. And I'm not with the FBI," Nick said calmly, letting the words linger.

"Not FBI? Then what? State police or something? Whoever you're with you still have to follow the rules." Landers O'Leary's brow furrowed.

"You're wasting valuable time that could be better spent sorting out an issue we have. I'm under an incredible amount of pressure to proceed with my investigation. And you have information I need."

"What the hell are you talking about?"

"Fentanyl. In particular, the shipments you've been making to some of Boston's inner-city gangs," Nick said.

"No idea what you're referring to," O'Leary said. His voice was less intense.

"Well, if you ever plan on getting back your sad existence of a life then you'd better start coming clean." Nick ran his finger over the tablet's screen. "I'd prefer not to bore you with all the capabilities of this room, but in short there are other ways of breaking you down and making you talk. Not particularly my favorite thing to do, but like I said I'm in the business of getting answers. Your choice as to how that is going to happen."

"I want a phone call!" O'Leary squealed.

"No phones. No lawyers. And no leaving until I have what I need," Nick said flatly. "We don't want you. You're just a pathetic middle-man. Your supplier is important to us."

"That's not happening. You can't bully me into talking. Ain't going to work on me. This conversation is over." O'Leary forced as much conviction into his words as he could muster, but the effort fell flat.

"Then I'll be leaving you to think on that. I'm pretty sure when I return, you'll be singing a different tune."

Nick stood without saying another word. He punched the keypad and exited the Cube. As soon as the doors closed, he activated the noise and light exposure sequence. Nothing could be heard through the soundproof walls, but judging from the obese man's biometric readout, he immediately experienced a high level of discomfort. His blood pressure spiked, and the movement detected by the chair's sensors showed him to be convulsing violently.

"How long do you think it'll take?" Nick asked Spider, who was standing nearby.

"Not sure, we'll need to keep an eye on him. His poor physical condition could exacerbate his reaction to the induced stress. We don't need him dying in there before he has a chance to tell us what we need."

An hour had passed and Nick continued a vigilant watch over the man subjected to the Cube's magic. O'Leary's heart rate was nearing one-hundred-eighty beats per minute, something you'd expect to see from a runner, not a man seated in a chair. Looking through the one-way mirrored window pane, Nick saw O'Leary's resistance had waned since the psychological torture began. Tears fell from the broken man's face, and Nick deemed it time to reconnect with the stubborn bar owner.

The light returned to its normal incandescence and the music stopped the moment the Cube's door rolled open. Nick entered and stood in quiet observation of the weakened shape of O'Leary's husky frame, hunching forwarded in unspoken defeat. The door slid closed behind him, and Nick resumed his position, seating himself across from the large, sweat-covered man. The odor of alcohol permeated the air around him.

Nick looked around at the walls and shook his head evenly from side to side. "This room is something else, huh? Not quite how you imagined your evening going?"

O'Leary said nothing. His head down, he let out a low whimper.

"Let's get back to what we were talking about earlier. Shall we?"

The man's beady, bloodshot eyes peered up at Nick. A long line of drool hung from the corner of his mouth and connected to the floor. He looked as though he'd just undergone a frontal lobe lobotomy. His face was painted in a combination of derangement and hopelessness.

"How long were you gone?" O'Leary asked, his voice a defeated whisper.

"One hour. I know it can feel a lot longer. Sadly, this could only be the beginning. Each time you force my hand, I will spend more time outside. And you will spend more time in here to reflect on your willingness to cooperate. You're in a really bad position right now and let me explain why. As I told you before, my team and I are looking for information. Your cooperation to that end is critical. Should you choose to meet me with the same resistance as you did previously, then I'll be forced to extend the next session until I'm satisfied that your willingness to cooperate has been reached. Do you understand? And before you say anything, know that what you say next determines whether I stay or go." Nick tapped the tablet as a subtle reminder of potential things to come.

O'Leary let out a long slow wheezy breath. "I understand."

"And?"

"And I'll cooperate."

"Good. So, back to my previous question. I'm interested in knowing the supplier who's been delivering the fentanyl to you. Everything you tell me will be verified by other members of my team in real time and therefore there's no point in trying to send me down the wrong path."

"There's this guy. He calls me up and tells me where to meet. And he makes the drop. Really, it's that simple. I never went looking for the stuff. It found me. You gotta believe that."

"You've got to do better than that. I hope you're not planning on making me continually ask for details. If that's the case, then I'm going to get tired real fast and end up having to take another long break." Nick leaned in closer.

"He contacted me a while back. Told me he'd heard I was a guy who could move product. I'm not a dealer. Did some petty stuff back in the day. Moved a little coke and weed, but nothing too heavy. Took a couple whacks in the pen for it. You can check my record. I haven't caught a case in over ten years. Learned my lesson, I guess. I found out I could make more money being a middle man. I just hold on to packages and ship them off to some of the local crews. No deals are made out of my bar. I run a legit business and use the other stuff as a side hustle. I keep the two separate. I don't need the boys in blue shutting down my bar."

"So, how did the fentanyl thing come into play? It's not like people go around asking bar owners if they'd be interested."

"I typically move coke and the occasional brick or two of heroin to a local crew called the Hoodstars. They must've told their connection. Then out of the blue this guy reaches out and offers me a pretty penny to sit on a stash of fentanyl. Seriously, he came to me. It's not like I'm in the phone book under drug courier," O'Leary said earnestly.

"Somebody you don't know asks you to hold a large quantity of a dangerous drug and you say yes? No questions asked? Seems a bit strange to me."

"I'm not lying. Look at your little computer thingy and tell me I'm not telling the truth. Like I said. It was good money. And easy too. I don't know where you come from, but where I grew up if somebody walks in with a bag full of money you usually don't ask too many questions. Sometimes the wrong questions land a bullet in your head."

"Okay, I'll bite. You get an offer to hold the fentanyl and are paid well for it. Then what?" Nick asked.

"He calls and tells me when and where to deliver it and I do. Simple. I make the drop and I'm done until he contacts me for the next load. Sometimes it's weeks. Sometimes days. There really isn't much of a pattern. I'm at his mercy."

"What's this guy's name?" Nick asked, knowing Wiz had already ripped the data from O'Leary's phone and was looking to match a name with the number.

"Don't know his real name. I just call him Stinky Pete," O'Leary said.

"Stinky Pete?"

"Yeah. The guy smells. I mean really smells. Looks like a homeless guy. But whenever the call is made, he's the guy that makes the drop. Personally, I think he's just a runner for them. Smart business. Using some schlep to do the deal. I probably should do the same, but thing is, I don't trust many people. Nature of the beast. Been burned a couple times in my life and now I like to hold all the cards."

"When was the last time you had a drop made?"

"About three days ago. It was only a quarter key of the stuff. Each time the amount's different, too. No rhyme or reason to the amount or timing of things. Not my place to question a fellow entrepreneur's business model." O'Leary shrugged.

"Have you ever called the number and requested anything from Stinky Pete?" Nick asked.

"Once. A little while back one of the crews I distribute to had run out earlier than expected and contacted me for more. So, I called it in."

"And?"

"He delivered."

"Well, I guess we found the way you're going to help us with this." Nick reached over and rested his hand on O'Leary's broken finger. He tried to pull away. Nick tightened his grip and a pained expression shot across the injured man's face.

"What are you talking about? How can I help?"

"You're going to make a call and set up a meet."

"No way, man. Absolutely not!" O'Leary began huffing and sweat began seeping out of his forehead. The trickle rolled along his grooved jowls down his neck to the stained collar of his shirt. "Are you out of your freakin' mind? Snitching is one thing but setting these guys up is a guaranteed death sentence! Do you understand?"

"I think you should be more worried about us. Remember, the little girl you met? The one who completely disabled you in a matter of seconds? Well, she's just one of many people in our employ. You might want to really consider which team might be more dangerous for you to piss off. And besides, if you play this right, then you won't have them to worry about afterward. Trust me when I say this, people we target typically do not have a very long shelf life." Nick removed his hand from O'Leary's.

Landers O'Leary sighed. "I'll make the call and then we're straight? I want to be done after that. Tell me that I do this thing and we're good."

"I'll let you know when we're straight. You just sit tight for a minute while I work out the details with my team."

Nick stood up, picking up the tablet. O'Leary flinched at the movement. Nick made his way to the door.

"Please don't turn it back on," O'Leary begged.

"Like I told you when we first talked, cooperation is a good thing. And as far as I can tell, you and I have come to an understanding with regard to that. Take this time to relax for a minute. You've got some work to do in a little bit."

Nick exited the Cube. The remaining members of the Valhalla Group were seated around the conference table. It was time to strategize the next phase of the operation.

18

Nick had a clear vantage point of the drop location. He was seated in a white plastic chair across from Declan in the outdoor seating area of The Clam Box, a Quincy Shore seafood restaurant, located on the Wollaston Beach shorefront. Blending in with their environment, both men ordered the fish and chips. Due to the cool temperatures, there wasn't anyone else out on the patio but the view from inside was obstructed and therefore the two endured the cold. The warm food helped. Nick leaned in taking a piece of the flaky-battered cod and shoveled it into his mouth. Declan munched a couple fried clam strips. The two men smiled at each with full cheeks.

"Take it easy. If you choke, I think I'll be too full to revive you," Declan said between bites.

Nick gave a chipmunk grin. "I think I'll pass on mouth-to-mouth from you. And this would be one hell of a last meal."

"I still say we should have got a beer or two to wash this down. It feels wrong to be eating this without."

"My God, it's bad enough you guys get to eat from your perch while we have to sit in the van. Do we really need to listen to your play-by-play as you gorge yourselves?" Barbie said through the earpiece.

"Save me some fries," Mouse added.

Landers O'Leary had cooperated fully after an additional reminder of the Cube's influential power. He'd called the number for Stinky Pete the night prior and requested another delivery, claiming a crew had run out of the last batch early and were looking to re-up. An arrangement was made, and O'Leary was given a noon meeting place of the Wollaston Beach Playground. Landers said he'd never met at that location, but explained each meet was at a different spot.

O'Leary had been given specific instructions and was told to sit under the gazebo and wait for the arrival. He'd been told not to bring anybody else. Again, this was explained as normal procedure. Nothing was out of the ordinary.

The plan was simple. Spider would accompany O'Leary and be present when the exchange was made. Nick and Declan would provide over-watch while Barbie and Mouse, tucked in a van up the road, would converge and assist Spider in snatching Stinky Pete.

"Spider, I've got good eyes on you," Nick said, chewing on a French fry and relaying the information to Spider's earpiece.

"Good to go. O'Leary is set," Spider said. "I'll call the takedown from here."

O'Leary was seated in a gazebo wearing the same clothes he'd had on the night before when he picked Mouse up in the bar. His hand was still bandaged, and Nick was confident the man's last eighteen hours would forever change his approach to young girls.

Spider sat on a bench at the edge of the park, reading a newspaper.

Spider looked down at his watch. It was two minutes past noon. He wasn't shocked the delivery wasn't punctual. A drug dealer would be a fool to meet at any set time. By doing so they would expose themselves to ambush. A smart dealer would do counter-surveillance and mark the target area prior to a meeting. Spider knew this, because he worked for such men in his previous life. The cartel he worked for required him to be a master of many talents. Interrogation was among them, and he excelled better than most. But he also was a part of a hand-picked security team for one of Mexico's biggest distributors of cocaine. He had carried out the orders of his employer. Some of those actions haunted him to this day. Jay had snatched him during a raid and given him an opportunity to start over.

"I haven't seen any cars loop. Nor have I picked up any surveillance on foot in the area," Spider said.

"Roger. It's quiet up here on our end of the street," Barbie replied.

Spider folded the paper, opening it to a new section. He did this every two and a half minutes to keep up the mystique of a man enjoying his lunch-break read. His eyes glanced from the paper to the surrounding area. He didn't move his head much, mostly acquiring the visual scan through his peripheral.

"Got a dark sedan. Just pulled past us. Heavy tints on the window. Couldn't get a positive on the driver. Stay sharp," Barbie said, broadcasting to the group.

Spider picked up the blue sedan as it pulled up to the left side of Sachem Street, the road that ran alongside the park. It came to a stop near the intersection with Quincy Shore Drive. The brake lights flashed, and a tall, muscular man exited. He wore a navy suit and held a thick yellow manila envelope in his hand.

"Heads-up. Male party. Tall. He's got something in hand. Doesn't look like the guy O'Leary described," Nick relayed.

"I don't like it," Declan said softly. "Get ready to move."

"Hold tight," whispered Spider. "Let's see where this goes. We jump the wrong guy and it may spook our only chance. Everybody stay put. I'm eyes on the ground and have control of the situation."

"Roger," Nick acknowledged.

The man in the suit paused for a moment, looking at Spider as he passed by. He then proceeded toward the gazebo where O'Leary was seated. Spider looked up from his paper casually sizing up the man in the suit. He gave a nod and the man in the suit returned the favor.

The man in the suit had a distinguished look about him. More of a businessman than a drug dealer. Although, Spider knew, some of the most dangerous of men wear a suit. He knew this because he was one of them. As the man walked by, Spider noticed a slight bulge along the hipline on the right side of the small of his back. The impression etched in the man's suit jacket was readily identifiable to Spider's trained eye.

"He's armed. Right rear hip," Spider announced. He folded the paper to mask his whispered transmission.

Spider watched as O'Leary shifted to face the approaching man. He looked around nervously.

"Who the hell are you? Where's Stinky Pete?" O'Leary asked.

"I'm personally delivering this today. Pete is now retired," the well-dressed man said quietly. He looked back at Spider again. "I see you brought company. Don't trust me?"

Spider was just out of earshot, but the glance back in his direction from the man in the suit worried him. O'Leary was beginning to sweat. All signs that something was definitely off with this meet.

"Look, just give me the damn package and let's get this over with," O'Leary barked.

"You stupid bastard! You set me up!" The man in the suit hissed and turned to leave, the package now tucked under his armpit.

Spider set aside the paper and stood. "The suit is the target. I'm moving in to intercept. Barbie on me. Now!"

The man moved adeptly, shoving his hand into the small of his back and removing a compact handgun. Spider made his move to withdraw his weapon, but he was on the losing end of an action versus reaction scenario. The suited man fired without a second's hesitation, delivering two rounds in Spider's direction. The impact slammed into Spider's chest. He smelled gunpowder and felt a burning sensation before falling backward striking the base of his skull on the hard wood of the bench. Immediately, his world cut to black.

Nick watched in horror from across the street as the shots rang out from the park. Spider was down and the man in the suit was on the move.

The shooter spun and fired back at O'Leary, who sat frozen in fear on the gazebo's bench seat. One round struck the obese bar owner in his forehead, just above his bulbous nose. The force rocked him back and forth like a Weeble Wobble until the big man collapsed face first into the playground's frozen turf.

Nick and Declan were already up and moving fast. Barbie closed the gap, coming to a stop behind the dark colored sedan.

"Spider's down. We're on point!" Barbie yelled over the screeching of her tires.

The man heard the sound of the approaching van and took aim, firing a barrage of bullets at the windshield. Blood spatter showered the splintered glass of the windshield. Declan took aim while on the move, firing a controlled burst from the patio. Nick hurdled the railing, landing hard on the sidewalk below. He was in a dead sprint toward the van. Declan emptied his magazine as the sedan sped away from the carnage.

Nick stood frozen, staring at the bullet-riddled van containing Barbie and Mouse. His heart pounded and his mind reeled to catch up. A man capable of maintaining a steely resolve under fire was paralyzed with fear, not for himself but for the brave girl he'd brought into this danger-filled unit. "We've got to go! Now!" Declan boomed, snapping Nick from his trance.

Declan was ahead of him, running toward the downed body of Spider, with Nick close behind. Nick grabbed his feet and Declan scooped Spider under the armpits. They ran, in step, toward the idling van. Spider groaned at the jostling motion—a good sign.

Nick opened the back doors and they slid Spider inside. Declan followed, closing the door behind them. Barbie was slumped to the side and her mangled head was being cradled by Mouse. Tears fell from the girl's blood-covered face. She shook her head slowly, answering Nick's unasked question.

Declan peeled Mouse's grip from the dead woman and pulled hard, hoisting her out of the driver's seat, into the open expanse of the truck's utility area where Spider lay moaning.

Nick applied direct pressure to Spider's wound as Declan pulled out of the area. The van raced along toward the Vault as the picturesque shoreline disappeared from view, leaving behind O'Leary's dead body and a slew of unanswered questions.

19

Spider was lying on the table inside the Cube where Nick had conducted his interrogation of the now dead O'Leary the previous day. Jay had managed to get the bleeding from his shoulder to stop using quick clot. The pressure Nick applied during the exfiltration assisted in saving his life. The bullet had entered and exited Spider's body, a through-and-through wound, tearing flesh and muscle but missing the bone. Jay acted as their resident medic, handling non-surgical trauma. His experience in such work had been honed during numerous clandestine ops overseas where limited access to medical facilities was the norm. The second bullet had struck Spider in the chest. Had Spider not been wearing a light-weight vest, he would be dead. The .40 caliber round struck the vest just left of his heart and the impact cracked his ribs. An excellent shot group from the man in the suit. It was the mark of an experienced shooter to be able to draw and shoot with accuracy while on the move facing multiple targets.

Jay exited the Cube. Spider's blood tainted his fingers and the sleeves of his white button-down shirt. "Let me get washed up and then we'll get started. Grab a mug."

Mouse turned to Nick. She'd showered and changed out of her blood-covered clothes. She absently rubbed her hands together as if still trying to remove invisible traces of Barbie's blood from her skin. "What did he mean by grab a mug?"

"You'll see. Have a seat and take a load off. I'll get you one from the break room," Nick said.

Mouse sat and then laid her head down on the table, her long, dark hair shrouding her face from view.

Nick opened an overhead cabinet in the Vault's break room. Declan stood by his side. Barbie's death had rocked both men, although admittedly neither man had really had much of an opportunity to learn much about her other than she was a stalwart companion on a mission. The unit's commitment to anonymity created an emotional disconnect. With the rate at which team members were killed or wounded, he understood its secondary purpose. It made dealing with the death of a teammate more tolerable.

"This unit's life expectancy is a lot shorter than I anticipated," Declan said.

Nick took a hard look at his friend. He knew the man's impressive military and police background, a man accustomed to life's tragedies. But there was something different about him today.

"You okay? You seem a bit off today."

"We've had two mission assignments since you and I came onboard. Two assignments and two deaths. Those are terrible odds, especially for a unit our size," Declan said flatly.

"You're right about that." Nick shook his head. "And I just brought Mouse into this group."

Declan sighed as he grabbed a mug at random—a plain-blue porcelain coffee mug.

Nick did the same, pulling two from the cabinet. He stared at one of the mugs in his hand. World's Best Dad was embossed on the outside. He slid the mug across the table to his friend.

"This one's more fitting for you."

Declan gave a weak smile. "I used to feel that way. My family is everything to me. You know the sacrifices I've made and would make for them. But lately, current circumstances being what they are, I'm starting to question my priorities."

Nick nodded. The two had first met because of one of Declan's more desperate decisions to provide for his family. A decision that could have had cataclysmic repercussions if not for Nick's intervention and subsequent redirection of the case investigation. Declan had made amends, atoning for his crime, but Nick knew the past still haunted him.

"This group is really starting to tear things apart in my family life. Laney's regressing. Her therapist has been applying some new coping strategies but integration into school has been extremely difficult. She's communicating more now, but her outbursts are still overwhelming, and Val's called to the school multiple times per week to assist. The meetings with social workers and her assigned paraprofessional are time consuming and occurring with more frequency lately. The energy Val expends on Laney leaves little left over for my two older girls. I used to be able to provide balance to that equation. Not so much lately. With the odds against us, I can't imagine leaving my girls to a life without their father. I'm truly conflicted. And that doesn't bode well for my focus."

"You need to do what you need to for your family. I know you risked a lot to get me here. Whatever debt you feel you owe me has been paid in full ten times over. You're the only person who can decide what you need to do, but I think you already know."

Declan was silent.

"Let's go say our goodbyes to Barbie," Nick said, turning and walking back out into the main office space.

Jay stood at the head of the table with a large bottle in hand. The remaining members of the group circled the table minus the empty chair normally occupied by Barbie. Jay released the champagne cork with a loud pop followed by a second bang as it struck the ceiling. The noise caused Wiz to jump.

Jay moved mug to mug, rounding the table and pouring the gold-tinged liquid for each member. The fizz of the carbonation was the only sound in the room.

Returning to his position at the head of the table, Jay held up his mug.

"To Ashley Crespin. She made the ultimate sacrifice. A death the world will never know about. A sacrifice understood only by those present here today. Until Valhalla!"

"Until Valhalla!" the rest said, each downing their glass.

"She was kind to me," Mouse said, her eyes watering from carbonation. "She treated me like I was family. I don't know much about her but during our little shopping trip she made me laugh. Not many people are able to do that. I'm going to miss her."

"You weren't going to wake me?" Spider asked. He entered the room with his IV holder in tow. He was pale and moved slowly.

"What are you doing up and about?" Nick asked.

"I'm not going to miss my only opportunity to pay my respects."

Declan hustled off and returned a moment later with a mug for Spider who took up a seat next to Wiz. Jay filled the wounded man's cup and gave him a knowing smile.

"She and I came into the unit at the same time. The adjustment to this new life didn't come easily for me, and on more than one occasion, I planned on making my escape back to the world I knew. Barbie...correction, Ashley...was the one who talked me down. Somehow she helped me see the bigger picture of what we do and ultimately where I belong."

Nick looked over at Declan and thought about the conversation they'd just had. His reasons for leaving trumped any for staying, and he worried his friend's loyalty would cloud his judgement. He made a mental note to revisit it when things settled.

Spider raised his mug with his uninjured arm. "Until Valhalla!"

The group clanged their mugs together and drained the remnants of their drinks.

"Let's waste no time in seeking our vengeance," Jay said.

"I've already pulled the footage from Jay's lapel camera." Wiz pushed back from the table and moved toward his workstation. "Give me a sec and I'll bring it up on the big screen."

Nick looked at the large flat screen television mounted on the wall adjacent to the conference table. It was muted, with a live newscast covering the recent shooting in Wollaston Beach Park. Behind the windswept hair of the blonde reporter the *do not cross* tape fluttered in the shore breeze. Police and crime scene techs were scattered about the backdrop in various positions of investigation. The caption read, *Shootout in Quincy Leaves One Dead.* A subheading stated that police were looking for any information on the shooters.

The image on the scene was replaced by a still image of the well-dressed man. He was facing toward the camera and had a small handgun pressed outward. Seeing him frozen in time, Nick was able to better process the man's features. The shooter was older than Nick had expected based on the athletic maneuvers he'd made during the altercation. His hair was tightly cut along the sides in military fashion with a touch of gray.

"This image was taken a millisecond before the first shot was fired," Wiz said.

"Does anybody recognize this man?" Jay asked.

"He looks familiar but not sure why. I can't specifically place him, but I definitely get the feeling I've seen him before," Nick said.

"I've got his image running through some facial recognition software, but the database of images is extensive and could take hours. If it manages to locate him at all," Wiz said.

"Keep at it until you do," Jay directed.

Wiz nodded and turned back to his monitors.

"This guy's a professional," Declan added.

"What makes you say that?" Mouse asked, speaking softly.

"I'd say by the look of that haircut and his shooting stance, he's ex-military, probably with some special operations experience. He was able to neutralize our attempt to snatch him with calculated efficiency. He killed two and injured a third in a matter of seconds. Most of his shooting was done on the move. Whoever we're dealing with isn't a simple street thug. Hit play and you'll see exactly what I'm talking about."

Wiz activated the playback function and the still image came to life. At full speed it was a blur of movement once the gunfire began.

"Slow it down." Declan waited for the slow-motion playback of the same scene. "Look at his target transition. He fires two quick shots. Before Spider's down he pivots and puts a headshot on O'Leary. That's a rare skillset you're witnessing."

Nick thought back to the bank robbery footage where he watched

Declan incapacitate two armored truck guards with such blinding speed. He remembered Izzy nicknaming him Flash as a result. Looking at the playback on the television it looked as though they were facing a similar adversary, and the thought was not a welcome one.

"Wiz, can you run the software through military databases as well?" Jay asked.

"It's all part of the program I designed, but it's still going to take some time. As good as this system is, we still haven't caught up to the imaginative level portrayed on television and in movies. I'll let you know as soon as I have any potential hits."

"Declan, reach out to Sorenson. Maybe they've got some info about the shooting that might be useful in identifying our guy."

"Sure thing, but not certain how cooperative he'll be since we pissed in his cornflakes when we stole his case out from under him," Declan said.

Jay retreated to his office and closed the door. Nick looked over at Mouse.

"How're you holding up, kiddo?" Nick asked.

Mouse shrugged. "I've seen a lot of bad things, but Barbie's killing caught me a bit unprepared. She was showing me the ropes. Took me shopping. She made this weird little group seem normal. Now she's gone."

Nick put his arm around her and pulled her in close. "I was so worried you'd been shot, too. I froze. It's never happened to me before. Seeing those rounds hit the windshield stopped me dead in my tracks. I don't know what I'd do if it had been you."

Mouse looked up at him from her position buried in his armpit. "Thanks."

"Thanks? For what?" Nick asked.

"For caring. Few people in my life have ever done that. You're a good man, Nick Lawrence."

It had been a long time since he'd felt as though he was a good person. The words struck him at the core. During his year in prison, he'd mentally punished himself for his failings. An abusive physical and psychological regimen aimed at recreating himself from the ashes. His self-image never fully recovered.

"She misses you, too."

"Who?" Nick asked.

"Anaya."

Nick sat back, derailed by the mention of her name. He still loved her, but managed to tuck those feelings, and the memory of the life he destroyed, into the deepest recess of his memory.

"Seriously Nick! I'm not messing with you. She came to visit me at my high school graduation. We talked."

"What'd she say?"

"She was hurt, physically and emotionally, after what happened to her. It was a lot for her to process, but she did sort out her feelings. She tried to set up visitations while you were incarcerated, but you denied access. She tried writing but the letters were returned unopened. You cut her out of your life. That may have been what hurt her the most. But even with all that, she's never stopped loving you."

"What life? I was serving consecutive life sentences. Was Anaya looking for a lifelong pen pal?" Nick snapped. He immediately regretted the outburst. "I'm sorry. I guess I haven't talked much about this with anyone. But, in my defense, I thought I was doing the right thing by her. It was also my way of dealing with my circumstances. Severing ties with the outside world was my only saving grace. Hard to understand, even for me, but it made sense then."

"You're not locked up anymore," Mouse said.

"She thinks I'm dead."

"But you're not."

"It's complicated."

"No, it's not. You showed up at my doorstep and look how everything turned out. Maybe your death was your first real chance at a life."

"When did you get so wise?"

"I'm an old soul." Mouse gave him a kiss on the cheek as she stood up from the table.

"Well, let's get going old soul. We've got a killer to catch."

20

He rubbed deeply at the gray patches framing his temples. The stress of the impending phone call was agonizing, but it was one he needed to make. He was sure his boss was already well aware of the recent turn of events, but an explanation was warranted.

He picked up the phone used for such calls. A phone that would be dumped after its one use. He let it ring twice and then hung up. He immediately redialed the number. The man on the other end picked up on the third ring. A simple but useful measure ensuring secrecy. If his boss did not answer on the second callback, he was to wait another hour and repeat the process until success. He was pleased he didn't have to forgo this conversation any longer.

"Explain," the gruff voice barked through clenched teeth.

"I was compromised," said the man softly. "Landers contacted me and said he needed some product to tide over one of the local crews until the next larger shipment. You told me to personally handle everything from this point forward, so I did the drop. When I got there, Landers had another guy with him. I wasn't sure at first, but then the guy made a move on me. I'm assuming he was a cop or a fed but can't be certain. I figured it'd look really bad for you if I was to get pinched with a quarter kilo of the stuff you're trying to get off the streets. So, I shot him and then I shot Landers. More responded, so I shot at them, too. Hit the driver and then escaped."

"You thought it'd be better to shoot a cop?" his boss asked. Without seeing the man, he knew his face was a deep red. Hearing the unspoken anger made him even gladder this conversation was not in person.

"Yes. Have you seen the news? No mention of a cop being shot or killed. Police are labeling this a mob hit or drug deal gone wrong, depending on which station you listen to. The Boston Police went on air asking for any witnesses to come forward. Does it sound like I killed a cop to you?"

"No."

"The more I think about it, I'm leaning toward the idea that maybe our fat bar owner wanted to cut himself a bigger piece of the pie and was trying to muscle his way out of the role as middle-man. Nothing else makes sense. He must've thought he could get the drop on me. I guess he underestimated the situation." He flicked some lint from the cuff of his expensive suit's sleeve.

"I guess that's a good thing. Because drug dealers typically don't call the police."

"Especially dead ones."

"That being said, you're going to need to make the next delivery to our friend, Mr. Caldwell. Because of your actions today, you're going to have to fill in for Landers."

"When?"

"It's going to have to be today. I want you to deliver a larger-than-normal shipment. Three kilos. Tell him it's an advance for all the great work he's been doing, and that we'll recoup it on the back end."

"Three kilos. It'll take him a while to offload that much product."

"I know. That's the plan. This is our last delivery. Everything else is in place. Tell Caldwell to sell the product uncut. I want the junkies to get their money's worth on this haul. We need our numbers to skyrocket over the next day or so. After you make the drop I want you to get word to our friend with Boston PD. Make sure everything is in place. I can't have any more debacles like today. Make it right. This is our chance to move up."

"Okay. I'll handle it."

21

He was still wearing the same suit from his encounter at Wollaston Beach as he stood outside the apartment door and knocked three times. He could hear the sounds of computer-generated gunfire and explosions, a far cry from the real thing he'd experienced both on and off the battlefield.

No answer. He banged louder, delivering his blows with the bottom pad of his balled fist. He was not a man accustomed to waiting, especially when the annoyance was caused by someone half his age.

A shout came through the door. "Who dat?"

"Open the door." He raised his voice louder than he'd intended, but he wanted to ensure being heard above the ruckus. He felt completely out of place in the rundown Roxbury apartment building.

The sound of the gameplay stopped, the person inside either paused or shut off the machine. He heard the creak of the floorboards on the other side of the door, and he could almost feel the eyes watching him through the peephole.

"You must have the wrong address," the voice said from within.

"Trust me, I'm at the right place. Now open the door."

"You the police? You know you need a warrant to come in here," the man said.

Is this idiot serious? What self-respecting cop would walk up and knock on a criminal's door?

"No, I'm not a cop. I have something for you, and I'd prefer we not discuss it through the door. It's a package that I can't leave on your doorstep," he said, trying to be as discrete as possible, but failing miserably.

"I ain't order no package," the man said.

"Landers isn't around to deliver it," the man seethed. He instantly regretted killing him earlier. This would've been much easier to delegate to the fat bar owner. "Now open the damn door!"

He heard the deadbolt slide, releasing the steel lock from the frame. The door opened and he was face to face with Sam Caldwell, a.k.a. Jinx.

"Mr. Caldwell, you and I need to talk." the man entered the apartment, pushing past the smaller-statured drug dealer. He did his best not to brush his suit against the tank top- wearing hoodlum.

The two-bedroom apartment was small but had an open layout connecting the kitchen area to the living room. It smelled of Cheetos and marijuana, two odors he despised. The man was standing in his own personal hell.

"Nobody calls me by my government name. Everybody 'round here calls me Jinx." He said his street name with boastful pride.

"Okay then, Jinx, let's you and me discuss some pertinent business matters."

The chairs and couches of the apartment were littered with various pizza boxes and a variety of other food cartons. After a quick assessment of his surroundings, he resigned himself to delivering the package and accompanying instructions from a standing position.

"Where's Landers?" Jinx asked suspiciously.

"Dead."

"Dead? When?"

"Don't you watch the news?" He shot a glance toward the fifty-two-inch flat screen television set with a paused image of an alien battleground and immediately realized the stupidity of his question.

"Nah. Too busy for that nonsense. I'm a business man," Jinx said, smugly.

"Right. I can see that. Let's get down to it. I'd hate to keep you from your demanding work schedule. I have three kilos of fentanyl here." The man unshouldered the leather satchel, sliding it off his suited shoulder, and rested it at his feet.

"Hey man, I don't got the money for that right now. I don't know what you're thinking walkin' in here with that much product. Landers ain't never brought that much before."

"I'm not Landers. Plus, my employer would like to compensate you for the little setback to your operation. With two of your employees in jail and you out of quite a bit of product, I thought you might be a bit more excited at this opportunity. I can, however, take it to someone else more willing to cooperate?"

"No, I'm straight as long as you can front me the keys. I can pay you back on the flip?" Jinx bartered.

"That's what we intended. This could be your big break. If you do right by us with this shipment, then we are going to be able to cut you in on a bigger piece of the operation."

"I can step on this stuff a hundred times and make us a killing," Jinx said, smiling.

"No. You're not to cut it with anything. My employer is adamant about this batch of product hitting the streets as is."

Jinx shook his head. "You know how powerful this crap is, right? This is pure fent! You want me to put it out as is? That could bust some people up. Junkies don't know how to handle this stuff. You could be killing off a bunch of your clientele."

"How about you stick to the dealing and I'll worry about the rest."

"Whatever man. It's your baby. You raise it the way you want."

"Also, I've placed a stamp for your bags. We're working on some brand recognition with this batch. We really want to stand out from the crowd." He bent down and retrieved the three wrapped packages, handing them to Jinx, who in turn placed them on the table behind him. He dipped his hand back into the satchel and then stood, holding the stamp and pad.

"What's the stamp?" Jinx asked, reaching out his hand.

"It's just the number eight." He handed it over to the drug dealer. He was glad this exchange would soon be complete and he could leave.

"Why the number eight?"

"Isn't that what you call it on the street? Murder 8? Like I said, we're looking for some brand recognition."

"Oh, I get it. Makes sense to me. But you know most of us don't stamp Murder bags. Especially with the cops crackin' down on bodies. That's bad for business. But do whatever you want, fancy man." Jinx tossed the stamp over with the packages.

The well-dressed man suppressed the desire to strike out and instead leveled a steady gaze at the young dealer. "It's important you start getting this out right away. Is that clear?"

"I'm a little short-staffed right now with some of my best members locked up."

"I'm sure a savvy businessman like yourself can figure it out." He turned and walked to the door.

"How do I get in touch with you?" Jinx asked.

"You don't. But worry not, I'll be back soon enough."

The man exited the apartment, closing the door behind him as he went. He felt the apartment's odor linger, and he moved briskly toward the exit, hoping the cool afternoon wind would wash the stink from his clothing.

Outside he walked the block to where his car was parked and left the Orchard Park neighborhood of Roxbury behind.

The man answered on the first ring. "Sorenson."

"I've got another tip for you," Wilcox said.

"How is it that a senator's aide gets intel on local drugs rings?" Sorenson asked.

"We've got a lot of concerned citizens in our constituency. They pass along plenty of information, but request anonymity, and I try to respect that. Would you prefer I call someone else in your PD? Have I not provided you with valuable information in the past?"

"Of course I appreciate it. I was just asking is all," Sorenson said, softening his tone.

"Listen. This next one could be a big one. I got a call from someone I trust implicitly. The senator is going to want to hold a press conference when it's all said and done. You and your team are going to be the face of his Hope Restored initiative. This could definitely benefit your career track." Wilcox knew Sorenson was on the Lieutenants' list and was confident his last statement would resonate with the career-oriented police officer.

"Sounds good. What do you got?"

"My constituent called me, frantic. He had information on a local dealer moving a lot of deadly crap. He is well established in the community and has his finger on the pulse of this sort of thing. I've been told there's a local group in the Roxbury neighborhood called the OP Hoodstars, or Hoodrats. Hood-something or other, but you get the gist. Kind of out of my element on this. Have you heard of them?" Wilcox asked.

"Of course. I'm very familiar with the group. We hit them the other day. Pretty good bust too. Until the Feds snatched it from us," Sorenson said.

"I didn't realize that was the same case you told me about when you said you were having jurisdictional issues. I've been looking into it on our end to see if we could cut the red tape for you, but so far no such luck. Nothing saying you have to tell the Bureau guys on this one."

"Not so sure about that. Orders came from high to cooperate in all aspects of this investigation with the FBI task force guys. So, I guess I'll have to send the info over to the other guys. Hopefully, they'll keep me in the loop, though."

"The senator would prefer this stayed local. Boston PD needs to take the credit for this one. It won't have as much impact with the voters if this is handed off to a federal task force. You're a smart guy. You can see what I'm driving at? You're the point man on this one, Danny. The senator's counting on you."

"You're putting me in a tough spot. I'll do my best. What's the intel?"

"Some guy named Jinx, lives in the Orchard Park neighborhood, supposedly just received a very large amount of pure fentanyl. Not quite sure what constitutes a large amount in the drug world, but if recent headlines are remotely accurate, then if that stuff hits the streets it'll be bad news."

"I'm on it!" Sorenson said, eagerly. "Tell the senator he can count on me and my team to get the job done."

"I expected nothing less. Good luck sergeant, and let me know how everything turns out on this one. I want to make sure you are rewarded for your great efforts."

Wilcox ended the phone call.

22

Sorenson sat at his desk and flicked the business card against his fingers, staring at the number on the back. Avery Wilcox had promised some big things with this raid, but he'd also received a direct order from his superior, instructing him to play nice with the feds. He weighed the potential fallout of his next move and made his decision.

"Smith," Sorenson called out through the open door.

A moment later the large frame of the gentle giant Scott Smith filled the doorway's threshold. Like a loyal pitbull, he stood ready to spring into action.

"You rang?"

"I've got a tip. Could be big. The Hoodstars just got re-upped on a large quantity of pure fentanyl. This could be an excellent opportunity for us to make a serious dent in the distribution. Maybe slow down some of the ODs. Not sure the exact quantity, but in the four hours since I received the tip our patrol division has been overwhelmed with overdoses. Last count, we've had twenty-seven overdoses, with eleven fatal. It's an unprecedented number; apparently these guys are putting uncut fentanyl on the street," Sorenson said, delivering the message rapid-fire with his thick Boston accent.

"I thought we are playing second fiddle to the Feds on this one?"

Sorenson leaned forward. "Not anymore. I want this one in a bad way. We don't need a bunch of FBI guys coming in and stealing our spoils."

Smith folded his massive forearms and nodded.

"Hell, look what they did on the Merc arrest. They let us do all the grunt work and swooped in after the hard stuff was done. Then they take them off to who-knows-where and interview them. Did we get any kickback from that? No! They shut us out completely."

"Aren't you worried about the fallout from the brass if we don't play nice?" Smith asked.

"I think I've got that angle covered." Sorenson winked. In the back of his mind he hoped the senator would keep his word.

"Your team, boss. You know we'd follow you to hell and back. Say the word and I'll rally the troops."

"Saddle up."

Smith gave a thumbs up and left to alert the other TNT members. Sorenson tossed the FBI agent's business card into the waste bin beside his desk and set to task, preparing his intel briefing for the upcoming operation.

"Hey guys, I think you need to check this out," Wiz called out from his workspace.

Nick and the others piled in around the computer wizard.

"As you know, Declan planted a couple bugs in the TNT office space during the briefing. I've also been up on Sorenson's cellphone. Just to make sure we're kept in the loop. They're an active unit to say the least, but nothing related to our investigation. Well, that was until today."

"What're they up to?" Jay asked.

"They got a tip on large quantity of fentanyl. Looks like they're keeping the intel to themselves on this one."

"Can you blame 'em? We pretty much came in and stole their thunder on their last big hit. If I were in their shoes not sure I wouldn't do the same thing," Declan said.

"Do we have a target location?" Nick asked.

"It's the same crew out of Roxbury. The target is a Sam Caldwell. I've located his apartment. The information is a few hours old. I was working on the facial recognition for our shooter from the park and had the bugs running in the background. I missed the software's keyword recognition alerts about the fentanyl. Sorry," Wiz said.

"How far behind the power curve are we?" Jay asked.

"A few hours. Looks like they secured a search warrant and are in the middle of briefing the op now. If you gear up now, you may be able to beat them to the target location, but it's going to be tight."

"Nick and I can handle this one. Get us up on comms. We'll be out the door in five minutes," Declan said.

Mouse gave Nick a look of dejection. He mussed her hair as he passed. "Next time, kiddo."

Nick and Declan each grabbed a black tactical ballistic raid vest and affixed Velcro patches to the front and back with the bright white letters FBI.

Wiz filled them in as they sped to the Hoodstar stash house. "Looks like their op plan is using relatively standard tactics. The decision had been made to use a ruse to open the door before trying to break it. Apparently, earlier in the week the TNT guys had encountered a formidably reinforced door, and they hoped to avoid repeating the same mistake."

"Are they mobile yet?" Nick asked as Declan took a corner hugging the curb as he raced along the GPS's trail.

"An undercover female police officer is going to knock, posing as an addict looking for a fix. The entry team will be stacked in the hall and once the door was open, they'll move in," Wiz said, his voice projected in their earpieces.

Nick had been impressed with Sorenson's command of his team and the tactical proficiency in executing the car takedown on Merc. It seemed as though the Boston team was capable of cleanly executing the raid. And they had the manpower to carry it out.

"Any idea on how far out their team is right now?" Nick asked.

"I'm pinging Sorenson's phone. It's going to be close. Definitely no way you get in and out before they're on scene," Wiz said.

"I'm calling an audible. We're going to meet up with them, but TNT will make the hit. No way around it at this point. We'll snatch Caldwell after the raid, just like we did with Powell," Nick said.

Nick watched the GPS and the red dot they were racing toward. He couldn't help but feel they were on a collision course, the result of which remained unknown.

23

Sara Blanche had been an officer with the Boston Police for nearly two decades. Most of that time had been spent on the street with various stints in vice, primarily working prostitution cases. She looked the part in her role tonight. Her makeup had been caked on, giving her a look as though it had been applied by a six-year-old, who'd just found her mother's beauty box for the first time. The bright red lipstick was smeared out at the edges. Her clothes came from a stash Sara kept just for occasions like these and hadn't been washed in several weeks.

She lit a cigarette and walked around from a side street onto Orchard Park Street, home of the OP Hoodstars. A couple staggers added to her subterfuge, giving the impression of intoxication.

She dropped the cigarette on the outside steps leading to the apartment complex's main entrance. It was the all-clear signal Sorenson had come up with during the briefing. The small squad of darkly dressed members of the Tactical Narcotics Team emptied out of their van, parked a few buildings away, and silently assembled behind Blanche as she entered the building.

Blanche ascended the stairwell ahead of them to the floor containing Jinx's apartment. She cleared her throat, signaling it was clear to come up.

Once on the floor the team moved quietly into position as Blanche readied herself at the door.

She knocked quietly, then said, "Hey man, open up!"

The television could be heard in the hallway. So, Blanche knocked louder. The team hugged the left side of the wall and the point man was less than a foot away from the door's frame.

"C'mon man, I need to get right!" Blanche pleaded. Her raspy voice and slight slur to her speech added weight to the character she portrayed.

"I don't know you!" A male voice yelled through the door.

"Yeah you do. C'mon man, it's me, Trixie," Blanche whined.

The voice behind the door, obviously speaking to someone else in the room, said, "Do you know a Trixie?"

"Hey brah, everybody knows a Trixie. Just open the door, fool!" another said.

The deadbolt clacked and the knob began to turn. The door opened and a young Hispanic teenager stood in the doorway.

"What you need?" Spaz asked.

Sara Blanche stepped back. A second later, the massive frame of the team's breacher, Scott Smith, filled the void. "Police! Search Warrant!" He boomed as he entered.

Blasting the teen's chest with his forearm, Smith knocked the thin juvenile backward. The force of the blow sent Spaz flipping backward over the arm of the living room couch. He landed, crashing into the cheaply made table and sending a large glass marijuana bong, followed by several video game controllers, into the air.

Smith stayed on the boy as the remaining members of the team, including Sorenson, filled the apartment. The second man in rolled a flash-bang grenade into the kitchen area where Jinx was seated at a table which was covered in the bright white powder being packaged into small bags.

Jinx popped up with a revolver in hand, raising it in the direction of the fast-moving team. The wild-eyed drug dealer fired blindly in the direction of the TNT entry team, ripping off several rounds in rapid succession. The cylinder spun on the long-barreled wheel gun as each deafening shot rang out.

Sorenson ducked low while simultaneously bringing up his Glock. The years of range training and experience kicked into drive. His mind, through countless hours of drills, activated his proprioception, allowing him the ability to fire instinctively and without aiming. He pulled the trigger, firing two successive shots, striking the dealer in the chest as the flashbang went off.

The concussive blast threw the opened package of fentanyl into the air. The powder clouded the small apartment as members of the team cleared the remainder of the apartment. Even with the two known threats neutralized, it was important to clear the unknown areas. Smith was on top of the gangly teenager, smothering him in his massive bulk.

Sorenson scampered across the floor as fine bits of powder drifted down around him. It was like a scene from a post-apocalyptic movie. Every movement forward came through labored effort as though he were moving in slow motion. He found the dealer sprawled against the refrigerator, surrounded by thousands of glassine bags, some bundled with black rubber bands and some loose. All were stamped with a black 8.

Sorenson was on all fours beside the dealer. The revolver was still gripped in the dealer's hand. His finger continued to mindlessly pull the trigger. The now empty chamber of the Smith & Wesson clicked loudly, an automated response of the dying man. Sorenson ripped the gun free from the man's hand and slid it along the floor.

He yanked hard on the outstretched arm of Sam Caldwell, a.k.a. Jinx, pulling him closer. The dealer flopped forward listless, offering no resistance. Sorenson pressed the dealer face down on the powder covered laminate floor of the kitchen. He climbed atop, awkwardly mounting the dealer's back. Sorenson's mind was cloudy, and it took more effort than it should have to complete this task. He manipulated each arm to the small of Caldwell's back and ratcheted the cuffs into place. The drug dealer's white tank top was now soaked in the deep red of his blood.

Sorenson slid his hand along Caldwell's neck. He pressed two fingers along the man's carotid artery and checked for a pulse. It was weak, but there.

Sorenson slid off the dying man and took a kneeling position alongside. He rolled Caldwell onto his back and immediately applied hard pressure on the young man's chest, trying to slow the bleeding.

"Medic up!" Sorenson bellowed.

Sorenson felt his efforts wane and the room began to spin. The woozy feeling intensified and he collapsed on top of the bloody body

As the world began to collapse around him, he heard one of his team members scream out in anguish. "Smith's down! It's bad! Oh God, no!"

Sorenson fought to get up but his body wouldn't respond. He was trapped under an invisible, dizzying weight. Other TNT members around him began wheezing and coughing. Some started vomiting, while others fell to their knees. Through the haze and confusion, Sorenson caught a glimpse of his larger-than-life friend sprawled on the floor. Smith's head was turned toward him, and Sorenson saw the vacant, expressionless eyes staring back at him. It was the last thing he saw as the world around him went dark.

Nick and Declan had arrived at the same time as the TNT group, as Wiz had predicted. After a brief and awkward exchange, Nick and Declan agreed to remain outside the apartment building with the perimeter security members of Sorenson's team.

As soon as they heard the shots and murmured screams, the two made entry. They ascended the staircase taking two and three steps at a time and sprinted down the short hallway to the door.

Sara Blanche was exiting the apartment. Her back was arced as she pulled one of the TNT members by his raid vest's shoulder straps into the hallway. She had wrapped her shirt around her face. She back peddled until she slammed her back into the wall opposite the entranceway. Blanche released the man to the ground with a thud. She took a knee beside him, exhausted from the effort.

"Don't breathe that crap!" she wheezed. "Stuff will take you out."

Nick and Declan took off their shirts. Tightly tying them to their faces, they entered the apartment.

One by one, the two strong men pulled the remaining members into the hallway. Medics filled the area with equipment bags and stretchers, extracting those in the worst condition and rendering on-site aid to those less impacted by the ingestion of the substance. Sorenson was hauled away on a stretcher, unconscious. Smith lay dead on the apartment floor. One of the rounds loosed by Caldwell had struck the big man in his exposed neck. He had bled out within seconds of the impact.

Sam Caldwell, the dealer known to the Orchard Park community as Jinx, was pronounced dead during his transport to the hospital.

Nick sat against the hallway wall surveying the carnage. He was taking shallow breaths through the mask attached to his face. The oxygen helped clear the fog in his head. His head was pounding like the day after an all-night bender.

Declan, sitting across from him, looked to be in the same shape. "Ever seen anything like this?"

"Never." Nick said. "I guess the reports weren't exaggerated about the dangers of fentanyl. That was something I'd have expected to see overseas. It was like a biochemical attack."

He was glad Mouse hadn't been here on this one. They needed to collect themselves and figure out their next move. With the target dead, Nick needed to find some answers, and had an idea of where to start.

24

Senator Buzz Litchfield watched the newscast covering the previous night's drug raid. Wilcox sat by silently. The anchor had phrased it as a daring raid aimed at stopping one of the deadliest drugs on the market. The news ping-ponged between the takedown operation and the previous day's spike in overdoses among the neighboring communities. It was the third station he'd watched, and all were taking a similar perspective on recent events.

Litchfield clicked the power button on the remote, turning his attention to the man seated before him. He evaluated his aide-de-camp and personal friend, choosing his words carefully.

"I've asked a lot of you lately, my old friend. I know that. At times, maybe my demands were too much. But, please understand, I did all of it with absolute faith you were the best man for the job." Litchfield paused. "This most recent task was carried out to absolute perfection. I couldn't have asked for a better result."

"Thank you, Buzz."

"Keep tabs on Sorenson. I'm having Baker organize the press conference for later this morning and I'd like him there."

"Last I checked, he was still being monitored at the hospital. The nurse I spoke to last night told me his prognosis was good, and he'd most likely be released sometime this morning. They were just keeping him overnight as a precaution. He may need some additional time to recover."

"Additional time?"

"One of his teammates was killed in that raid. Might be best to wait until he's had time to process that and bury his friend before we parade him around the city as a hero."

"No time like the present. I didn't wait after my daughter was buried. I didn't go into hiding. I stood up and took my stand. And I think, looking at the polls, that decision was a game-changer. I think the same will be said for jumping on this right away. Press and public opinion are fickle beasts and we must strike when opportunity presents. This is one of those times. You understand?"

"Yes, sir. I do."

"Excellent. As soon as he is physically able, notify me so we can finalize the time for a press release," Litchfield said excitedly. "This is it, Avery. This is going to be the big one."

"I'm just glad to have been a part of your rise. It's been my absolute pleasure to serve you, sir. And hopefully, I'll continue to have a place and earn my keep."

"Don't worry, my friend, you're coming all the way to the top when I go." Litchfield stood and walked around his desk, resting his hand on his friend's taut shoulder. "Seriously, I don't know what I would've done without you. With Amber gone, you're really the only family I've got left now."

Litchfield had been given little time to grieve for the loss of his beloved Amber, and the thought of her now gave him pause. He personally hated using her death to his political advantage, but knew that his best chance at making the world a better place resided with him in the ultimate position of power. She'd have understood. At least he placated himself with that thought.

Wilcox stood. "I'll check on Sorenson and get back to you as soon as I hear something. Do you want me to send Baker in when I leave?"

"Yes, please do. There's much to discuss."

Gloria Baker was standing outside the door as it opened, like a loyal puppy excitedly awaiting the return of her owner. She entered the room as Wilcox departed.

"It looks like your opioid reform is taking hold. The seizure in Boston is going to really be a feather in your cap going forward. The timing of that raid couldn't have been better. Especially with all of the recent overdose deaths. People will see the importance of your initiative. As tragic as yesterday's events were, it could be the big break we've been looking for."

"I'm glad you see it that way. To that end, I need you to set another press event. We are going to capitalize on this. Ride this wave of media attention to drive forward the importance of my reform efforts. I've got Wilcox trying to reach out to that sergeant in charge of orchestrating the seizure. He should be commended for his bravery, as well as the team member who gave his life in the execution of that raid. And I plan to do just that."

Gloria Baker smiled. Litchfield knew the woman loved a positive-spin campaign. She made several quick notations in her notebook and the senator knew the wheels were turning and Baker was beginning to map out the ebb and flow of this political push.

"Today is the day we're also making the announcement," Litchfield said, returning her smile.

"Wow! This is it, then? I guess its timing is perfect. You delivered a knockout speech the other day after your daughter's funeral. The quotes are still being used as taglines, which, in the world of twenty-four-hour news coverage, is an amazing thing. So I think you're absolutely right to strike while the iron's hot, sir."

"As soon as Avery gets back to me on the status of Sergeant Sorenson, I'll let you know. But get the word out. It's happening today. Sooner, rather than later."

"Will do, sir. We can really take advantage of this opportunity. I'll begin generating a buzz. My media connections will be clamoring for this kind of thing. I'm very excited for you."

"Thank you. We're going to effect some real change in this country."

Baker turned and departed.

Litchfield embraced the silence and took the time to add some notes about the bust in Roxbury to his speech. It was one he'd been preparing for a long time, and now he had the final details in place to make it absolutely perfect. Even in the wake of yesterday's chaos, he couldn't help but smile at the prospect of what the future held.

25

Nick stood outside the room. Several nurses and doctors had entered and exited over the past half hour while Sorenson completed his discharge from the hospital. Nick noted no family in the waiting area. He felt bad for the detective sergeant and at the same time could empathize, knowing he too had made similar choices in his career. Putting the job ahead of his personal life had been a broken road.

The entire team was evaluated for the fentanyl exposure. The drug was dangerous on multiple fronts. It could be ingested intravenously, transdermally, or by inhalation. The latter proved to be the most detrimental to the entry team members. The flashbang created an aerosol dispersal of the opioid. Proximity to the kitchen and the amount breathed in correlated to the severity of symptoms. Sorenson had taken the worst of it while the others only sustained flu-like symptoms.

Nick watched Sorenson step out of the room with a blue folder containing his discharge paperwork, along with an information packet on the risks of fentanyl. Nick slipped in next to him as the narcotics sergeant made his way past the nurses' station toward the elevators.

"How you feeling?" Nick asked.

"Been better. Feel like I woke up on the wrong side of some bad seafood. What about you?"

"Nothing more than a headache. I was treated on scene by a medic. But Blanche warned us and we made a makeshift facemask before entering. I think it saved us from taking the brunt of the exposure."

"Smart thinking. I'm glad you did. Thanks for pulling me and the other guys out of there."

"You'd have done the same."

Sorenson stopped walking and faced Nick. "I'm not sure what the hell you guys are up to, but I reached out to my friends in the Bureau and they've never heard of you."

"It's a big agency. And, like I said when we first met, our unit operates out of D.C. No big surprise somebody from the Boston office doesn't know me."

"I've got a million questions for you. For starters, how the hell did you guys know about tonight's raid?'

"We've got an excellent intelligence source."

"Only way you knew was through my source, which I highly doubt, or you bugged my office."

"Maybe someone from your side kept us in the loop," Nick said, hoping to throw off the detective.

"Fat chance. My guys are loyal. They'd never pass on info behind my back."

"I'd be less worried about how I got my intel and more about who gave you yours."

"Meaning?' Sorenson squared his chest to Nick's.

"Meaning you've got one dead bad guy and one dead cop from the tip you received. Whenever something in my world breaks bad like that I start looking at all angles."

"Maybe I am. Maybe I'm looking at you. That brings me to my next question. Why'd you come over here and wait for me to get discharged?"

Nick looked around to ensure they were out of earshot of the others meandering about the wing. Satisfied, he said, "I'm going to need the name of your informant who gave the tip on that address."

"Ain't happening. Not sure how you do things where you come from, but 'round here we don't give up our sources. Bad for business."

"You seem like a bright guy. So, I'm going to run something by you and tell me if something's off."

"I'm all ears."

"How is it that a small crew operating primarily out of a run-down neighborhood happens to be sitting on close to three kilos of fentanyl hours after you receive your tip? A tip that came to you immediately after the big spike in overdoses. It doesn't add up to me."

"I've got good snitches."

"That's your answer. You've got good informants? I'm not buying it. It's more than that and you know it."

"You're just pissed because I didn't keep you in the loop."

"No, I'm pissed because you shot and killed Jinx. He was our best chance at finding the source. A cop gets a tip on the biggest raid and the most valuable commodity, the drug dealer, is dead, and therefore unable to answer any questions. Do you know how that looks to me?"

Sorenson's eyes flashed with anger and he leaned in. "I'm not dirty if that's what you're getting at."

"Then who gave you the information?"

"Piss off!"

"Then I'm going to have to assume it wasn't a legitimate source and your fast-track to promotion is going to be derailed."

Sorenson took a moment and began pacing in short steps back and forth in front of Nick. He muttered some indiscernible expletive and then said in a hushed tone, "Avery Wilcox."

"Who the hell is that?"

"Senator Litchfield's aide."

"You're telling me the Opioid Reform Committee Senator's aide is giving you intel on a major bust and you're not seeing anything strange about that?"

Sorenson face went slack. "He's well connected with lots of different types of people. Some of them run shelters and halfway houses. It's plausible they may have valuable information. It makes sense he'd reach out to me if it had to do with drugs. I'm not seeing an issue."

"How many times have you received information from the senator's aide?"

"A couple. In my defense, it always helped us get a scumbag off the street. I didn't really question it after the first one panned out."

"Were the busts always fentanyl related?"

"Yes. I mean, there were usually other drugs on scene, but the tips were always with regard to fentanyl. It's been getting a lot of media attention lately. Maybe his constituency felt a call to action."

Sorenson rubbed the lines on his forehead and closed his eyes. His cellphone rang. Sorenson looked at the incoming number and then at Nick. "Speak of the devil."

"Answer it. Let's see what the senator's aide has to say."

Sorenson accepted the call and put his phone to his ear. "Hello. Yes, I'm doing much better. Thanks for asking. I'm actually on my way out now. It's a little soon for that, don't you think? Smith's body's not even in the ground yet. I'd prefer we wait until things settle before proceeding in that fashion, but it's not my area of expertise. Okay. Two o'clock? I'll be there."

Sorenson pocketed the phone. "The Senator is holding a press conference today and he wants me to be there."

During the call Nick had done a quick google search on his cellphone. He froze when he saw the image of the man. "Well, let's make sure we don't disappoint him."

"I thought you had concerns about the senator's information. Now you want me to share the limelight with him?"

"Keep your friends close and your enemies closer."

"Enemies?"

"There's a lot you don't know about Mr. Wilcox. How fast can you walk an arrest warrant through?"

"Depends. What for?"

"Murder."

Nick had spent the elevator ride down giving Sorenson as much information on the Wollaston Beach shooting as he could. He told him his unit had acquired video of the shooting. Of course, he lied about how he acquired it, telling the narcotics detective it was received from an FBI tip line. Nick knew Sorenson didn't buy it, but also knew enough not to press further. As the two parted ways in the hospital's first floor lobby, a team of medics barreled through the emergency room's entrance. Nick heard a call out to the receiving party of medical personnel, "He coded on the ride. Six blasts of Narcan. Unresponsive. No pulse."

Sorenson shot a glance at Nick. "It never ends."

"Sometimes we're just putting our fingers in the dike."

Nick walked out into the late-morning gray light of day. Only a few hours until the press conference. He got into the passenger seat of the idling car, Declan at the wheel.

"How'd it go?" Declan asked.

Nick pulled out his cellphone, holding the image of Avery Wilcox in front of his friend. "This thing just took a turn."

"Well, I guess we have our next target."

"I've got an idea on how to play our hand."

Nick minimized the image on his phone's display and called Jay.

"Put me on speaker," Nick said as soon Jay answered.

"Okay, go ahead. We're listening," Jay said.

"Wiz, run the name Avery Wilcox. Get ready to have your mind blown."

Nick waited. A second later he heard Mouse gasp.

"It's him," Wiz said. "I don't believe it, but he's our shooter from the park. Senator Buzz Litchfield's right-hand man is doing wet work and drug deals. Seems there's more to the senator's reform plan than we thought."

"That's the understatement of the century. Wiz I'm going to need you to clean the video footage, so it only shows the few seconds where Wilcox starts shooting."

"Okay. What's the plan?" Wiz asked.

"Sorenson's going to help us out."

"Do you trust him or think he's in cahoots?" Jay asked.

"Seems as though Wilcox has been feeding the TNT guys the intel for their recent fentanyl cases. I guess he was thirsty enough to believe the info without questioning too deeply. In light of last night's raid, I think it's something that's going to haunt him for a very long time. So trust me when I say this, Daniel Sorenson is just as pissed as we are. Maybe more so."

"I'll put together an informational briefing on the good senator's aide. I'm sure the FBI might be interested," Jay said.

"Let's get moving on this. We've got some work to do before two," Nick said.

"What's happening at two?"

"The senator is holding a press conference about last night's bust. I for one think we should be there to show our support."

26

The room was crowded. Gloria Baker had done her job in spreading the word. She'd leaked that the senator would address the recent police action taken in response to the increased fentanyl-related overdoses and it would be followed by an announcement. The press inferred the second part and were already discussing the implications on several stations. It was creating a frenzy among political correspondents, with people weighing in on the senator's impact within the Commonwealth of Massachusetts and his potential to apply his leadership to the country as a whole. She'd masterfully manipulated the media beast. The room's attendance was a testament to her efficiency.

Sergeant Daniel Sorenson sat behind the podium, slightly left of where the senator would address the crowd. This was done so intentionally, to ensure photographers and video cameramen picked up the two together. Litchfield wanted to be visually connected to the man responsible for taking down the dealer responsible for the recent death toll. He wanted the images to represent a synergy of big government and local law enforcement. It was the key ingredient in his reform and an ideal he planned to carry forward into his presidency.

Sorenson sat next to Avery Wilcox. The well-dressed senator's aide absently picked at a small bit of lint on his pants.

"This is a big day for you, Danny," Wilcox said, leaning in.

"For you and the senator as well, I imagine."

"You have no idea."

"I'm just happy to be a part of this. Thank you again for the opportunity."

"Don't mention it."

"And thank you for all of the valuable intel you were able to provide me and my team."

"Don't mention that, ever." Wilcox stopped picking at his suit and narrowed his eyes. His words were delivered in a measured tone, but the implied meaning was undeniable.

Gloria Baker moved across the raised stage to the podium. She stood on her toes instead of bringing the microphone down to her. Litchfield hated to make adjustments in front of an audience. He'd been out on stage earlier and personally arranged the speaking platform to his preferences. She steadied her balance, gripping the wood sides of the podium before speaking. "Thank you all for coming today on such short notice. The senator will be out momentarily." She stepped down and took a seat on the opposite side of Avery Wilcox.

Senator Litchfield heard Baker's voice as the podium microphone reverberated her message through the walls as he waited in the back hallway outside the press room. The cue had been given and the senator readied himself. A tingle ran along his spine and his stomach fluttered. He hadn't felt nerves like this since the first time he put boots on the ground during a firefight. The return felt good, a reminder of the importance of this moment. He embraced it.

His hand firmly gripped the door handle. Litchfield paused, exhaling loudly, before entering.

Applause erupted from the crowd. This speech was a long time coming and Baker had worked tirelessly on his behalf in its preparation. Litchfield knew paid supporters were planted in the sea of reporters. People, for the most part, were reactionary by nature, and strategically placing actors scripted to evoke emotion was already proving a worthy investment. Reporters, who in the past, had chosen to disagree with him, now stood in support. Litchfield's political chess match effectively dissolved party lines. The room was a microcosm of what national polls were saying with regard to his approval rating. Overnight, Buzz Litchfield became the front runner in the next presidential campaign, and he hadn't even made his announcement to run.

Litchfield crossed the raised stage purposefully. He gave a nod to the row of people seated left of the podium. The clapping subsided and the room settled.

"I stood at this podium only a few days ago. Many of you here today were present at that time. I spoke of my daughter, Amber. As a father, I'm still grieving her loss and forever will. As much as her death pains me, I put aside my anguish to honor her memory. Harnessing my rage as a father and citizen of this great commonwealth, I focused on putting the full might of my Hope Restored initiative into effect. So, I'm back to tell you a story of success and bravery. Hopefully, when I'm done, you'll see the true power of this program and realize that we, not only here in Massachusetts, but as a nation, have a real chance at turning the tide in taking back our streets."

Litchfield stopped and turned his head, eyeing Sorenson. "This young man behind me will be joining me up here under the spotlight shortly, but before he does, I'd like to take a moment to introduce him. For those of you in this room that don't know, that's Sergeant Daniel Sorenson of the Boston Police Department. This man runs an elite unit of dedicated personnel tasked with going after the city's most dangerous drug dealers. The word hero is thrown around quite a bit without much substance to back it up. Not in this case, though. Sergeant Sorenson received a tip about a large quantity of fentanyl being distributed out of the Roxbury neighborhood. His team sprang into action."

Litchfield paused, taking a sip from the glass set on the podium. He'd made sure Baker put seltzer in the cup. The carbonation would cause his eyes to water slightly. Returning the glass to its original position, he looked out at the crowd and leaned in.

"Yesterday this city was devastated by an unprecedented loss of life. Not in a large-scale terrorist attack, but it might as well have been. When I last checked with the medical examiner's office, thirteen people were confirmed dead, and it's been reported three times that number were admitted to local hospitals on overdose-related symptoms in varying degrees. All of this devastation was caused by fentanyl, or Murder 8, as they affectionately call it on the street. Thirteen dead! Four times the number of lives taken during the murderous bombing during the 2013 marathon. Yet we don't treat it with the same seriousness. Why? Because the victims are drug users and therefore less worthy of our sympathy? Was my daughter less worthy?" Litchfield choked up. His voice cracked and a single tear rolled down his face.

"Sergeant Sorenson didn't feel that way. He didn't turn a blind eye. His team learned of the stash house location, in the Orchard Park section of Roxbury, and brought the full strength of the fine men and women of the Boston Police Department down on the criminals. The search warrant service was dangerous, to say the least. Danny and his team put their own personal safety aside for the greater good. The cost was heavy. One of the team members, Scott Smith, a veteran of the force, with over fourteen years of service, was cut down in the line of duty. In the course of his duties yesterday, and in an effort to prevent further loss of life, Sergeant Sorenson was forced to discharge his firearm to stop the armed dealer from harming any additional members of his team. Although that piece of the investigation is under review, it is my understanding that Sorenson acted in accordance with both the law and departmental policy."

Litchfield gave a nod of approval to the Narcotics sergeant seated behind him. "The injuries sustained by the other members of Tactical Narcotics Team weren't caused by any weapon, but by a drug. All of those involved in the takedown were exposed to the fentanyl. I'm glad to tell you all that as of this press conference, each member of his team has been discharged from the hospital and is back home with family."

The actors in the audience began their cued applause. As before, the rest of the group followed their lead. Litchfield himself began to clap and turned to direct it at Sorenson.

"Sorenson and his team are a shining example of how the second prong of my initiative is to work. They recovered nearly three kilos of fentanyl from the Orchard Park stash house. That may not seem like much when compared to other drug seizures, but I'll explain why it is. Fentanyl is one of the only drugs measured in micrograms because of its potency. A fatal dose can be delivered by the equivalent of a couple grains of sand. Now, think about that in kilograms. Scary stuff. Had Sorenson and his team not jumped into action the way they did, we'd be looking at a much higher body count."

Litchfield let the number sink in. He straightened his posture, gripping the podium on both sides.

"I've shown here today what a few dedicated law enforcement officers can do under my initiative. This program started here and we're going to deploy it nationwide. I want to see an end to this scourge and to bring about a true change. This is one of many reforms that I will be supporting in my campaign for the presidency."

Litchfield smiled and looked back. This time he eyed his best friend and loyal aide, Avery Wilcox. There was a commotion in the room and Litchfield turned his attention to it. A group of FBI agents entered the room, wearing their navy-blue windbreakers stenciled with gold lettering identifying them. They were accompanied by uniformed members of the Boston Police.

The door Litchfield used to enter the conference room opened and two more members of the FBI, similarly dressed, entered. The nervous senator bounced his attention between the group at the front and the newest additions in the rear.

"I see we've been joined by members of the FBI and Boston PD. I'm glad to see them here in support of Sergeant Sorenson and of my campaign initiative. Let's give a round of applause to show our support of these remarkable men and women."

The clapping began and Litchfield took this momentary distraction as an opportunity to cast a glance at his aide-de-camp. Wilcox rubbed his thighs nervously and looked at the two agents closest to him.

Sorenson reached into his pocket and pulled out a folded slip of paper. Litchfield eyed the detective sergeant curiously as he watched him slide the paper over to Wilcox.

Wilcox unfolded the paper and his eyes widened. Wilcox stood and began to sweat. He dropped the paper to the ground. Litchfield could see it was a picture. Upon more careful inspection, he noticed it was a picture of his best friend and political aide pointing a gun. He looked up at his friend in shock.

Wilcox staggered in a panicked daze toward Litchfield as the senator instinctively backed away. The senator looked back at the two federal agents standing at the steps to his right. They looked past him and he realized all of the now-approaching agents were focused intently on his aide-de-camp.

"Avery Wilcox, step away from the podium with your hands where we can see them," the agent near the rear door and closest to Litchfield said.

The agents stepped slowly, their hands hovering near the bulges at their waistlines.

The normally composed Wilcox looked wild-eyed and anxious.

Baker whispered, "What the hell is going on here?"

Sorenson slid his chair back, exposing a clear line of sight for the approaching feds. "Looks to me as though the end of a political career. I hope for your sake you're not involved."

Wilcox slowly turned away from the agents and raised his hands to ear-level. The two agents crossed the podium quickly as Sorenson slipped behind and placed him in custody, locking the stainless-steel handcuffs into place. "You're under arrest for the murder of Landers O'Leary, among other things."

Cameras flashed, and a loud rumble of chatter arose.

Wilcox was led off stage. As he passed, Litchfield feigned shock, the sight of which must've evoked a primal response, because Wilcox pulled away from Sorenson and lunged at Litchfield with his chest pressed out.

"Everything I did was at this man's command! Everything!" Wilcox yelled. His words were amplified by the podium's microphone but would've been easy enough to hear without it.

The two agents assisted Sorenson in regaining control of Wilcox and forcefully extracted him from the stage, where they were met by uniformed members of the Boston PD.

Amidst the clamor, Sorenson had slipped away to assist in ushering the aide-de-camp to jail, leaving Litchfield alone onstage with only Gloria Baker.

Litchfield's brow moistened. He took another sip of the seltzer, trying to calm his nerves. Looking out at the reporters' faces, he saw the palpable shift. In the fickle world of politics, he'd gone from presidential candidate to scandal in the blink of an eye.

For the first time in Senator Buzz Litchfield's career, he was speechless.

27

The group gathered in the Vault, seated around the conference table. The news ran on the television without volume. No need to hear the one-millionth recap of the recent events.

The Valhalla Group had amassed quite a bit on the Senator's operation. Wilcox, operating on his orders, used The Onion Router (TOR), or more commonly called the Dark Web, to purchase the fentanyl. From the information gathered, they'd purchased somewhere in the range of ten kilos of fentanyl using campaign money. The dirty work was carried out by Wilcox, but facing a heavy prison term, he decided to cooperate with the investigation. The former aide-de-camp was a very organized person and kept an exact accounting of all his extra-curricular activities performed at the senator's behest. That ledger would be Litchfield's undoing.

"My contact in the Bureau has informed me that the indictment of Senator Litchfield is underway. Wiz helped connect the dots on this and we submitted our detailed report. He should be in custody within the hour," Jay said.

"I wish I could be there to see his face," Nick said.

"I think we're well represented on that front." Declan slapped the back of Nick's shoulder.

Senator Litchfield sat at his desk. He'd been alone for the last hour, refusing to take calls. Gloria Baker was busy fielding the influx of calls from reporters and fellow members of Congress. It was a tidal wave of inquisition and the woman was haggard from it.

She opened the door and entered. Her security blanket of a notepad was clutched tightly.

"I thought I told you I don't want to be disturbed!" Litchfield slammed his fist on the desk. The impact sent a teetering stack of pages off the edge and onto the ornamental braided rug encircling his desk. The picture frame holding his daughter's photo fell with it, and the glass shattered. He leapt out of his seat.

Baker cowered as if fearing a blow. Litchfield ignored his assistant and rounded the desk. He kneeled at the broken picture frame. The senator shook the loose shards free onto the floor as he stood. Leaning against his desk he looked at the picture as if seeing it for the first time. It was taken a few years back after one of his daughter's high school soccer games. The lime green jersey brought out the brightness in her eyes. He remembered the game as if it were yesterday. Amber's team had lost, but it was the grace with which she'd faced that defeat he respected. She had told him, *Sometimes your best isn't always good enough. As long as you give it everything and leave it all on the field, then you can hold your head high.* It was a profound statement and it meant more to him now than ever before.

"I'm sorry, sir," Baker said meekly. "But there are some people here to see you."

"What part of no visitors is so hard for you to understand? We're not making any statements until we get a handle on this Wilcox catastrophe."

"These people aren't here to interview you."

"Well, what the hell do they want?"

"I'm not completely sure, but they're with the FBI."

Litchfield looked back at the window and seriously considered diving out in hope that the five-floor drop to the busy sidewalk below would be enough to do him in. The thought evaporated as soon as it entered his mind. He was not a coward and would not act in such a way now.

The senator straightened his crimson tie and returned to his seat. He set the shattered frame back in its place on the desk. He eyed the closed door behind Baker and then calmly said, "Show them in."

The doors opened and three men entered. Two wore dark navy suits and had matching lapel pins affixed with a miniaturized FBI emblem. The third man, entering last, was dressed more casually, and Litchfield recognized him. Detective Sergeant Daniel Sorenson of the Boston Police Tactical Narcotics Unit was statuesque behind them. The two locked eyes and it was Litchfield who broke first, looking away.

"Senator Litchfield, we have a signed warrant for your arrest. We need you to come with us," the tall, thin agent said.

"This is preposterous! There must be some mistake."

The three men said nothing.

"I'm not going anywhere until I speak to my attorney." Litchfield looked past the men to Baker, who was standing timidly in the outer office area. "Gloria, get Sam Waters on the phone, and tell him I need him here immediately!"

"You'll have an opportunity to speak with your attorney after processing. We're going to need you to come with us. We've arranged to take you out the back to minimize your exposure, but let me make this clear, this is not up for debate."

"Danny? Talk to these guys. Straighten this out for me. There's obviously some misunderstanding. Whatever Wilcox told you is an outright lie," Litchfield whined.

"Senator, you're also facing local charges as well," Sorenson said. He stepped deeper into the room and now only the desk separated the two men. "You mobilized my team to enforce your Hope Restored initiative. You gave us the power to go after the dealers and distributors responsible for overdose-related deaths."

Litchfield's heart was beating uncontrollably. Sorenson held out a piece of paper with the medical examiner's emblem in the header.

"What's this?" Litchfield asked, taking the paper in hand.

"It's a list compiled of the deaths attributed to the recent fentanyl distribution. It took a lot of leg work on Homicide's part to link the drugs to the dealers, but I think you'll note the list is quite extensive."

"What does this have to do with me?"

"These are the bodies we're laying at your feet. And you might want to read down that list to the very bottom." Sorenson folded his arms and waited.

Litchfield held his intimidating gaze on the detective for a few moments before giving in to the request. His eyes scanned the list of names. Fifteen in total. His heart stopped as he read the last name at the bottom of the list. Amber Litchfield.

The senator dropped the paper and felt as though he were going to vomit. His daughter's bright eyes stared back at him through the broken glass.

"Was it worth it?"

Litchfield didn't answer.

The two agents gathered the weakened Litchfield by his elbow. He was cuffed in front and a suitcoat was laid over top to mask it from view. The three escorted the former presidential front-runner out of his office. Buzz Litchfield's head hung low and he wept silent tears as he began his silent procession.

———

"The craziest thing in all this is the drug Litchfield used to move forward his political agenda was the same one that killed his daughter. So, he's actually responsible for his daughter's death," Nick said.

"I doubt he's even made the connection. Guys like him rarely, if ever, see the fault in their actions," Declan said.

"The biggest irony is the Senator's Hope Restored initiative is going to be used against him and Wilcox. Boston PD has a solid case against them for the fifteen overdose-related deaths. And Sorenson is heading that investigation. He's a bit peeved to have been duped by Wilcox," Nick added.

"I don't get it. The Senator wanted to change drug culture, but he did it by bringing in more drugs?" Mouse asked. She added with a giggle, "Heck, where I came from, he probably would've been president."

"He needed the visibility of the overdoses and the ability to control the outcome. Each of his speeches had been timed with the deliveries of fentanyl. He was able to manipulate Sorenson's team to tie in arrests and build his initiative's platform," Nick said.

"Like I said. The guy would've been president where I'm from."

Declan opened the door, exiting Jay's office into the main space of the Vault. Nick saw his friend's face and knew something was up. Declan walked over to the back to the locker room. Nick followed.

"So?" Nick asked.

"I'm out, brother. My family needs me. I know I've pled my case to you. I laid everything out to Jay. He understands. Not to say he isn't disappointed. But I've done a lot of soul searching on this one and my decision stands. You're not going to be able to talk me out of it. So, don't even try."

"I know you're a stubborn bastard. I wouldn't waste the effort in trying to convince you otherwise. Like I said before. Whatever debt you feel is owed has been paid. I would never hold you back. Your family, Val and the kids, are the single most important thing. Go home. Be the father I know you are. This crazy life is way too short."

"Thanks for understanding."

"I'm not sure we'll be able to keep in touch. Me being dead and all. But I'll try to check in from time to time."

"Hopefully this isn't the last goodbye."

"When are you planning on taking off?"

"Soon. I want to say goodbye to Mouse and the guys. But no need in delaying the inevitable. Like pulling off a Band-Aid, best to do it quickly."

"Listen, you ever need anything, and I mean anything, then you call me. I'll be there."

Nick and Declan shared a quick embrace, slapping each other firmly on the back.

The ice cream swirled atop the cone wasn't melting. That's because it was freezing outside. But this is where Mouse had asked to go. She sat on the same bench Spider was sitting on when Wilcox launched his assault.

Mouse made Nick get her an ice cream cone from The Clam Box. The lady eyed him like he was crazy. He shrugged it off. The will of his teenage companion obviously was beyond reason.

The two sat on the cold bench. Looking down, he saw a dark brown circular spatter on the bench seat. He knew it was blood and most likely from Spider's gunshot wound to the shoulder. It was odd enjoying peace in a place where they'd experienced such violence, but in the same breath he welcomed it.

A short while passed before the two spoke. Nick understood, better than most, that each person processed grief differently. Apparently, Mouse did so by eating ice cream, regardless of the temperature or season. For a child born into violence, Mouse took Barbie's death hard. It concerned Nick, and he worried the girl had reached her breaking point.

"I'm not quite sure what I brought you into. You joining the group may have been a mistake. I've been questioning myself a lot lately, in light of recent events. I pulled you from a normal life and a family that cares. Look at Declan. He's going back to his wife and children. This is no place for someone who's got a chance at some normalcy," Nick said.

"First off, normal doesn't exist. Second, I have a family. You," Mouse said.

Nick didn't know what to say.

"But as far as you go, there's much work to be done. You're broken. And I think we need to do some major repairs."

"Major repairs?" Nick scoffed.

"Don't worry about it. I already talked to Jay about this and told him my plan."

"I'm totally lost. Talked to Jay about what?"

"This place is no good for you, just like it was no good for Declan. So, I gave Wiz a little project and now it's all set."

"Has that ice cream frozen your brain?"

"Nope. I'm right as rain." Mouse took a lick of her ice cream.

She reached into her pocket. Mouse pulled out a driver's license and slid it across the bench to Nick.

He held it up and then looked over at the girl who'd handed it to him.

"Why did you have Wiz make me a new driver's license? And why Texas?"

"He didn't just create a new license. He did a lot more than that. It's a complete package. Birth certificate, social security number, the works."

"Is there another mission I don't know about?"

Nick looked at the name on the license. Nicholas Anderson. The picture was of him, but with short hair. The same one Wiz used to forge his recent FBI credentials.

"Sort of. I call it Project Nick. You've done a lot in your life. You've put the lives of others ahead of your own. Some of that came with a major price. Without you, I'd be dead or worse. Jay said the same for him. He realized the second chance he gave you at life wasn't a fair trade for the debt he owes you."

Mouse pulled out another license from her pocket. She handed it to Nick. This one was of her. Maria Anderson with Mouse's picture. He looked at her with a furrowed brow.

"Maria was my first name. And now we have the same last."

"What's the mission?"

"Family." Mouse tapped on the license's address. "It's time for us to go home. That's where we are going to live. Jay's purchased a house using funding from the group. Apparently, there's quite a bit of money. He's also loaded an offshore account with enough money to keep us afloat until you can find a job. He will give you the details on that. The banking stuff was a little too much for me to understand."

"Did you say we?"

"Yes. I think you're right. This is not the life for either one of us. I've come up with a way for us to start over. But, there is something we're missing."

"What's that?"

"Not a what. A who – Anaya."

Nick felt dizzy. Mouse apparently arranged a deal with Jay, releasing him from the group to go back to a life he thought he'd lost forever. It was a lot to take in. He didn't know how to react.

Mouse took another lick of her ice cream and gave him a cavalier grin. "It's going to be okay. Trust me. And don't worry, I'll be with you every step of the way."

28

The weathered paint on the exterior of his house begged him to repaint it. He had ignored it long enough and vowed to begin repairing the damaged surface in the spring. The more pressing repairs lay within and had nothing to do with the house and everything to do with the people inside.

Declan walked toward the side door. A dusting of snow lined the concrete walk and crunched underfoot. He stopped outside the door and listened. He heard his Abby and Ripley giggling. He couldn't hear what caused the joyous uproar, but the sound of it lightened his burdensome decision to walk away from the group.

He knew he'd have to enter to hear the sound of his youngest daughter Laney. She typically didn't speak, but on the rare occasion when she did it was powerful.

There were times in the past when he would come home from work and he'd just stand by and listen to his family. He'd peek in at them. He loved watching them when they didn't know they were being watched. It was an unfiltered look into his family's unique dynamic.

But he'd been away too long to wait outside for an extended period of time. He jostled the loose doorknob. The sound alerted his middle daughter, who was seated at the kitchen table, drawing one of her uniquely creative caricatures. Seeing him, she threw her crayon in the air and made a mad dash for the door.

Declan was barely able to drop his duffle bag before bracing for impact. Ripley coiled herself tightly around his neck. She screamed, "Daddy's home!"

A pitter patter of feet echoed throughout the small colonial's wood floors. Abigail rushed out from the living room, running down the short hallway to him. She joined in the hug fest. The girls battled for position.

"I missed you so very much," Declan said, kissing each girl on their soft cheeks. "Where's your sister?"

"In the living room."

Declan gently shook off his girls as he stood upright. He then walked into the living room. Laney was seated on a small love seat, wearing her noise-cancelling headphones. She didn't look up from her book. Laney had a focused intensity as she scanned the glossy page of her dinosaur book. Declan approached and took up a seat next to his youngest. His body brushed against her arm. The jostling interrupted her process and she looked over at him. She cocked her head, analytically evaluating him, as she did everything. Her lips curled upward into a smile.

"Daddy," she said.

Declan rested his forehead against hers. It had become their custom for welcoming him back home.

Val scampered down the stairs. "Babe, you're back? I hadn't heard from you and was worried."

"Sorry. It's been a crazy couple days."

He stood and the two hugged. "God, I missed you. How long do we have you home this time?"

"How does forever sound?"

Mouse rang the doorbell. A short time later there was movement on the other side of the door. It opened and Anaya Patel stood in the entranceway.

"Mouse? What are you doing here?"

"Hi Anaya."

"Oh my goodness! What a wonderful surprise!" Anaya exclaimed, throwing her arms wide and swallowing Mouse in her grasp.

"I missed you, too!"

Anaya released Mouse from her hug and turned to go inside. "Well, come on in so we can catch up. I just threw a lasagna in the oven if you're hungry. Silly of me, you're always hungry."

"Got room for one more?" Mouse asked.

Anaya turned back toward Mouse as Nick stepped into view. Her jaw dropped and she stared in disbelief.

"Nick?"

Hearing his name roll off her tongue buckled his knees. He worked up the courage to smile. Anaya rushed to him, wrapping her arms tightly around his neck.

She pressed her face into his chest and the familiar smell of coconut wafted from her smooth skin. Anaya's body shook and she whimpered softly. Nick said nothing, silently absorbing this moment in time, forever etching it in his mind.

He picked his head up and saw Mouse standing behind Anaya, smiling broadly. "I told you the haircut was a good move."

"What's she talking about?" Anaya asked, pulling back enough to look up at Nick, her eyes wet with tears.

"Long story."

"But I thought – I mean the funeral – you were," Anaya fumbled with the words.

"Dead? I know. Even longer story. But I guess you could say I did die on that day." Nick knew exactly what she was referring to. "Mouse helped bring me back. There's so much I need to explain. But, I'm here now, if you'll have me?"

"On one condition."

"Name it."

"Promise me you'll never leave me again."

"Never again."

Anaya took his hand and the three ambled inside. Nick closed the door behind him, ending his previous life and potentially beginning a new one.

MURDER BOARD
A BOSTON CRIME THRILLER NOVEL

On the tough streets of Boston, justice requires a detective who isn't afraid to break the rules.

The crime sent shockwaves through the entire city.

But for Boston homicide detective Michael Kelly, the case hits particularly close to home.

Kelly was born and raised only a few blocks from where the girl's body was found. He still has friends living in the old neighborhood.

Some are cops.

Others run the Irish mob.

And when Kelly's investigation uncovers a shocking conspiracy, he realizes that he'll need to use all of his unique connections to solve the case.

Because Kelly is determined to bring the killer to justice.
Whatever the cost...

Get your copy today at BrianChristopherShea.com

JOIN THE READER LIST

Never miss a new release! Sign up to receive exclusive updates from author Brian Shea.

Join today at
BrianChristopherShea.com

Sign up and receive a free copy of
Unkillable: A Nick Lawrence Short Story.

YOU MIGHT ALSO ENJOY...

The Nick Lawrence Series

Kill List

Pursuit of Justice

Burning Truth

Targeted Violence

Murder 8

The Boston Crime Thriller Series

Murder Board

Bleeding Blue

The Penitent One

Never miss a new release! Sign up to receive exclusive updates from author Brian Shea.

BrianChristopherShea.com/Newsletter

Sign up and receive a free copy of

Unkillable: A Nick Lawrence Short Story

ABOUT THE AUTHOR

Brian Shea has spent most of his adult life in service to his country and local community. He honorably served as an officer in the U.S. Navy. In his civilian life, he reached the rank of Detective and accrued over eleven years of law enforcement experience between Texas and Connecticut. Somewhere in the mix he spent five years as a fifth-grade school teacher. Brian's myriad of life experience is woven into the tapestry of each character's design. He resides in New England and is blessed with an amazing wife and three beautiful daughters.

facebook.com/BrianChristopherShea

twitter.com/BrianCShea

instagram.com/BrianChristopherShea

CPSIA information can be obtained
at www.ICGtesting.com
Printed in the USA
LVHW100959100522
718400LV00010B/70